ADVENTURE TIME™

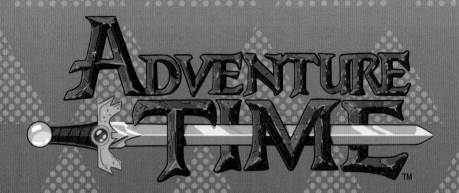

MASKED MAYHEM

ROSS RICHIE CEO & Founder • MATT GAGNON Editor-in-Chief • FILIP SABLIK President of Publishing & Marketing • STEPHEN CHRISTY President of Development • LANCE KREITER VP of Licensing & Merchandising
PHIL BARBARO VP of Finance • BRYCE CARLSON Managing Editor • MEL CAYLO Marketing Manager • SCOTT NEWMAN Production Design Manager • IRENE BRADISH Operations Manager • CHRISTINE DINH Brand Communications Manager
SIERRA HAHN Senior Editor • DAFNA PLEBAN Editor • SHANNON WATTERS Editor • ERIC HARBURN Editor • IAN BRILL Editor • WHITNEY LEOPARD Associate Editor • JASMINE AMIRI Associate Editor • CHRIS ROSA Associate Editor
ALEX GALER Assistant Editor • CAMERON CHITTOCK Assistant Editor • MARY GUMPORT Assistant Editor • KELSEY DIETERICH Production Designer • JILLIAN CRAB Production Designer • KARA LEOPARD Production Designer
MICHELLE ANKLEY Production Design Assistant • DEVIN FUNCHES E-Commerce & Inventory Coordinator • AARON FERRARA Operations Coordinator • ELIZABETH LOUGHRIDGE Accounting Coordinator • JOSÉ MEZA Sales Assistant
JAMES ARRIOLA Mailroom Assistant • STEPHANIE HOCUTT Marketing Assistant • SAM KUSEK Direct Market Representative • HILLARY LEVI Executive Assistant • KATE ALBIN Administrative Assistant

Created by Pendleton Ward

Written by **Kate Leth**

Illustrated by **Bridget Underwood**

with **Drew Green & Vaughn Pinpin**

Inks by **Jenna Ayoub**

Colors by **Lisa Moore**

Letters by **Aubrey Aiese**

"Starchy Cleans Up"
Written & Illustrated by **Meredith McClaren**

Cover by **Drew Green**

Designer **Kara Leopard**
Associate Editor **Whitney Leopard**
Editor **Shannon Watters**

With Special Thanks to Marisa Marionakis, Rick Blanco, Nicole Rivera, Conrad Montgomery, Meghan Bradley, Curtis Lelash and the wonderful folks at Cartoon Network.

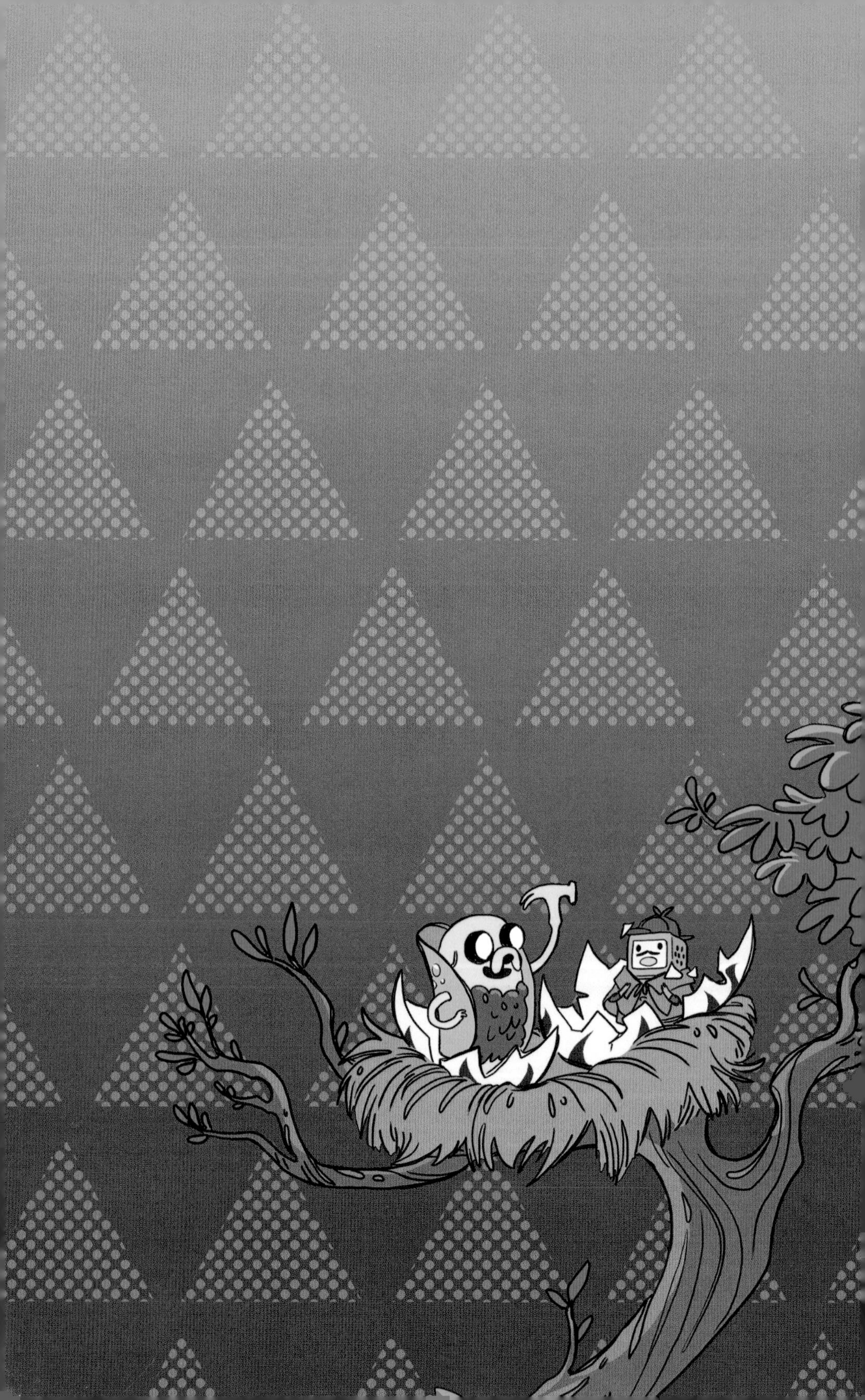

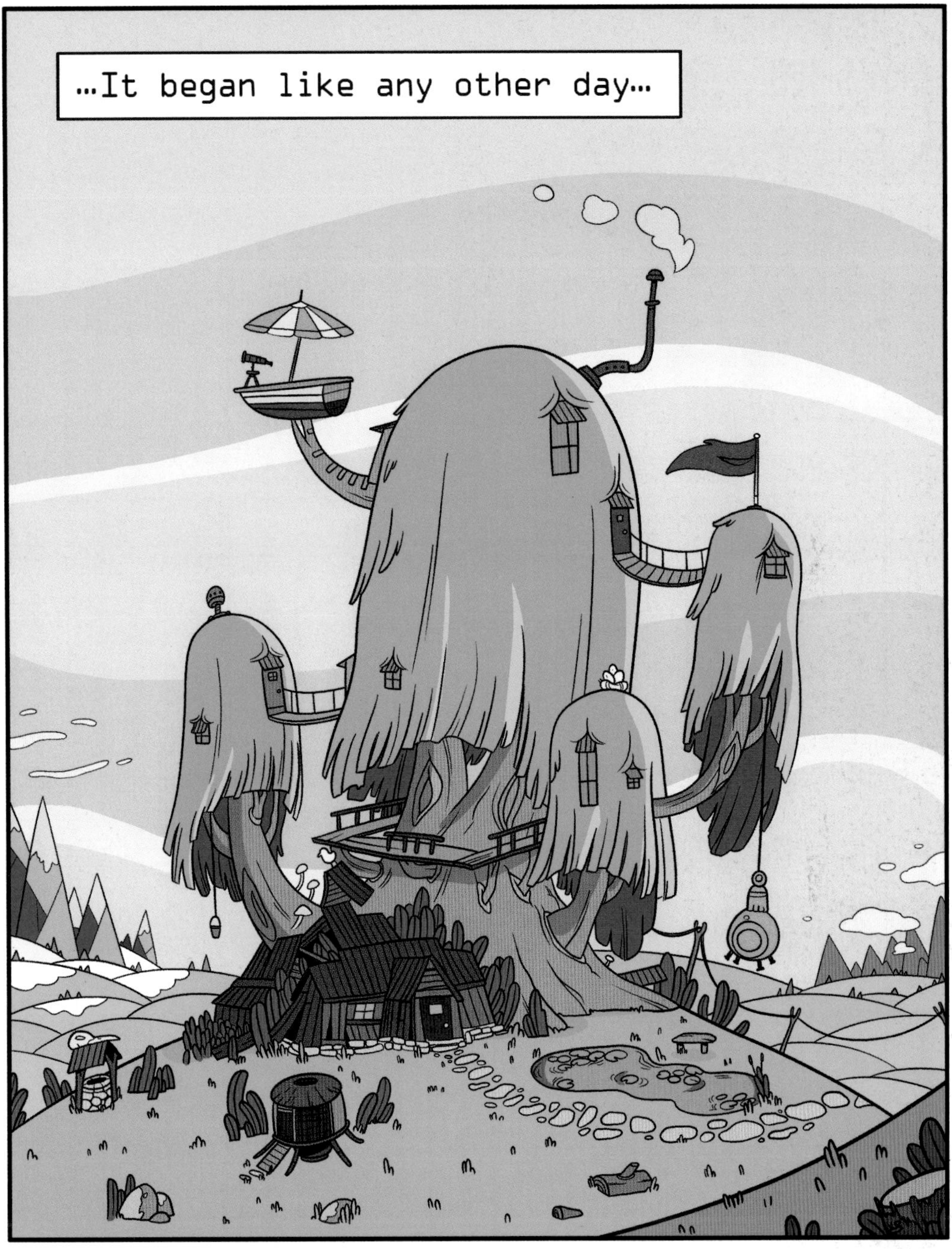
...It began like any other day...

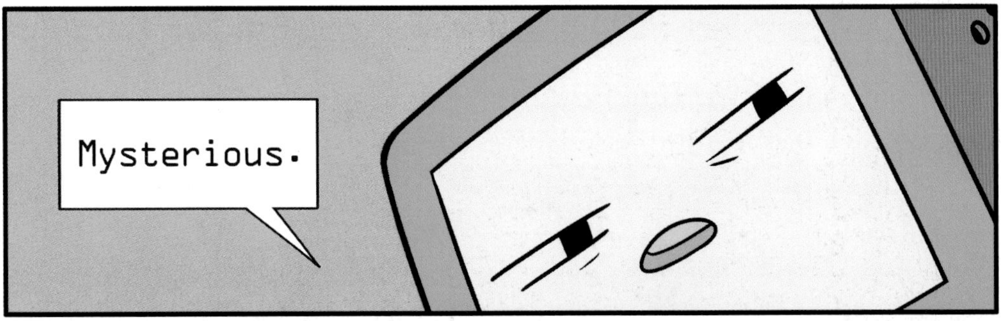
Mysterious.

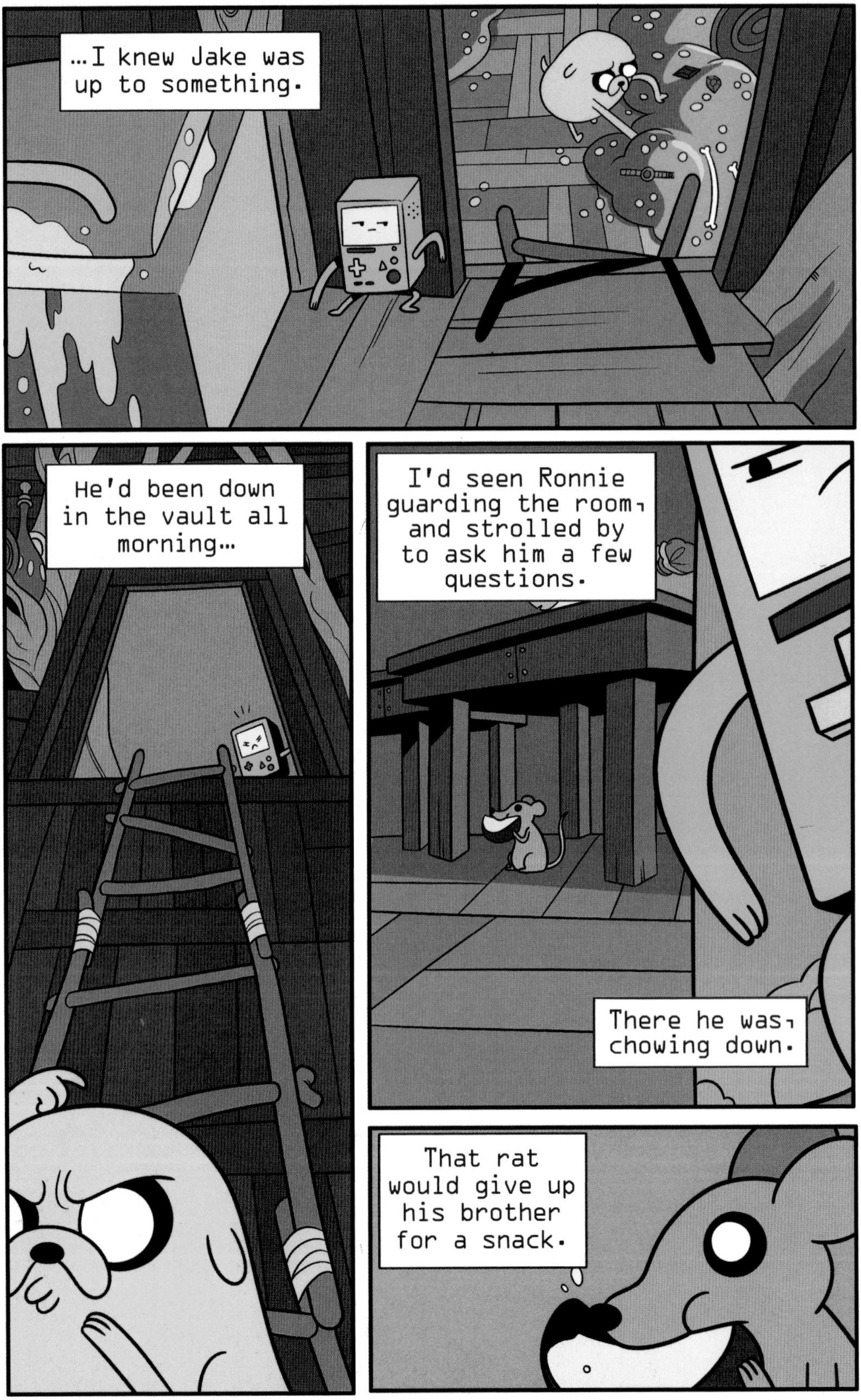
...I knew Jake was up to something.
He'd been down in the vault all morning...
I'd seen Ronnie guarding the room, and strolled by to ask him a few questions.
There he was, chowing down.
That rat would give up his brother for a snack.

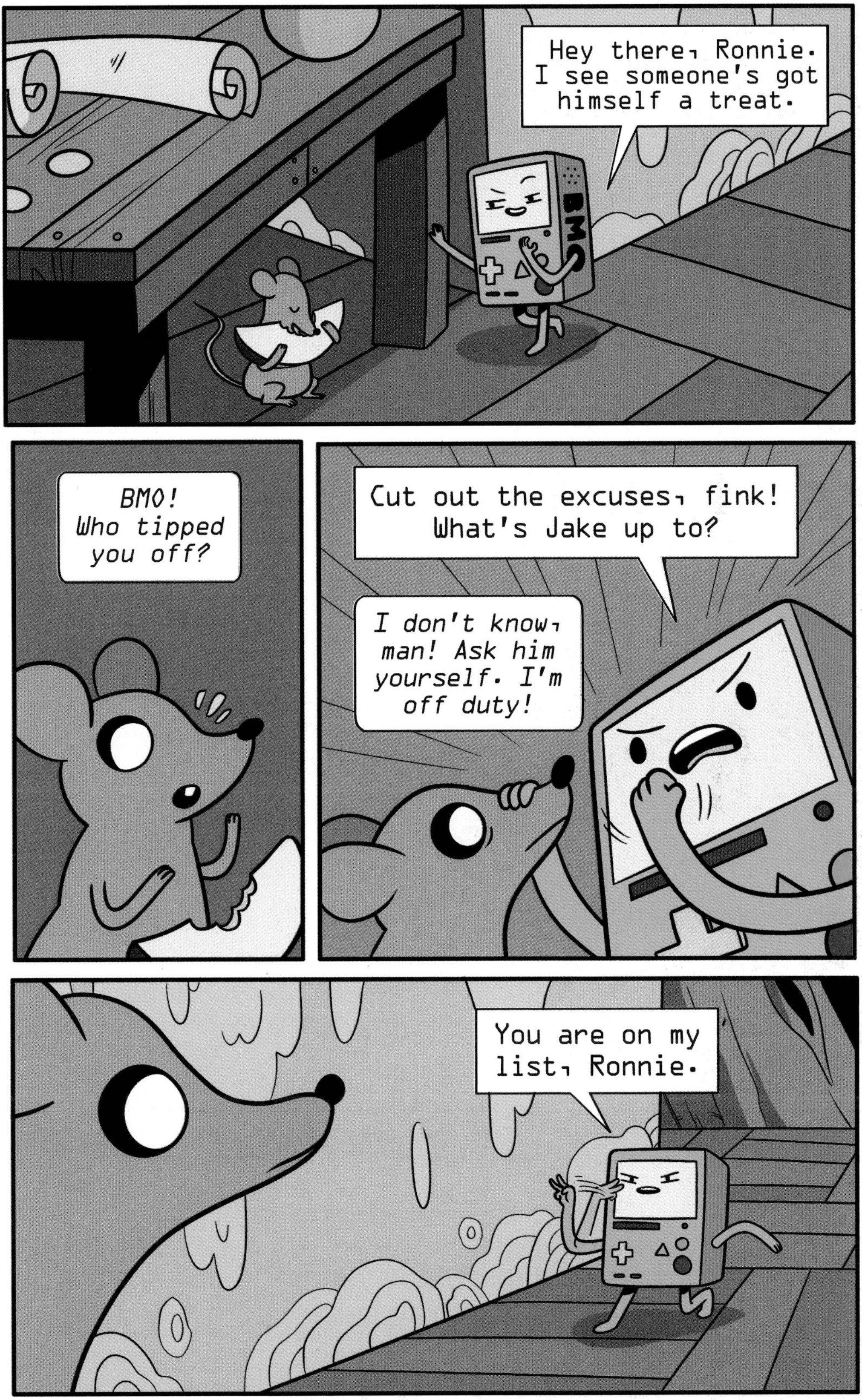
Hey there, Ronnie. I see someone's got himself a treat.
BMO! Who tipped you off?
Cut out the excuses, fink! What's Jake up to?
I don't know, man! Ask him yourself. I'm off duty!
You are on my list, Ronnie.

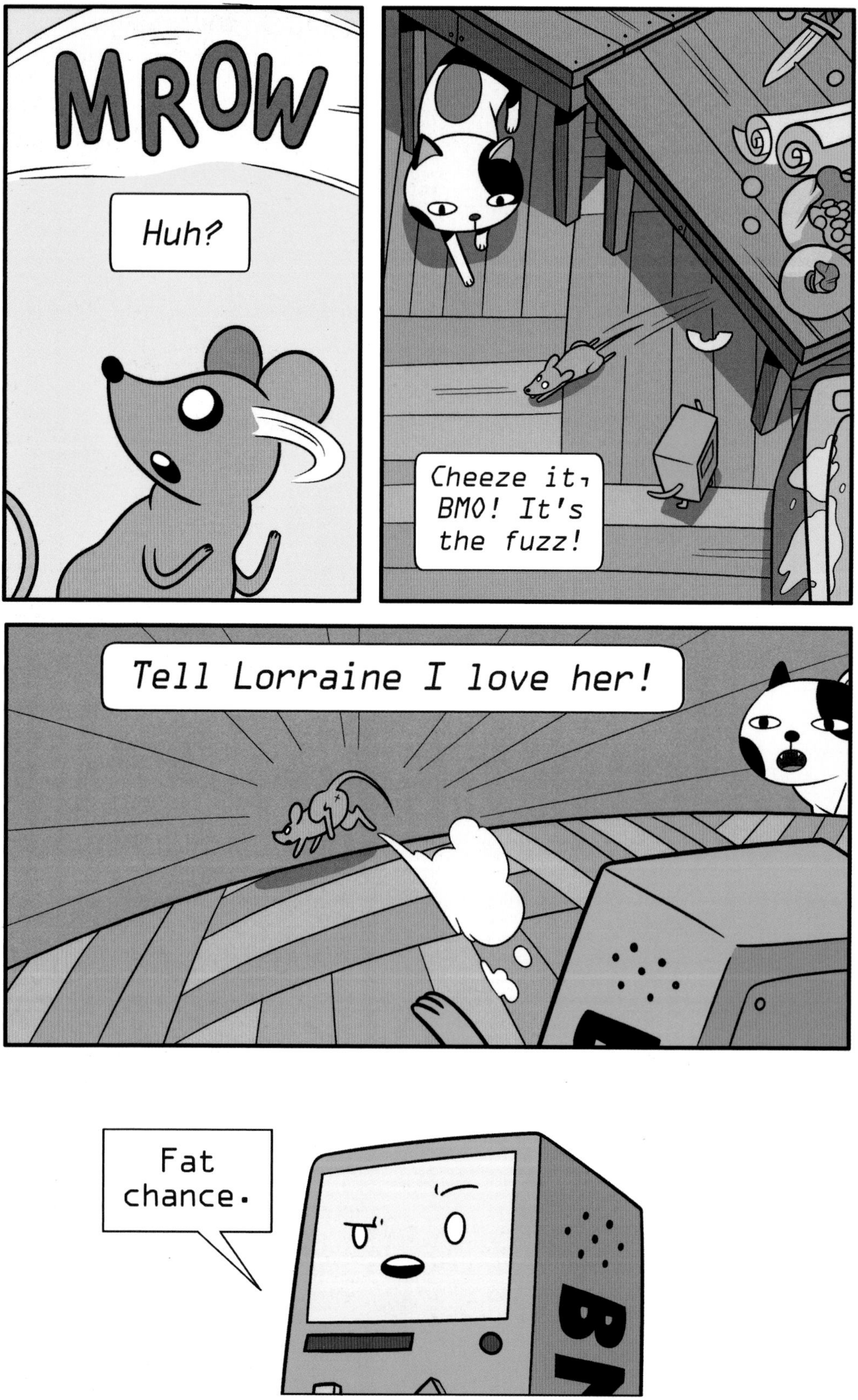
MROW
Huh?
Cheeze it, BMO! It's the fuzz!
Tell Lorraine I love her!
Fat chance.

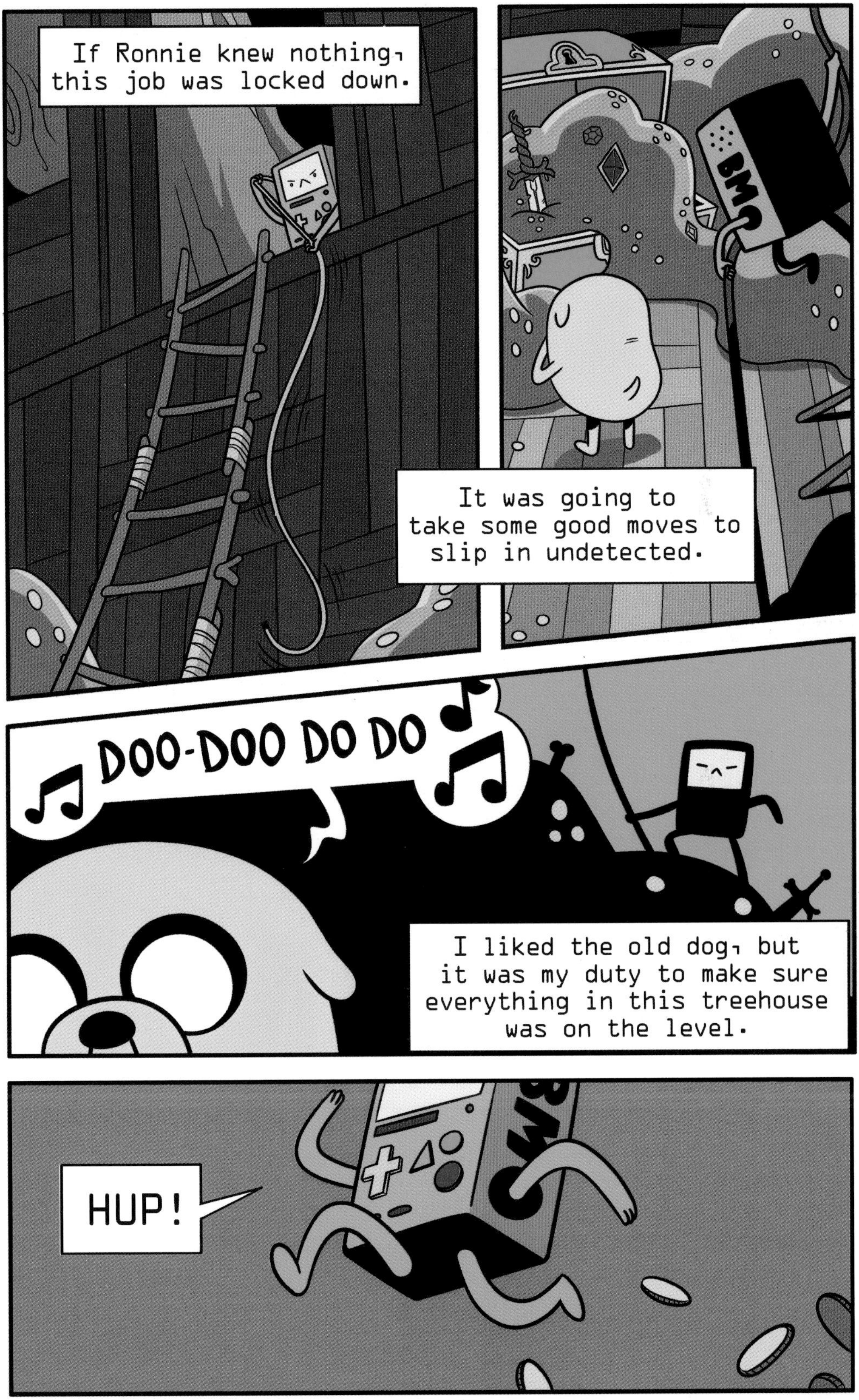
If Ronnie knew nothing, this job was locked down.
BMO
It was going to take some good moves to slip in undetected.
DOO-DOO DO DO
I liked the old dog, but it was my duty to make sure everything in this treehouse was on the level.
HUP!

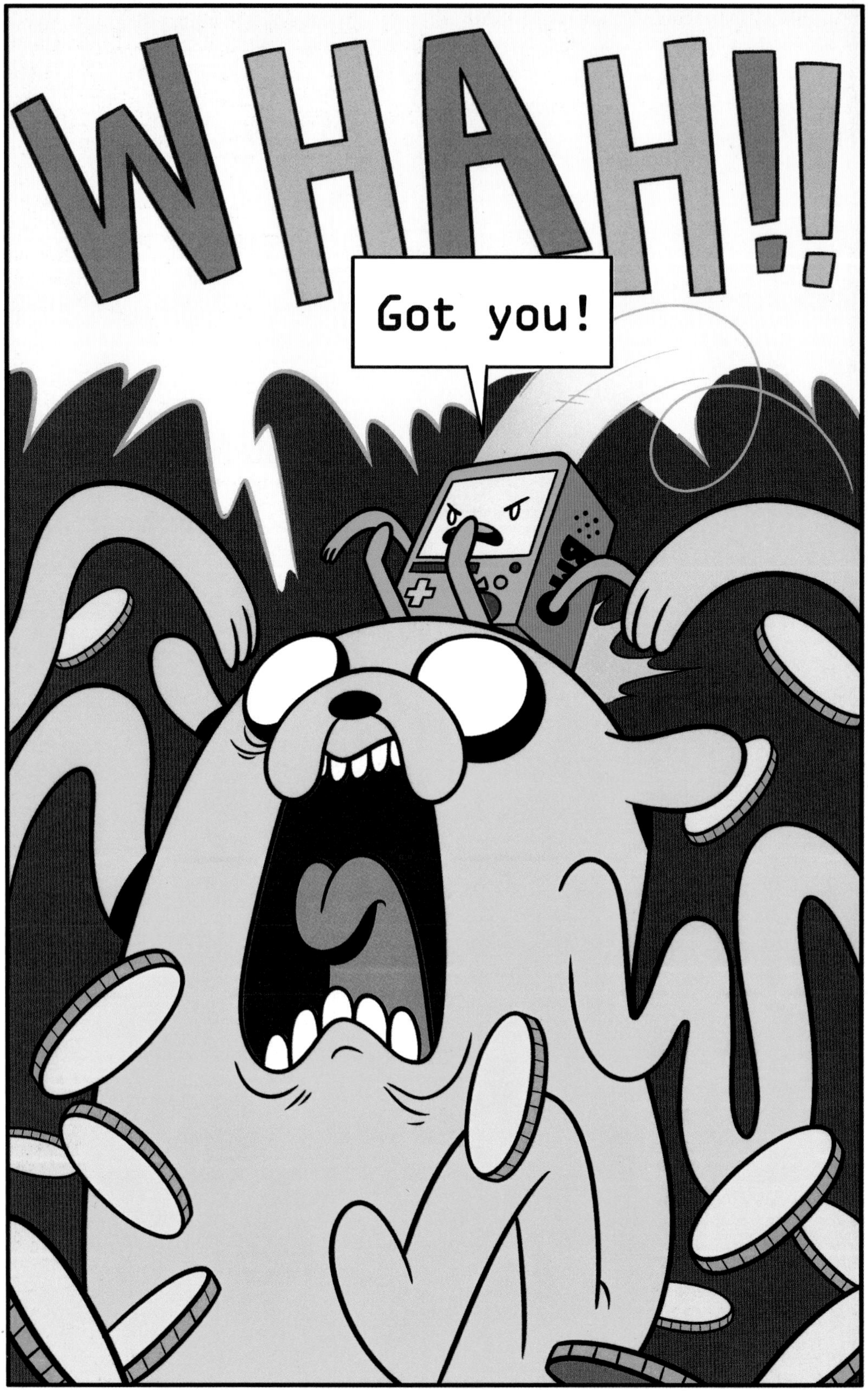
WHAH!!
Got you!

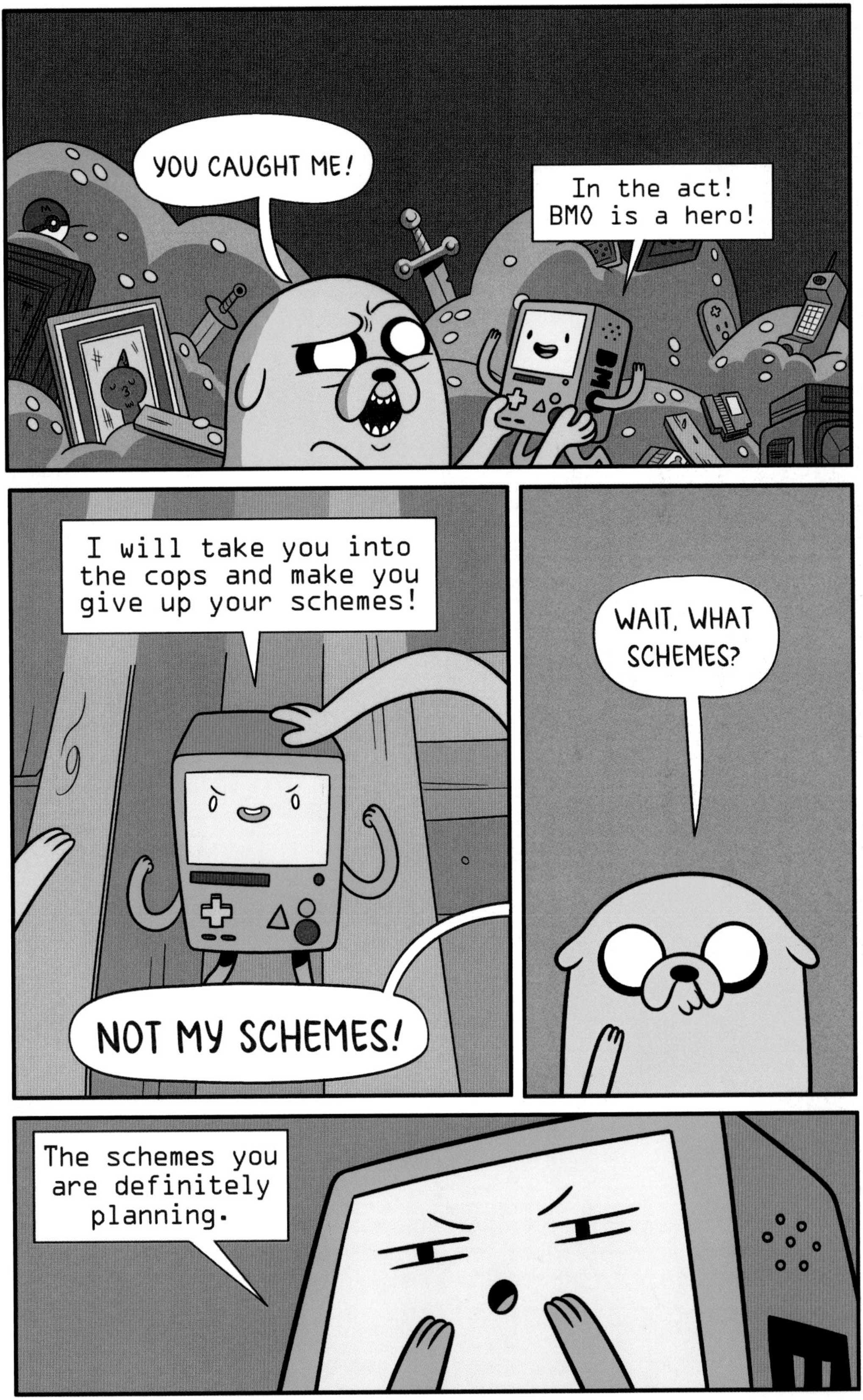
YOU CAUGHT ME!
In the act! BMO is a hero!
BMO
I will take you into the cops and make you give up your schemes!
WAIT, WHAT SCHEMES?
NOT MY SCHEMES!
The schemes you are definitely planning.

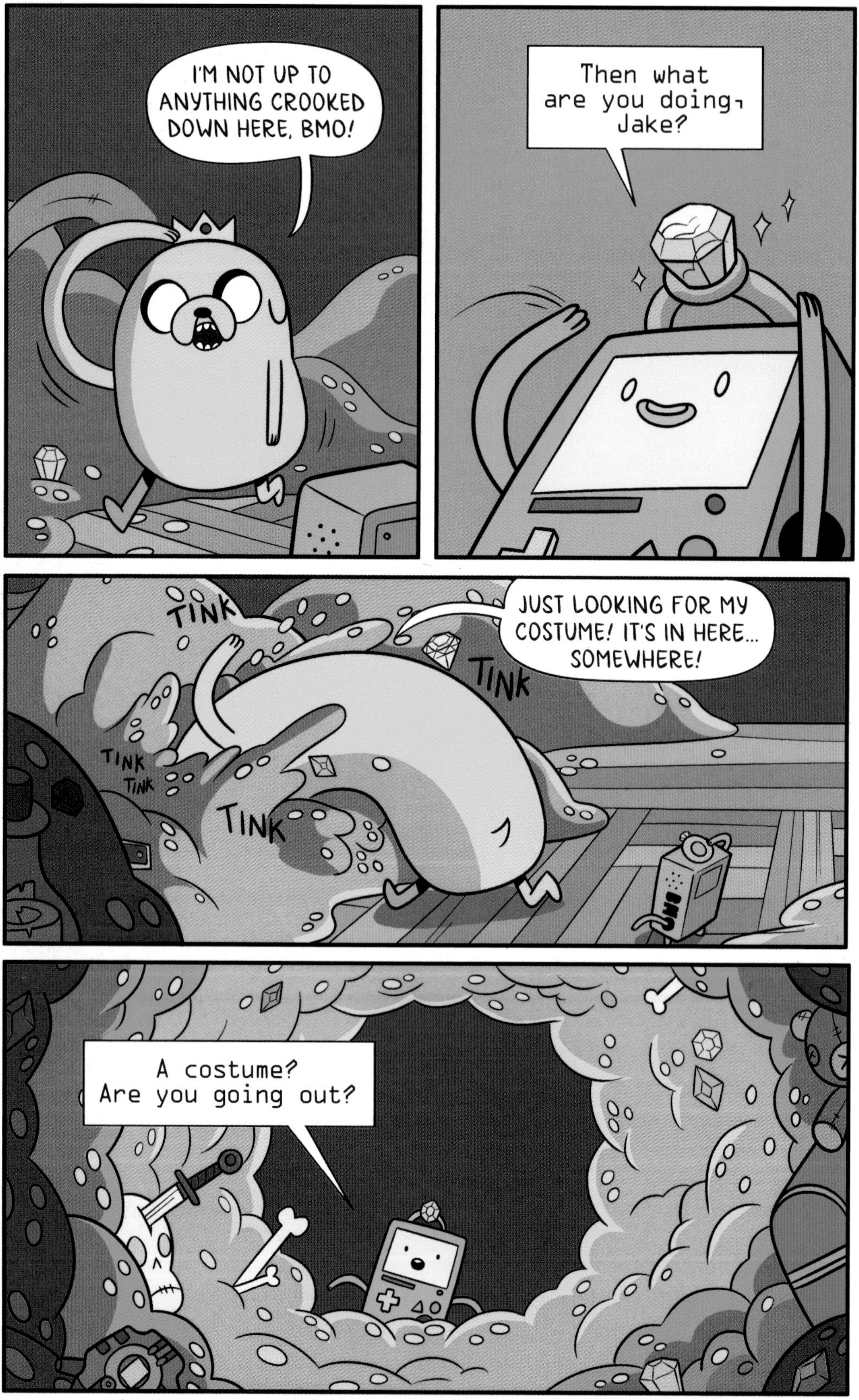
I'M NOT UP TO ANYTHING CROOKED DOWN HERE, BMO!
Then what are you doing, Jake?
TINK
JUST LOOKING FOR MY COSTUME! IT'S IN HERE... SOMEWHERE!
TINK
TINK
TINK
TINK
BMO
A costume? Are you going out?

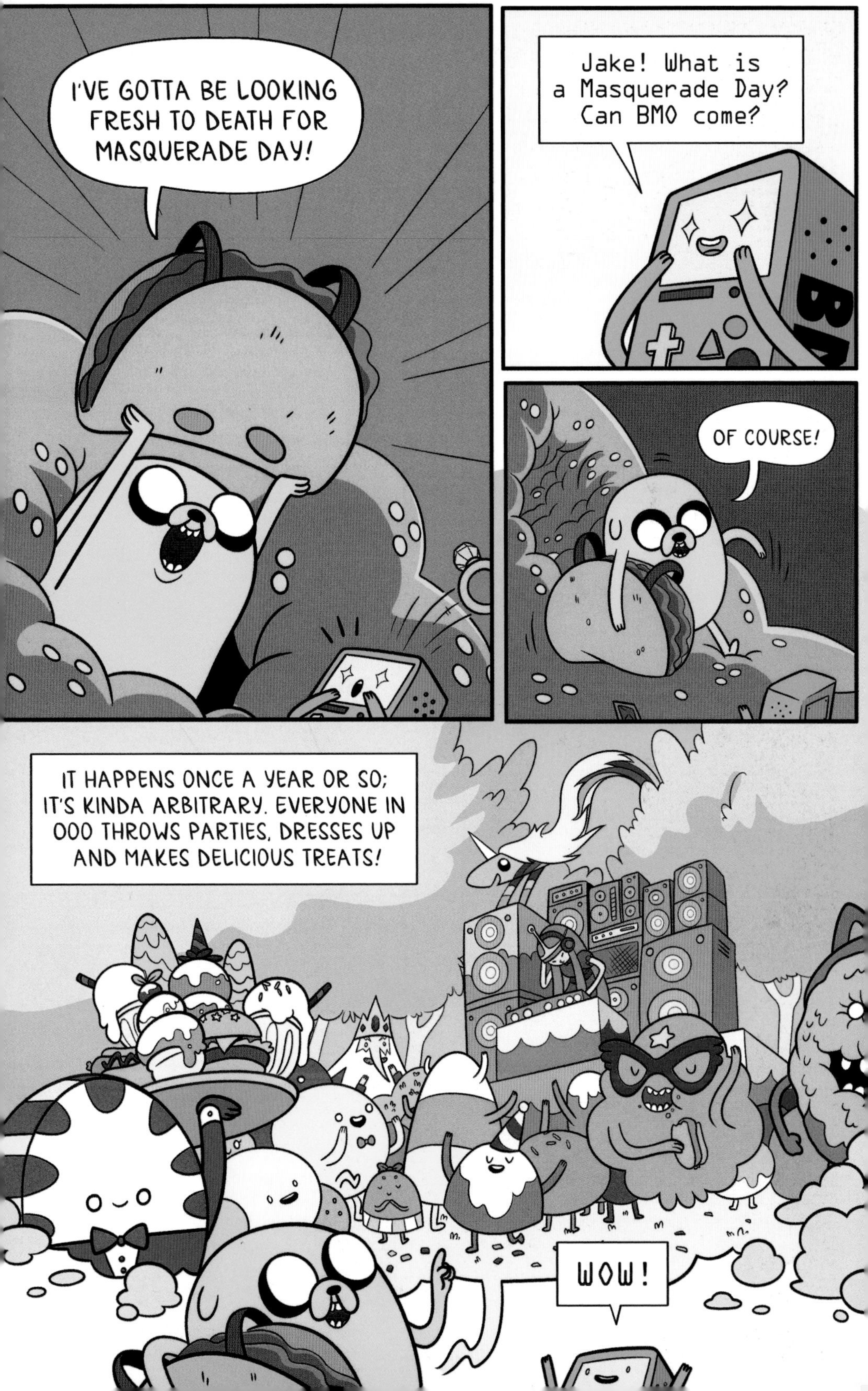
I'VE GOTTA BE LOOKING FRESH TO DEATH FOR MASQUERADE DAY!
Jake! What is a Masquerade Day? Can BMO come?
OF COURSE!
IT HAPPENS ONCE A YEAR OR SO; IT'S KINDA ARBITRARY. EVERYONE IN OOO THROWS PARTIES, DRESSES UP AND MAKES DELICIOUS TREATS!
WOW!

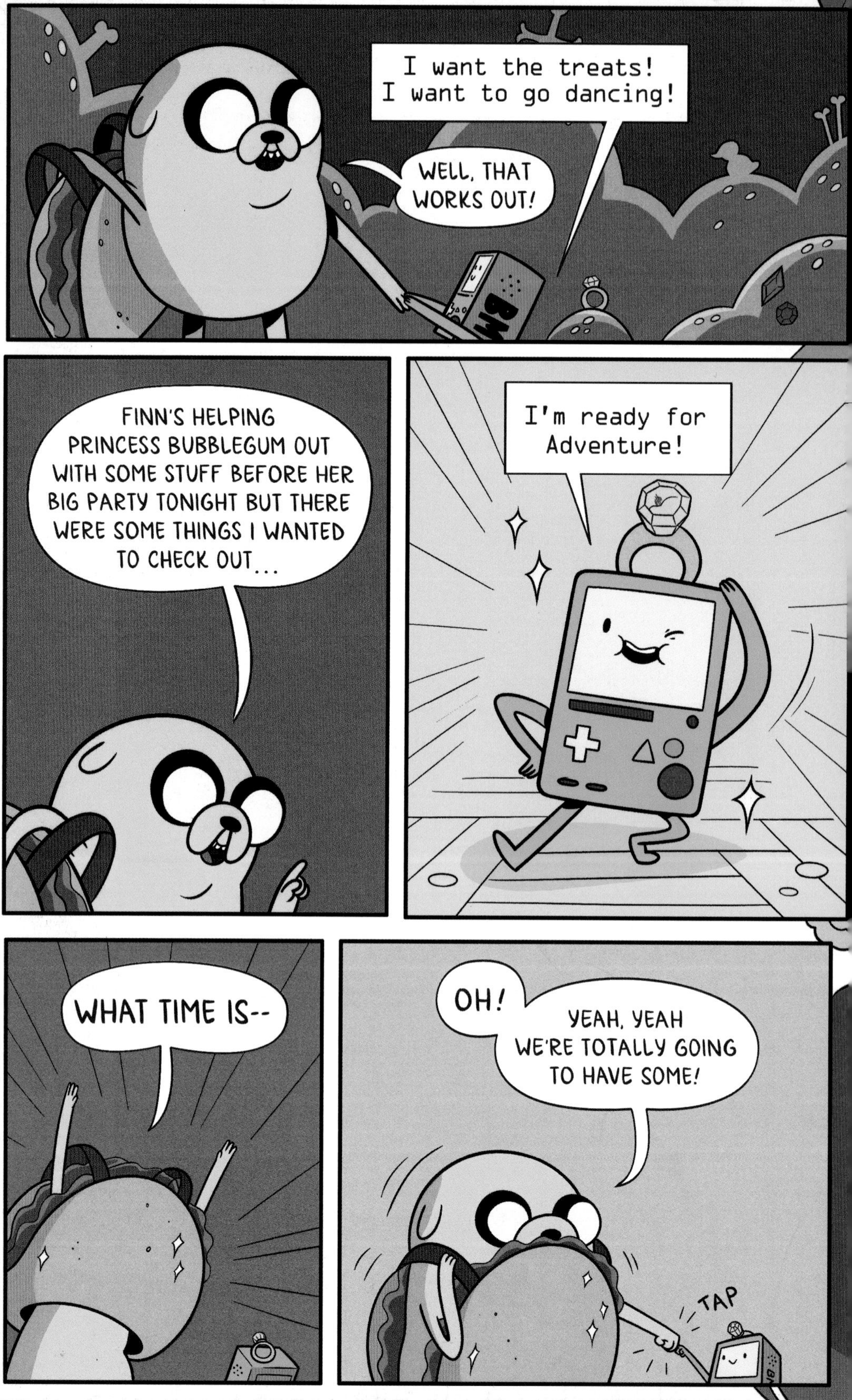
I want the treats! I want to go dancing!
WELL, THAT WORKS OUT!
FINN'S HELPING PRINCESS BUBBLEGUM OUT WITH SOME STUFF BEFORE HER BIG PARTY TONIGHT BUT THERE WERE SOME THINGS I WANTED TO CHECK OUT...
I'm ready for Adventure!
WHAT TIME IS--
OH!
YEAH, YEAH WE'RE TOTALLY GOING TO HAVE SOME!
TAP

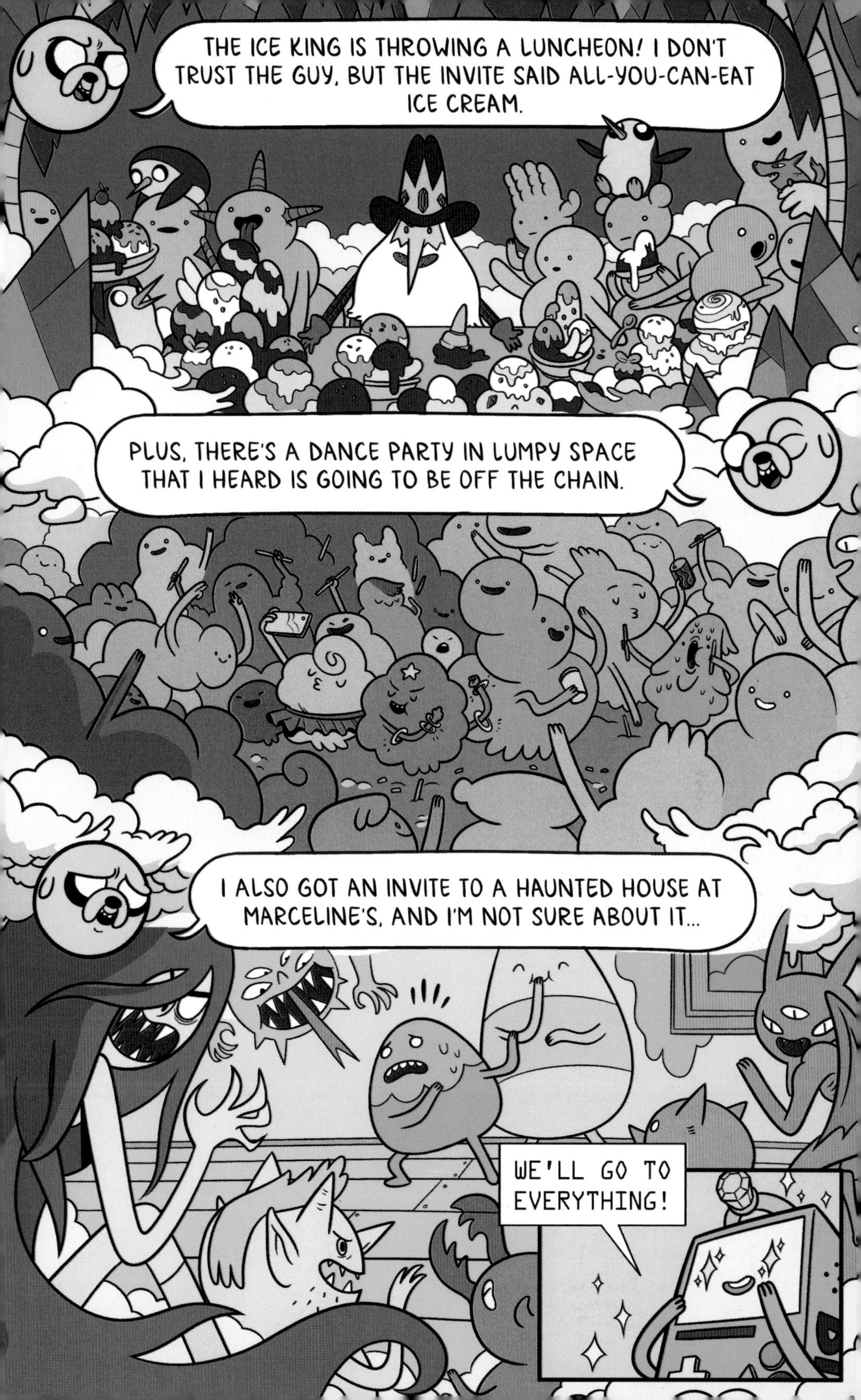
THE ICE KING IS THROWING A LUNCHEON! I DON'T TRUST THE GUY, BUT THE INVITE SAID ALL-YOU-CAN-EAT ICE CREAM.
PLUS, THERE'S A DANCE PARTY IN LUMPY SPACE THAT I HEARD IS GOING TO BE OFF THE CHAIN.
I ALSO GOT AN INVITE TO A HAUNTED HOUSE AT MARCELINE'S, AND I'M NOT SURE ABOUT IT...
WE'LL GO TO EVERYTHING!

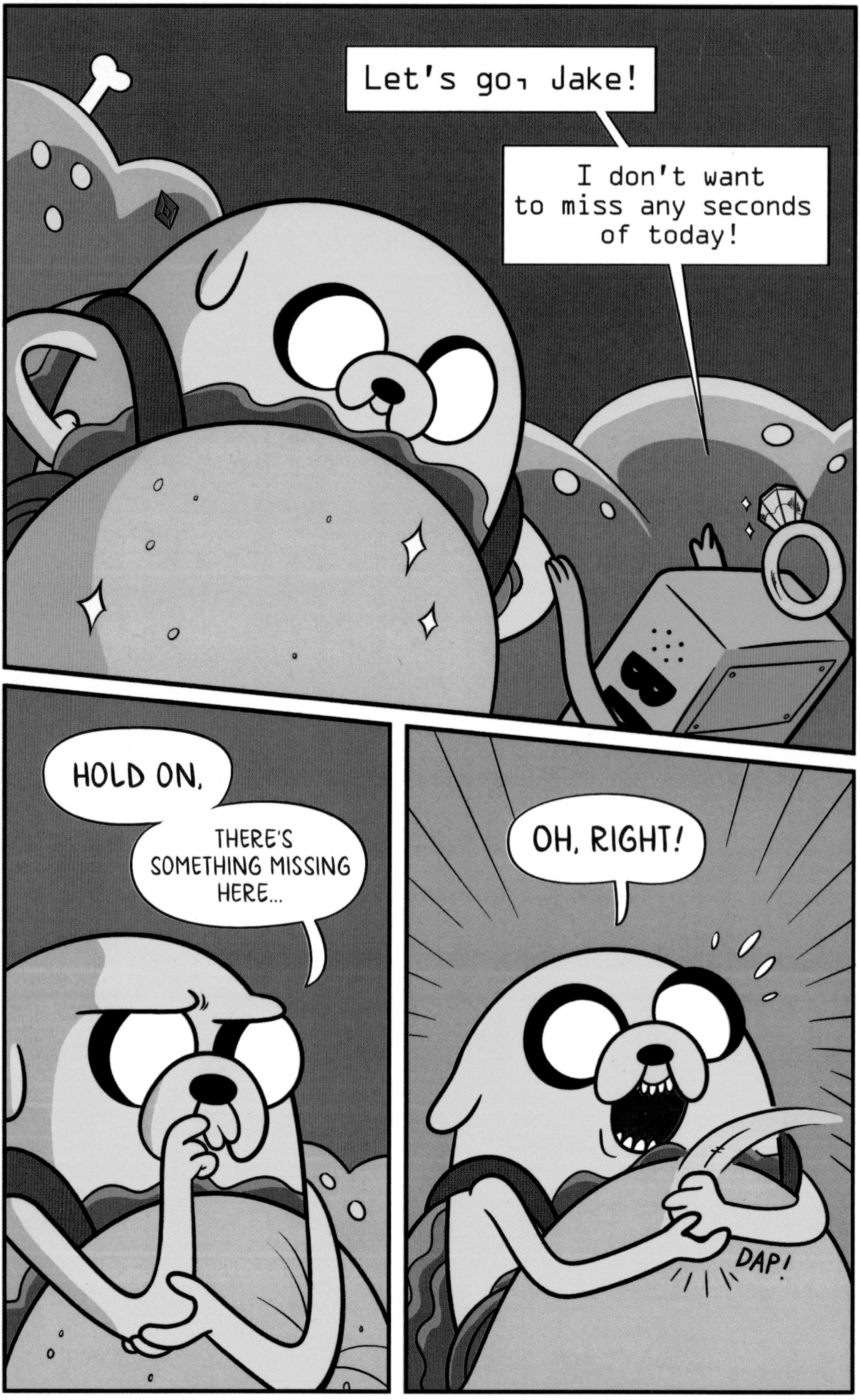
Let's go, Jake!
I don't want to miss any seconds of today!
HOLD ON.
THERE'S SOMETHING MISSING HERE...
OH, RIGHT!
DAP!

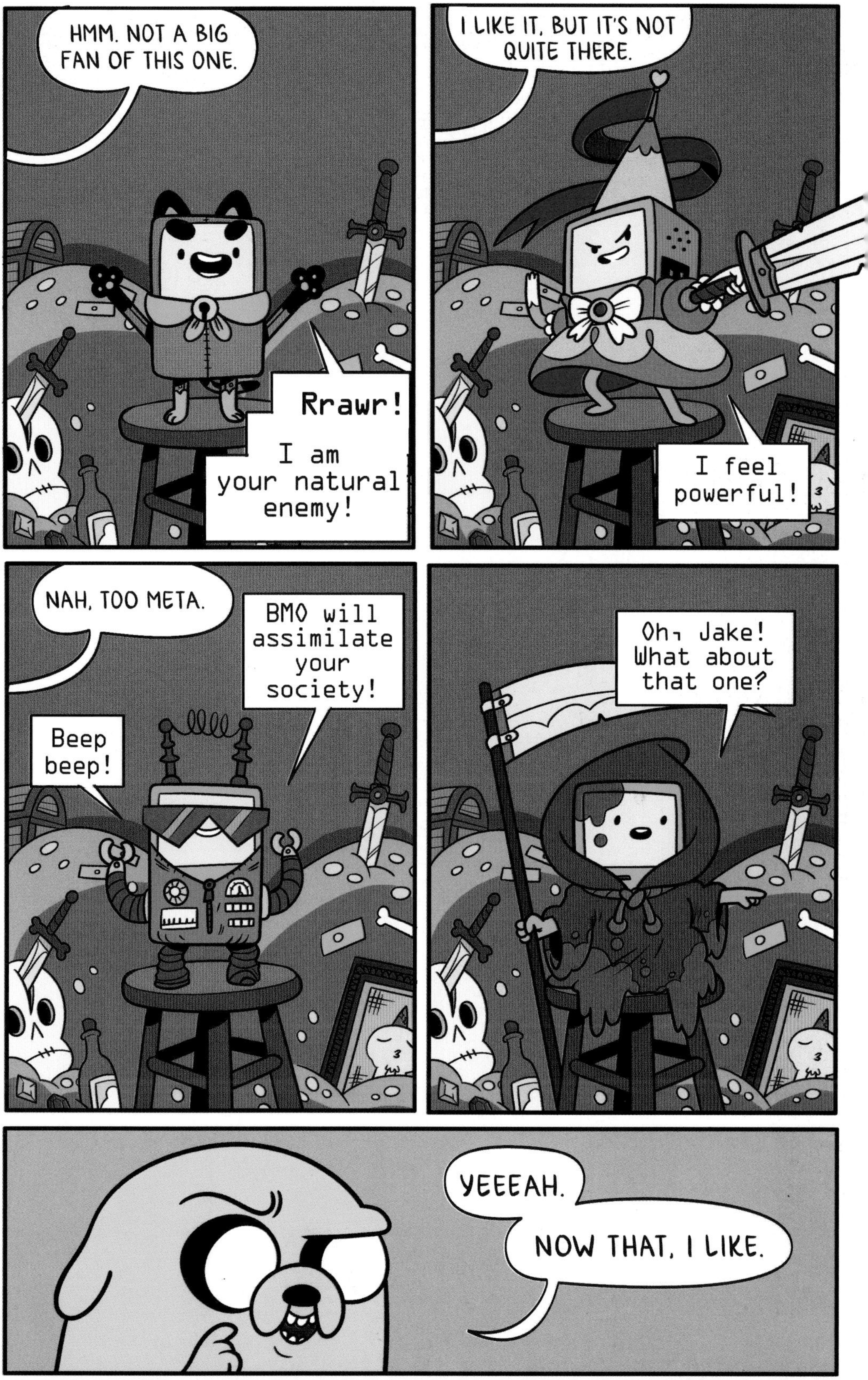
HMM. NOT A BIG FAN OF THIS ONE.
Rrawr!
I am your natural enemy!
I LIKE IT, BUT IT'S NOT QUITE THERE.
I feel powerful!
NAH, TOO META.
BMO will assimilate your society!
Beep beep!
Oh, Jake! What about that one?
YEEEAH.
NOW THAT, I LIKE.

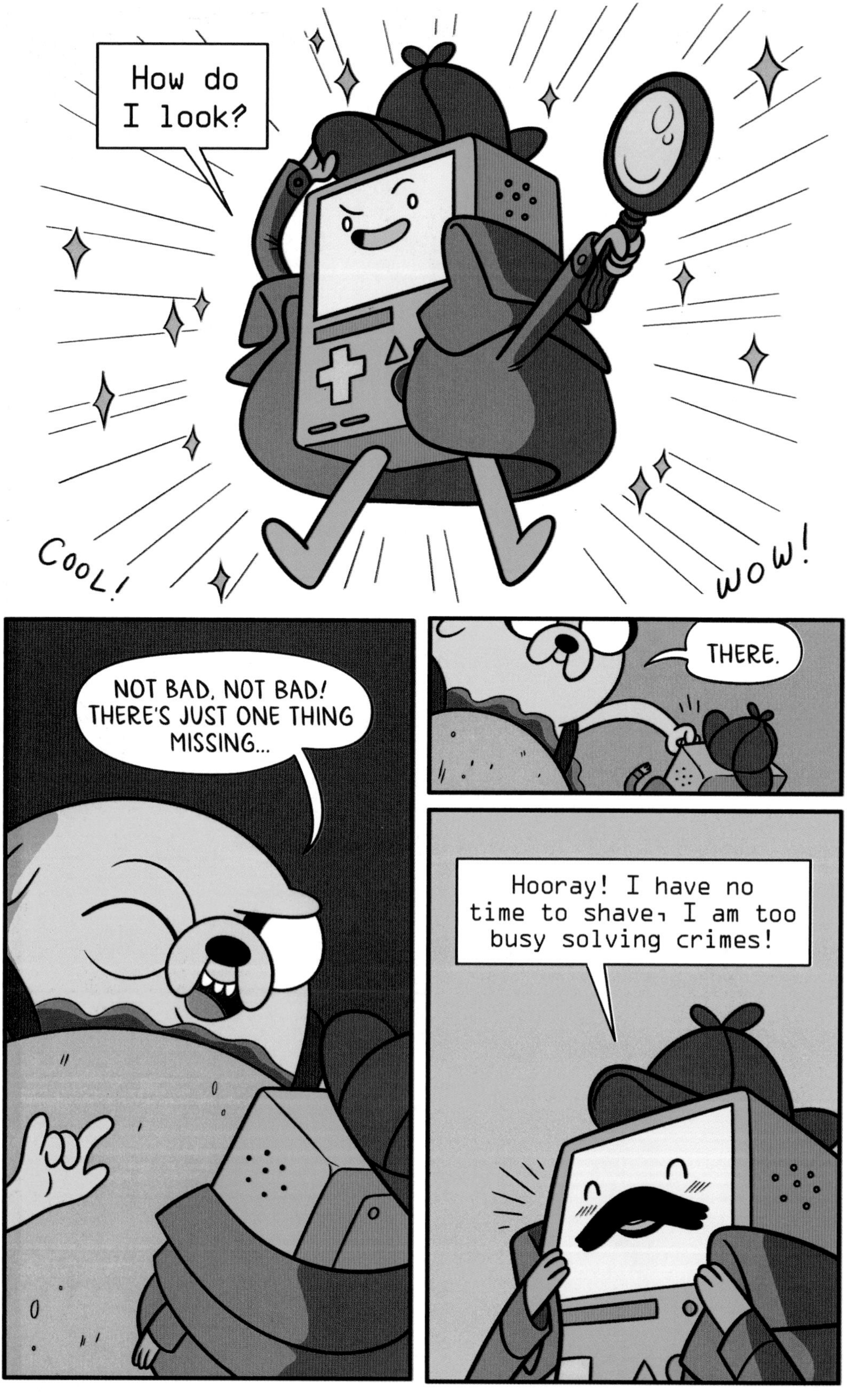
How do I look?
COOL!
WOW!
NOT BAD, NOT BAD! THERE'S JUST ONE THING MISSING...
THERE.
Hooray! I have no time to shave, I am too busy solving crimes!

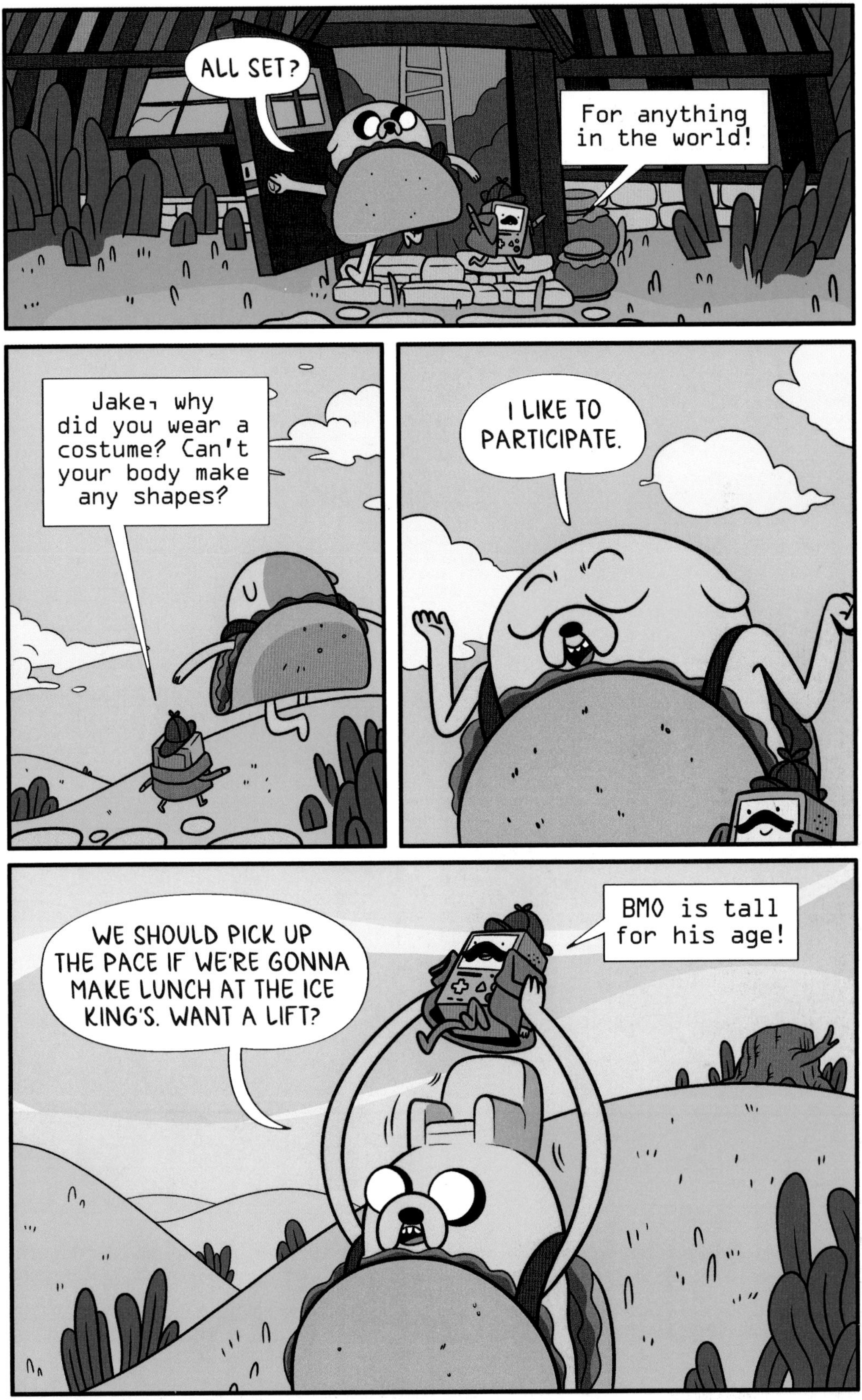
ALL SET?
For anything in the world!
Jake, why did you wear a costume? Can't your body make any shapes?
I LIKE TO PARTICIPATE.
WE SHOULD PICK UP THE PACE IF WE'RE GONNA MAKE LUNCH AT THE ICE KING'S. WANT A LIFT?
BMO is tall for his age!

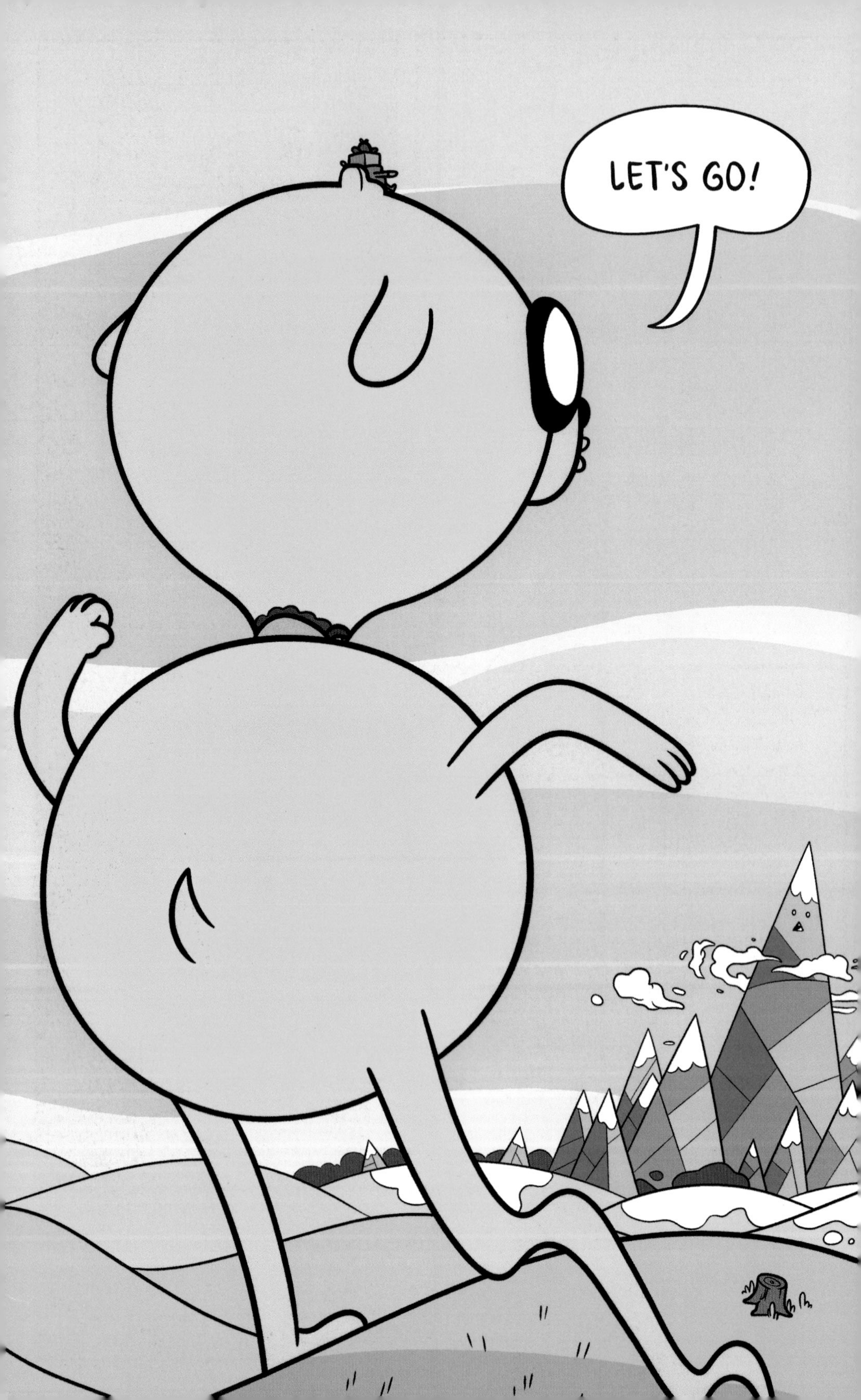
LET'S GO!

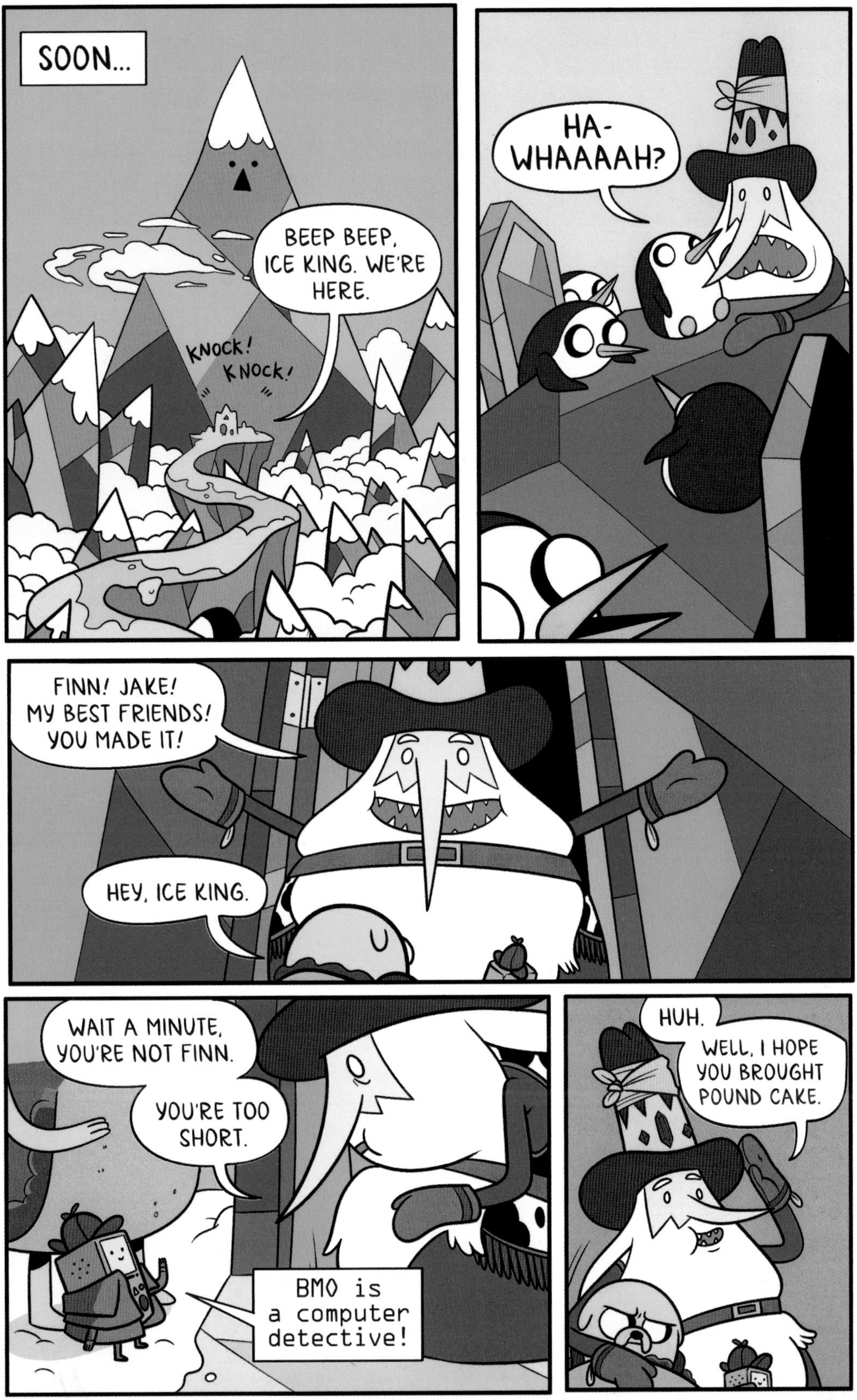
SOON...
BEEP BEEP, ICE KING. WE'RE HERE.
KNOCK! KNOCK!
HA-WHAAAAH?
FINN! JAKE! MY BEST FRIENDS! YOU MADE IT!
HEY, ICE KING.
WAIT A MINUTE, YOU'RE NOT FINN.
YOU'RE TOO SHORT.
BMO is a computer detective!
HUH.
WELL, I HOPE YOU BROUGHT POUND CAKE.

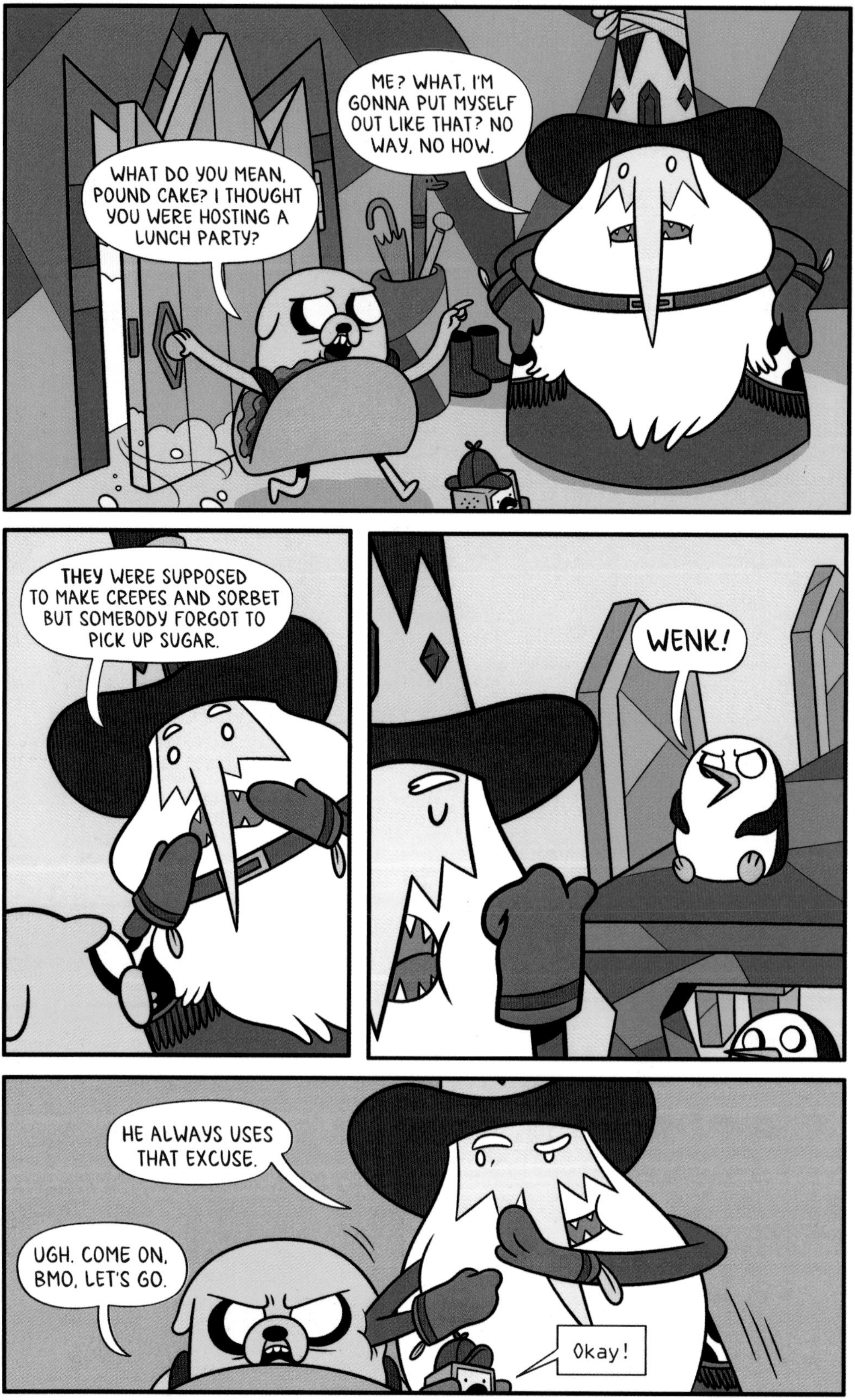
WHAT DO YOU MEAN, POUND CAKE? I THOUGHT YOU WERE HOSTING A LUNCH PARTY?
ME? WHAT, I'M GONNA PUT MYSELF OUT LIKE THAT? NO WAY, NO HOW.
THEY WERE SUPPOSED TO MAKE CREPES AND SORBET BUT SOMEBODY FORGOT TO PICK UP SUGAR.
WENK!
HE ALWAYS USES THAT EXCUSE.
UGH. COME ON, BMO, LET'S GO.
Okay!

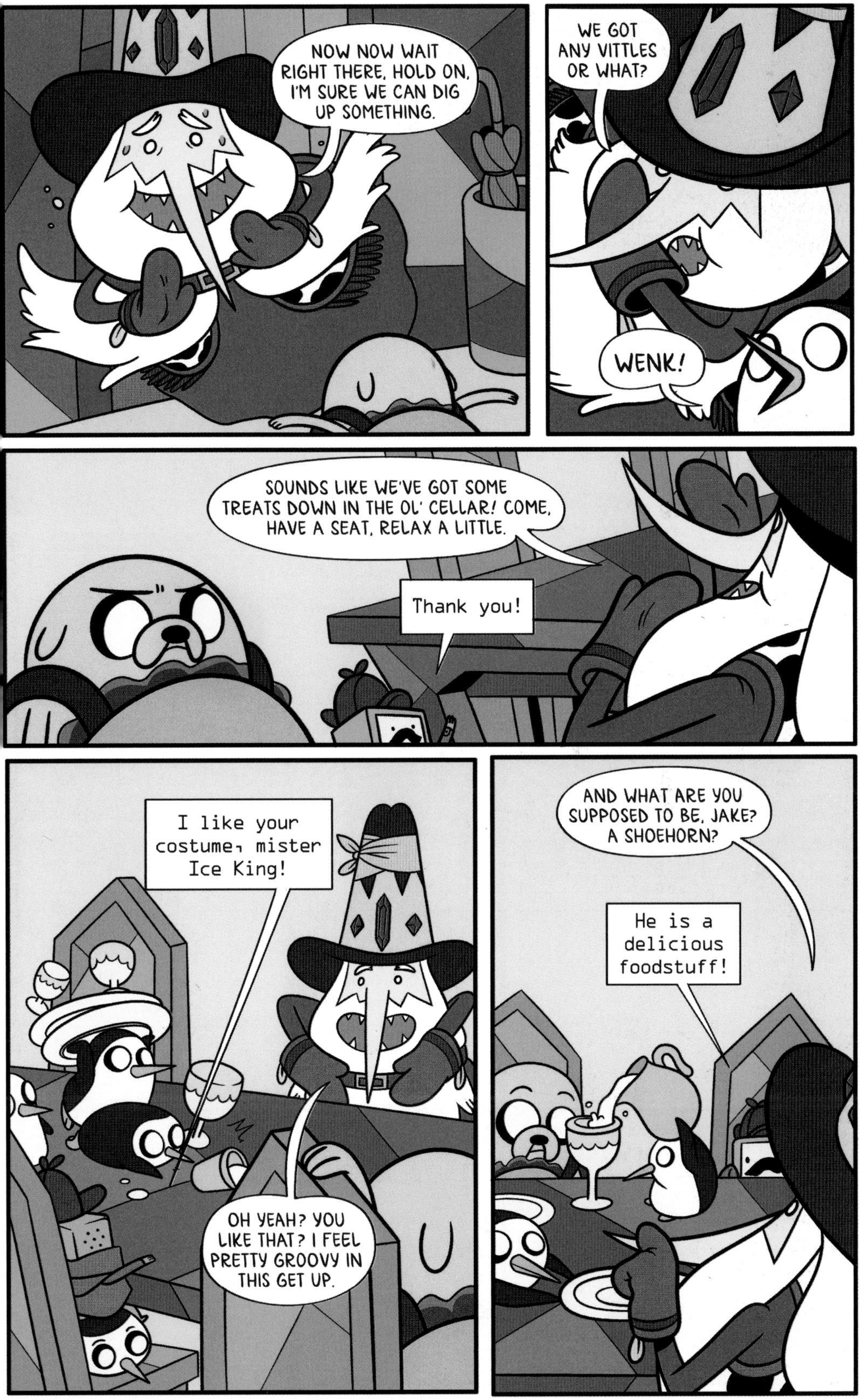
NOW NOW WAIT RIGHT THERE, HOLD ON, I'M SURE WE CAN DIG UP SOMETHING.
WE GOT ANY VITTLES OR WHAT?
WENK!
SOUNDS LIKE WE'VE GOT SOME TREATS DOWN IN THE OL' CELLAR! COME, HAVE A SEAT, RELAX A LITTLE.
Thank you!
I like your costume, mister Ice King!
OH YEAH? YOU LIKE THAT? I FEEL PRETTY GROOVY IN THIS GET UP.
AND WHAT ARE YOU SUPPOSED TO BE, JAKE? A SHOEHORN?
He is a delicious foodstuff!

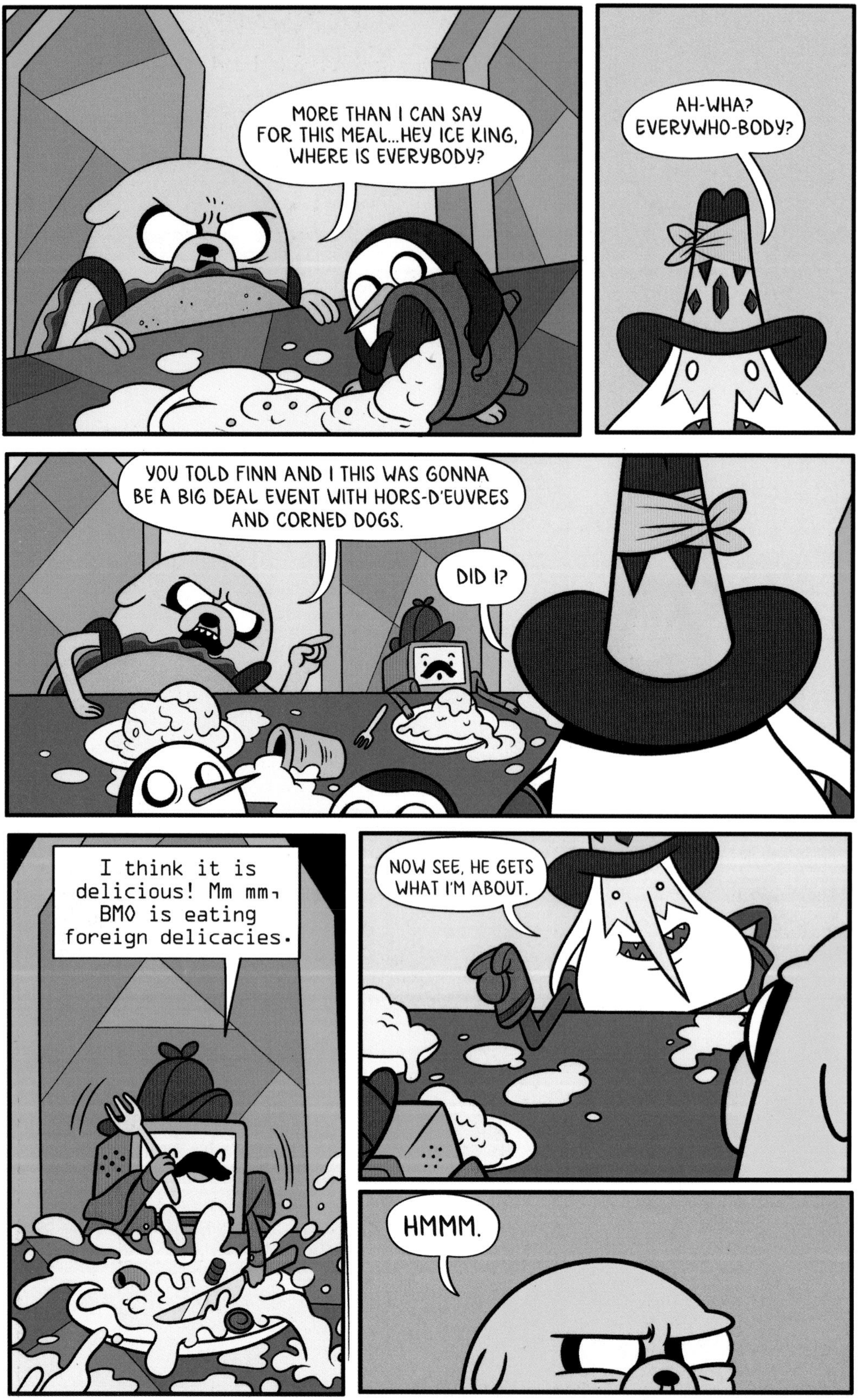
MORE THAN I CAN SAY FOR THIS MEAL...HEY ICE KING, WHERE IS EVERYBODY?
AH-WHA? EVERYWHO-BODY?
YOU TOLD FINN AND I THIS WAS GONNA BE A BIG DEAL EVENT WITH HORS-D'EUVRES AND CORNED DOGS.
DID I?
I think it is delicious! Mm mm, BMO is eating foreign delicacies.
NOW SEE, HE GETS WHAT I'M ABOUT.
HMMM.

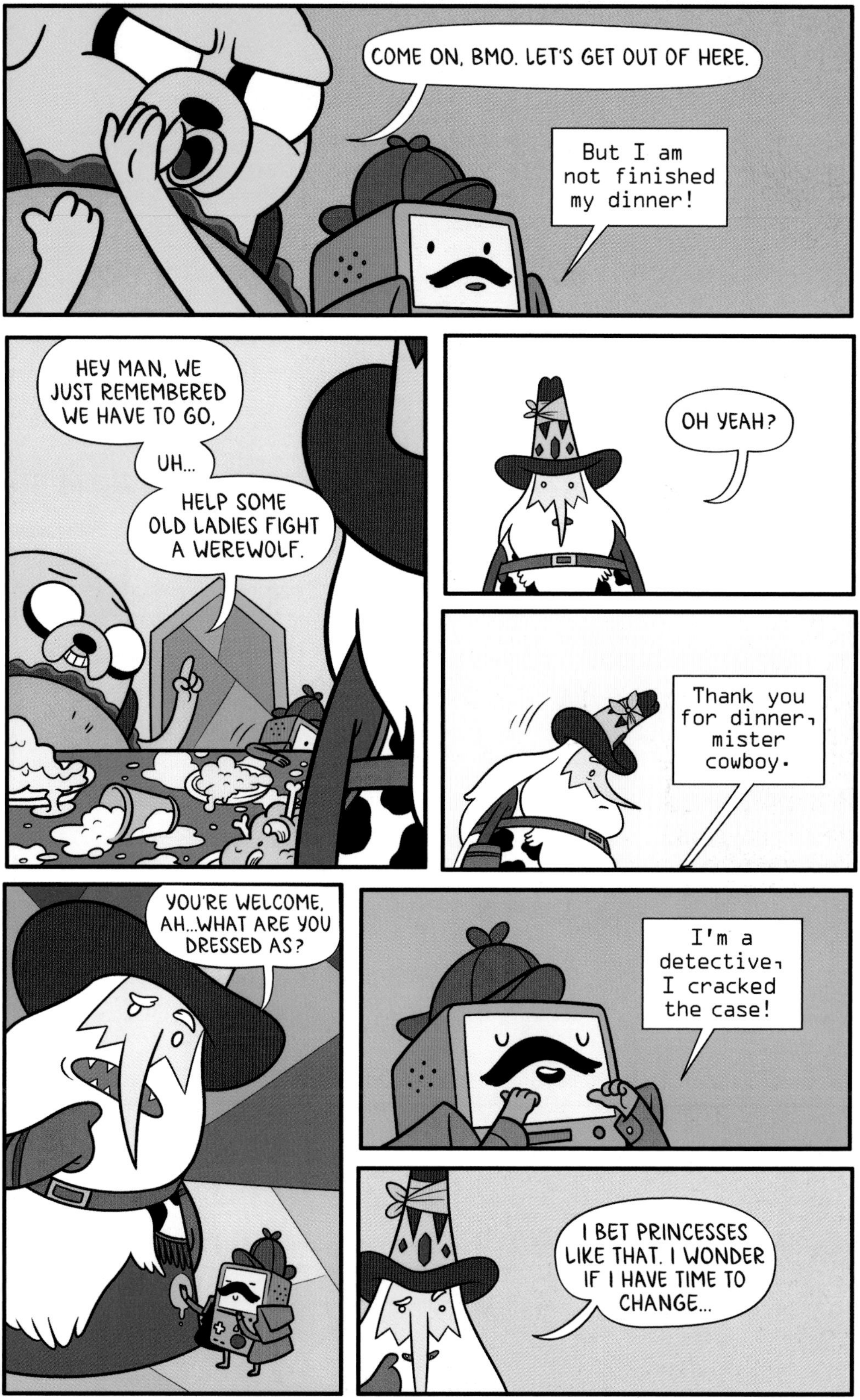
COME ON, BMO. LET'S GET OUT OF HERE.
But I am not finished my dinner!
HEY MAN, WE JUST REMEMBERED WE HAVE TO GO,
UH...
HELP SOME OLD LADIES FIGHT A WEREWOLF.
OH YEAH?
Thank you for dinner, mister cowboy.
YOU'RE WELCOME, AH...WHAT ARE YOU DRESSED AS?
I'm a detective, I cracked the case!
I BET PRINCESSES LIKE THAT. I WONDER IF I HAVE TIME TO CHANGE...

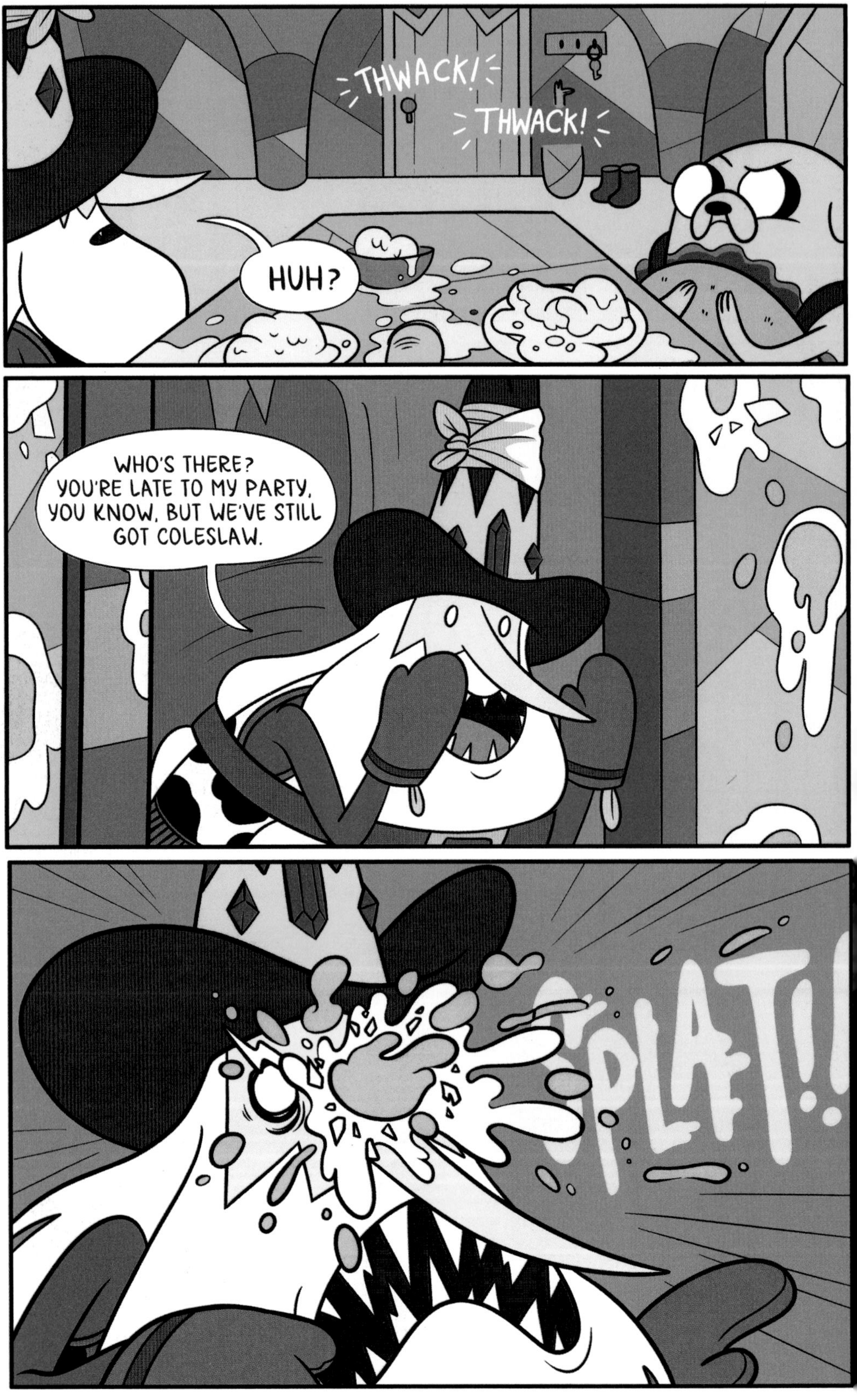
THWACK!
THWACK!
HUH?
WHO'S THERE? YOU'RE LATE TO MY PARTY, YOU KNOW, BUT WE'VE STILL GOT COLESLAW.
SPLAT!!

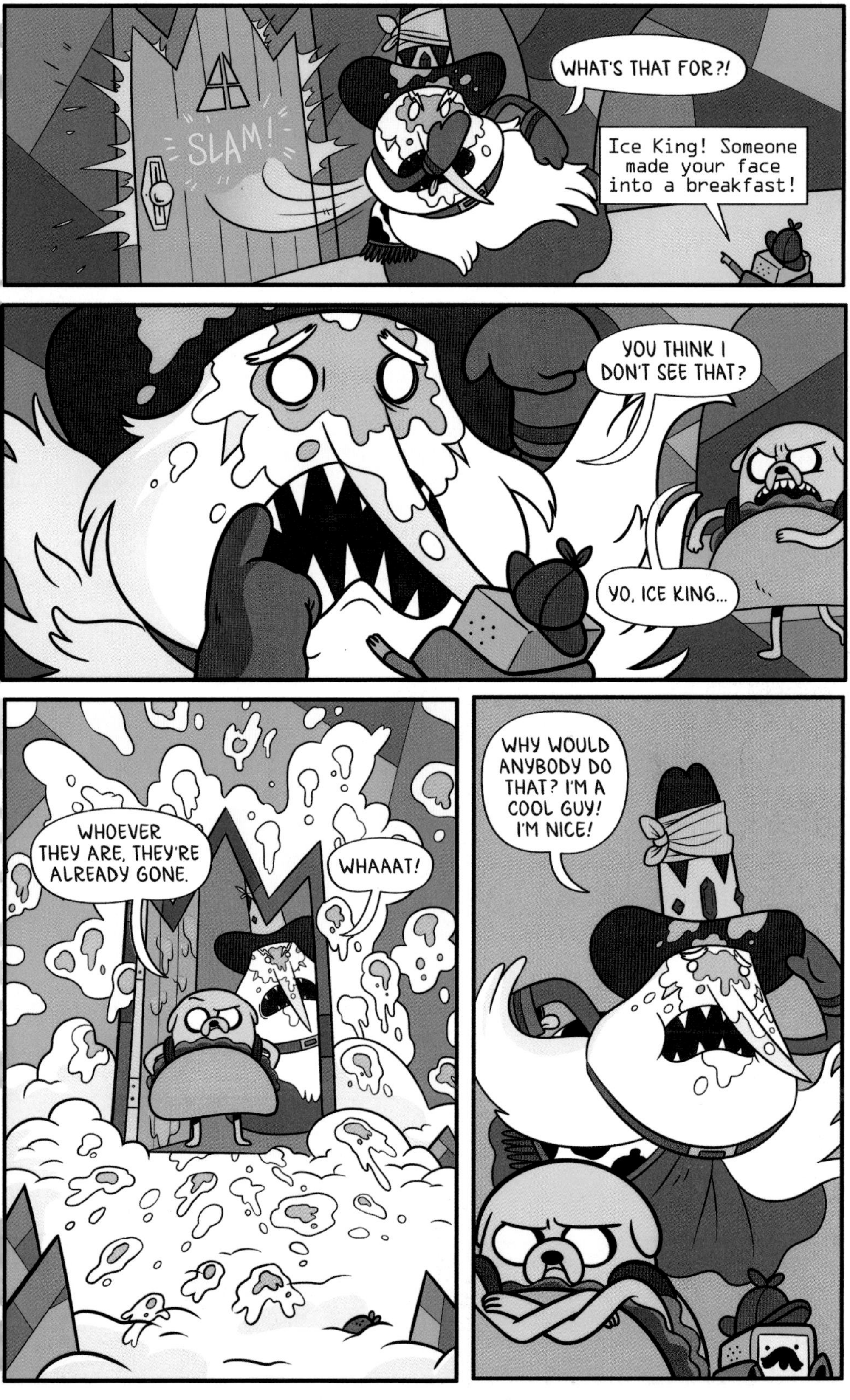
SLAM!
WHAT'S THAT FOR?!
Ice King! Someone made your face into a breakfast!
YOU THINK I DON'T SEE THAT?
YO, ICE KING...
WHOEVER THEY ARE, THEY'RE ALREADY GONE.
WHAAAT!
WHY WOULD ANYBODY DO THAT? I'M A COOL GUY! I'M NICE!

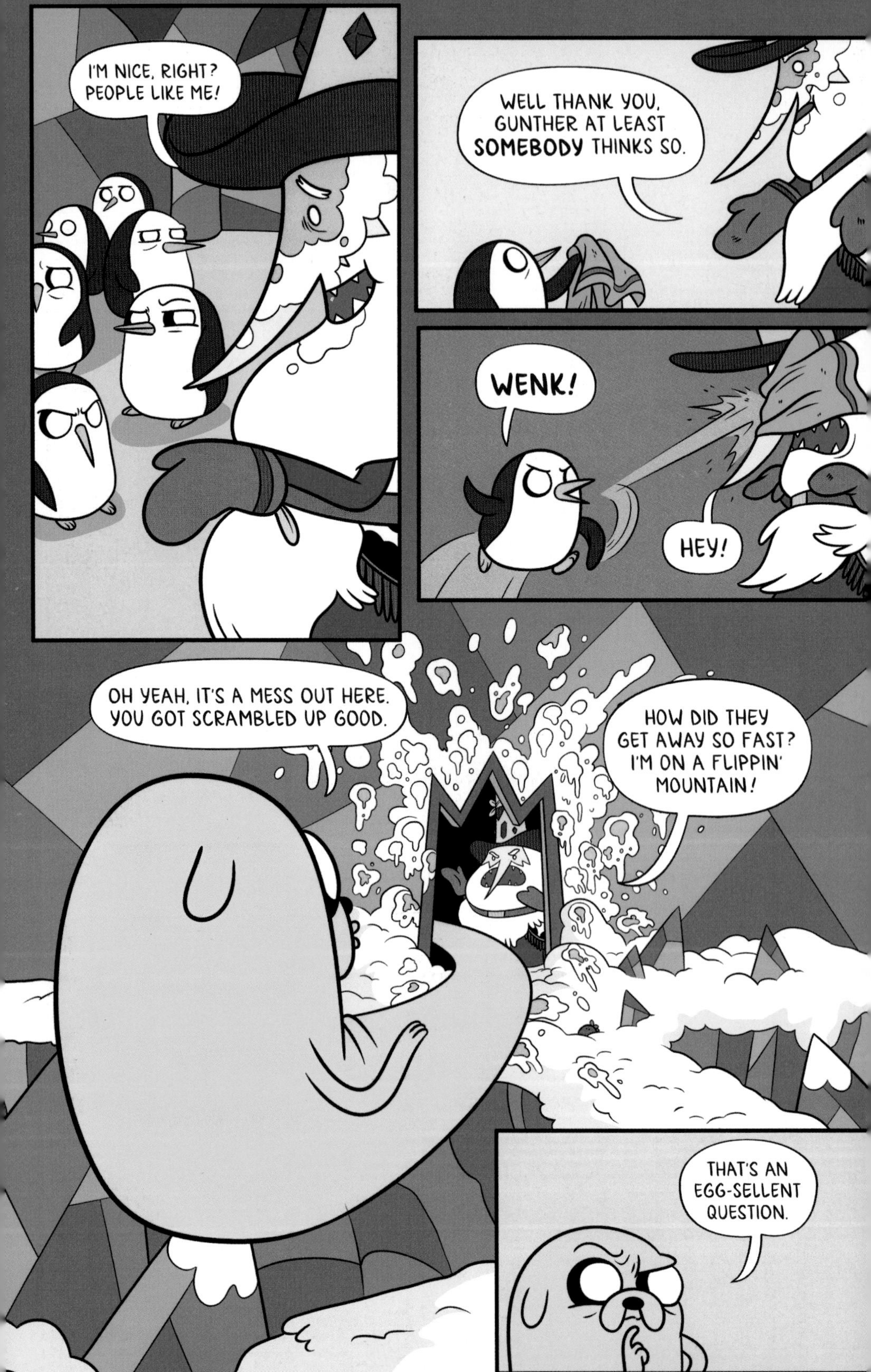
I'M NICE, RIGHT? PEOPLE LIKE ME!
WELL THANK YOU, GUNTHER AT LEAST SOMEBODY THINKS SO.
WENK!
HEY!
OH YEAH, IT'S A MESS OUT HERE. YOU GOT SCRAMBLED UP GOOD.
HOW DID THEY GET AWAY SO FAST? I'M ON A FLIPPIN' MOUNTAIN!
THAT'S AN EGG-SELLENT QUESTION.

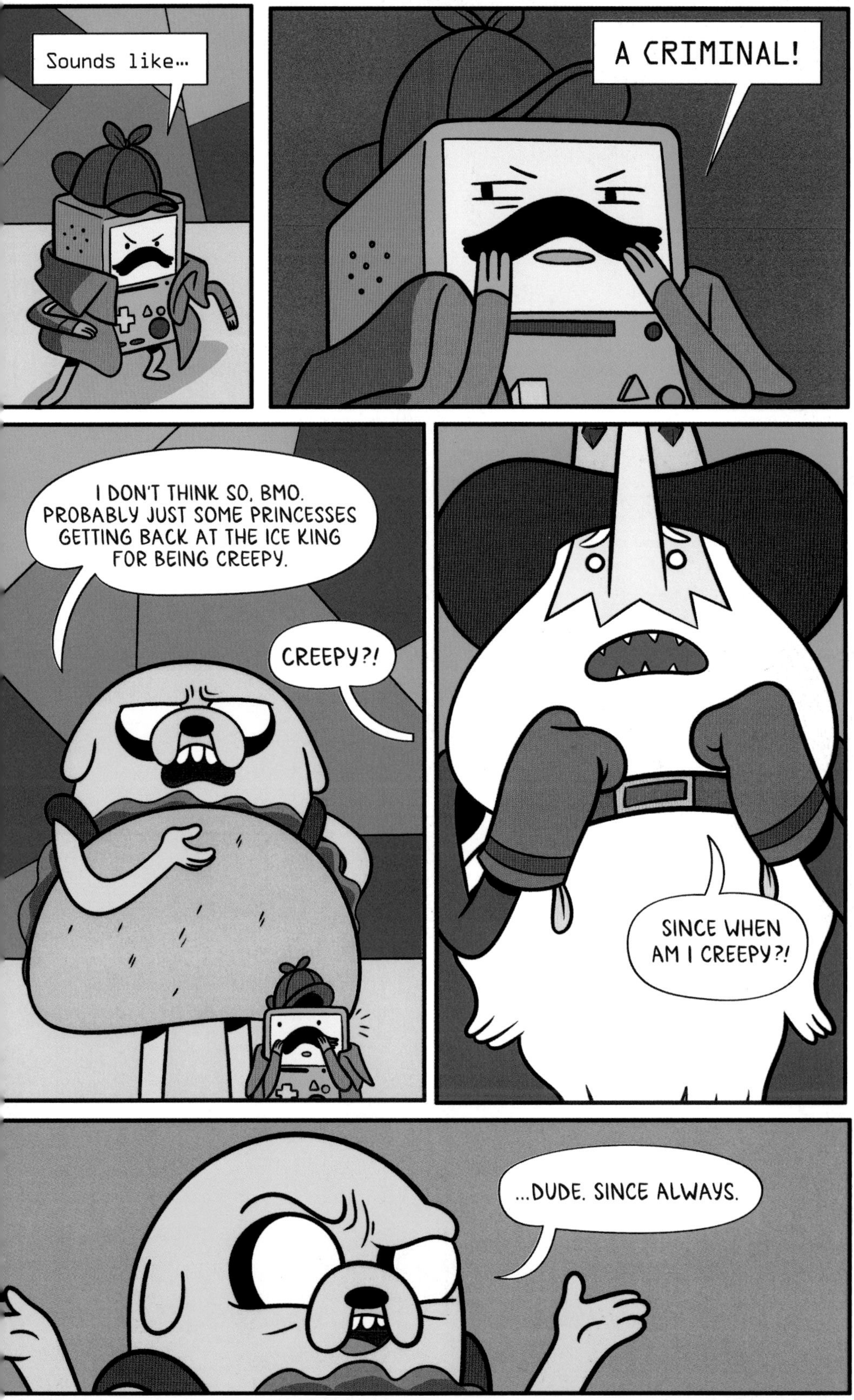
Sounds like...
A CRIMINAL!
I DON'T THINK SO, BMO. PROBABLY JUST SOME PRINCESSES GETTING BACK AT THE ICE KING FOR BEING CREEPY.
CREEPY?!
SINCE WHEN AM I CREEPY?!
...DUDE. SINCE ALWAYS.

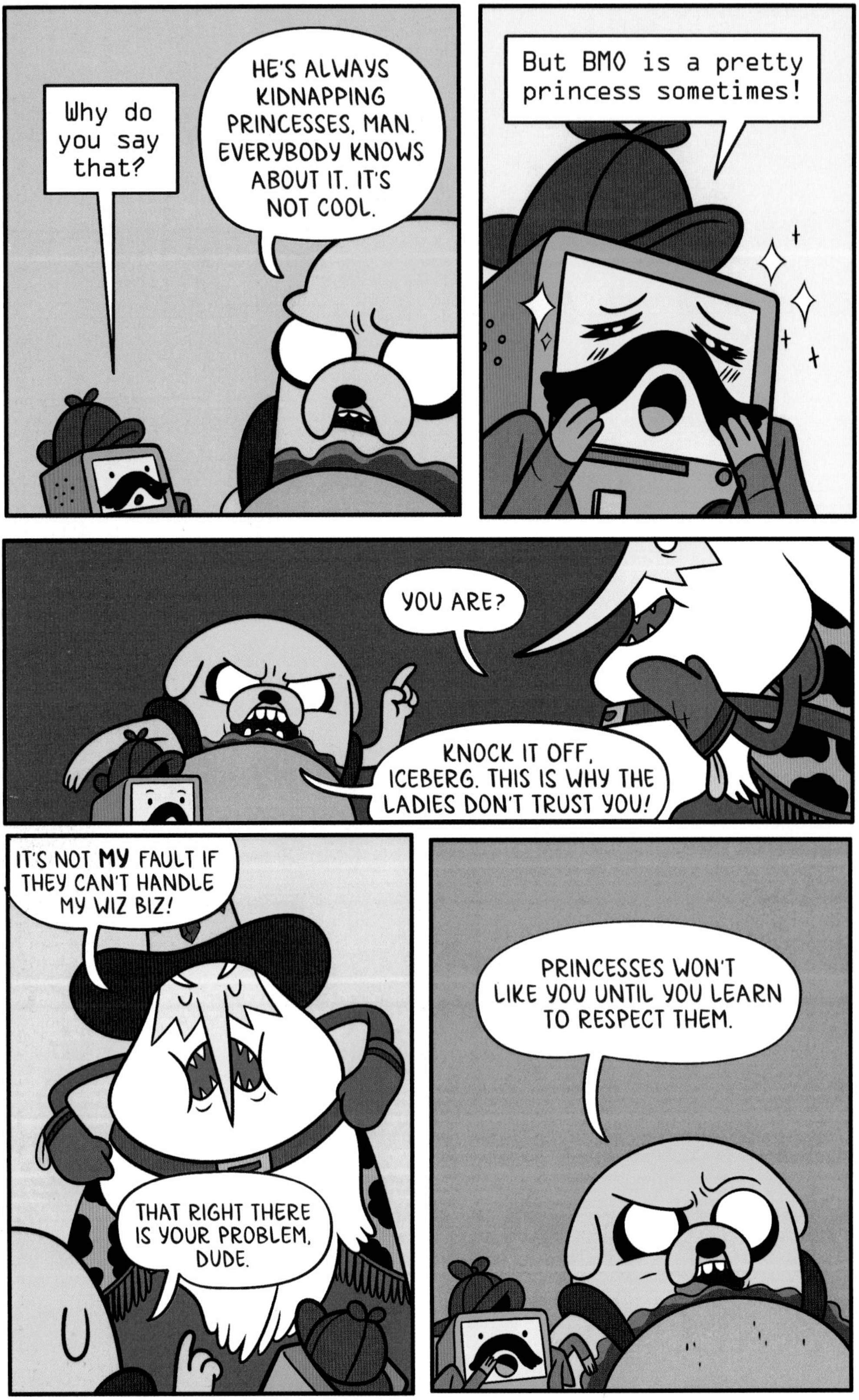
Why do you say that?
HE'S ALWAYS KIDNAPPING PRINCESSES, MAN. EVERYBODY KNOWS ABOUT IT. IT'S NOT COOL.
But BMO is a pretty princess sometimes!
YOU ARE?
KNOCK IT OFF, ICEBERG. THIS IS WHY THE LADIES DON'T TRUST YOU!
IT'S NOT MY FAULT IF THEY CAN'T HANDLE MY WIZ BIZ!
THAT RIGHT THERE IS YOUR PROBLEM, DUDE.
PRINCESSES WON'T LIKE YOU UNTIL YOU LEARN TO RESPECT THEM.

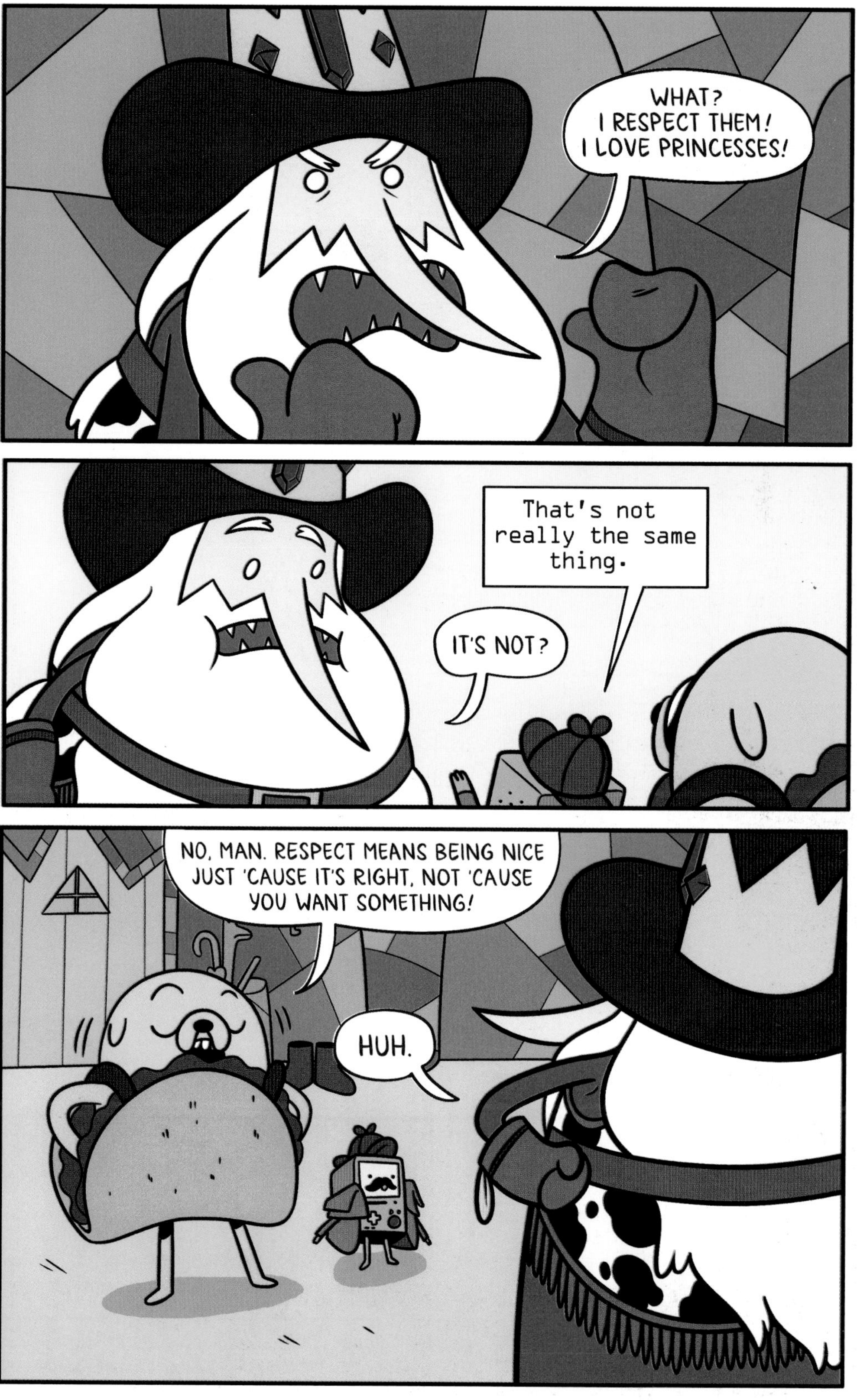
WHAT?
I RESPECT THEM!
I LOVE PRINCESSES!
That's not really the same thing.
IT'S NOT?
NO, MAN. RESPECT MEANS BEING NICE JUST 'CAUSE IT'S RIGHT, NOT 'CAUSE YOU WANT SOMETHING!
HUH.

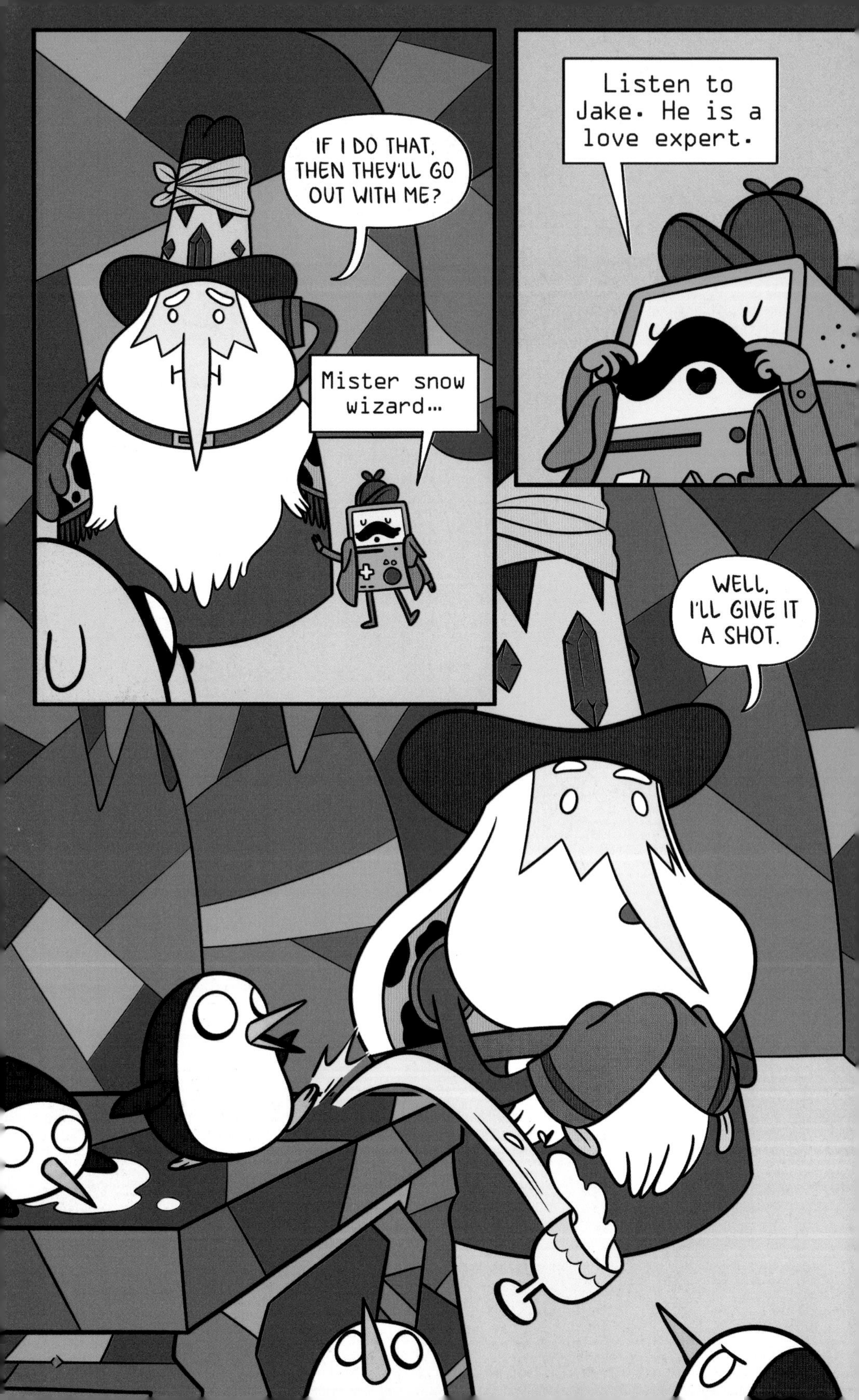
IF I DO THAT, THEN THEY'LL GO OUT WITH ME?
Mister snow wizard...
Listen to Jake. He is a love expert.
WELL, I'LL GIVE IT A SHOT.

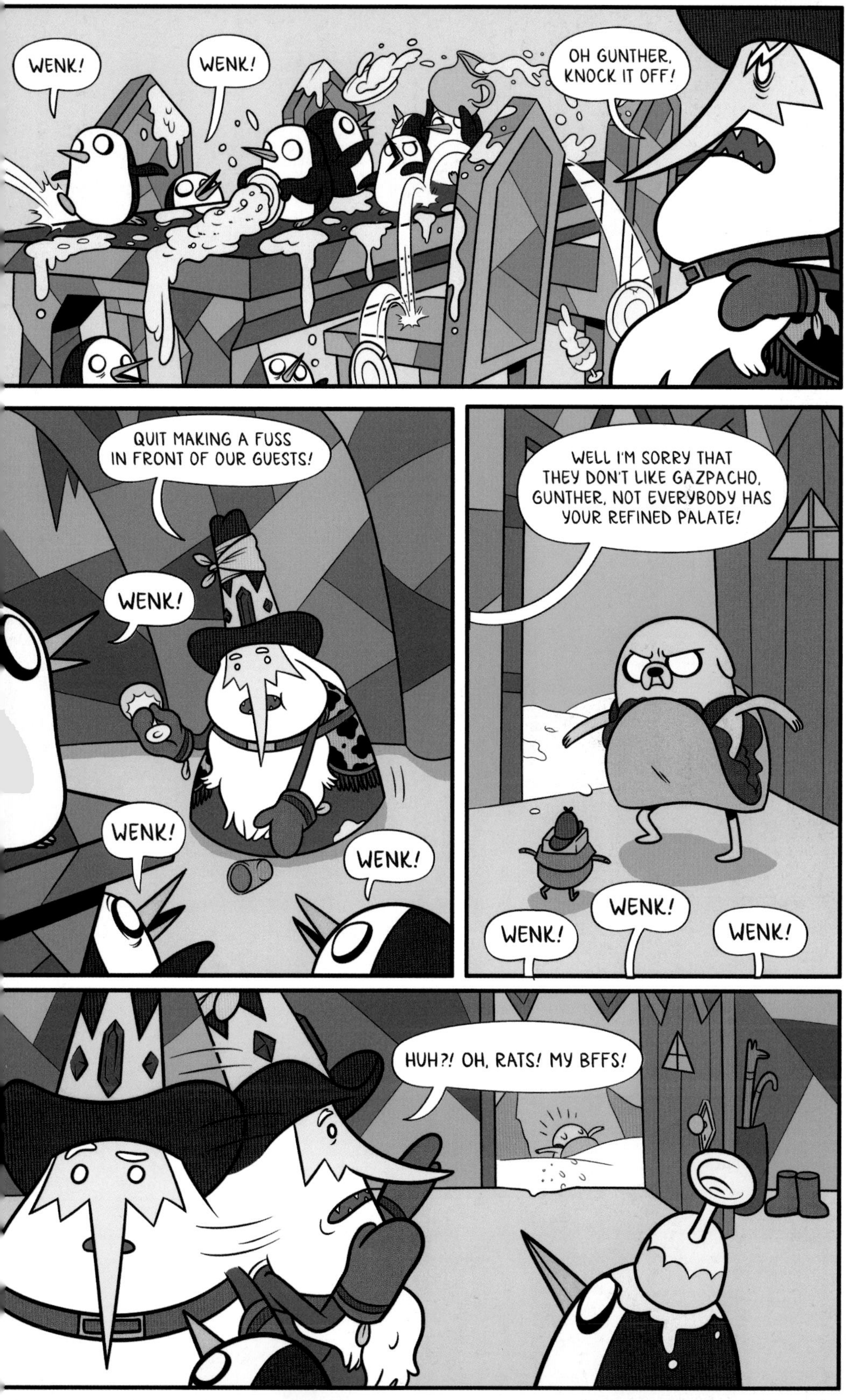

WENK!
WENK!
OH GUNTHER, KNOCK IT OFF!
QUIT MAKING A FUSS IN FRONT OF OUR GUESTS!
WENK!
WENK!
WENK!
WELL I'M SORRY THAT THEY DON'T LIKE GAZPACHO, GUNTHER, NOT EVERYBODY HAS YOUR REFINED PALATE!
WENK!
WENK!
WENK!
HUH?! OH, RATS! MY BFFS!

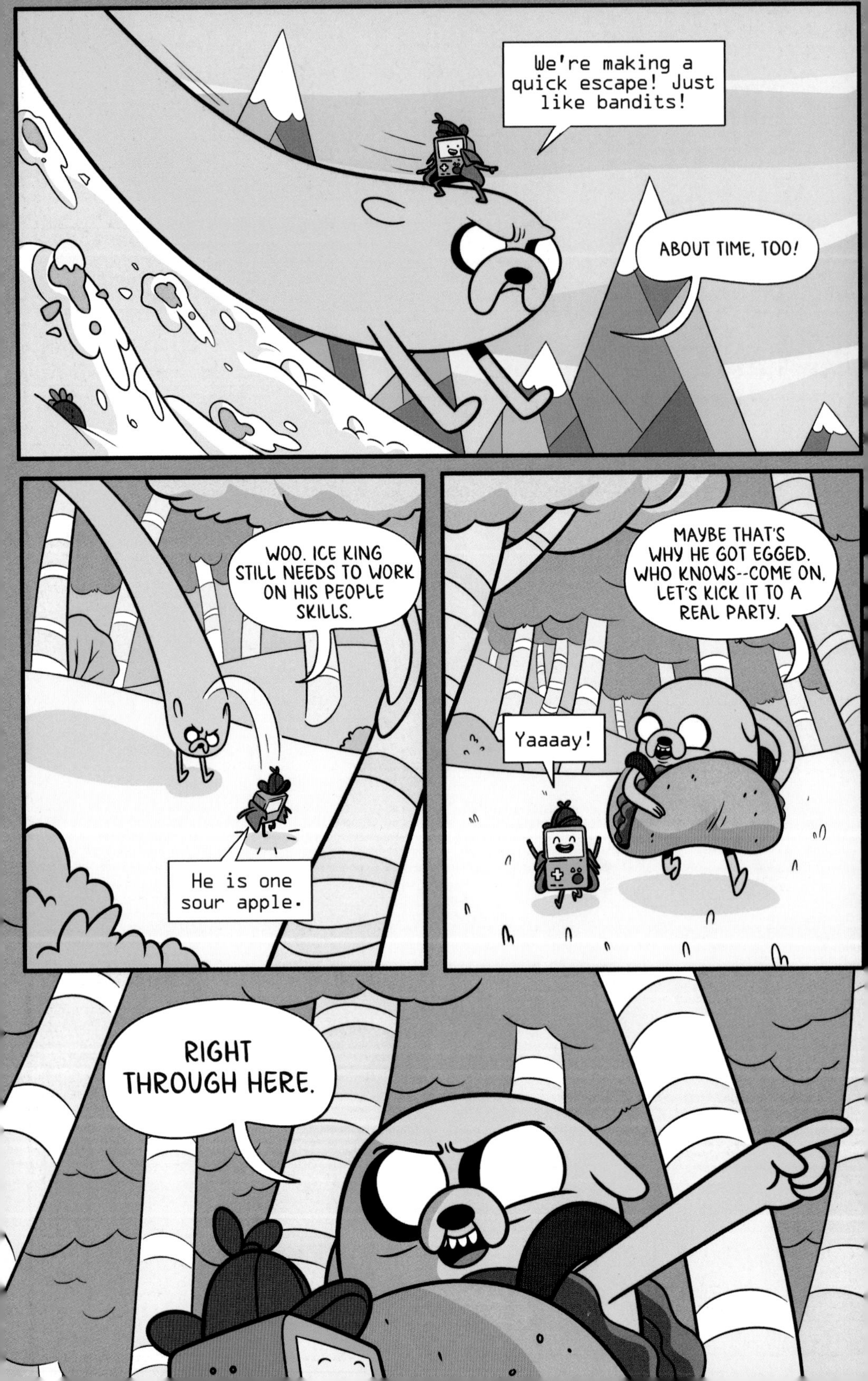
We're making a quick escape! Just like bandits!
ABOUT TIME, TOO!
WOO. ICE KING STILL NEEDS TO WORK ON HIS PEOPLE SKILLS.
He is one sour apple.
MAYBE THAT'S WHY HE GOT EGGED. WHO KNOWS--COME ON, LET'S KICK IT TO A REAL PARTY.
Yaaaay!
RIGHT THROUGH HERE.

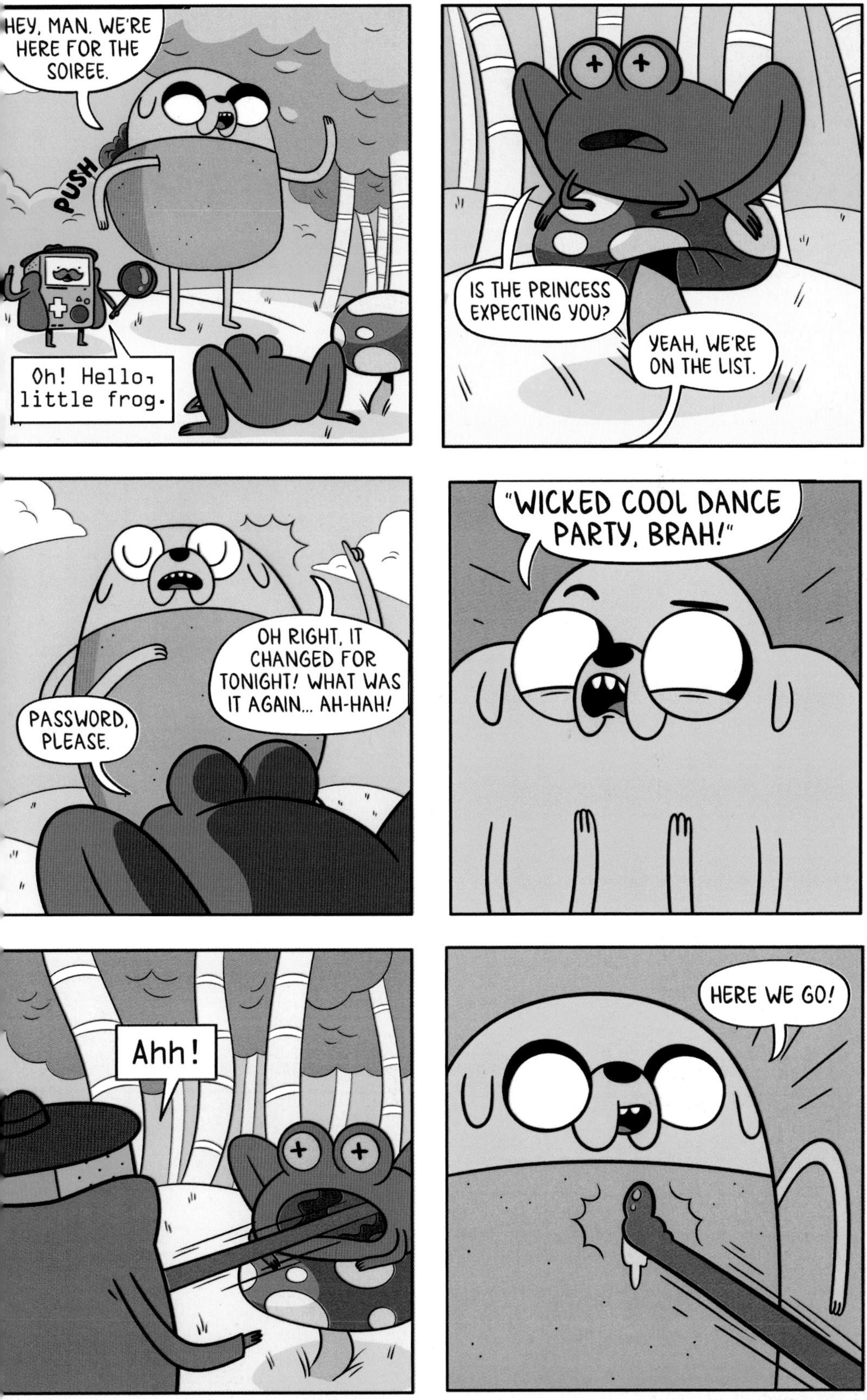
HEY, MAN. WE'RE HERE FOR THE SOIREE.
PUSH
Oh! Hello, little frog.
IS THE PRINCESS EXPECTING YOU?
YEAH, WE'RE ON THE LIST.
PASSWORD, PLEASE.
OH RIGHT, IT CHANGED FOR TONIGHT! WHAT WAS IT AGAIN... AH-HAH!
"WICKED COOL DANCE PARTY, BRAH!"
Ahh!
HERE WE GO!

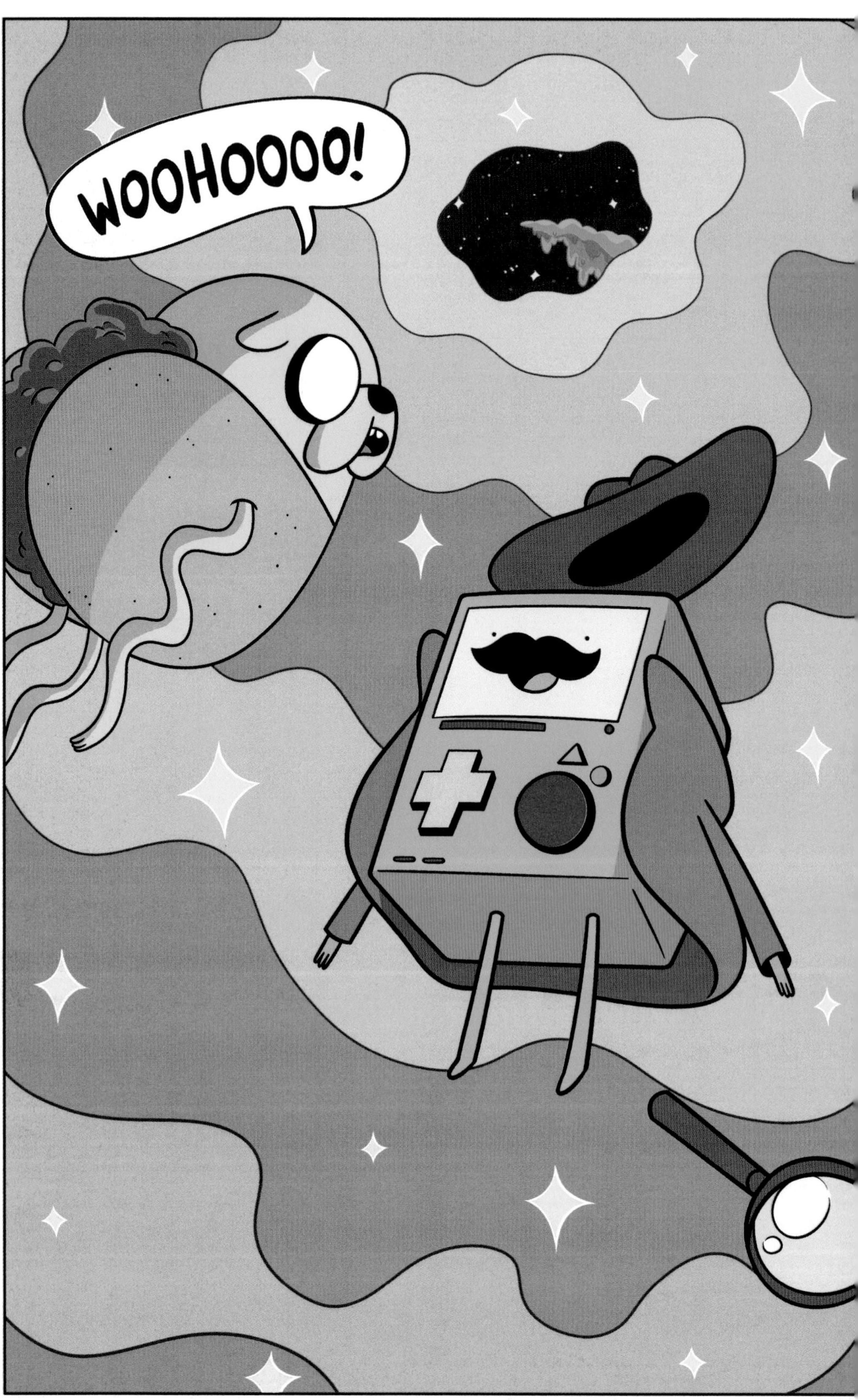
WOOHOOOO!

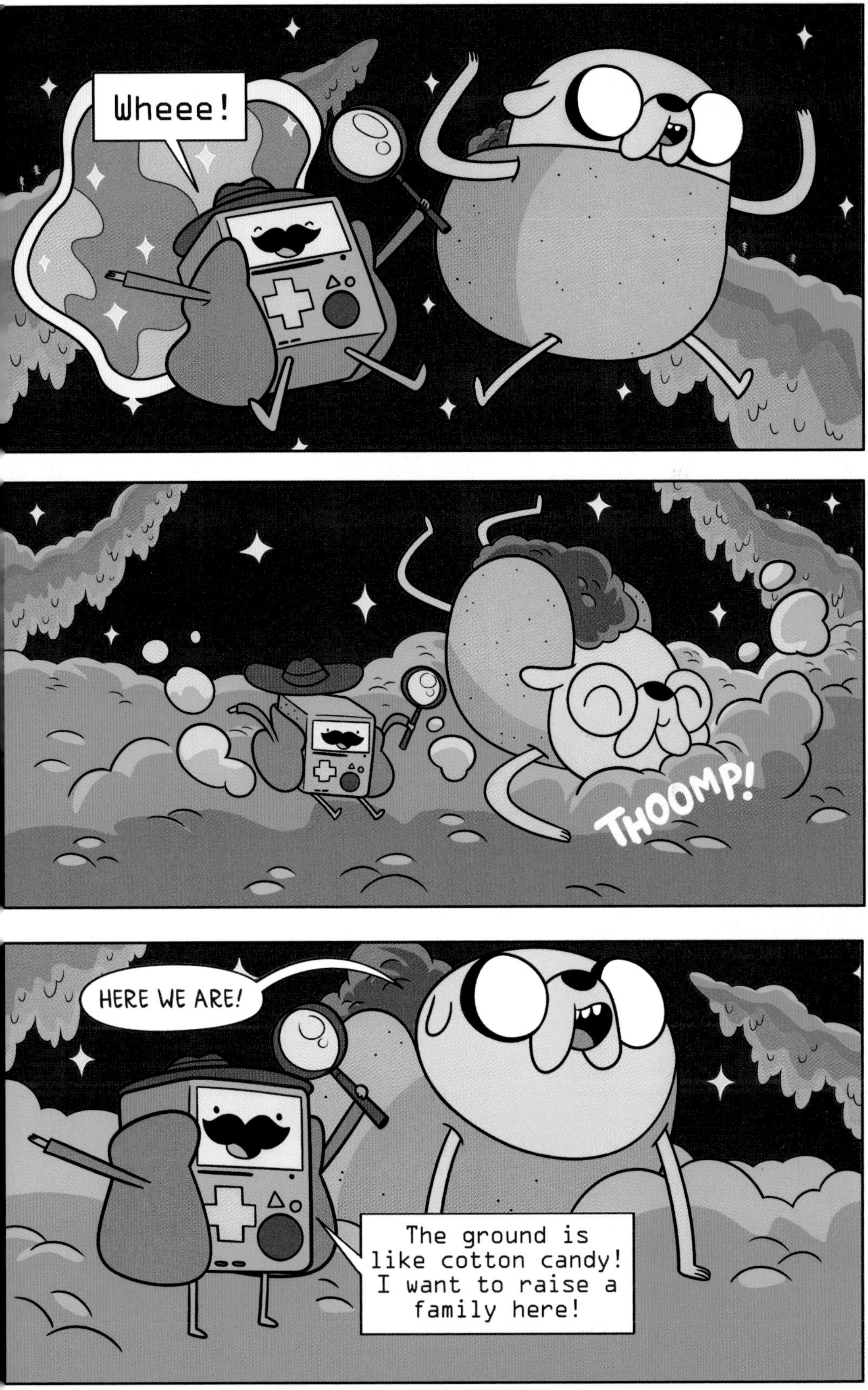
Wheee!
THOOMP!
HERE WE ARE!
The ground is like cotton candy! I want to raise a family here!

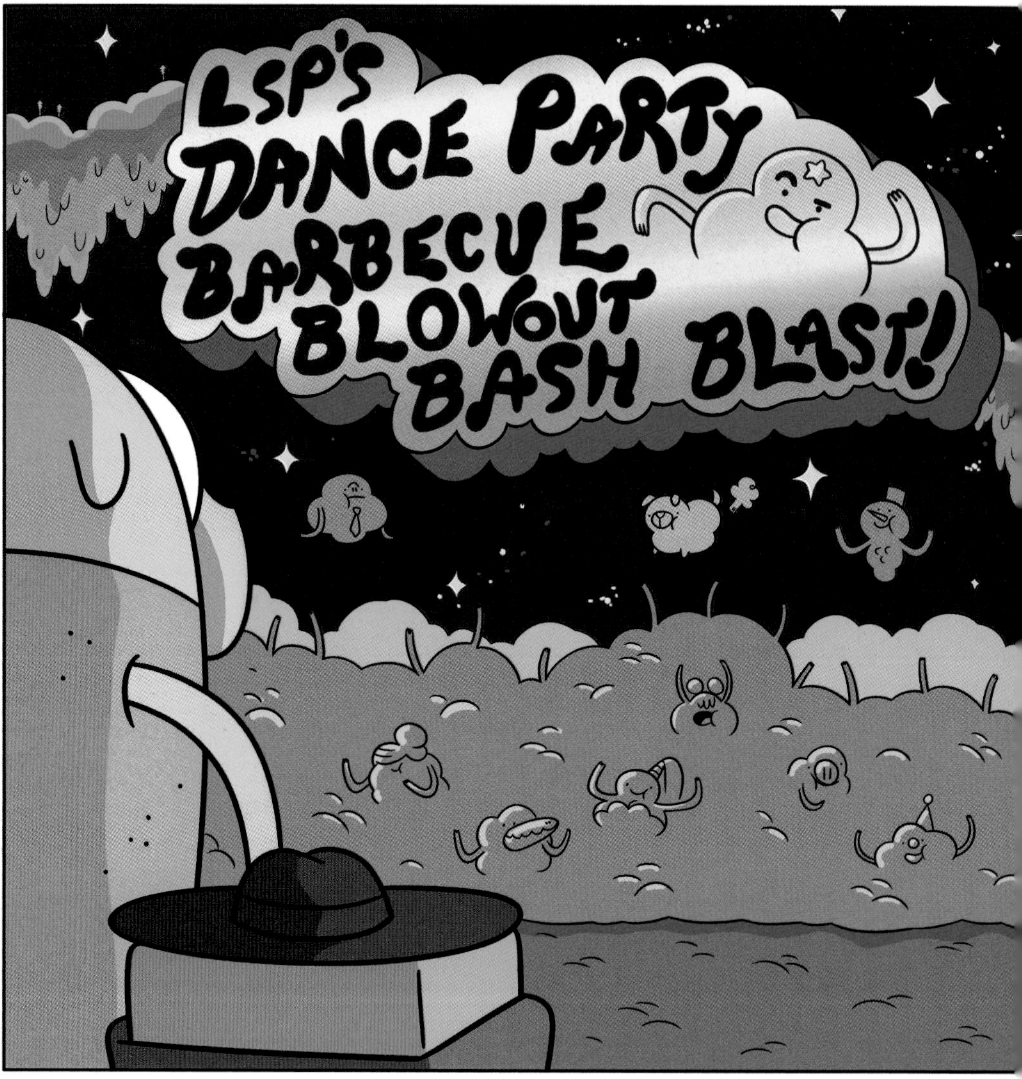
LSP'S DANCE PARTY BARBECUE BLOWOUT BASH BLAST!

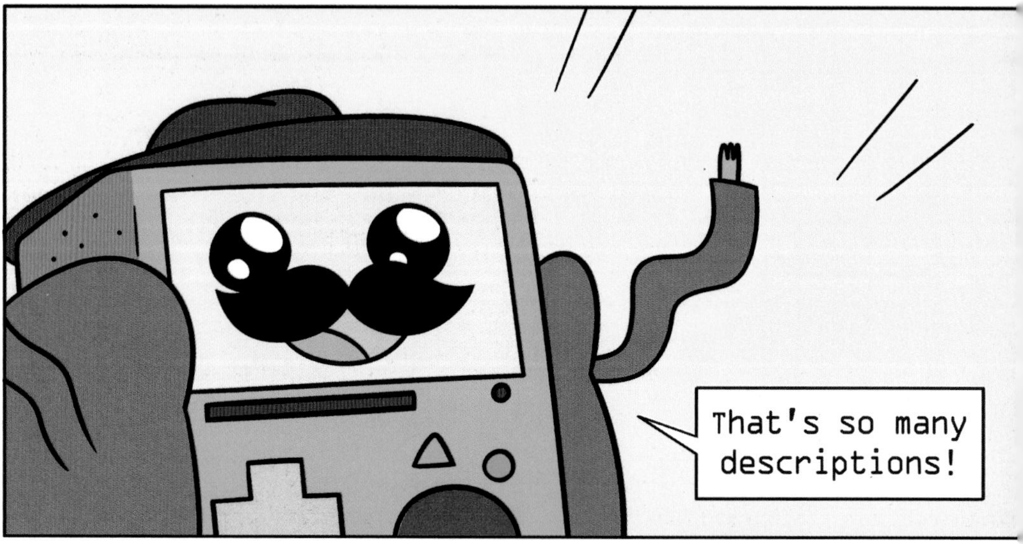
That's so many descriptions!

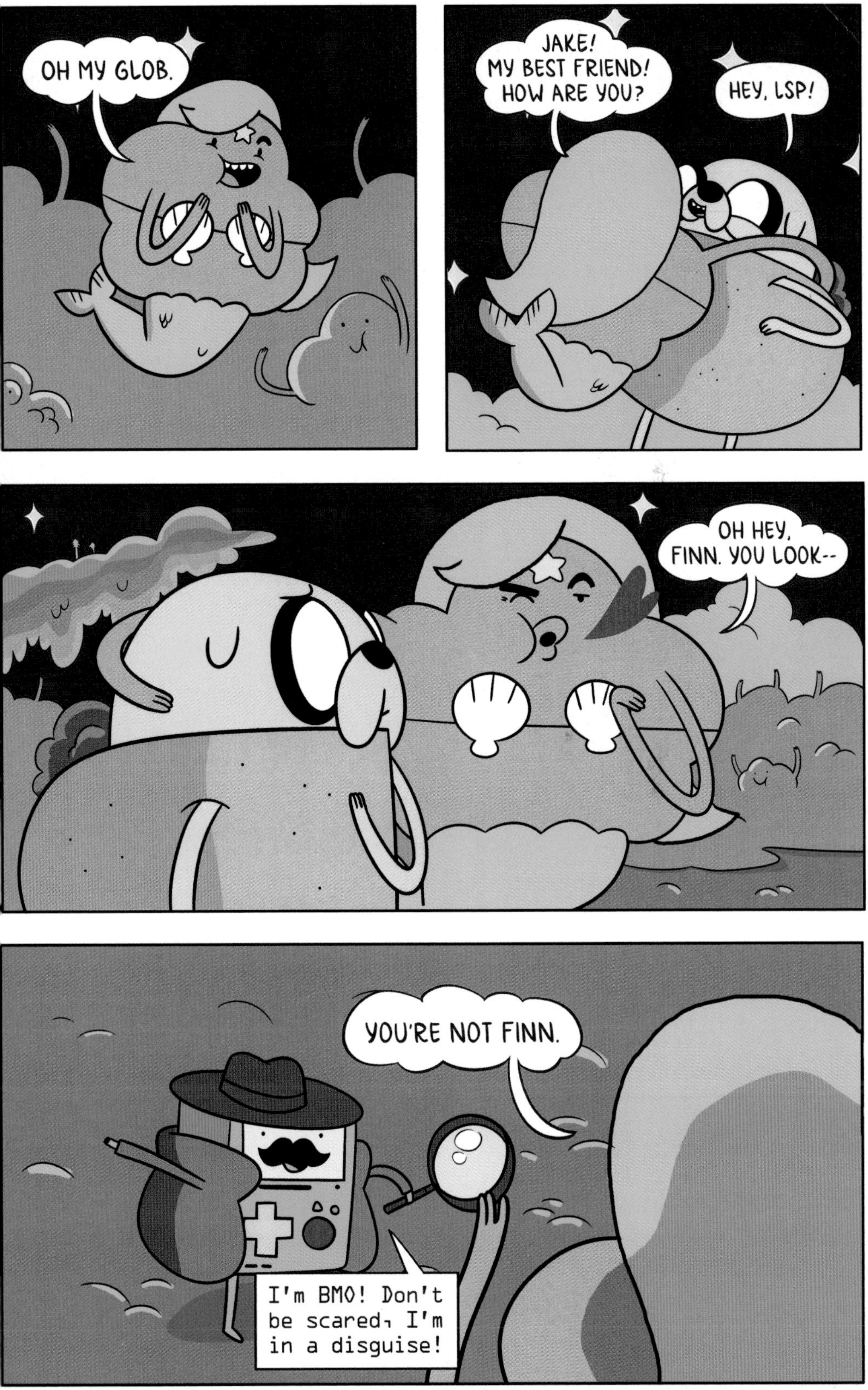
OH MY GLOB.
JAKE! MY BEST FRIEND! HOW ARE YOU?
HEY, LSP!
OH HEY, FINN. YOU LOOK--
YOU'RE NOT FINN.
I'm BMO! Don't be scared, I'm in a disguise!

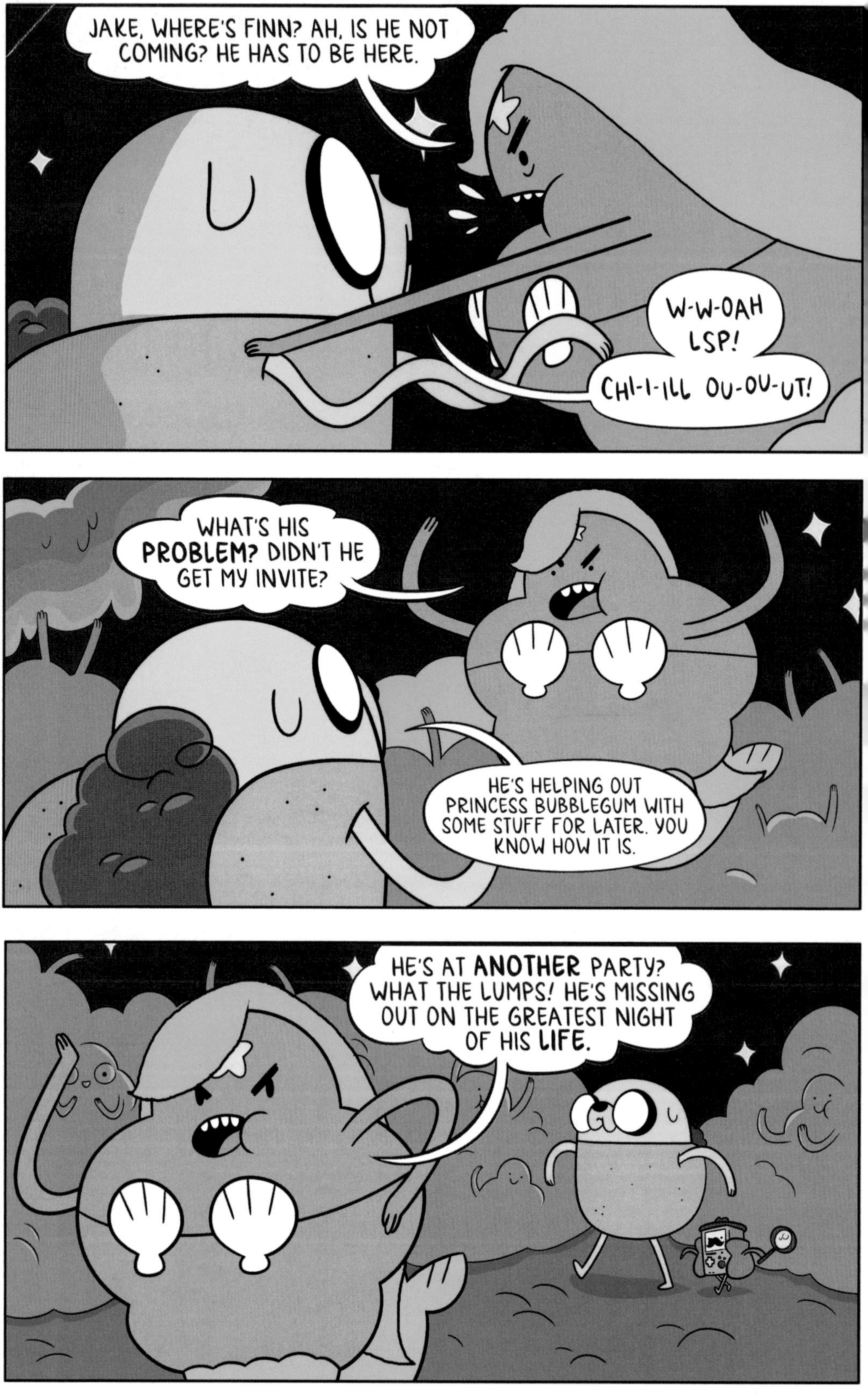
JAKE, WHERE'S FINN? AH, IS HE NOT COMING? HE HAS TO BE HERE.
W-W-OAH LSP!
CHI-I-ILL OU-OU-UT!
WHAT'S HIS **PROBLEM?** DIDN'T HE GET MY INVITE?
HE'S HELPING OUT PRINCESS BUBBLEGUM WITH SOME STUFF FOR LATER. YOU KNOW HOW IT IS.
HE'S AT **ANOTHER** PARTY? WHAT THE LUMPS! HE'S MISSING OUT ON THE GREATEST NIGHT OF HIS **LIFE.**

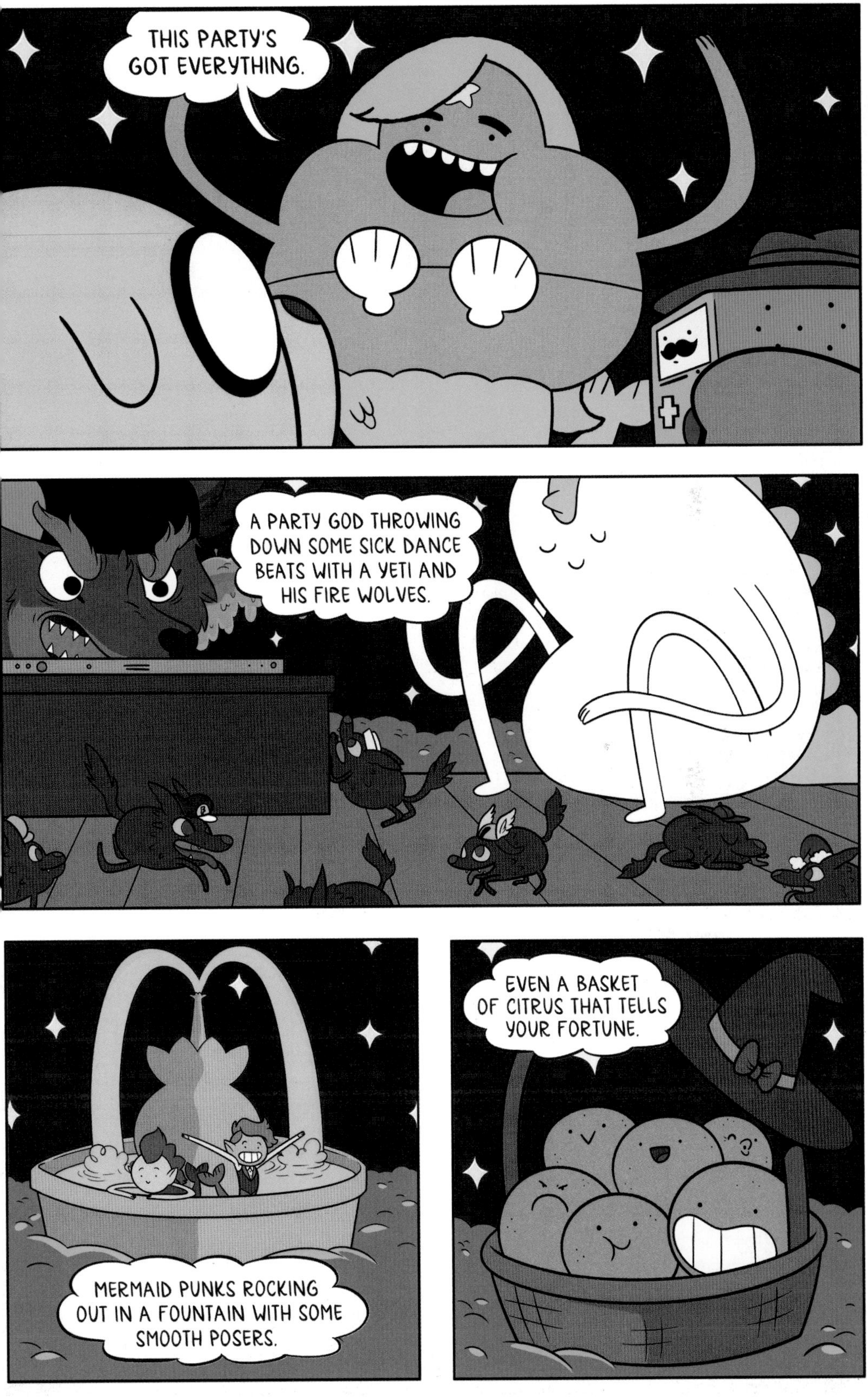
THIS PARTY'S GOT EVERYTHING.
A PARTY GOD THROWING DOWN SOME SICK DANCE BEATS WITH A YETI AND HIS FIRE WOLVES.
MERMAID PUNKS ROCKING OUT IN A FOUNTAIN WITH SOME SMOOTH POSERS.
EVEN A BASKET OF CITRUS THAT TELLS YOUR FORTUNE.

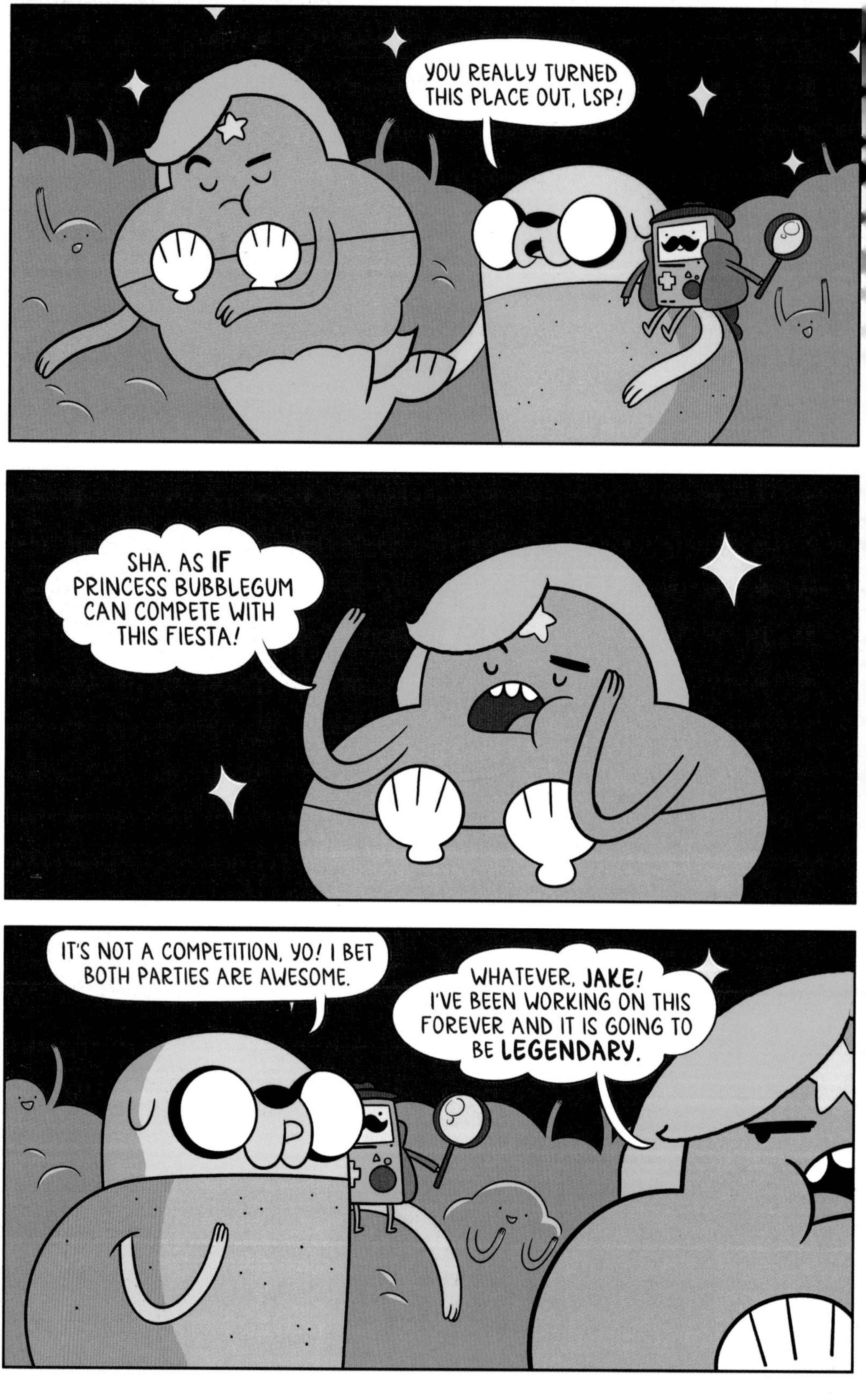
YOU REALLY TURNED THIS PLACE OUT, LSP!
SHA. AS IF PRINCESS BUBBLEGUM CAN COMPETE WITH THIS FIESTA!
IT'S NOT A COMPETITION, YO! I BET BOTH PARTIES ARE AWESOME.
WHATEVER, JAKE! I'VE BEEN WORKING ON THIS FOREVER AND IT IS GOING TO BE LEGENDARY.

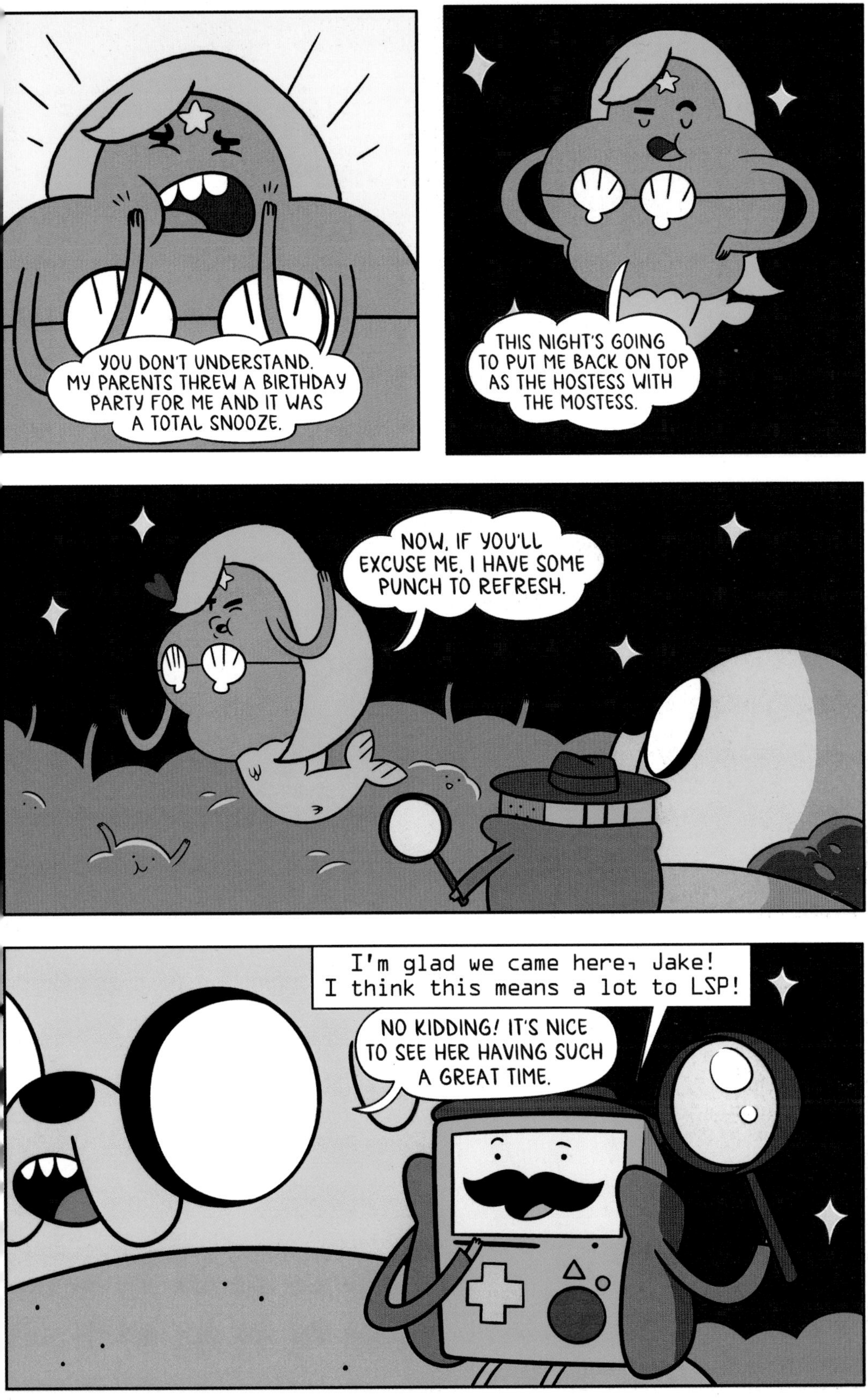
YOU DON'T UNDERSTAND. MY PARENTS THREW A BIRTHDAY PARTY FOR ME AND IT WAS A TOTAL SNOOZE.
THIS NIGHT'S GOING TO PUT ME BACK ON TOP AS THE HOSTESS WITH THE MOSTESS.
NOW, IF YOU'LL EXCUSE ME, I HAVE SOME PUNCH TO REFRESH.
I'm glad we came here, Jake! I think this means a lot to LSP!
NO KIDDING! IT'S NICE TO SEE HER HAVING SUCH A GREAT TIME.

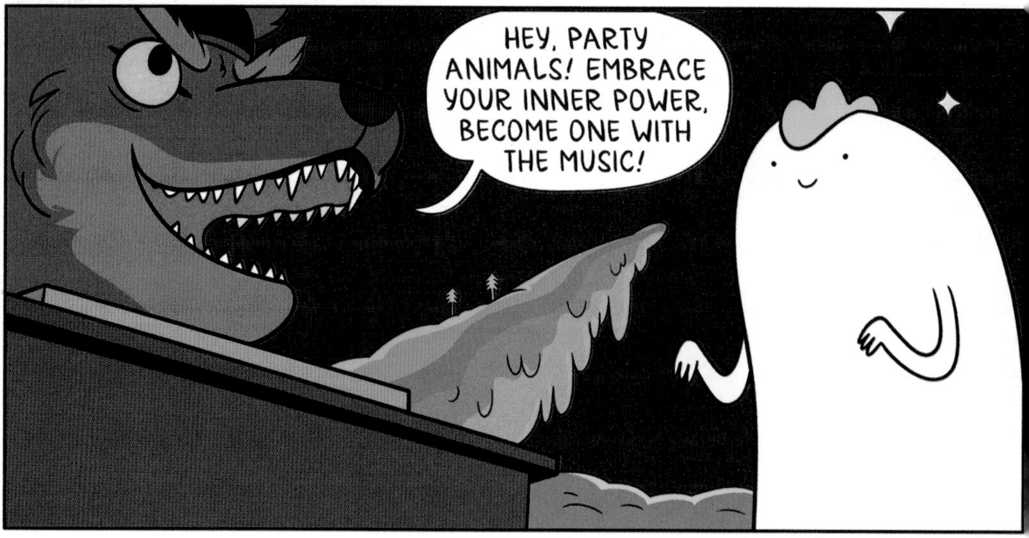
HEY, PARTY ANIMALS! EMBRACE YOUR INNER POWER, BECOME ONE WITH THE MUSIC!

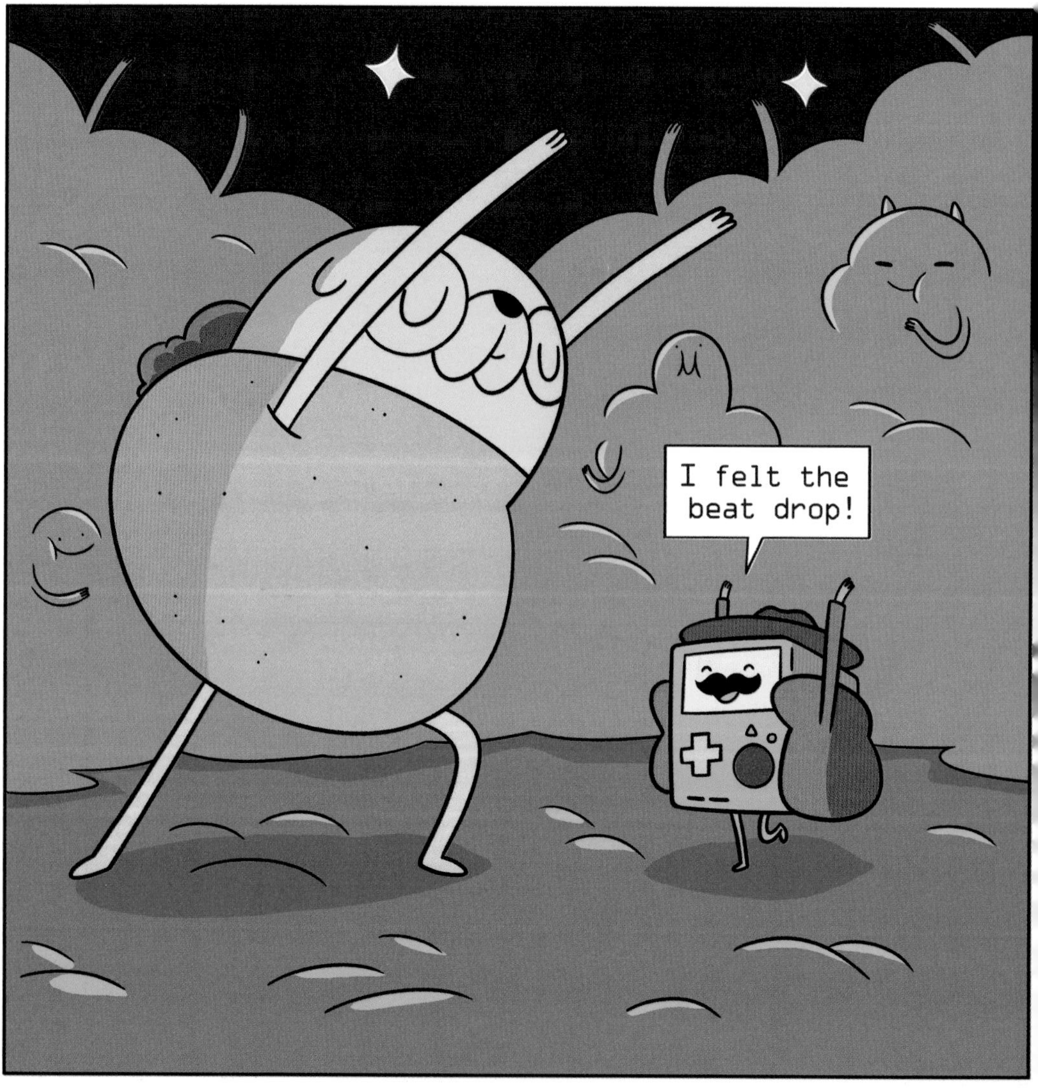
I felt the beat drop!

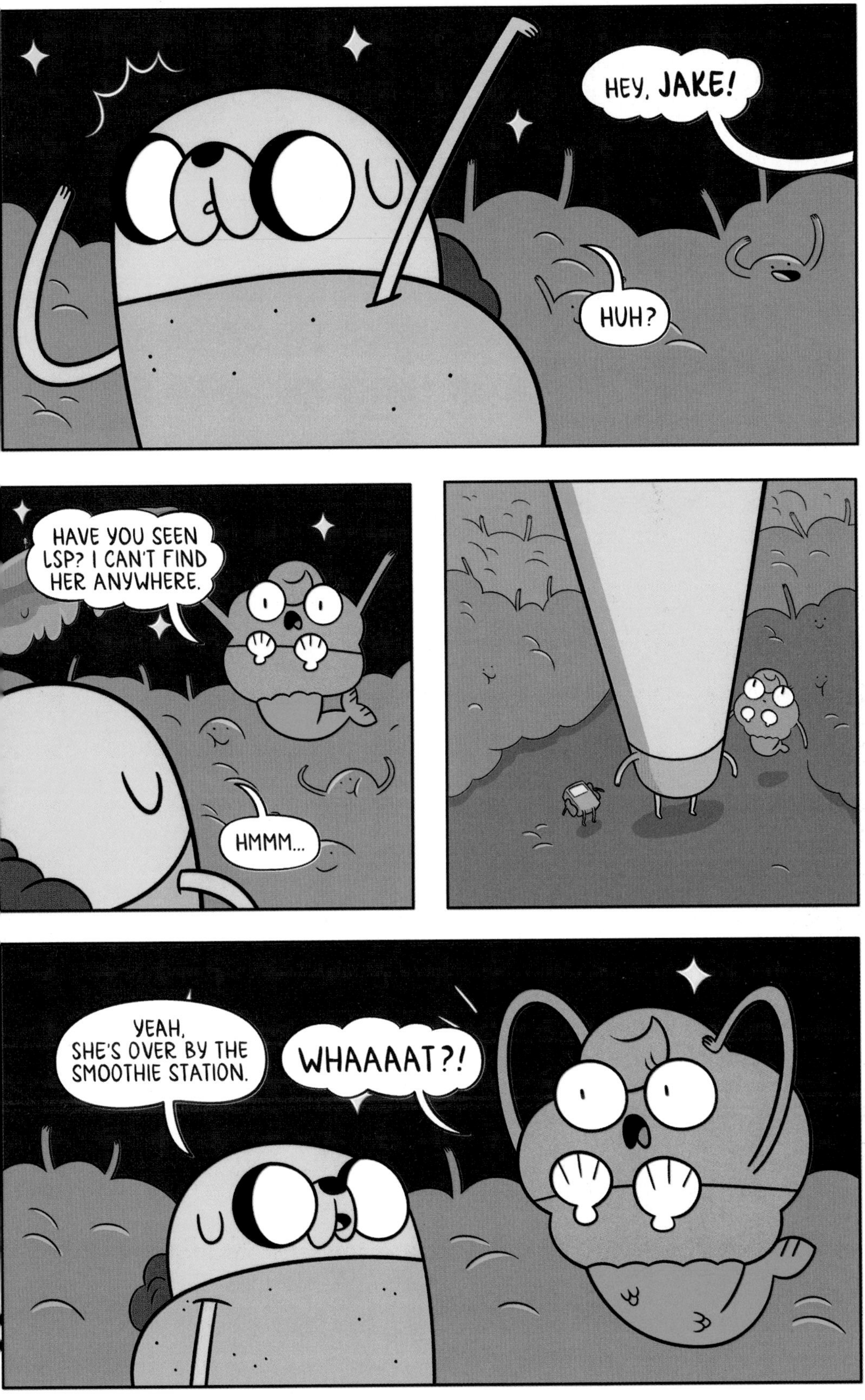
HEY, JAKE!
HUH?
HAVE YOU SEEN LSP? I CAN'T FIND HER ANYWHERE.
HMMM...
YEAH, SHE'S OVER BY THE SMOOTHIE STATION.
WHAAAAT?!

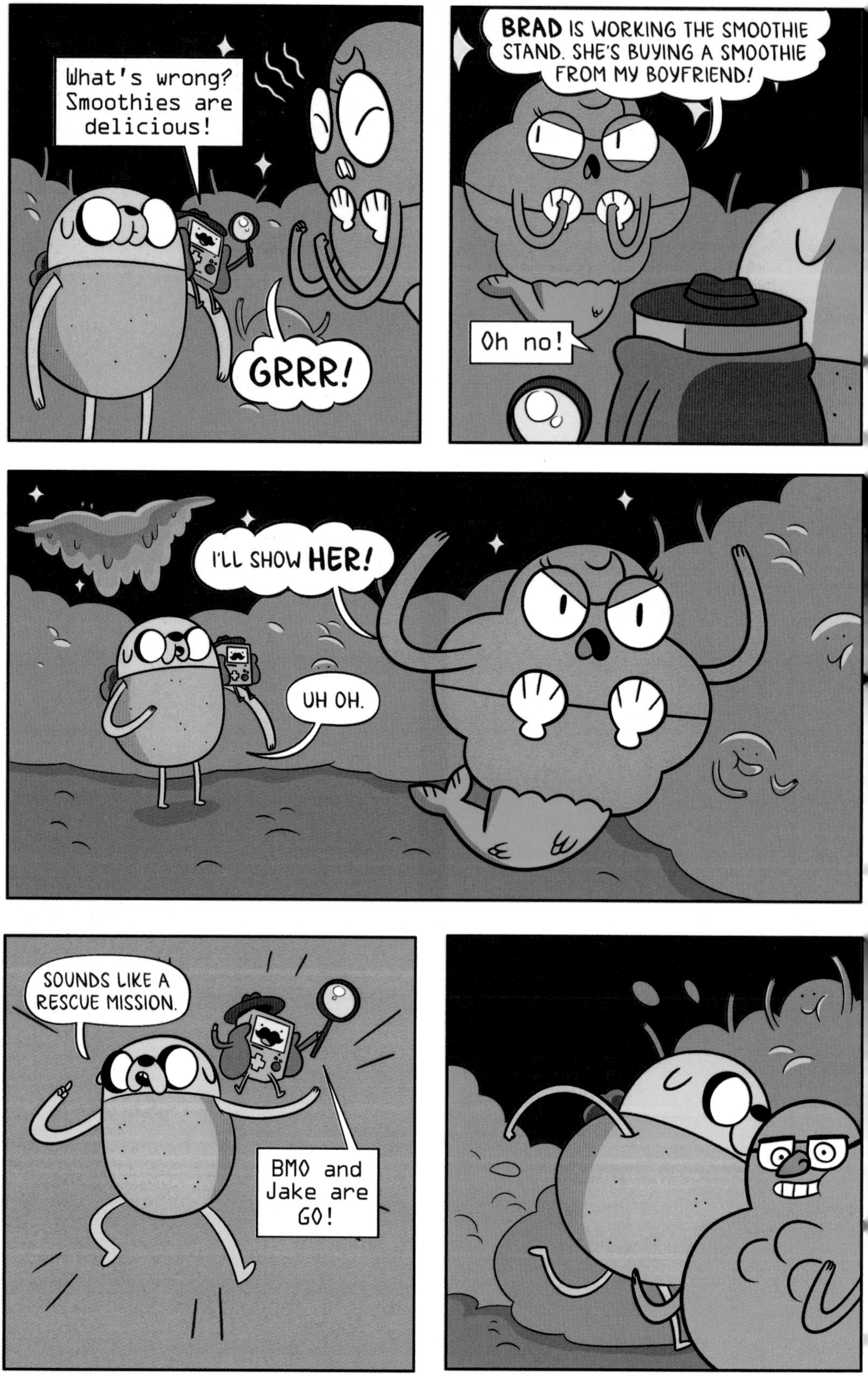
What's wrong? Smoothies are delicious!
GRRR!
BRAD IS WORKING THE SMOOTHIE STAND. SHE'S BUYING A SMOOTHIE FROM MY BOYFRIEND!
Oh no!
I'LL SHOW HER!
UH OH.
SOUNDS LIKE A RESCUE MISSION.
BMO and Jake are GO!

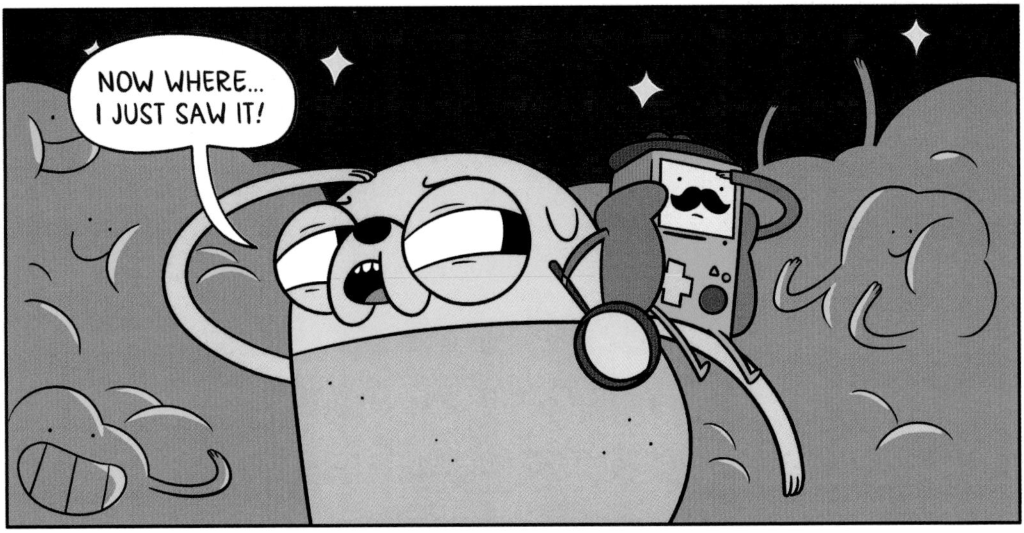
NOW WHERE...
I JUST SAW IT!

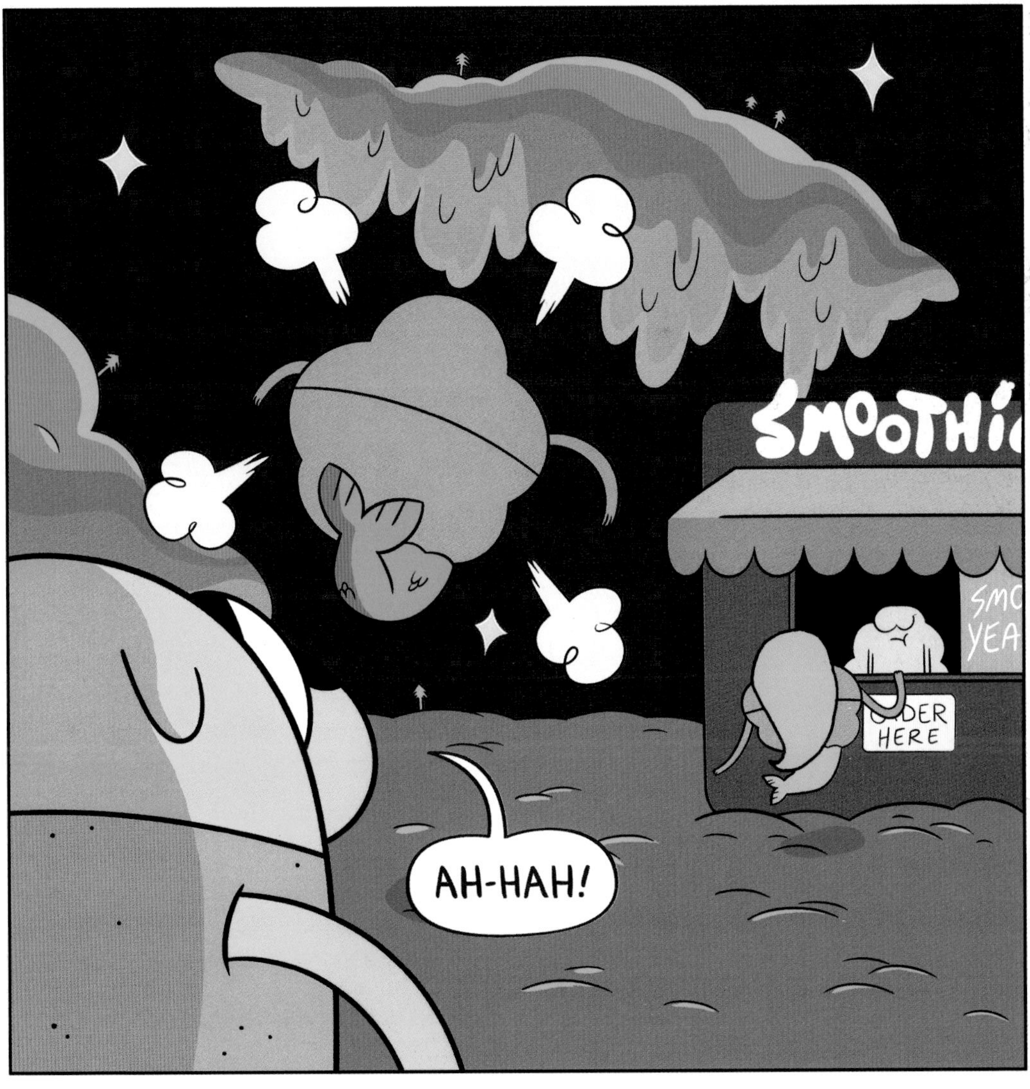
HERE
AH-HAH!

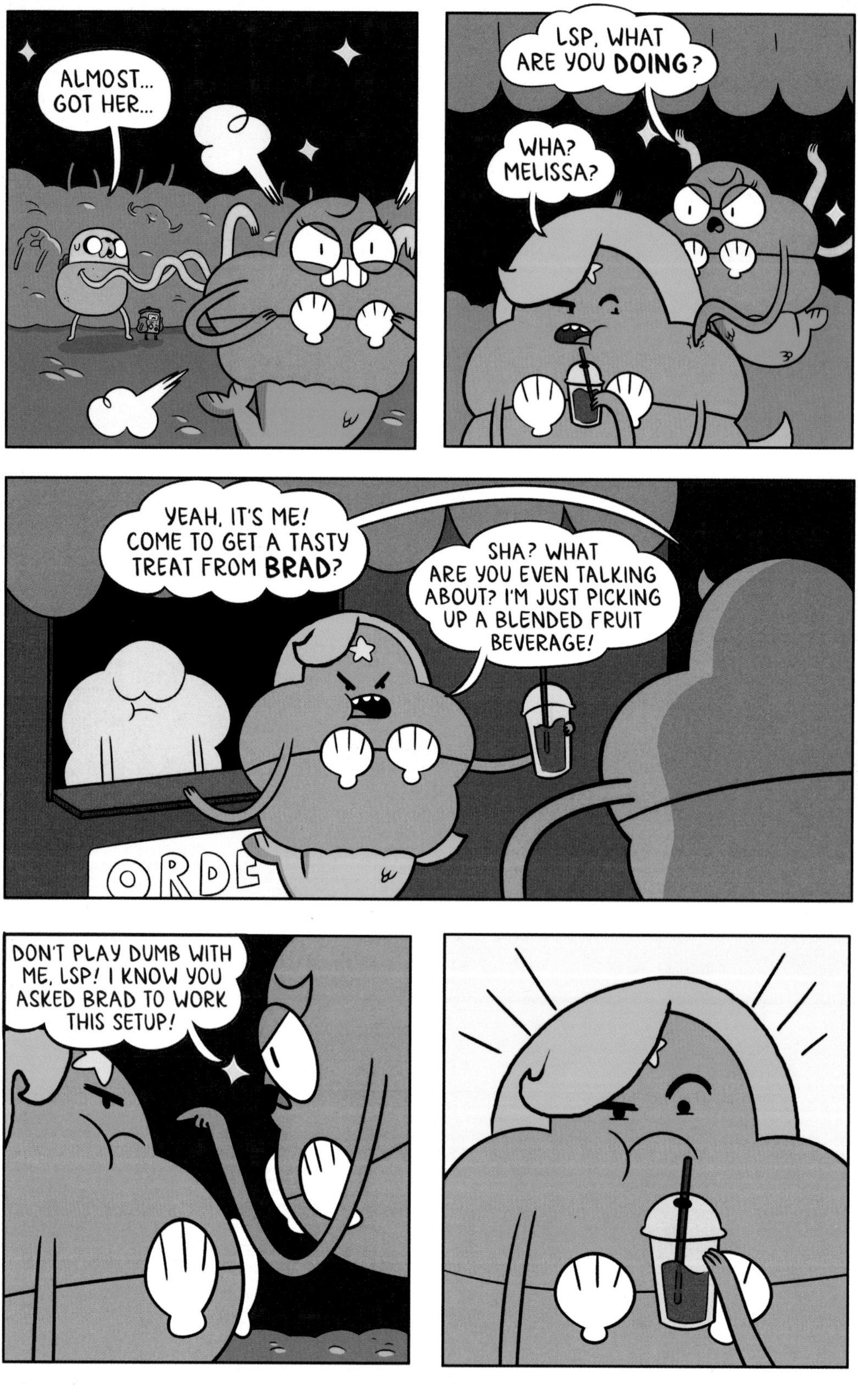
ALMOST... GOT HER...
LSP, WHAT ARE YOU **DOING**?
WHA? MELISSA?
YEAH, IT'S ME! COME TO GET A TASTY TREAT FROM **BRAD**?
SHA? WHAT ARE YOU EVEN TALKING ABOUT? I'M JUST PICKING UP A BLENDED FRUIT BEVERAGE!
ORDE
DON'T PLAY DUMB WITH ME, LSP! I KNOW YOU ASKED BRAD TO WORK THIS SETUP!

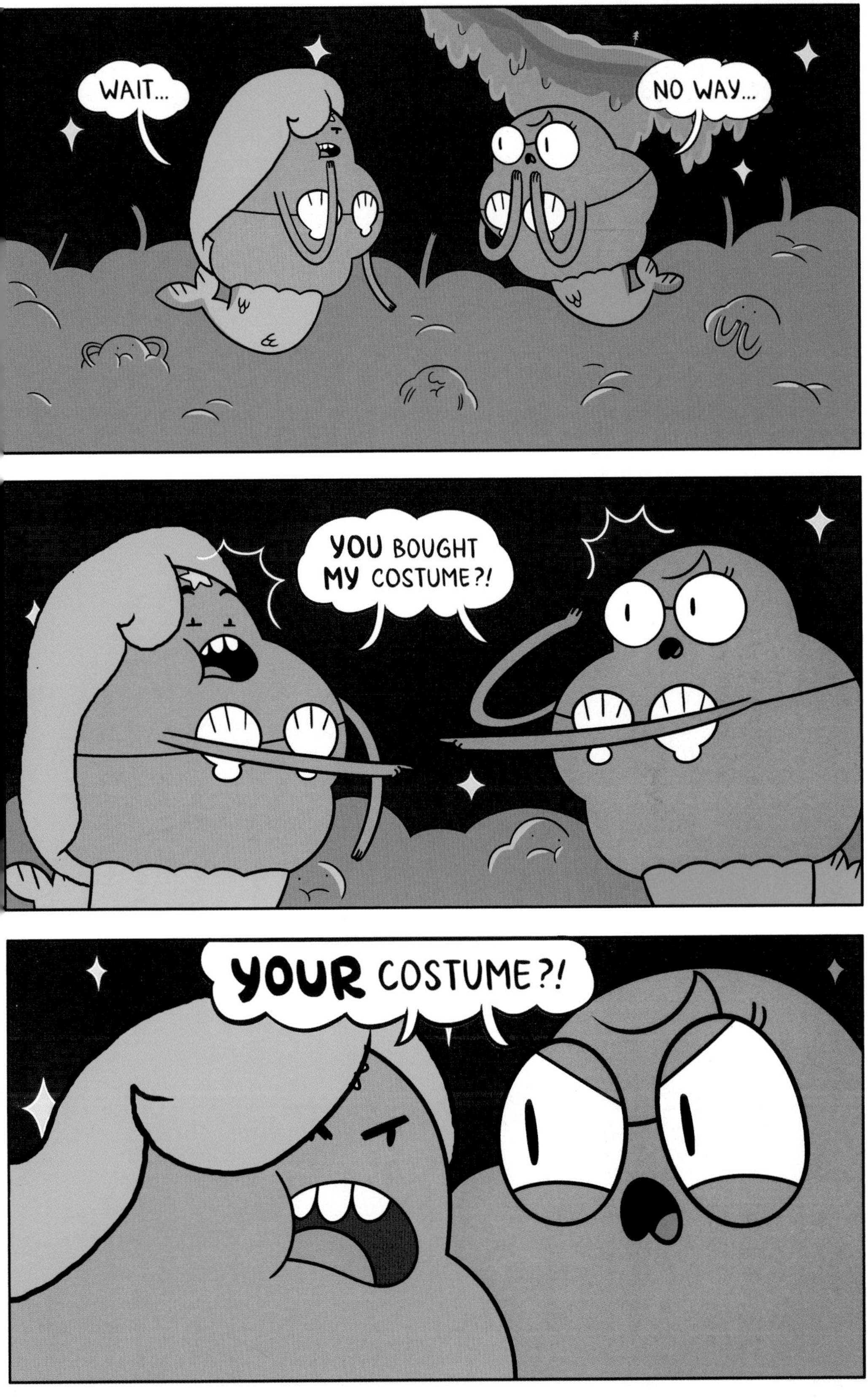
WAIT...
NO WAY...
YOU BOUGHT MY COSTUME?!
YOUR COSTUME?!

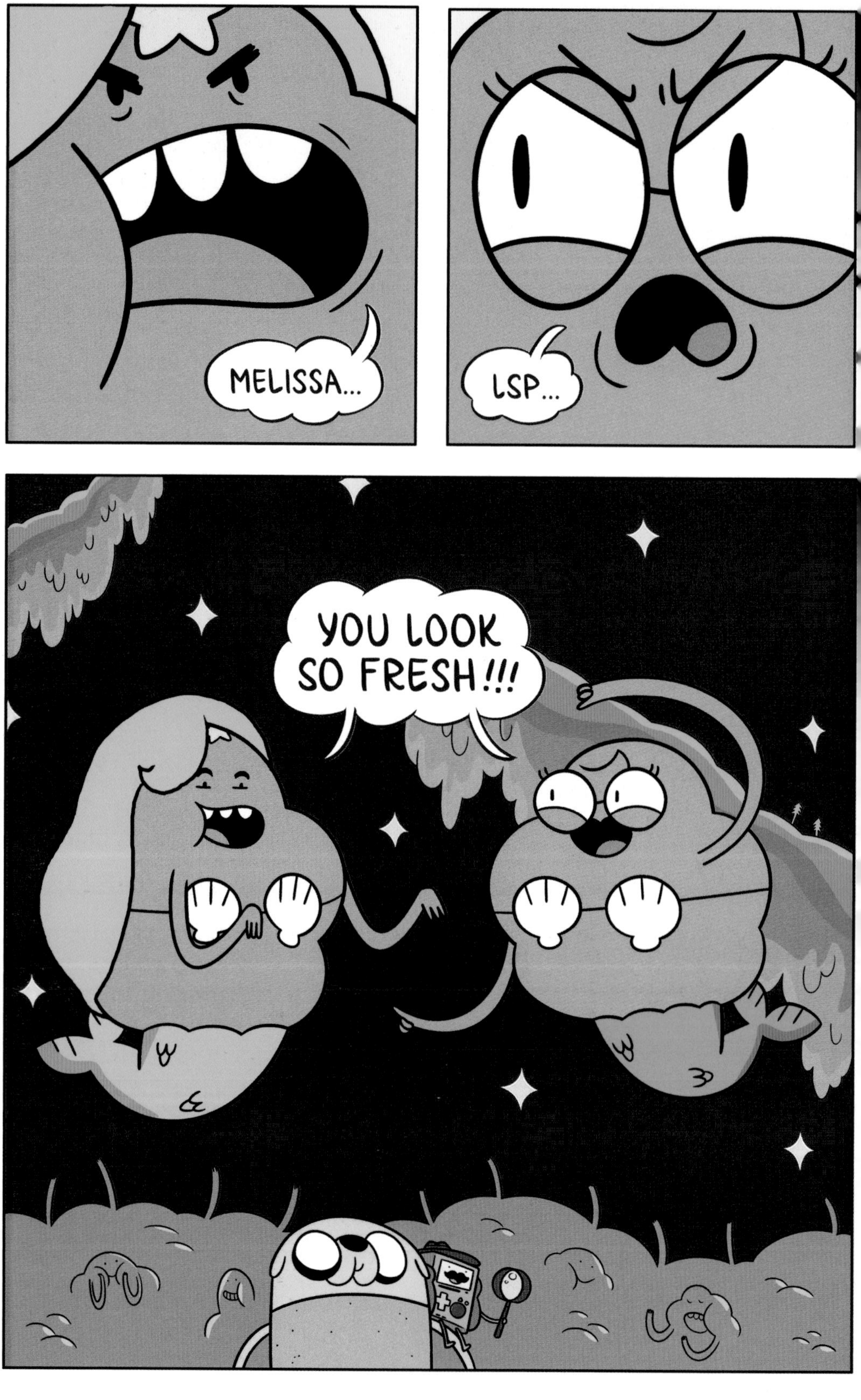
MELISSA...
LSP...
YOU LOOK SO FRESH!!!

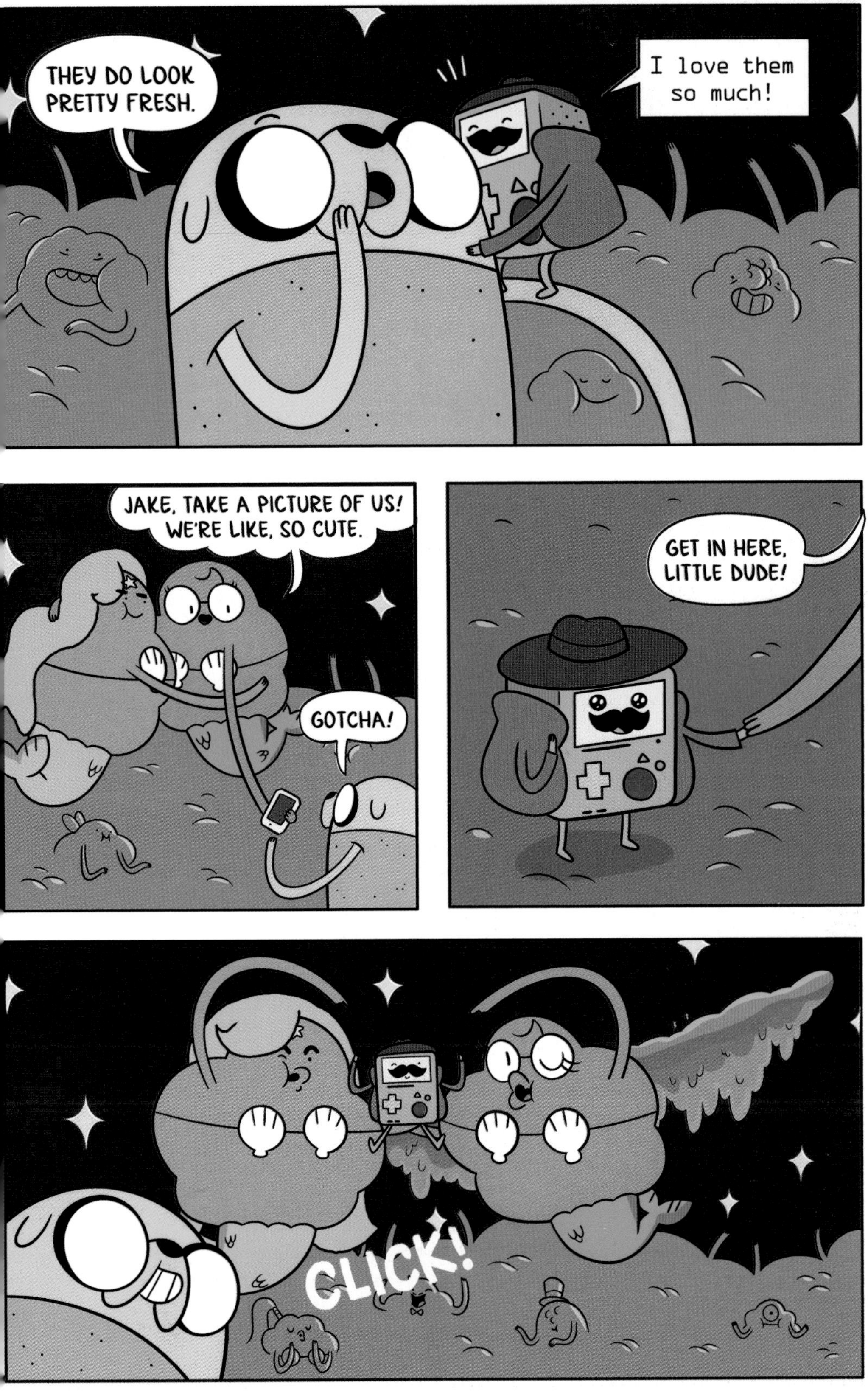
THEY DO LOOK PRETTY FRESH.
I love them so much!
JAKE, TAKE A PICTURE OF US! WE'RE LIKE, SO CUTE.
GOTCHA!
GET IN HERE, LITTLE DUDE!
CLICK!

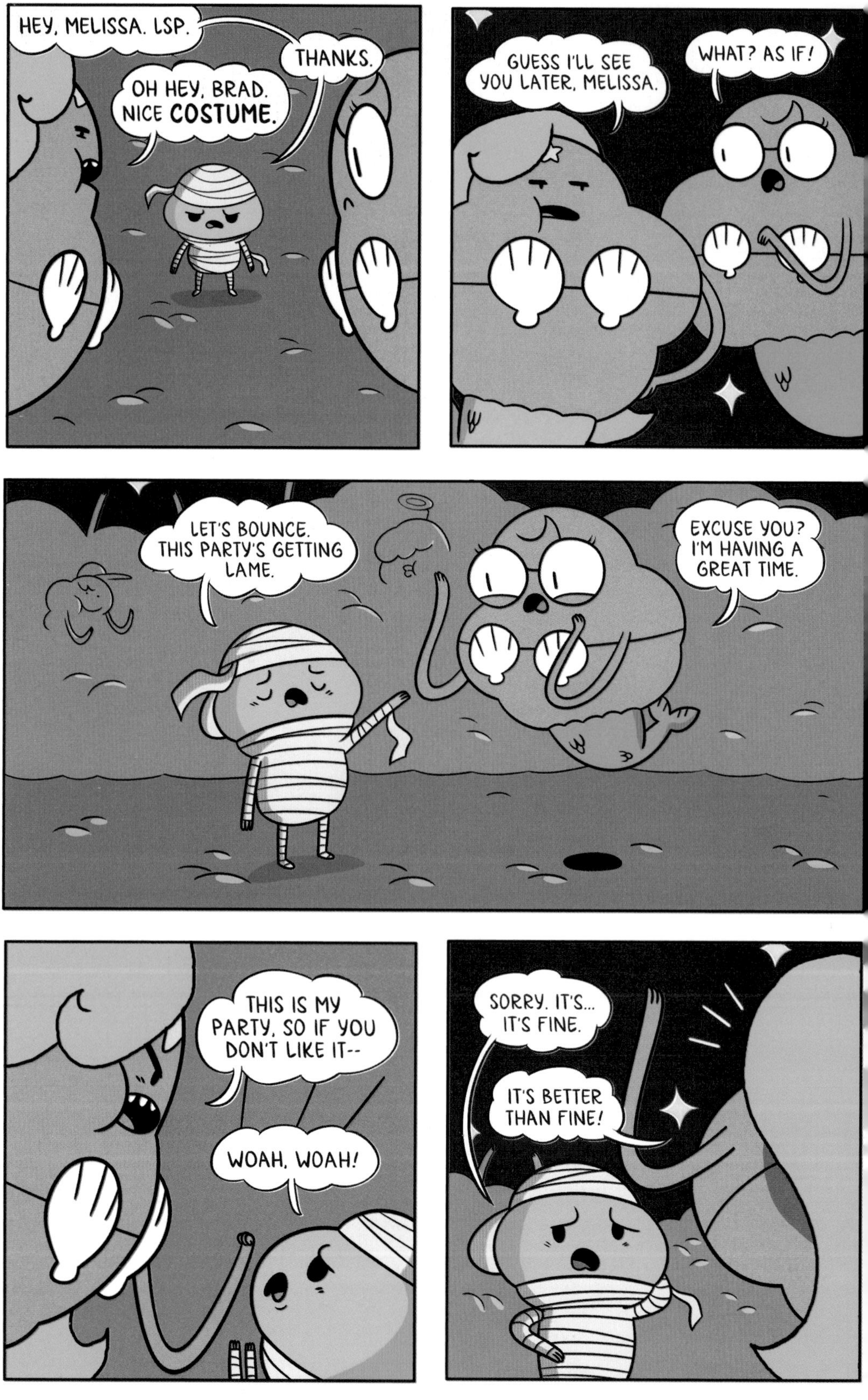
HEY, MELISSA. LSP.
OH HEY, BRAD. NICE **COSTUME.**
THANKS.
GUESS I'LL SEE YOU LATER, MELISSA.
WHAT? AS IF!
LET'S BOUNCE. THIS PARTY'S GETTING LAME.
EXCUSE YOU? I'M HAVING A GREAT TIME.
THIS IS MY PARTY, SO IF YOU DON'T LIKE IT--
WOAH, WOAH!
SORRY. IT'S... IT'S FINE.
IT'S BETTER THAN FINE!

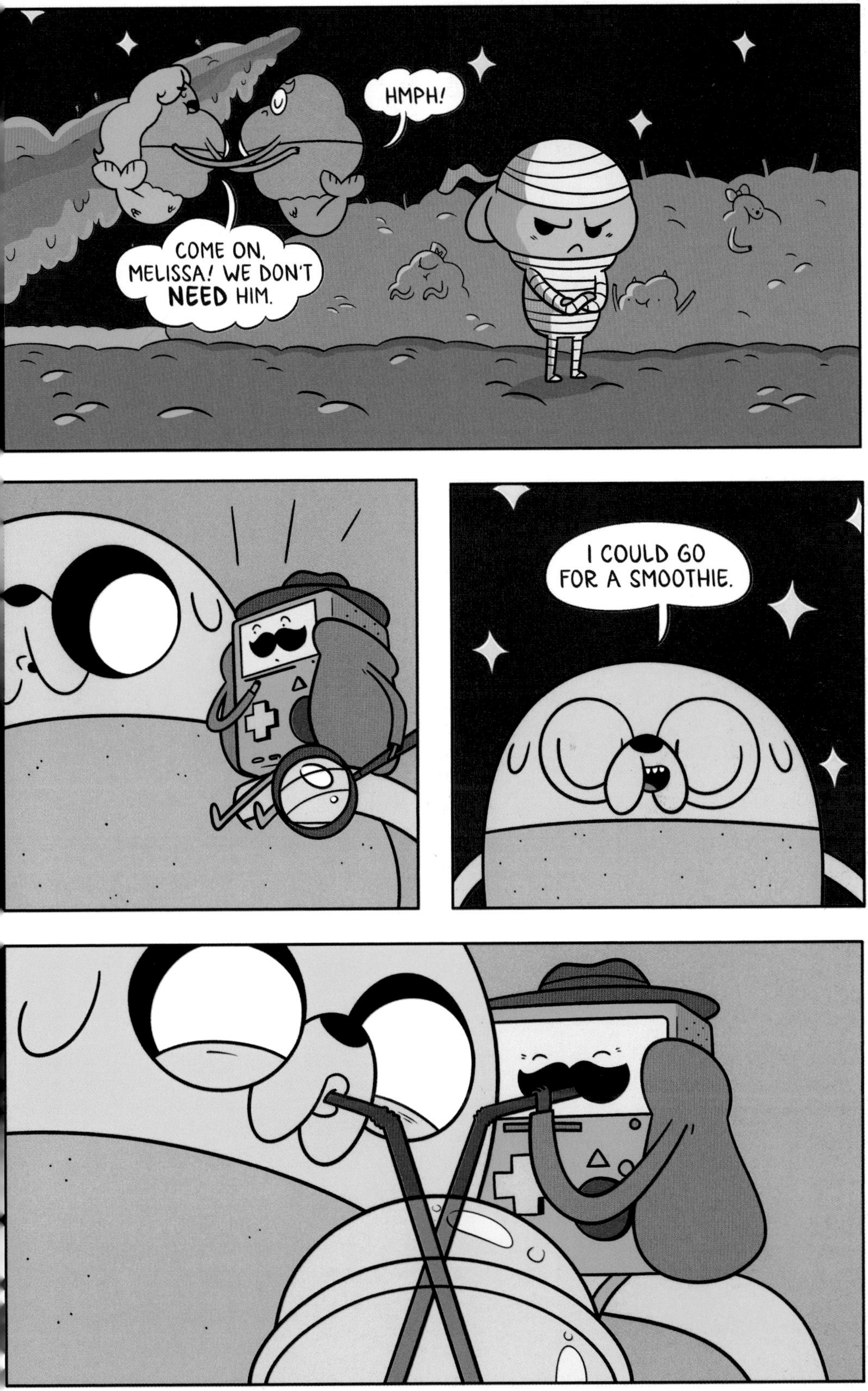
HMPH!
COME ON, MELISSA! WE DON'T **NEED** HIM.
I COULD GO FOR A SMOOTHIE.

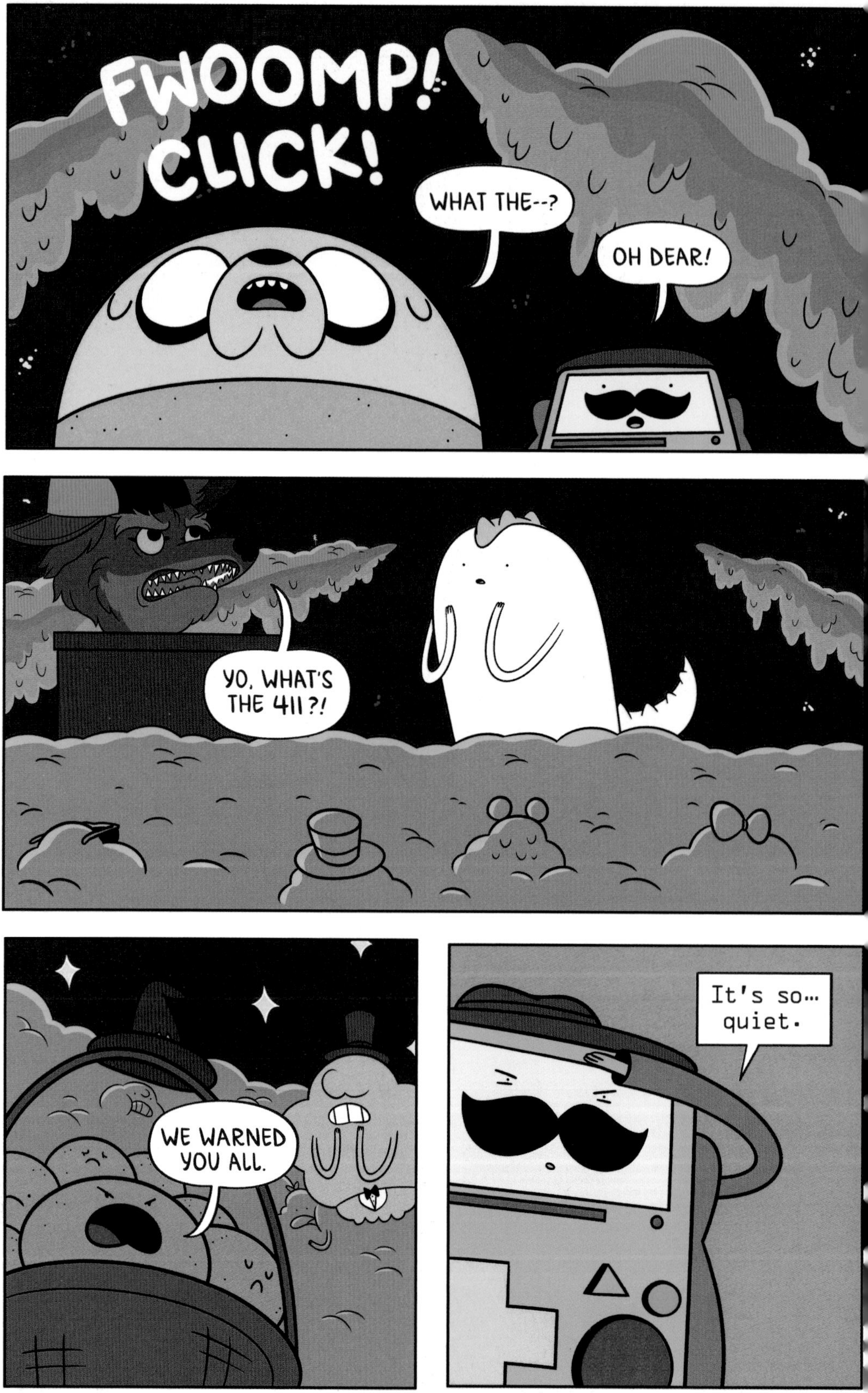
FWOOMP!
CLICK!
WHAT THE--?
OH DEAR!
YO, WHAT'S THE 411?!
WE WARNED YOU ALL.
It's so… quiet.

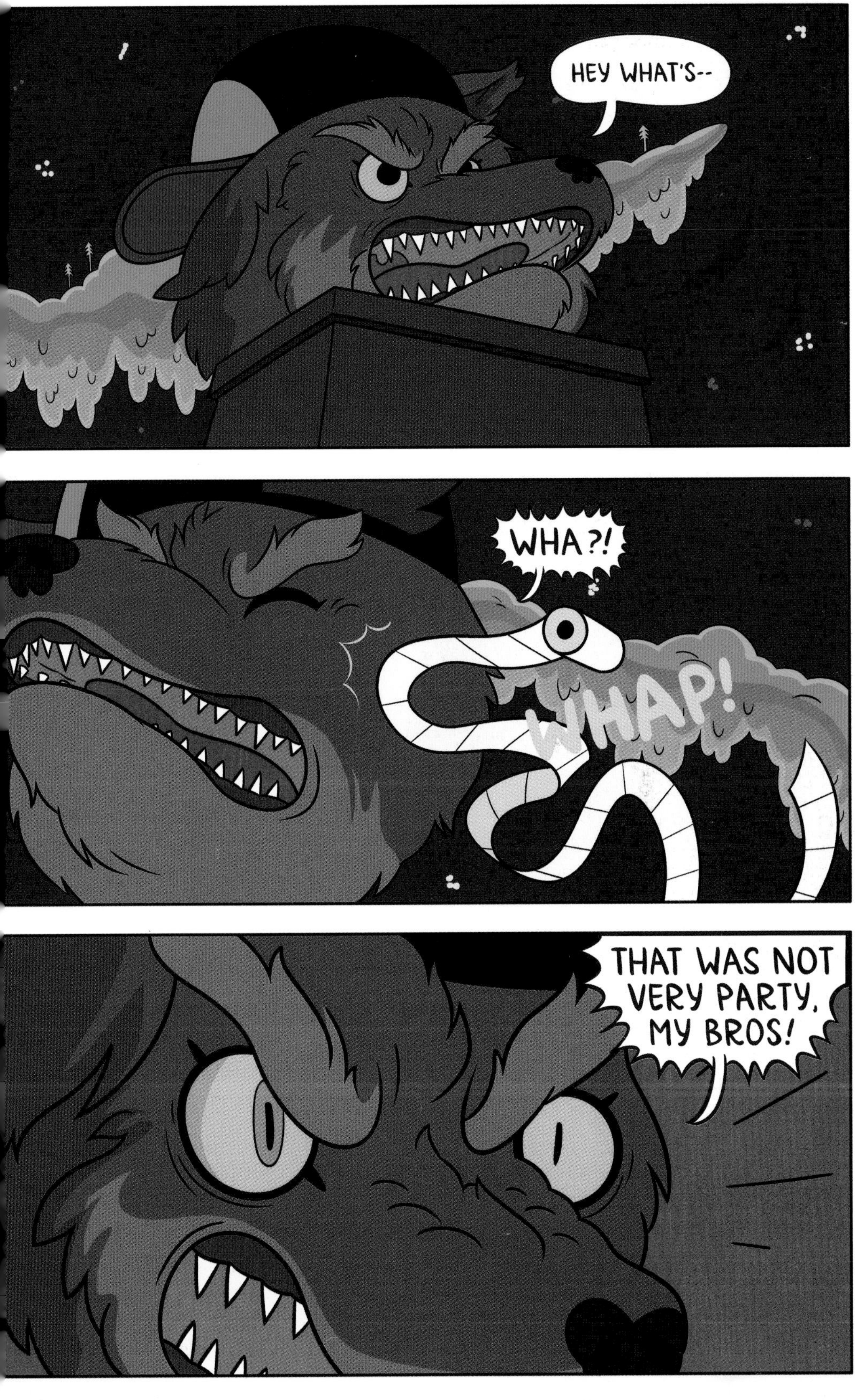
HEY WHAT'S--
WHA?!
WHAP!
THAT WAS NOT VERY PARTY, MY BROS!

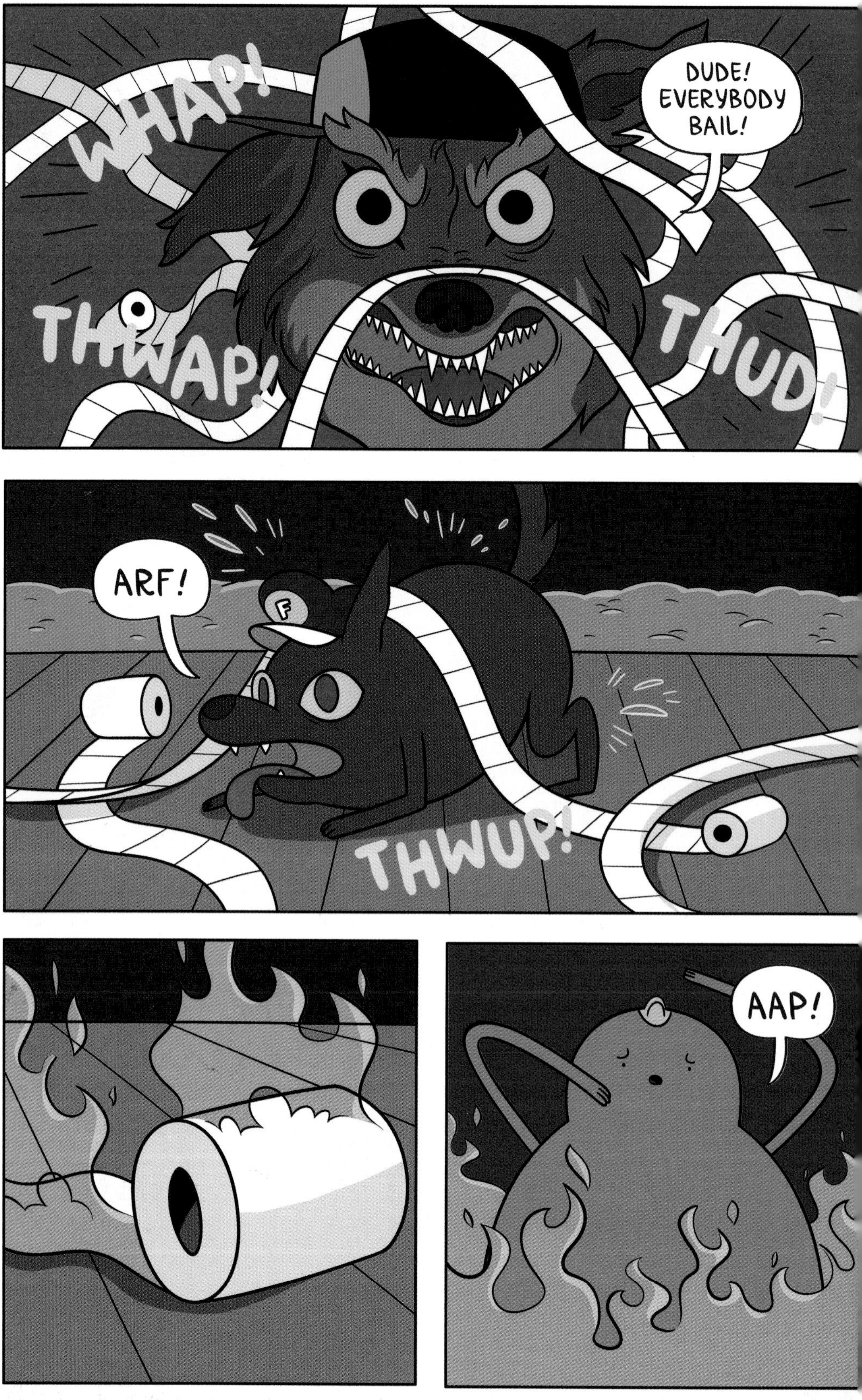
WHAP!
THWAP!
THUD!
DUDE! EVERYBODY BAIL!
ARF!
THWUP!
AAP!

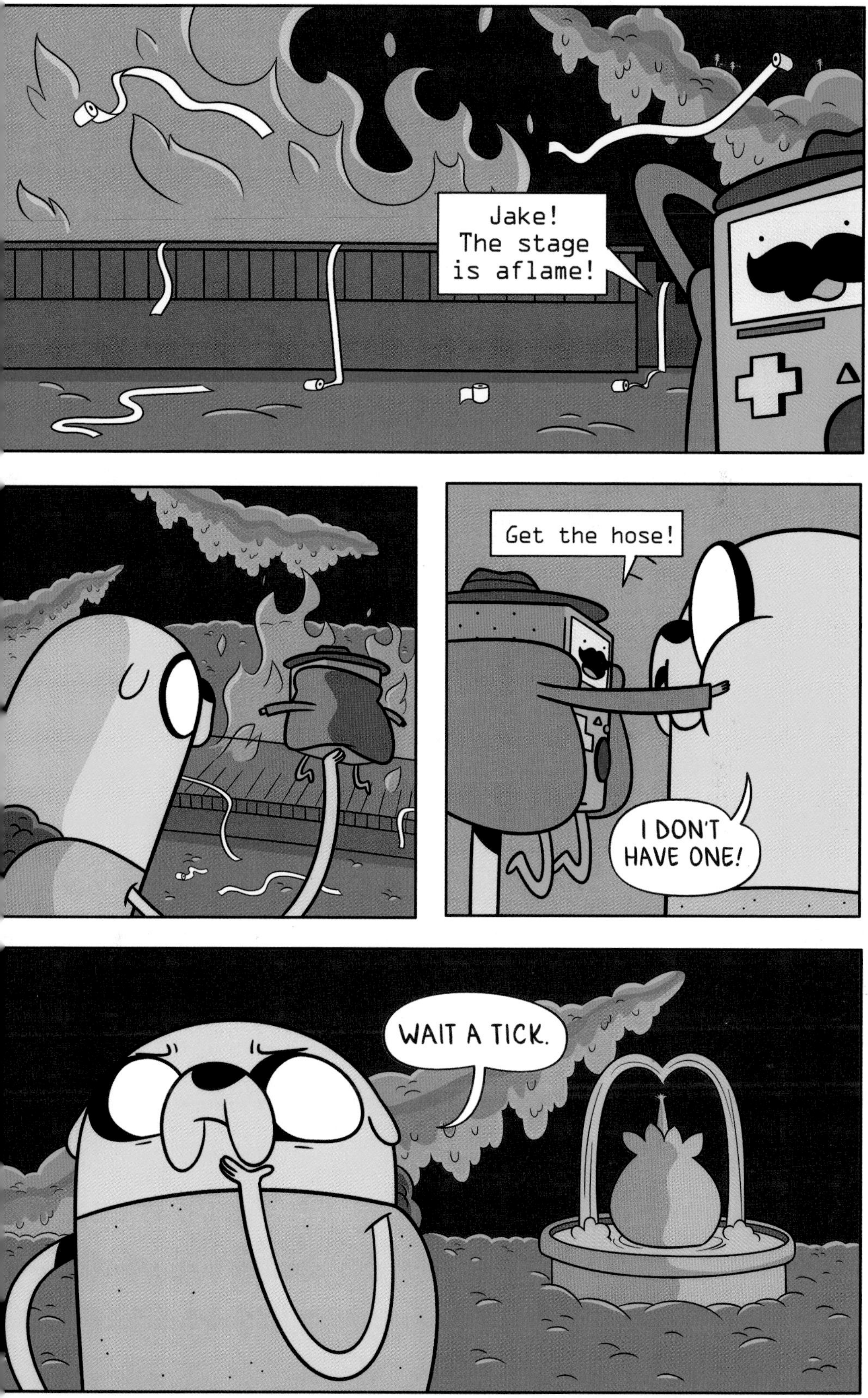
Jake!
The stage
is aflame!
Get the hose!
I DON'T
HAVE ONE!
WAIT A TICK.

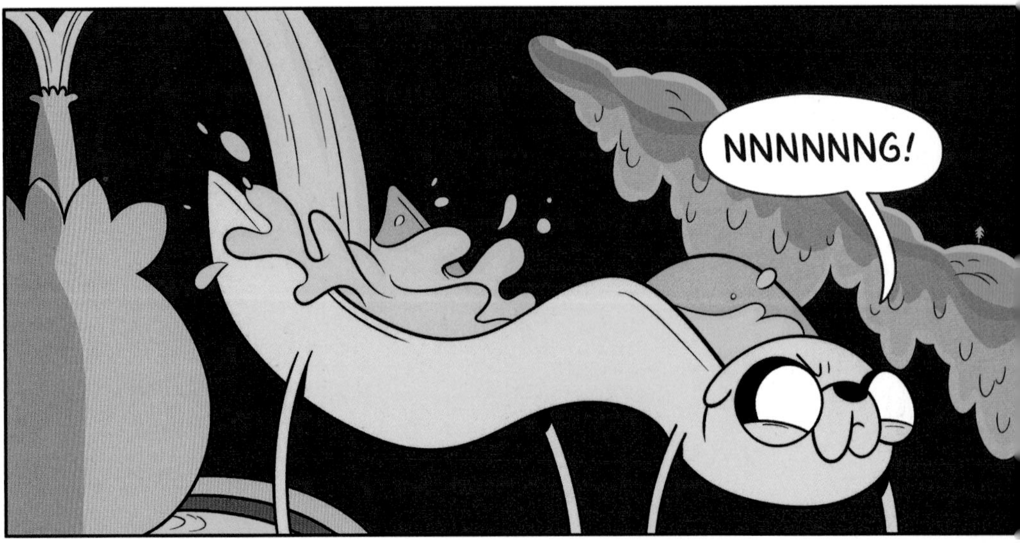
NNNNNNG!

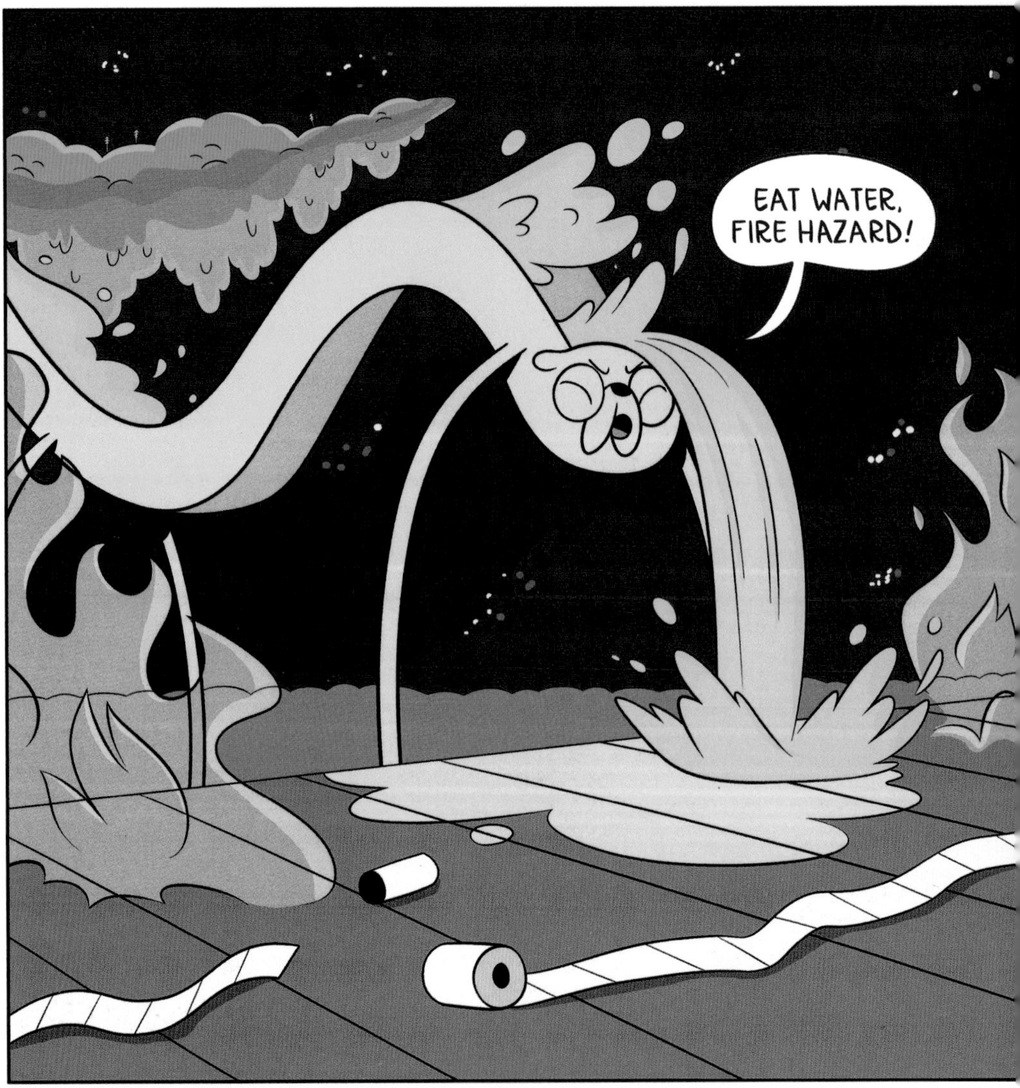
EAT WATER,
FIRE HAZARD!

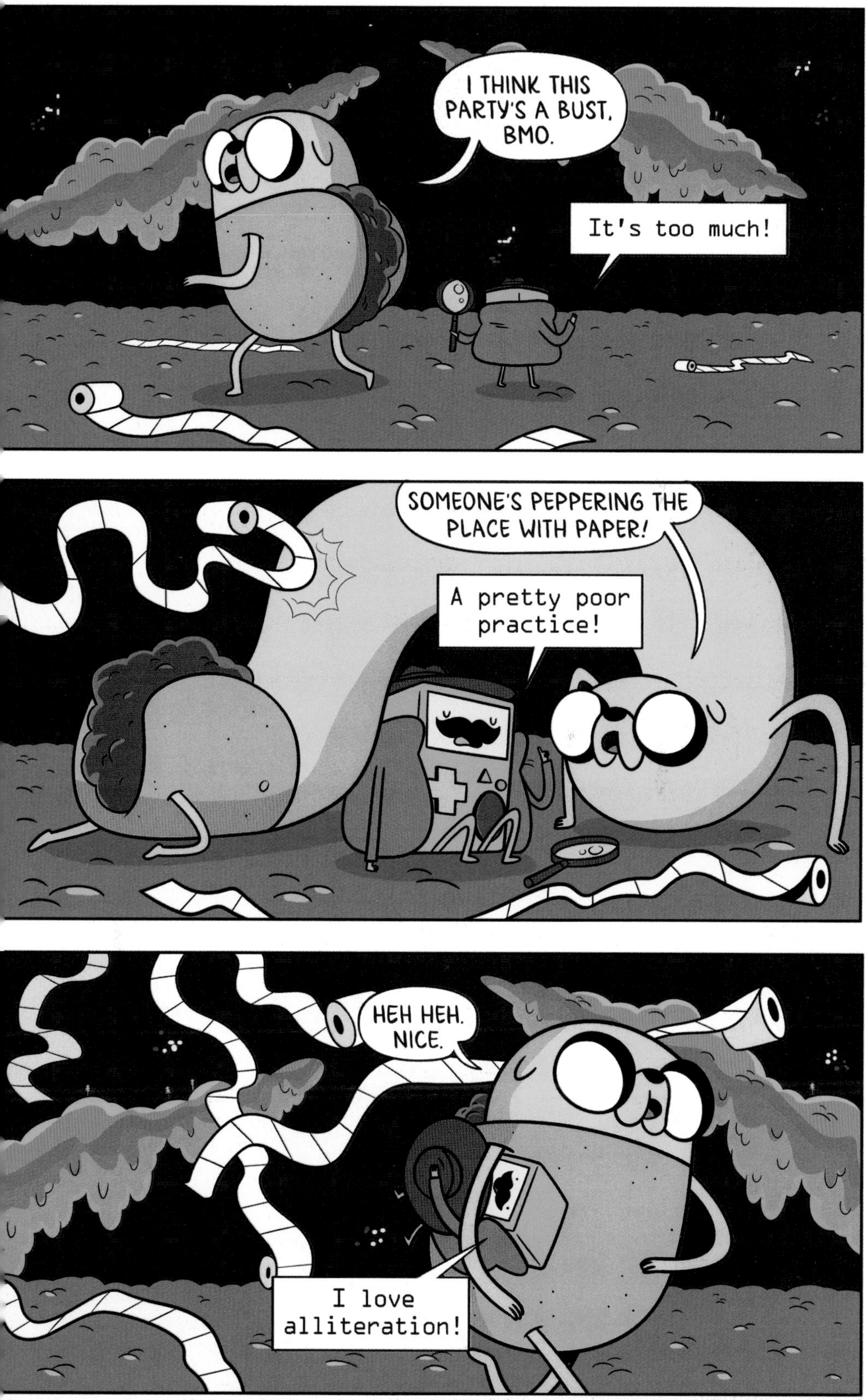
I THINK THIS PARTY'S A BUST, BMO.
It's too much!
SOMEONE'S PEPPERING THE PLACE WITH PAPER!
A pretty poor practice!
HEH HEH. NICE.
I love alliteration!

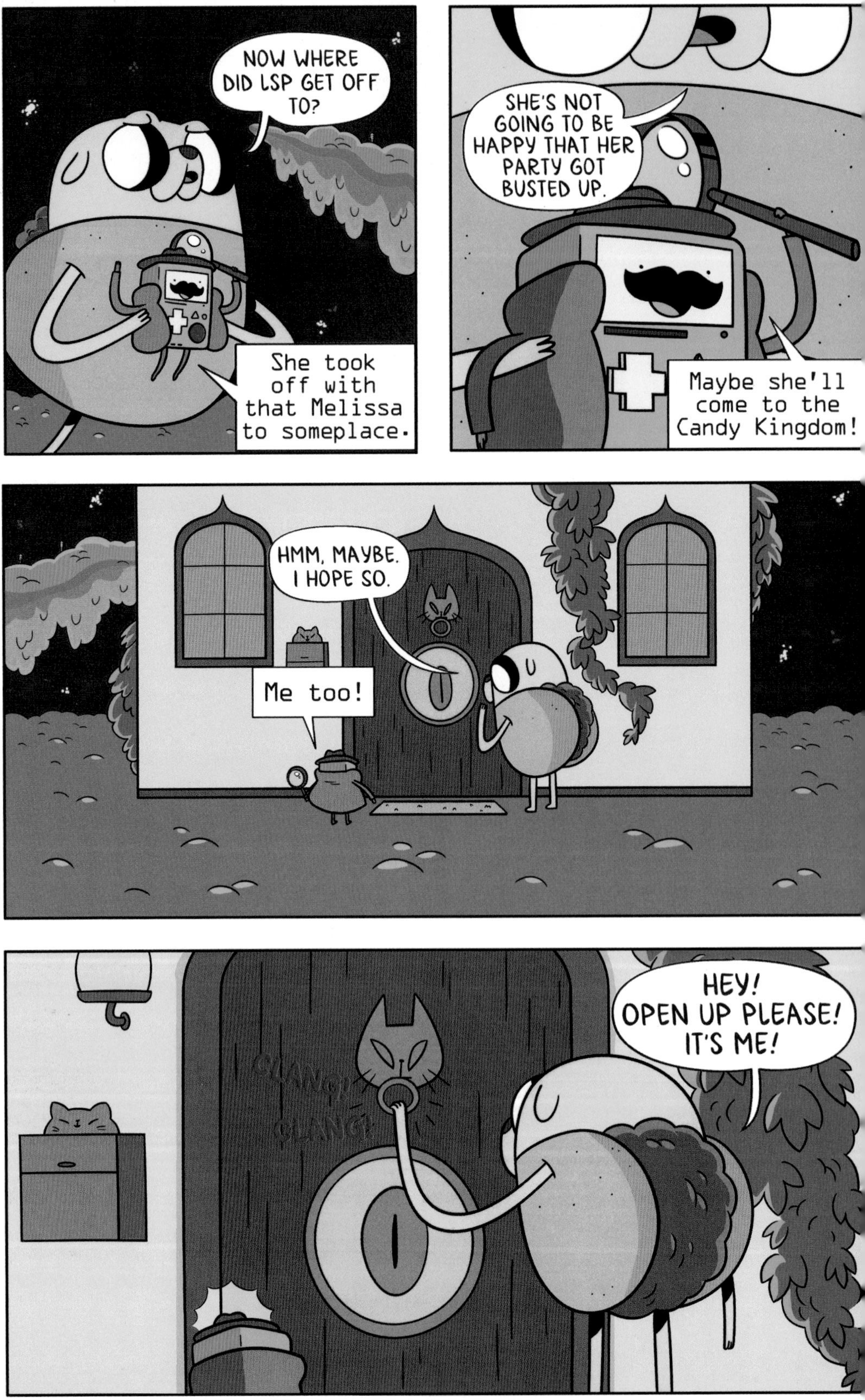

NOW WHERE DID LSP GET OFF TO?
She took off with that Melissa to someplace.
SHE'S NOT GOING TO BE HAPPY THAT HER PARTY GOT BUSTED UP.
Maybe she'll come to the Candy Kingdom!
HMM, MAYBE. I HOPE SO.
Me too!
CLANG!
CLANG!
HEY! OPEN UP PLEASE! IT'S ME!

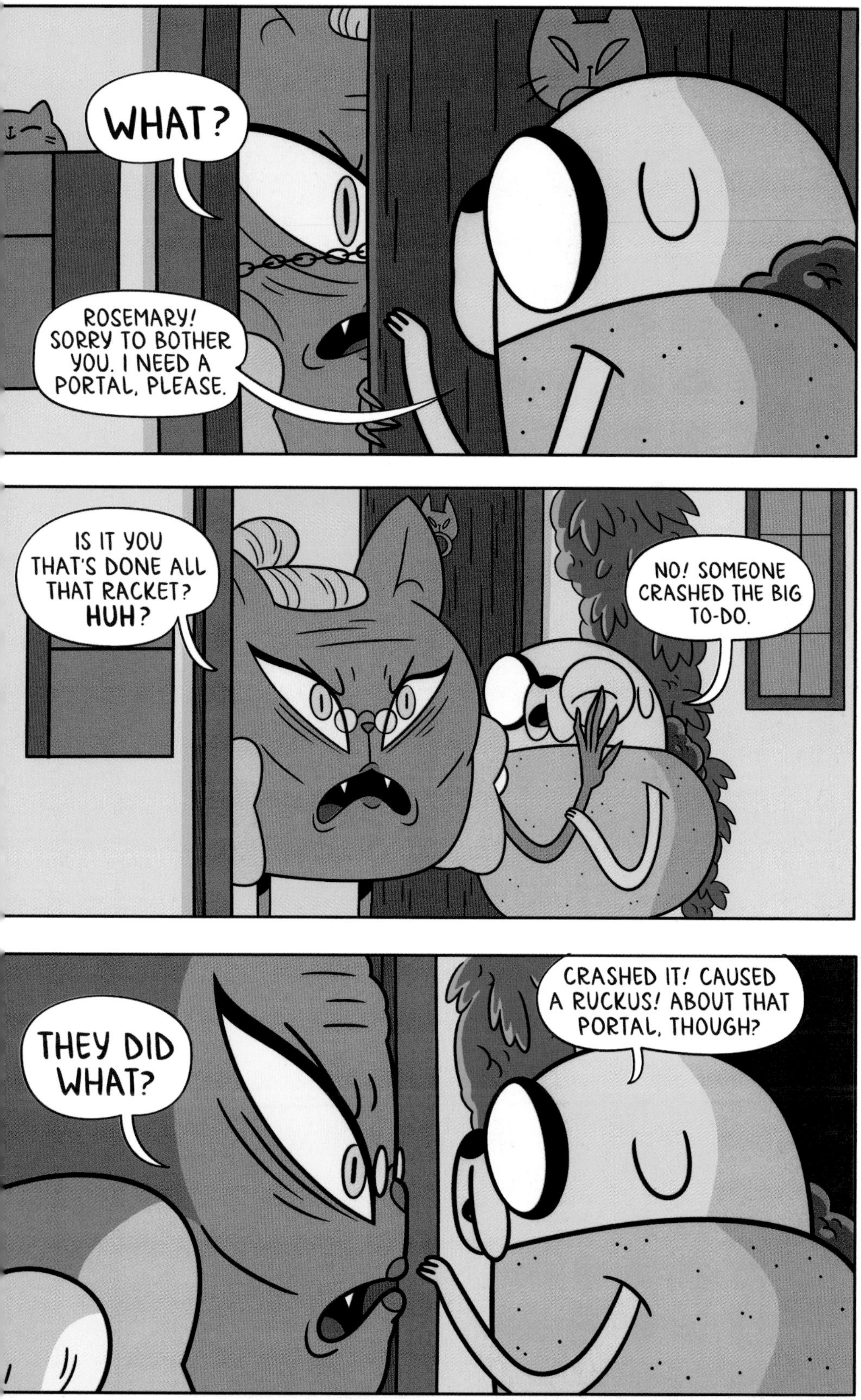
WHAT?
ROSEMARY! SORRY TO BOTHER YOU. I NEED A PORTAL, PLEASE.
IS IT YOU THAT'S DONE ALL THAT RACKET? HUH?
NO! SOMEONE CRASHED THE BIG TO-DO.
THEY DID WHAT?
CRASHED IT! CAUSED A RUCKUS! ABOUT THAT PORTAL, THOUGH?

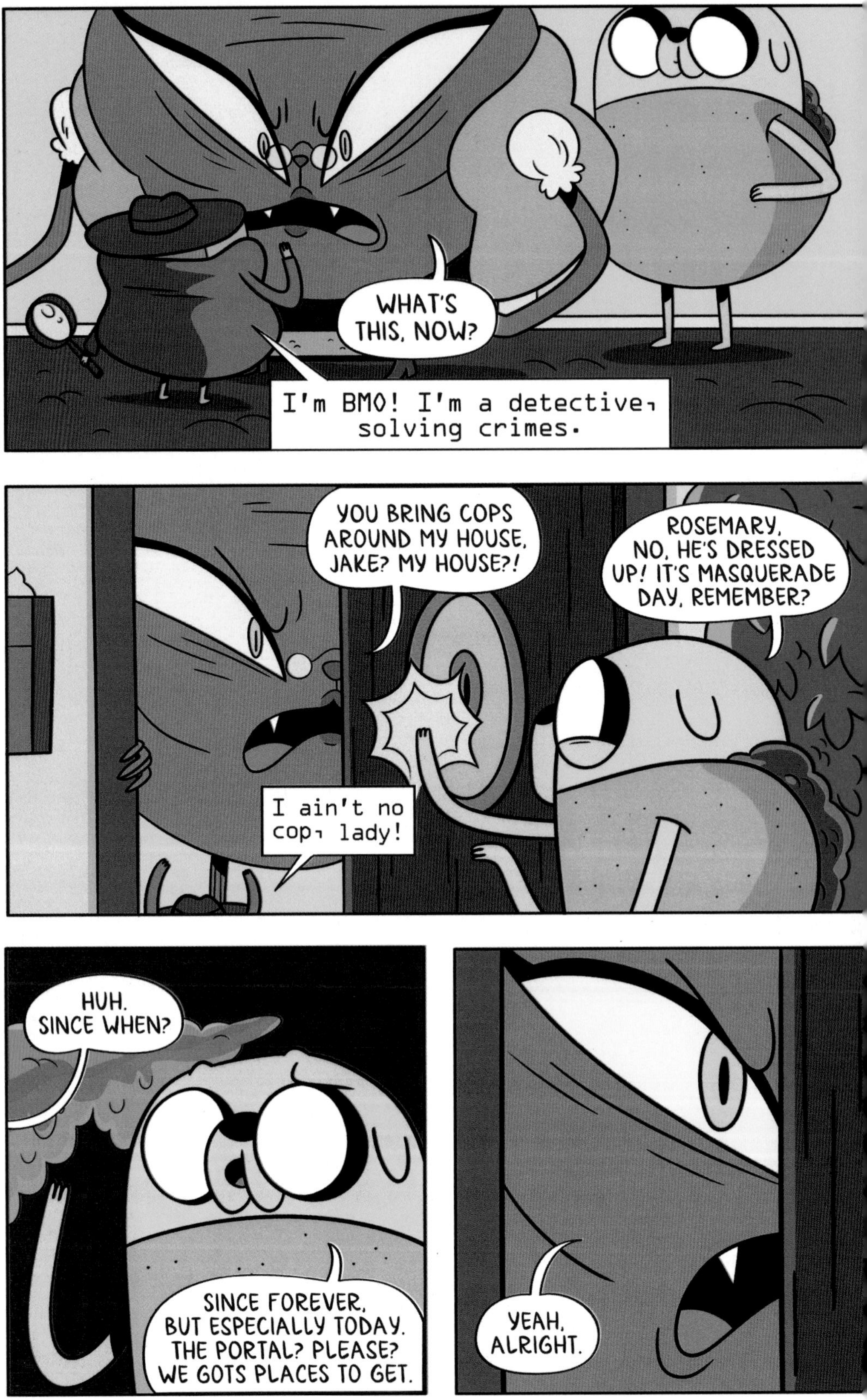

WHAT'S THIS, NOW?
I'm BMO! I'm a detective, solving crimes.
YOU BRING COPS AROUND MY HOUSE, JAKE? MY HOUSE?!
ROSEMARY, NO, HE'S DRESSED UP! IT'S MASQUERADE DAY, REMEMBER?
I ain't no cop, lady!
HUH. SINCE WHEN?
SINCE FOREVER, BUT ESPECIALLY TODAY. THE PORTAL? PLEASE? WE GOTS PLACES TO GET.
YEAH, ALRIGHT.

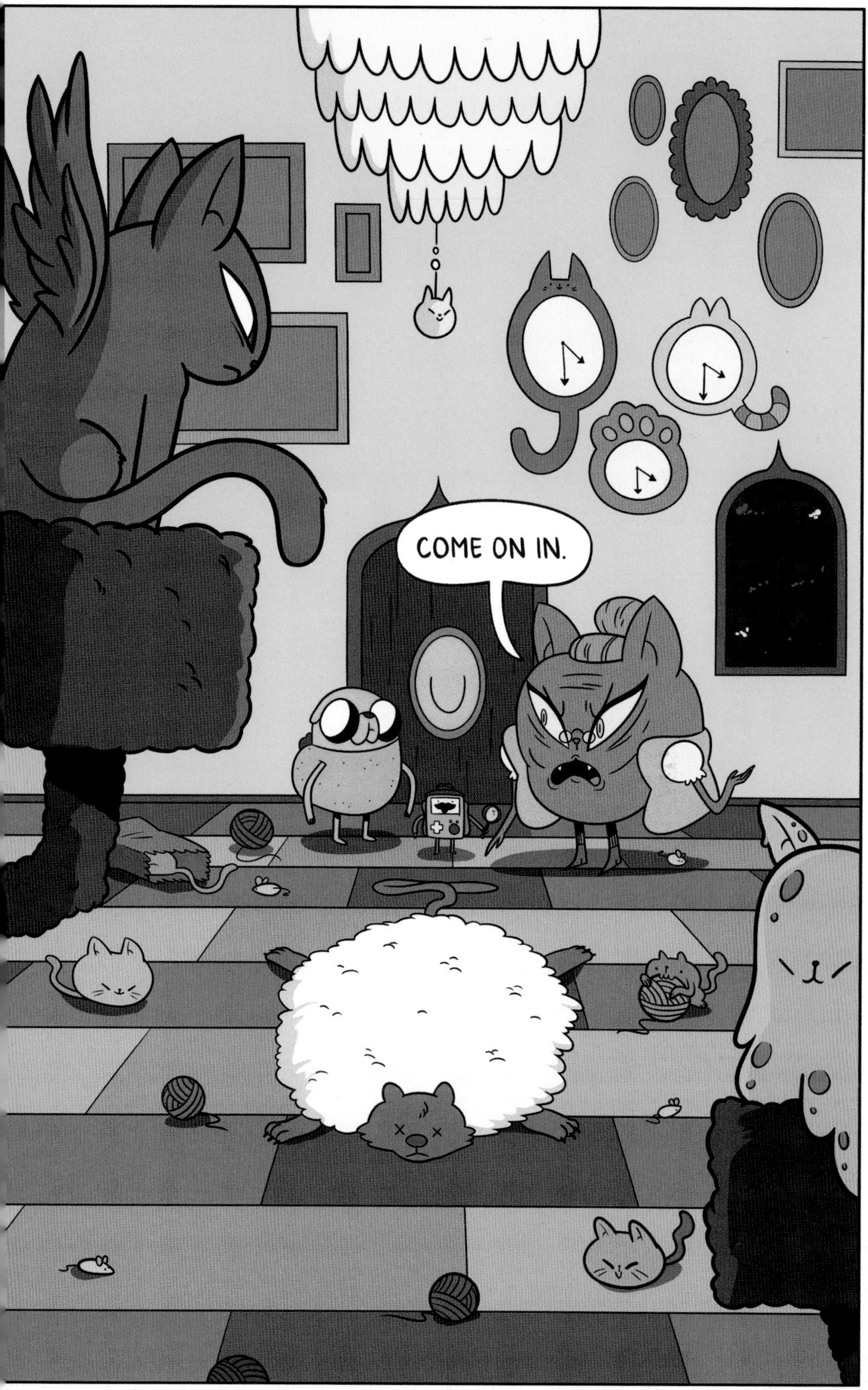
COME ON IN.

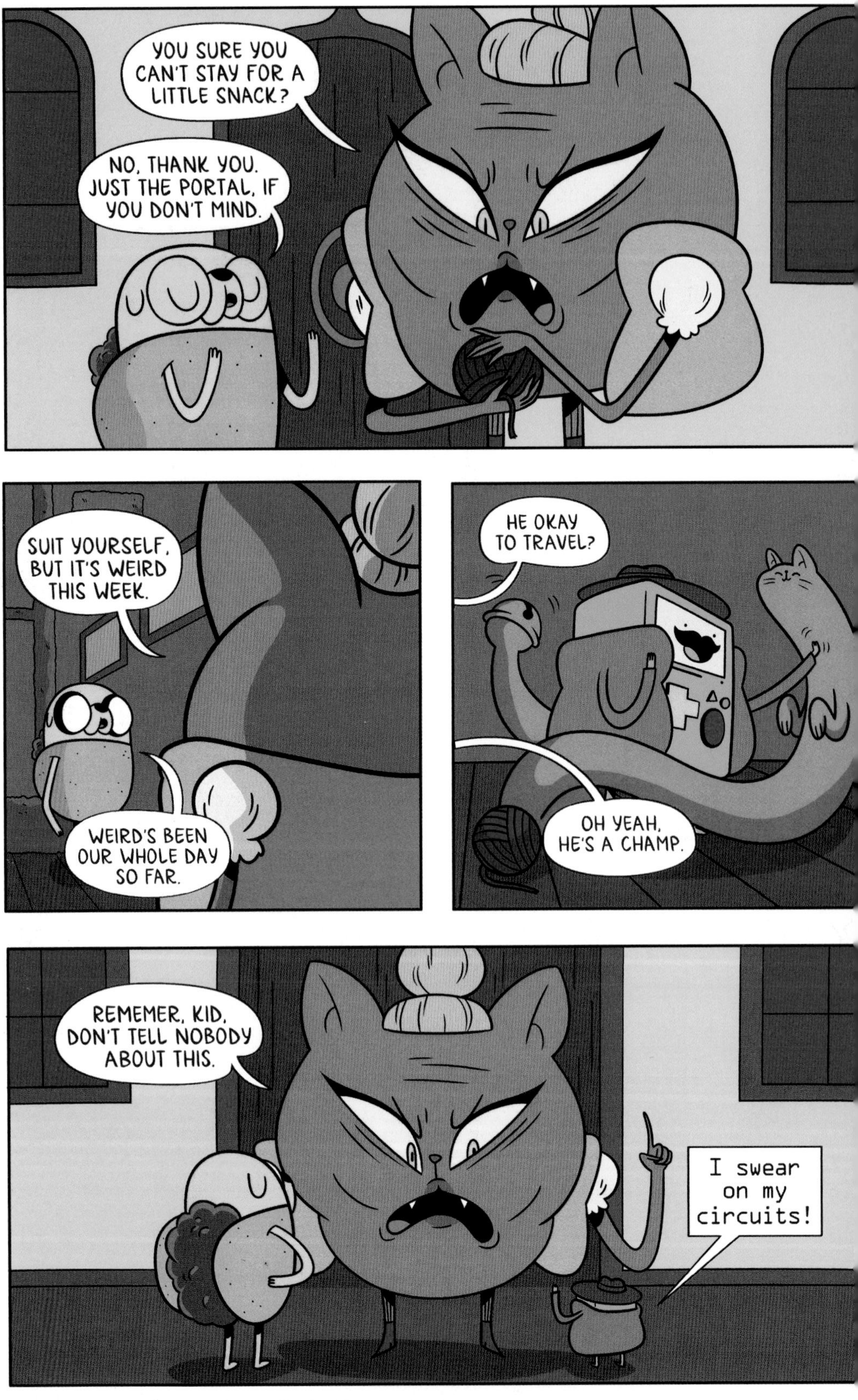
YOU SURE YOU CAN'T STAY FOR A LITTLE SNACK?
NO, THANK YOU. JUST THE PORTAL, IF YOU DON'T MIND.
SUIT YOURSELF, BUT IT'S WEIRD THIS WEEK.
WEIRD'S BEEN OUR WHOLE DAY SO FAR.
HE OKAY TO TRAVEL?
OH YEAH, HE'S A CHAMP.
REMEMER, KID, DON'T TELL NOBODY ABOUT THIS.
I swear on my circuits!

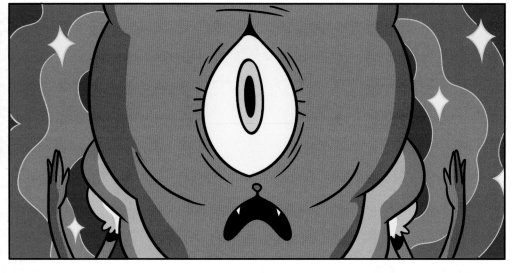

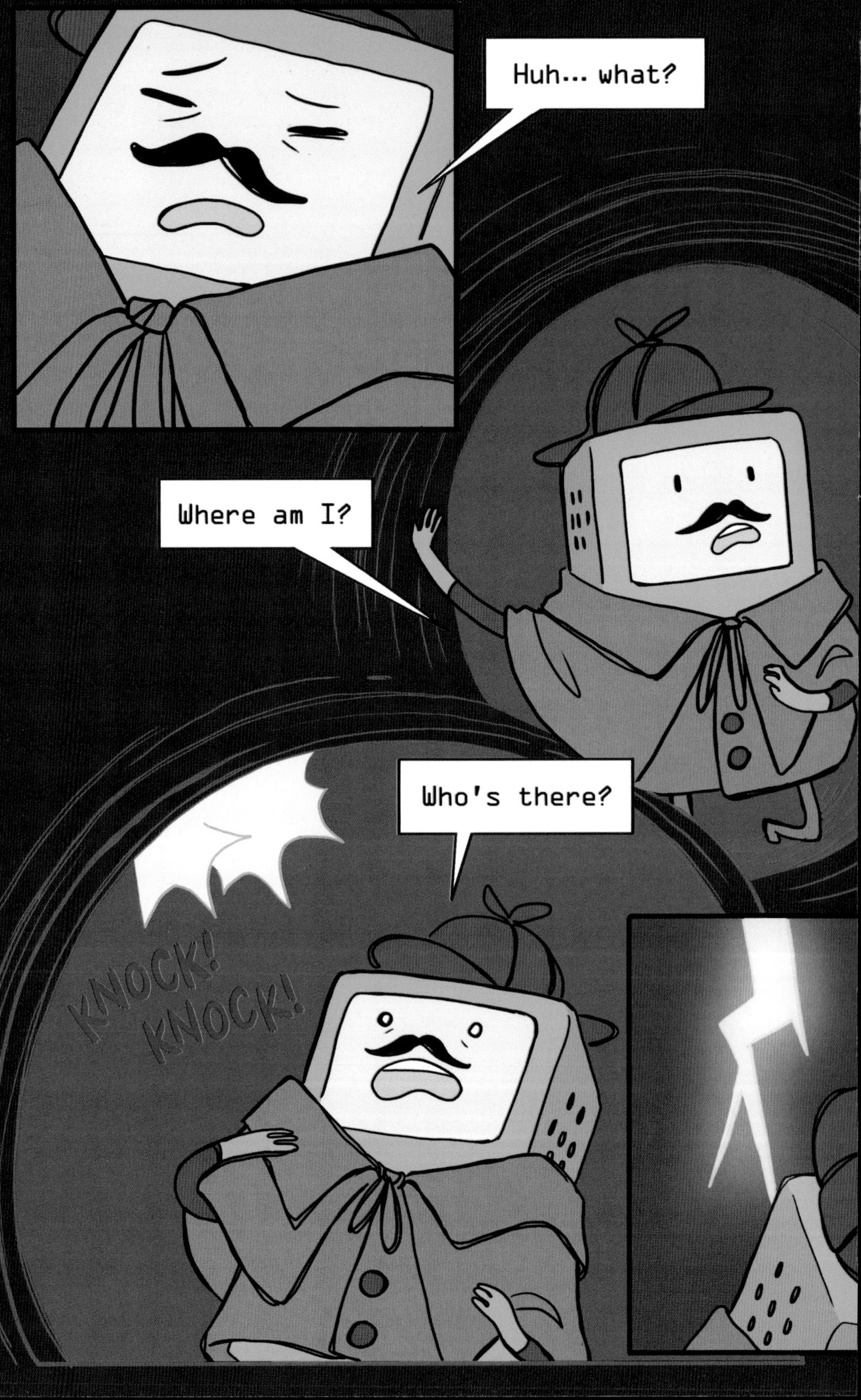

Huh... what?
Where am I?
Who's there?
KNOCK! KNOCK!

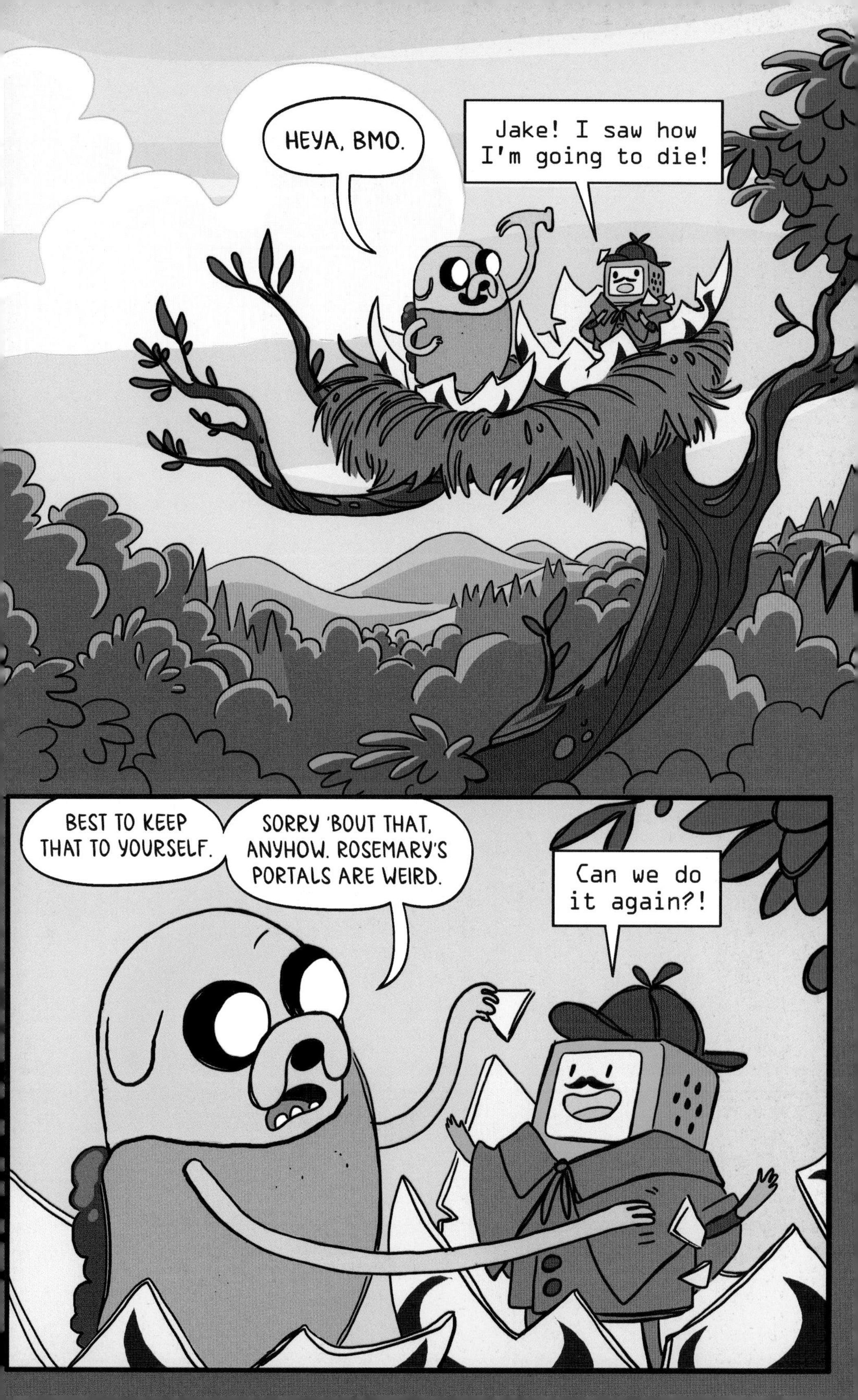
HEYA, BMO.
Jake! I saw how I'm going to die!
BEST TO KEEP THAT TO YOURSELF.
SORRY 'BOUT THAT. ANYHOW. ROSEMARY'S PORTALS ARE WEIRD.
Can we do it again?!

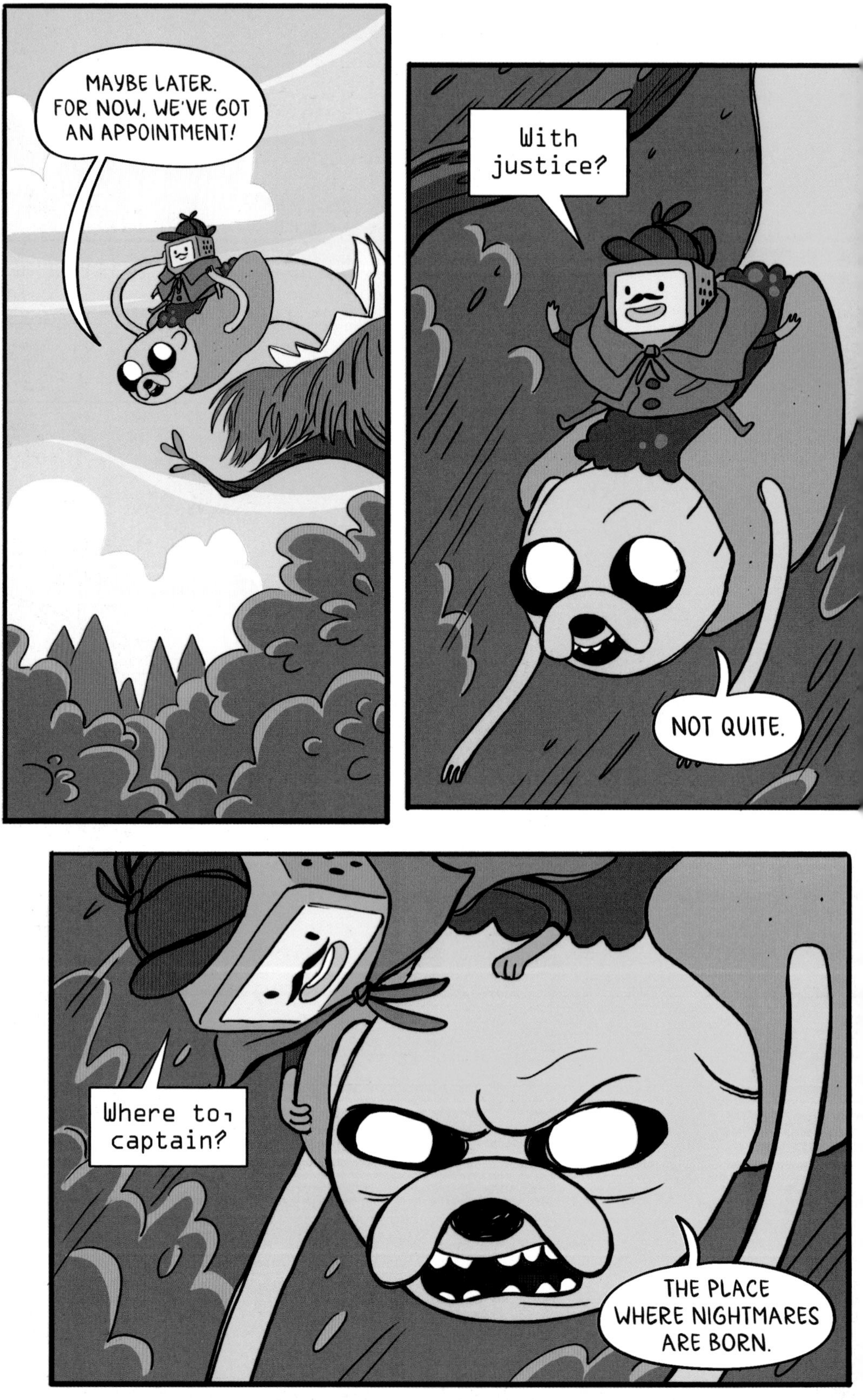
MAYBE LATER. FOR NOW, WE'VE GOT AN APPOINTMENT!
With justice?
NOT QUITE.
Where to, captain?
THE PLACE WHERE NIGHTMARES ARE BORN.

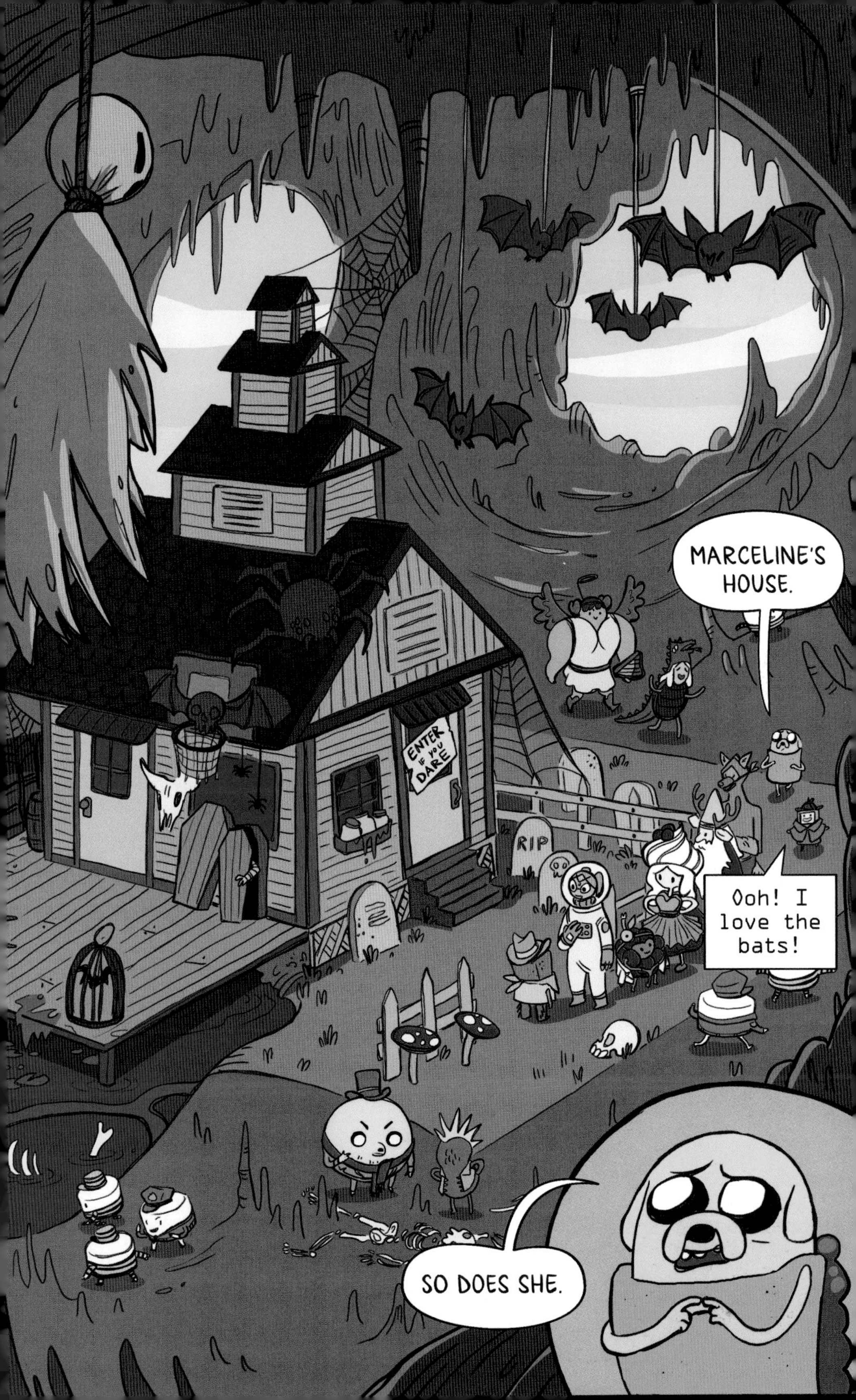
MARCELINE'S HOUSE.
ENTER IF YOU DARE
RIP
Ooh! I love the bats!
SO DOES SHE.

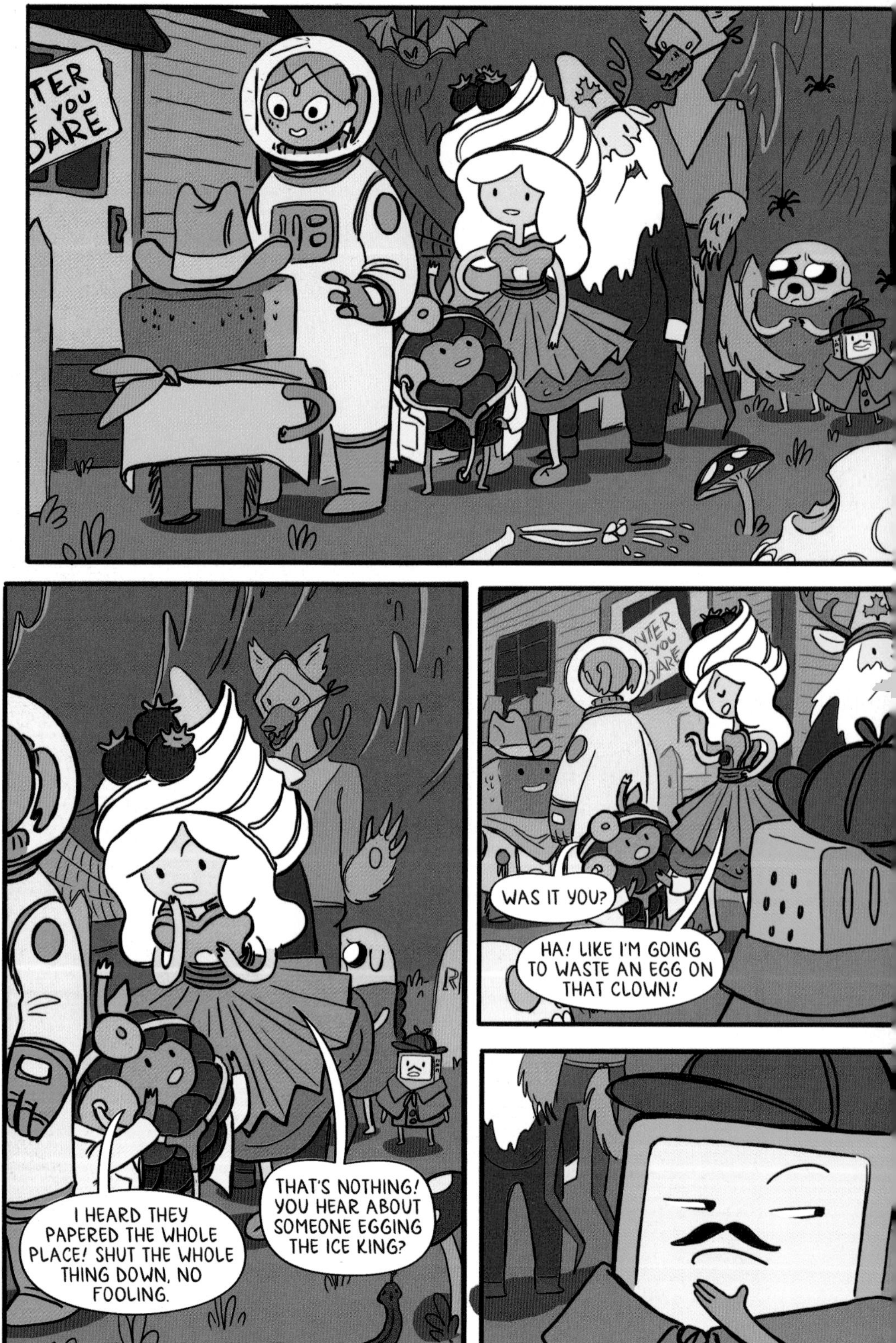
I HEARD THEY PAPERED THE WHOLE PLACE! SHUT THE WHOLE THING DOWN, NO FOOLING.
THAT'S NOTHING! YOU HEAR ABOUT SOMEONE EGGING THE ICE KING?
WAS IT YOU?
HA! LIKE I'M GOING TO WASTE AN EGG ON THAT CLOWN!

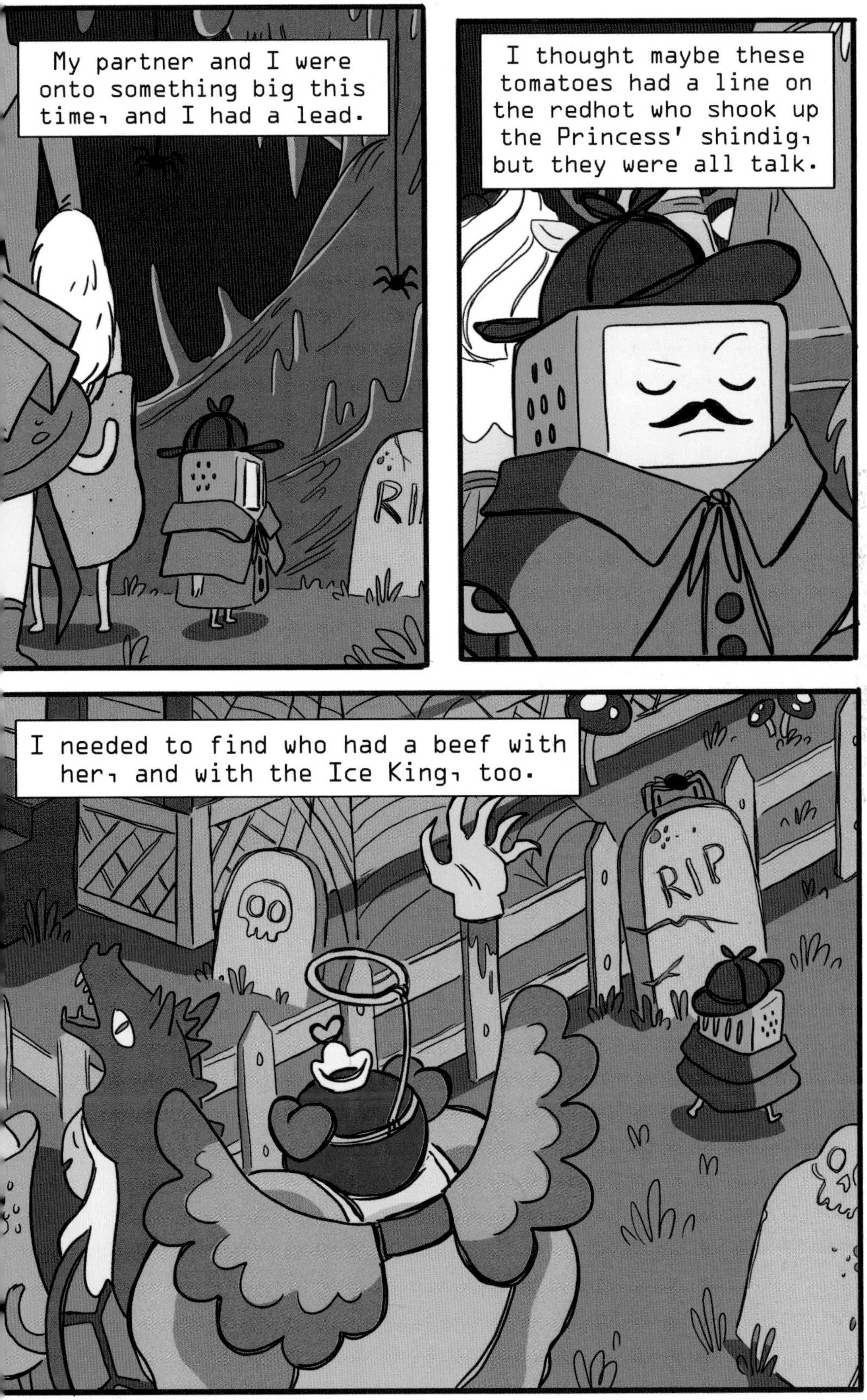
My partner and I were onto something big this time, and I had a lead.
RI
I thought maybe these tomatoes had a line on the redhot who shook up the Princess' shindig, but they were all talk.
I needed to find who had a beef with her, and with the Ice King, too.
RIP

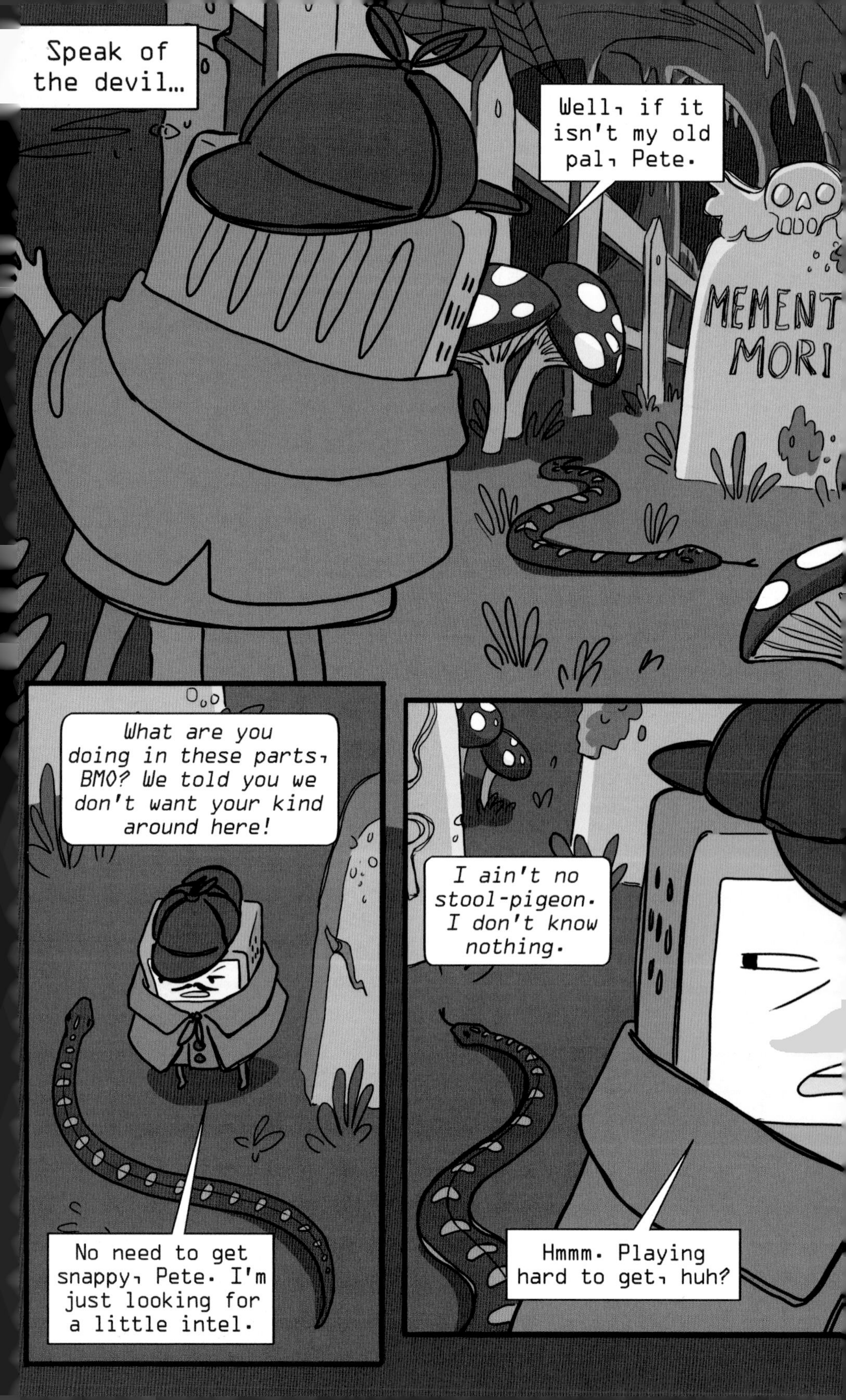
Speak of the devil...
Well, if it isn't my old pal, Pete.
MEMENTO MORI
What are you doing in these parts, BMO? We told you we don't want your kind around here!
No need to get snappy, Pete. I'm just looking for a little intel.
I ain't no stool-pigeon. I don't know nothing.
Hmmm. Playing hard to get, huh?

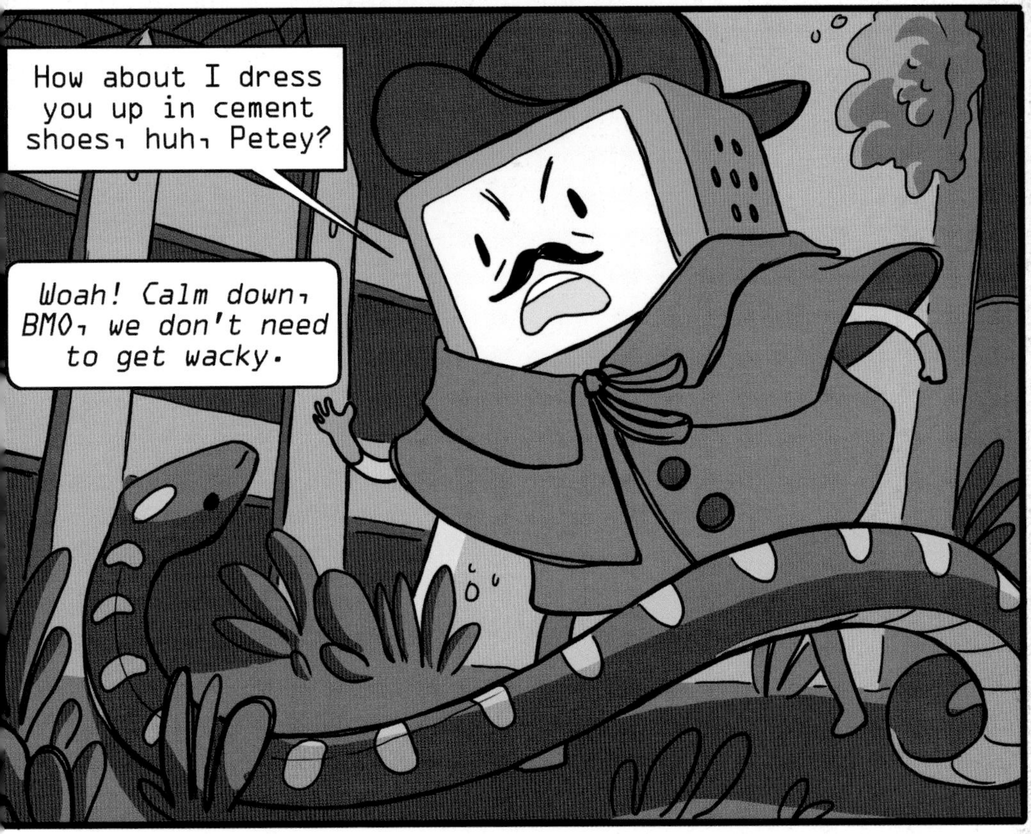
How about I dress you up in cement shoes, huh, Petey?
Woah! Calm down, BMO, we don't need to get wacky.

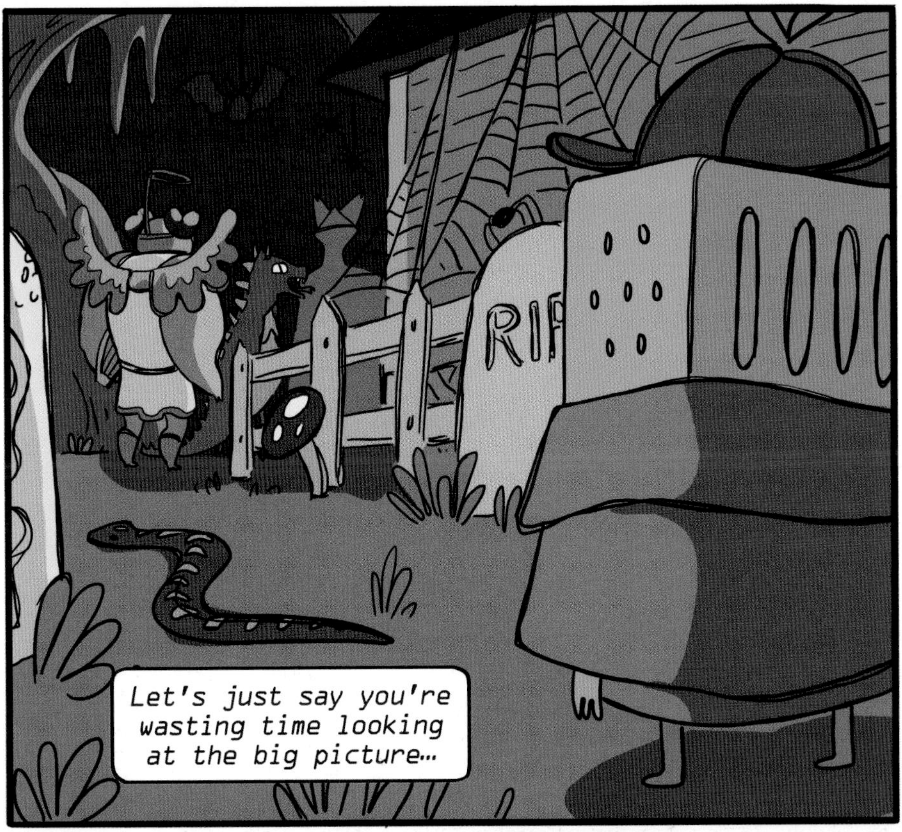
RIP
Let's just say you're wasting time looking at the big picture...

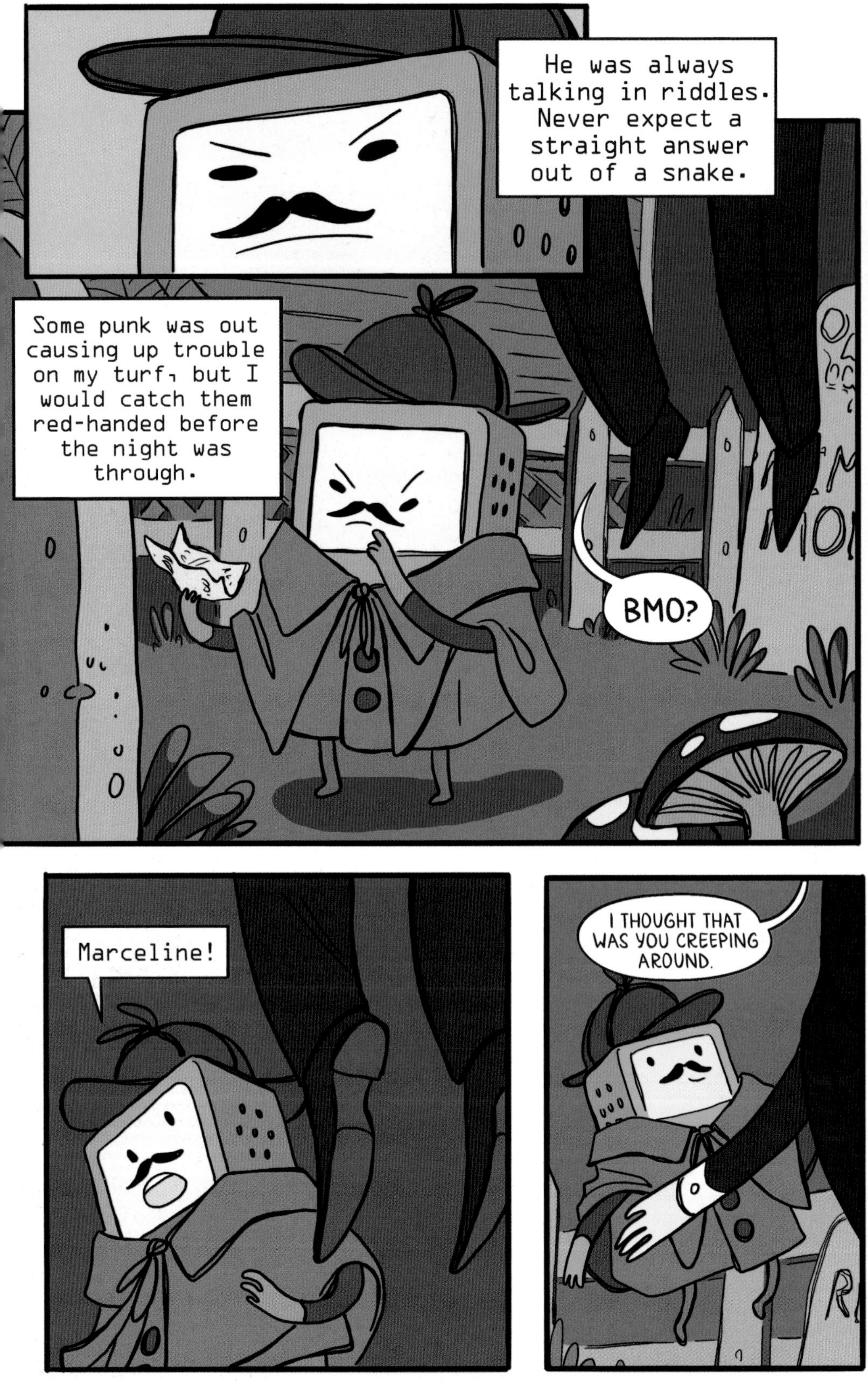
He was always talking in riddles. Never expect a straight answer out of a snake.
Some punk was out causing up trouble on my turf, but I would catch them red-handed before the night was through.
BMO?
Marceline!
I THOUGHT THAT WAS YOU CREEPING AROUND.

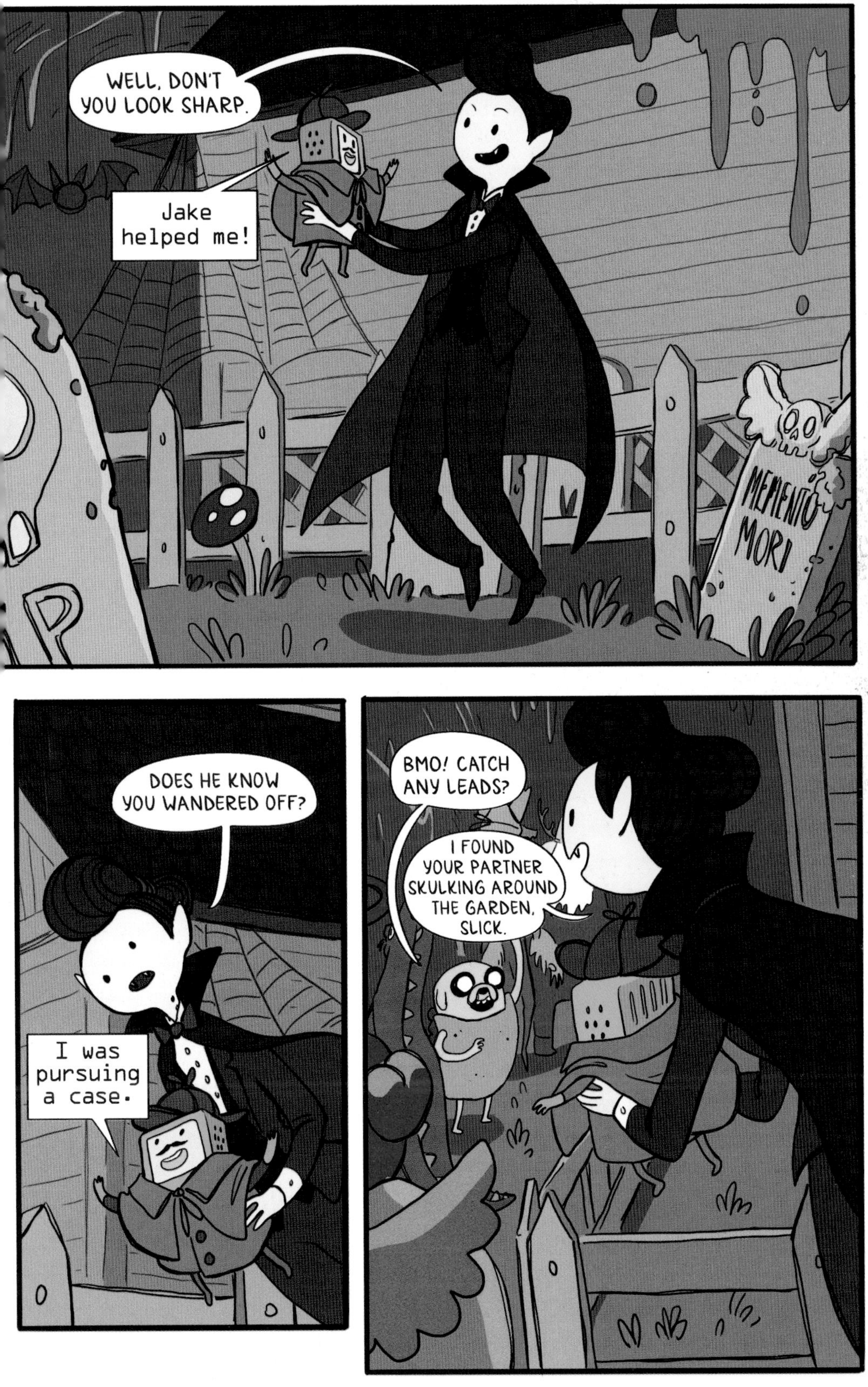
WELL, DON'T YOU LOOK SHARP.
Jake helped me!
MEMENTO MORI
DOES HE KNOW YOU WANDERED OFF?
I was pursuing a case.
BMO! CATCH ANY LEADS?
I FOUND YOUR PARTNER SKULKING AROUND THE GARDEN, SLICK.

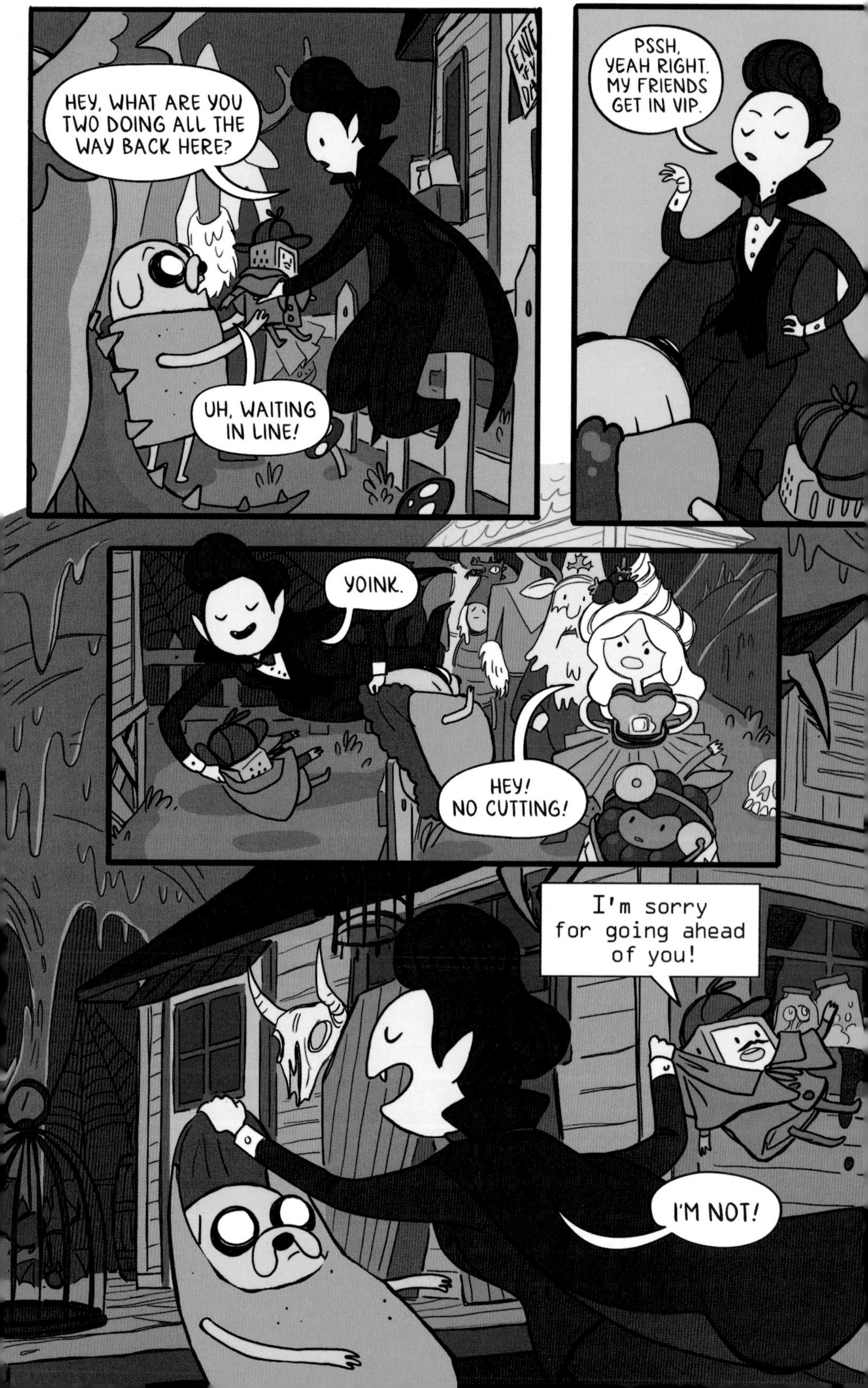
HEY, WHAT ARE YOU TWO DOING ALL THE WAY BACK HERE?
UH, WAITING IN LINE!
PSSH, YEAH RIGHT. MY FRIENDS GET IN VIP.
YOINK.
HEY! NO CUTTING!
I'm sorry for going ahead of you!
I'M NOT!

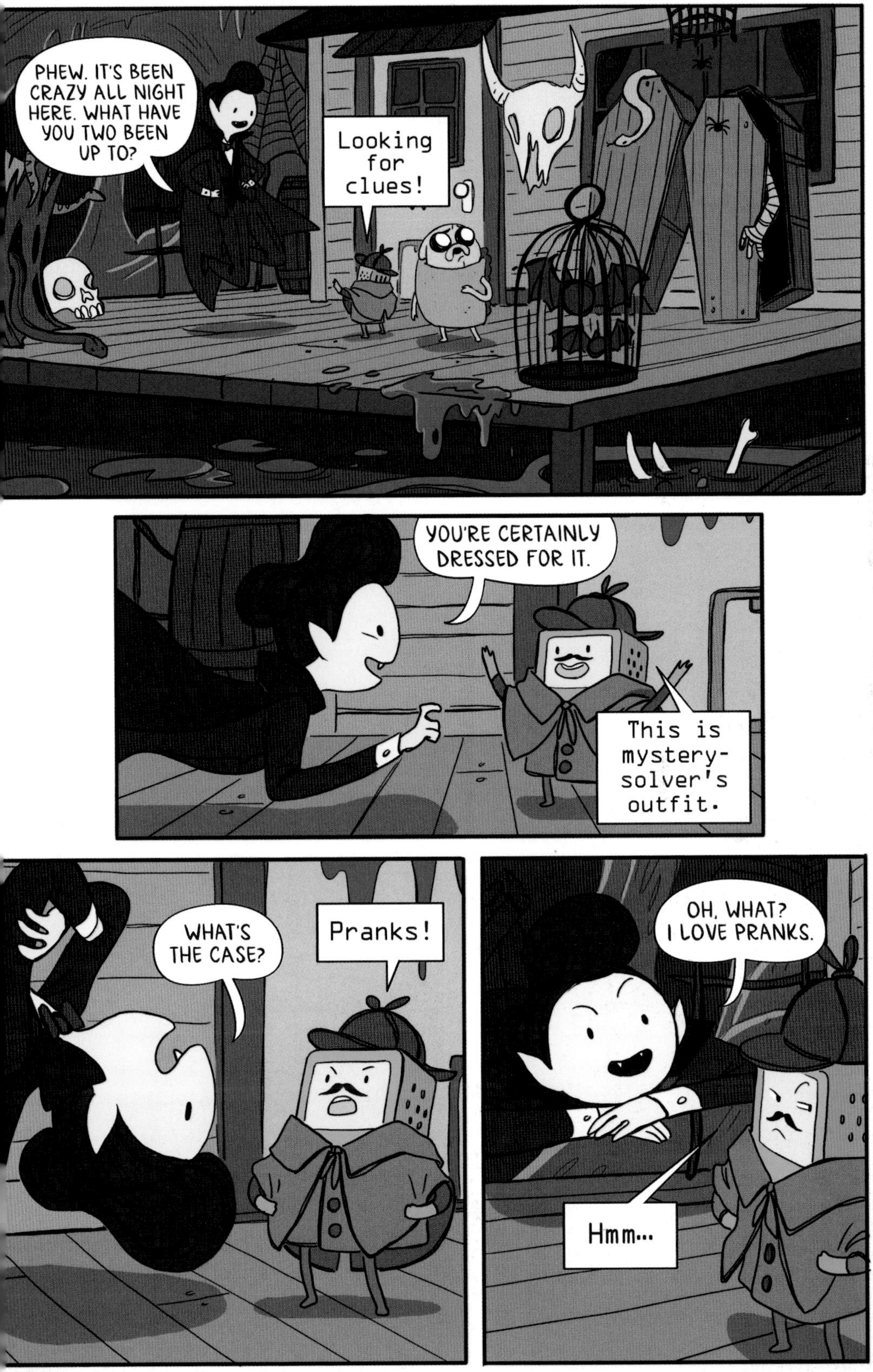
PHEW. IT'S BEEN CRAZY ALL NIGHT HERE. WHAT HAVE YOU TWO BEEN UP TO?
Looking for clues!
YOU'RE CERTAINLY DRESSED FOR IT.
This is mystery-solver's outfit.
WHAT'S THE CASE?
Pranks!
OH, WHAT? I LOVE PRANKS.
Hmm...

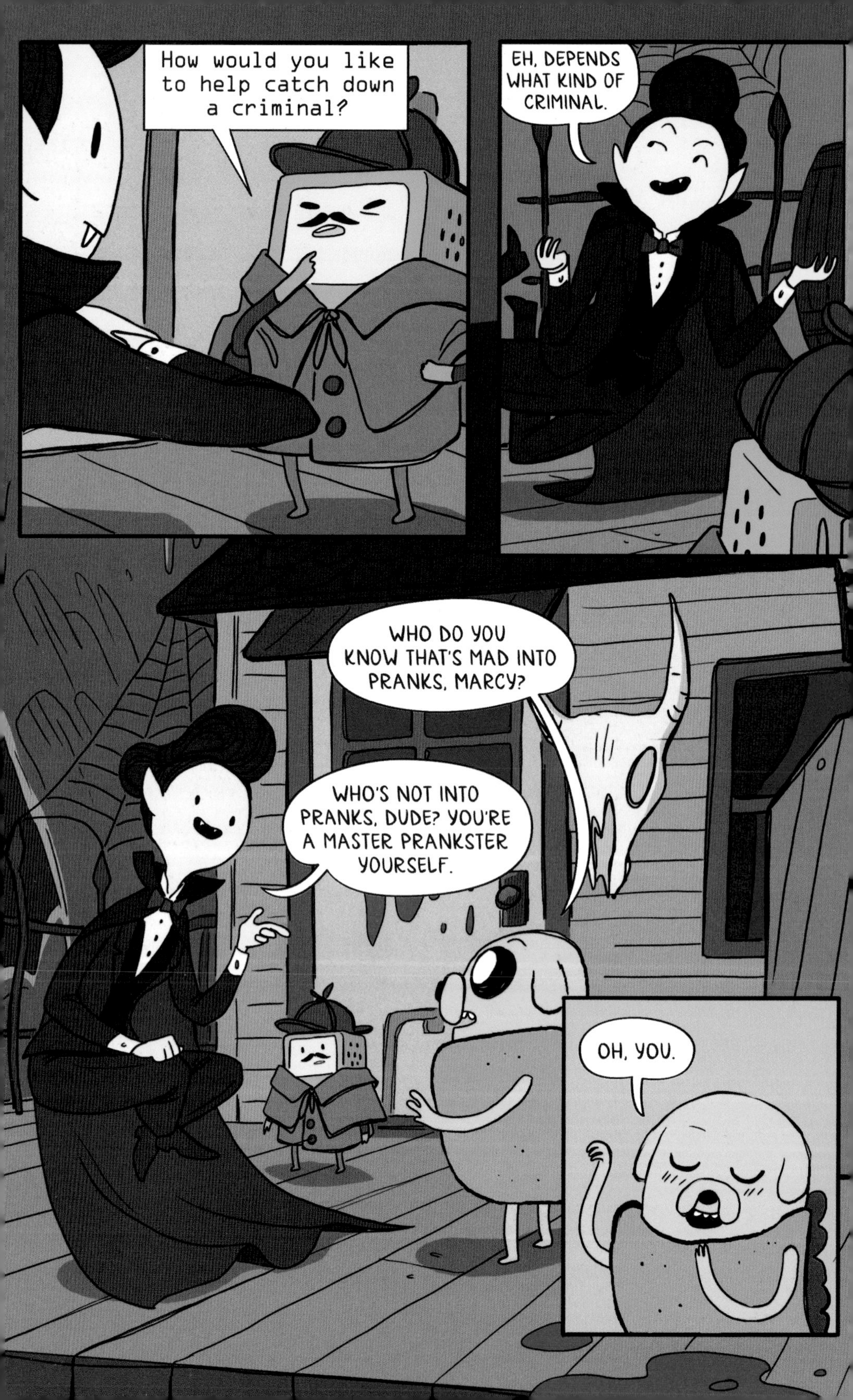
How would you like to help catch down a criminal?
EH, DEPENDS WHAT KIND OF CRIMINAL.
WHO DO YOU KNOW THAT'S MAD INTO PRANKS, MARCY?
WHO'S NOT INTO PRANKS, DUDE? YOU'RE A MASTER PRANKSTER YOURSELF.
OH, YOU.

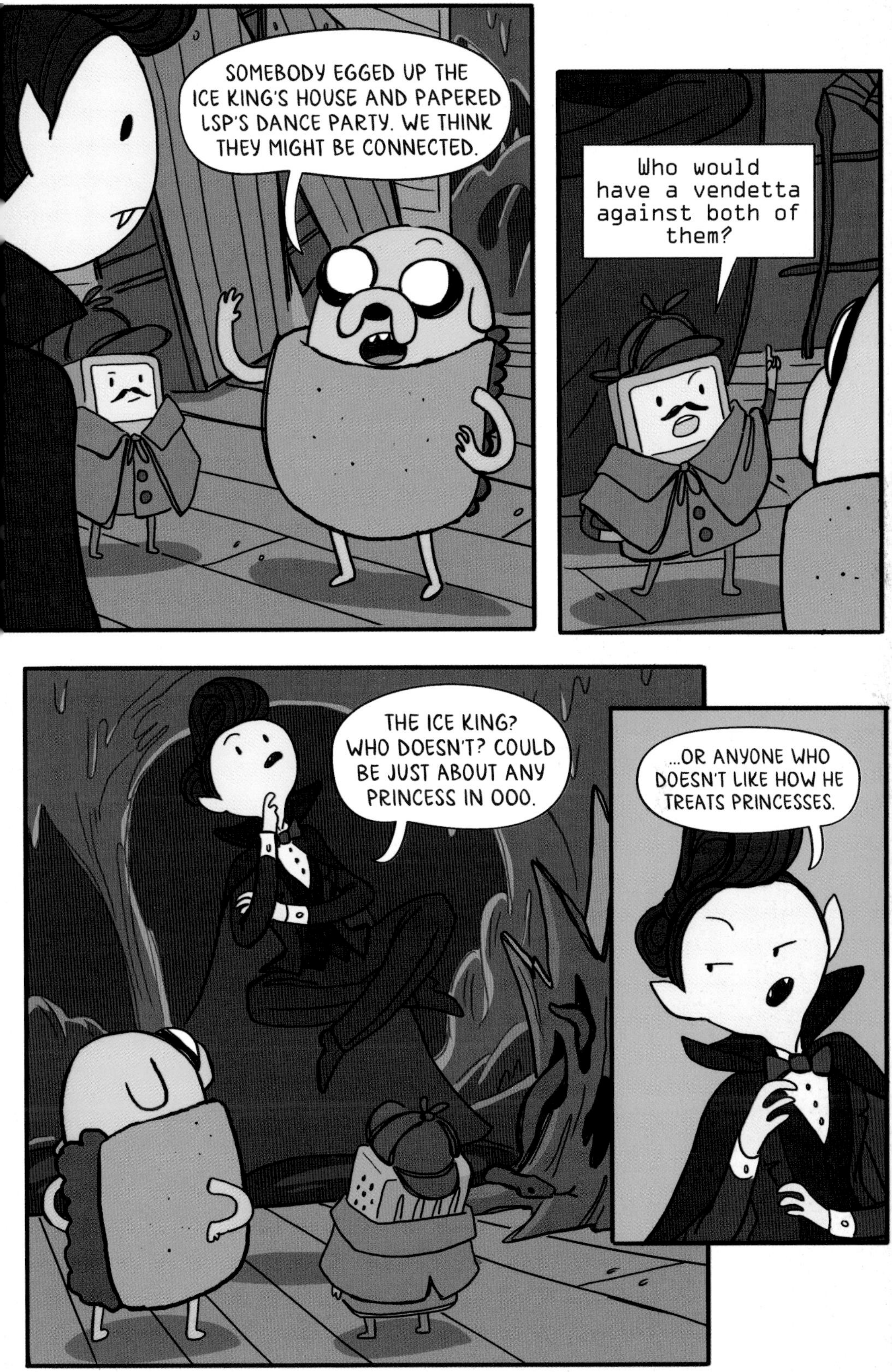
SOMEBODY EGGED UP THE ICE KING'S HOUSE AND PAPERED LSP'S DANCE PARTY. WE THINK THEY MIGHT BE CONNECTED.
Who would have a vendetta against both of them?
THE ICE KING? WHO DOESN'T? COULD BE JUST ABOUT ANY PRINCESS IN OOO.
...OR ANYONE WHO DOESN'T LIKE HOW HE TREATS PRINCESSES.

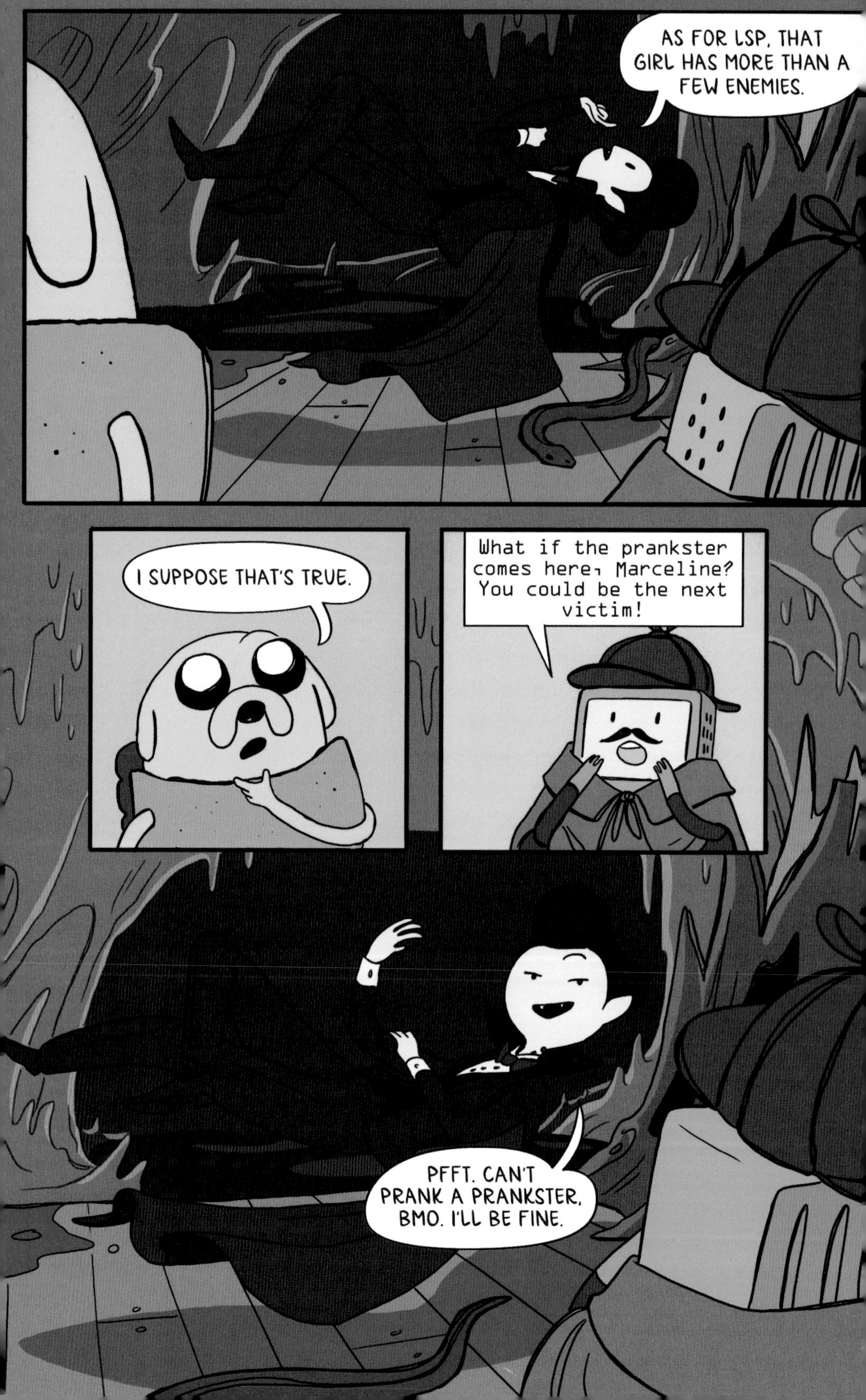
AS FOR LSP, THAT GIRL HAS MORE THAN A FEW ENEMIES.
I SUPPOSE THAT'S TRUE.
What if the prankster comes here, Marceline? You could be the next victim!
PFFT. CAN'T PRANK A PRANKSTER, BMO. I'LL BE FINE.

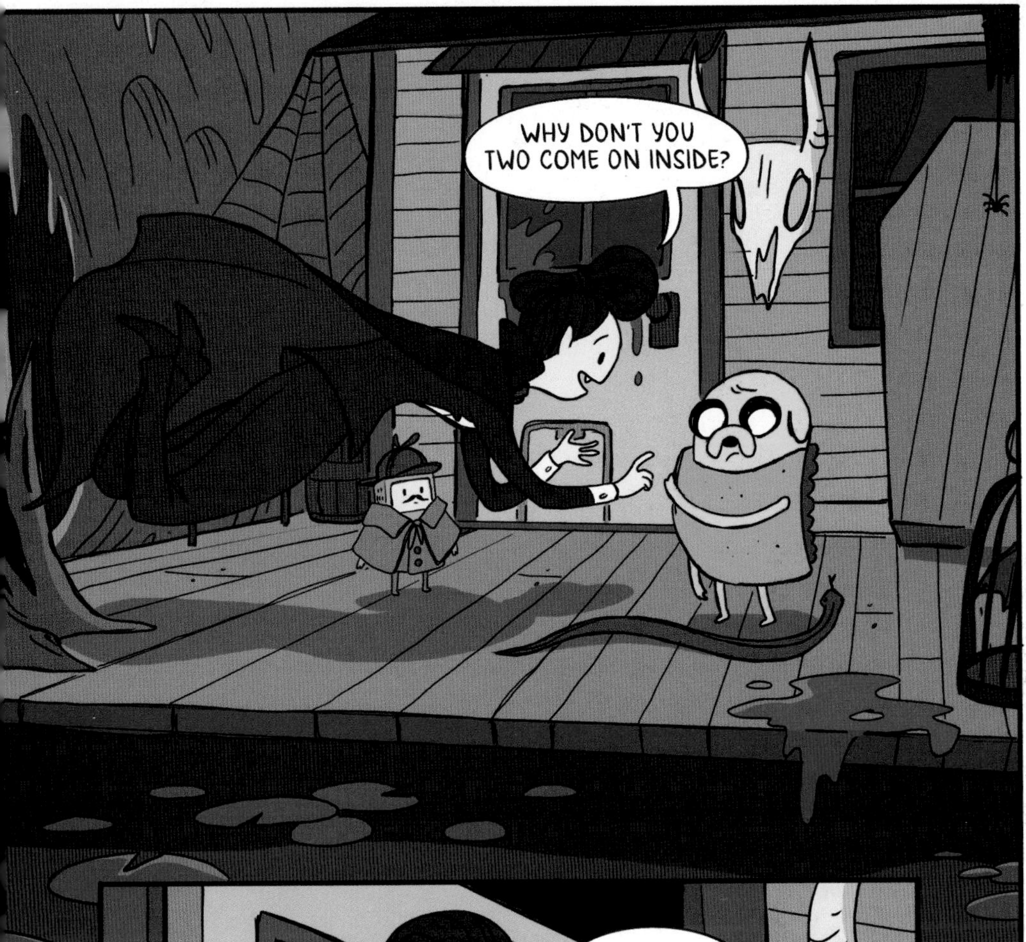
WHY DON'T YOU TWO COME ON INSIDE?

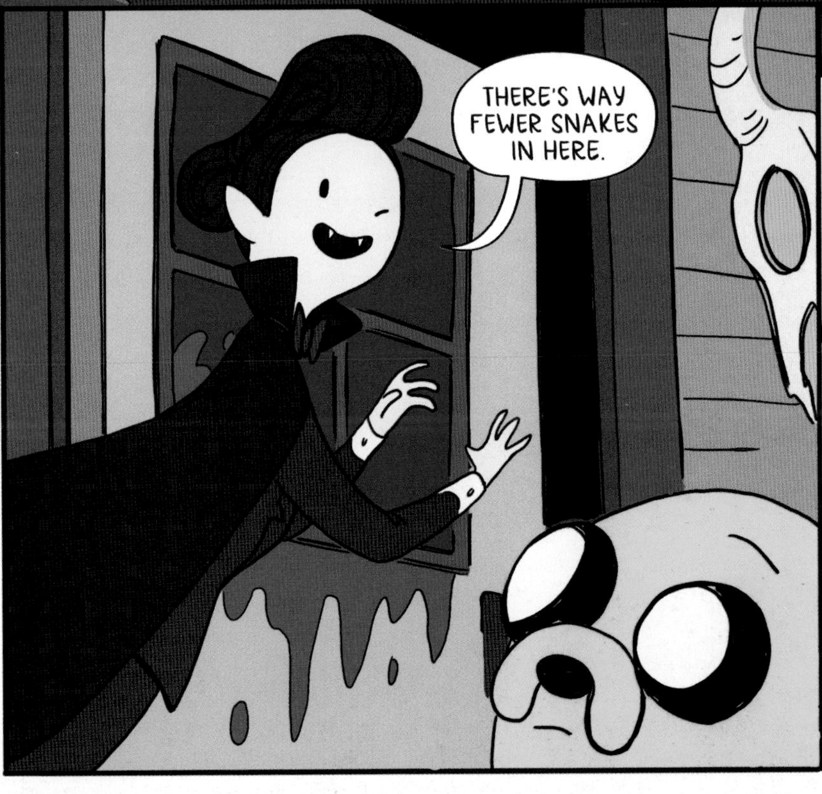
THERE'S WAY FEWER SNAKES IN HERE.

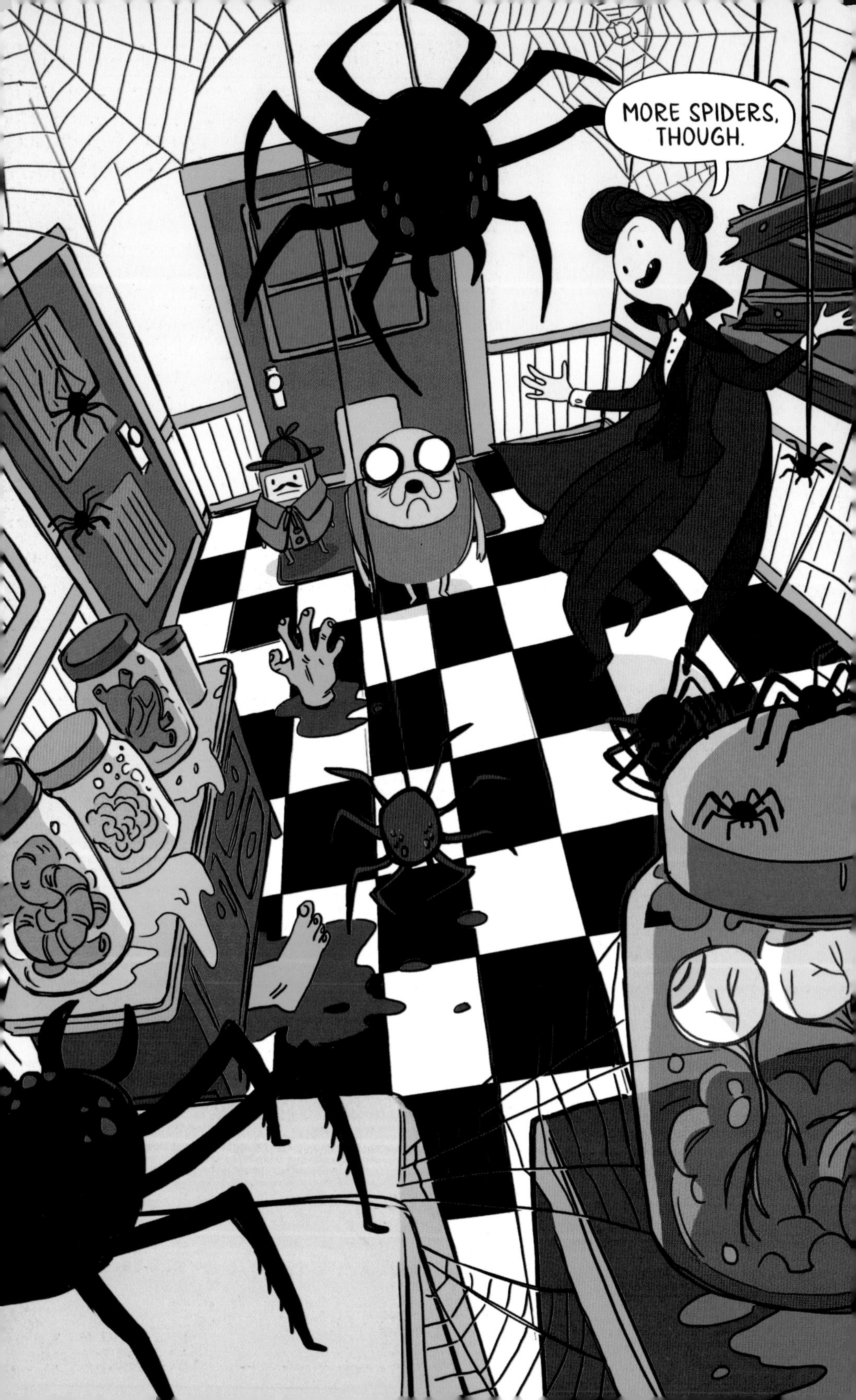
MORE SPIDERS, THOUGH.

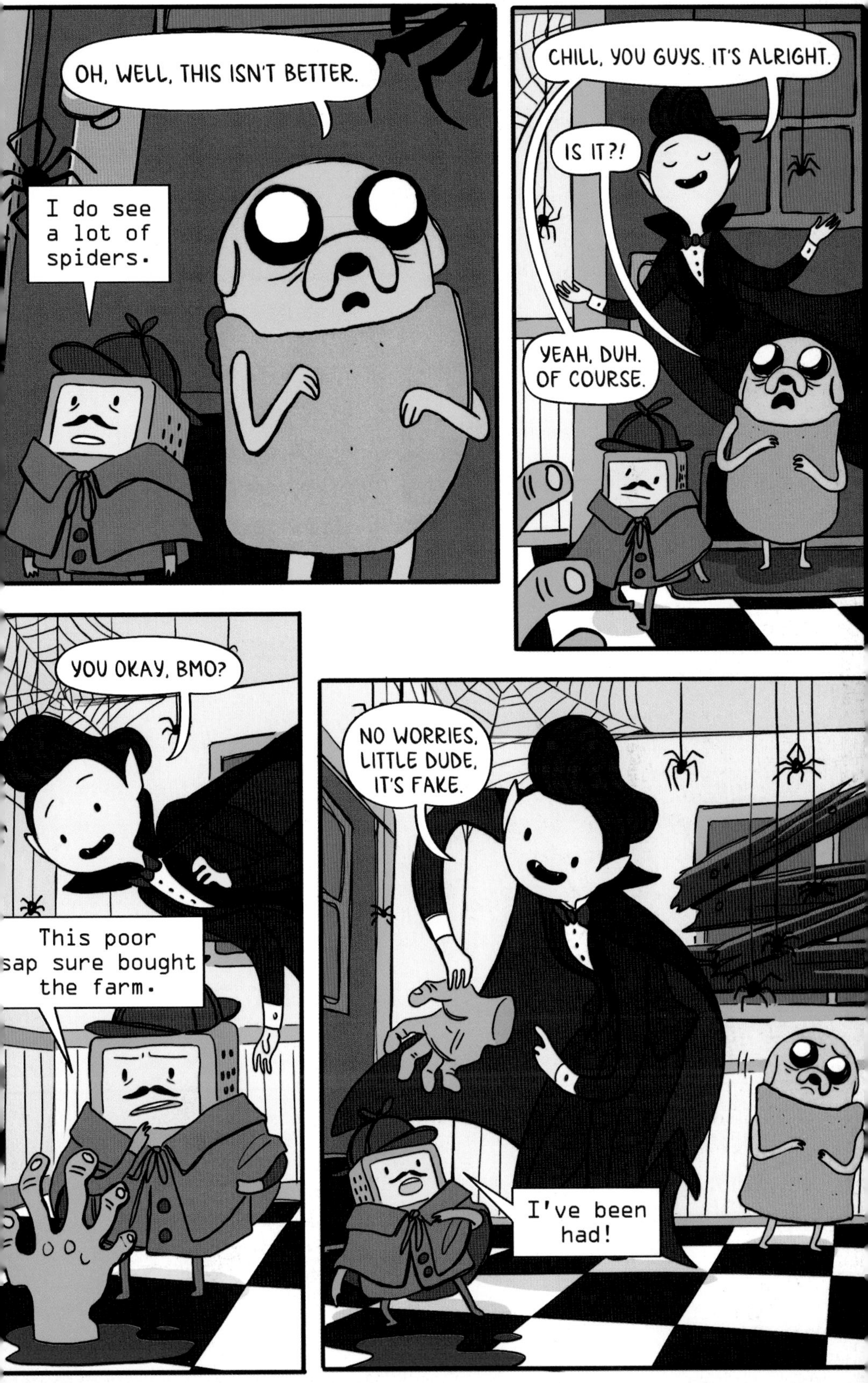
OH, WELL, THIS ISN'T BETTER.
I do see a lot of spiders.
CHILL, YOU GUYS. IT'S ALRIGHT.
IS IT?!
YEAH, DUH. OF COURSE.
YOU OKAY, BMO?
This poor sap sure bought the farm.
NO WORRIES, LITTLE DUDE, IT'S FAKE.
I've been had!

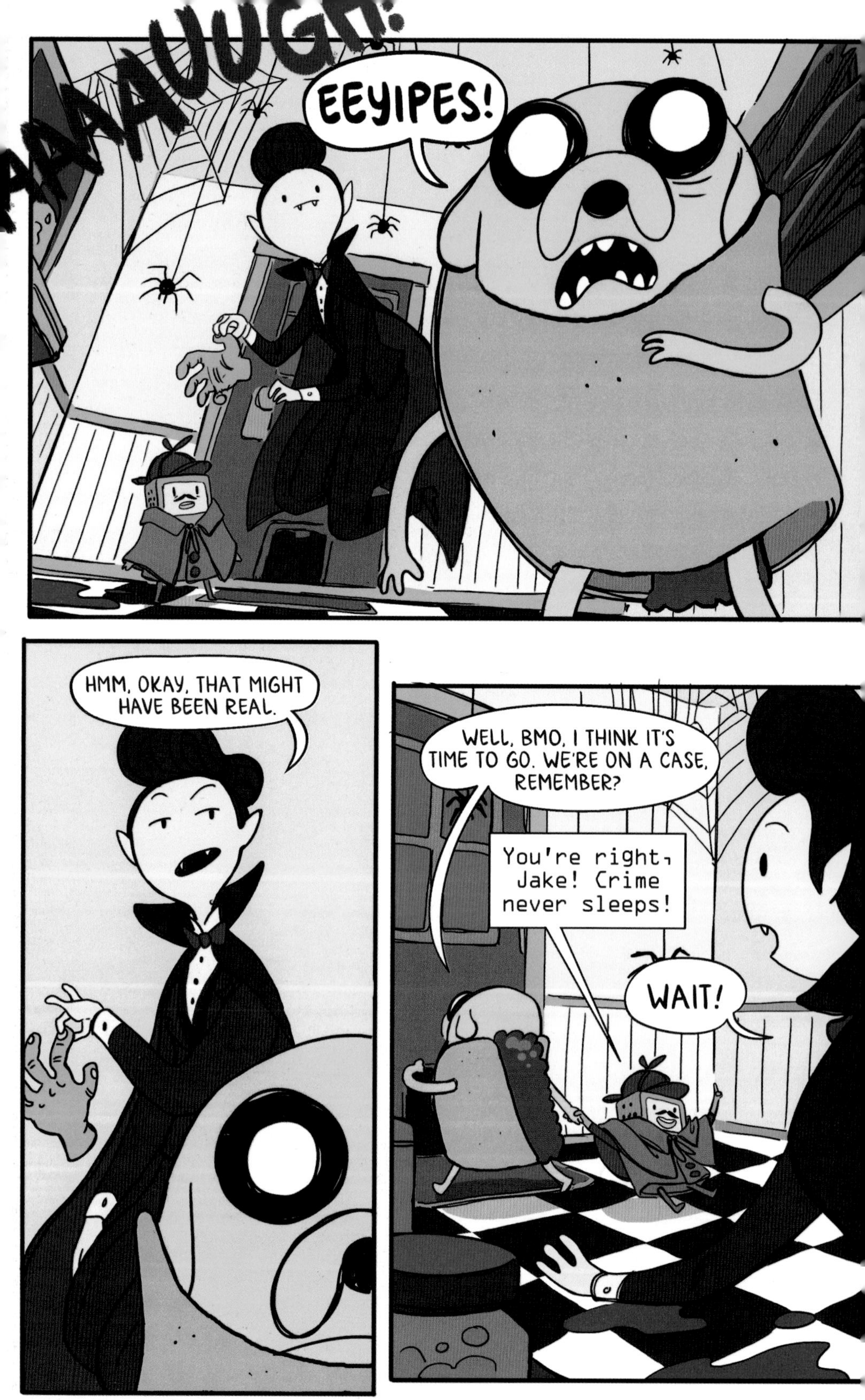
AAAAUUGH!
EEYIPES!
HMM, OKAY, THAT MIGHT HAVE BEEN REAL.
WELL, BMO, I THINK IT'S TIME TO GO. WE'RE ON A CASE, REMEMBER?
You're right, Jake! Crime never sleeps!
WAIT!

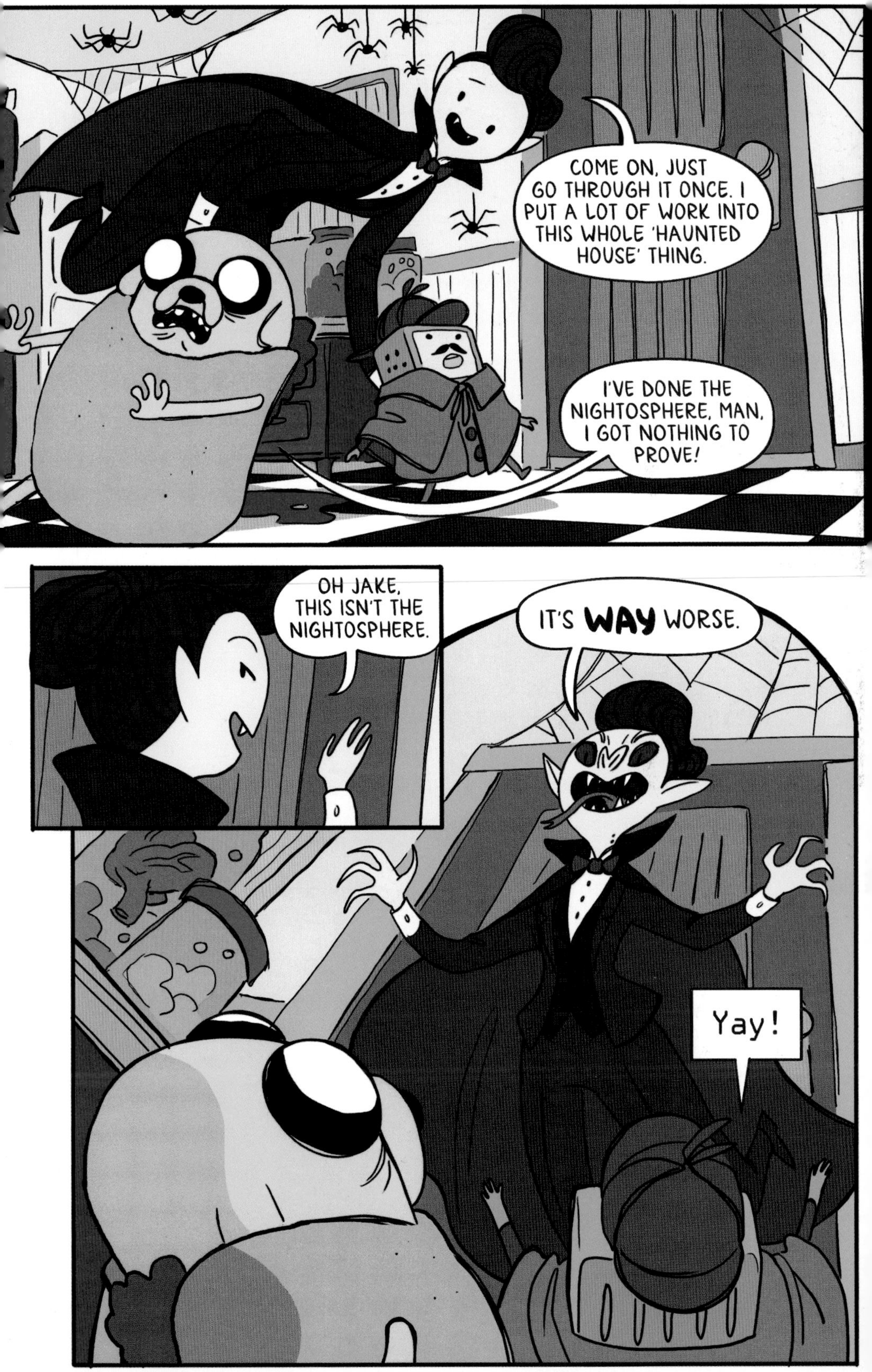
COME ON, JUST GO THROUGH IT ONCE. I PUT A LOT OF WORK INTO THIS WHOLE 'HAUNTED HOUSE' THING.
I'VE DONE THE NIGHTOSPHERE, MAN, I GOT NOTHING TO PROVE!
OH JAKE, THIS ISN'T THE NIGHTOSPHERE.
IT'S **WAY** WORSE.
Yay!

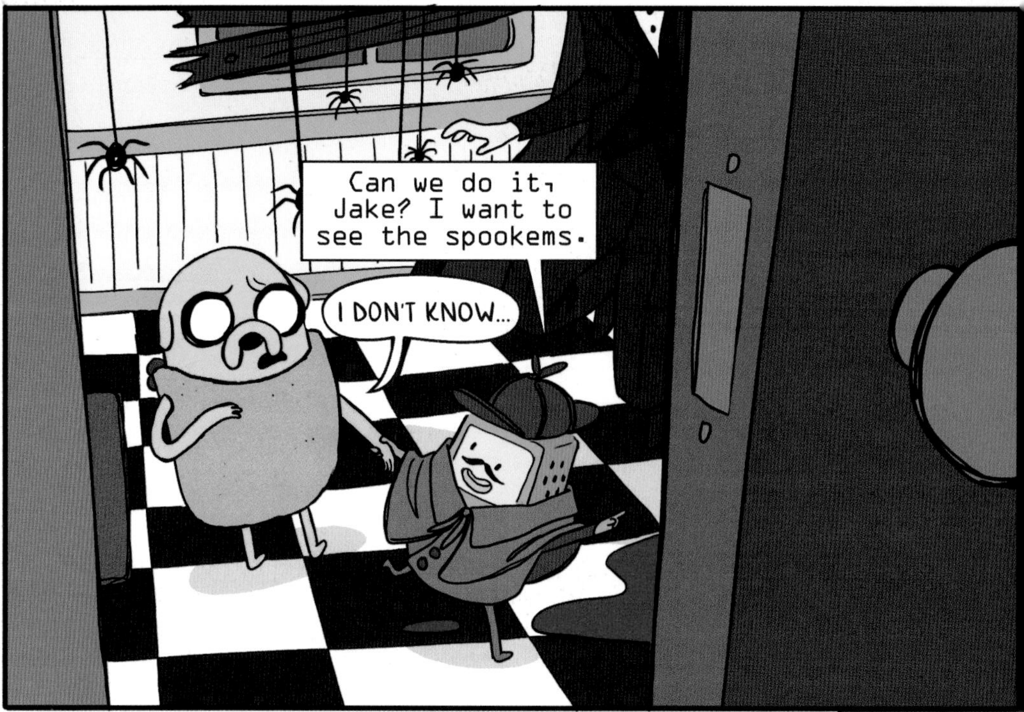
Can we do it, Jake? I want to see the spookems.
I DON'T KNOW...

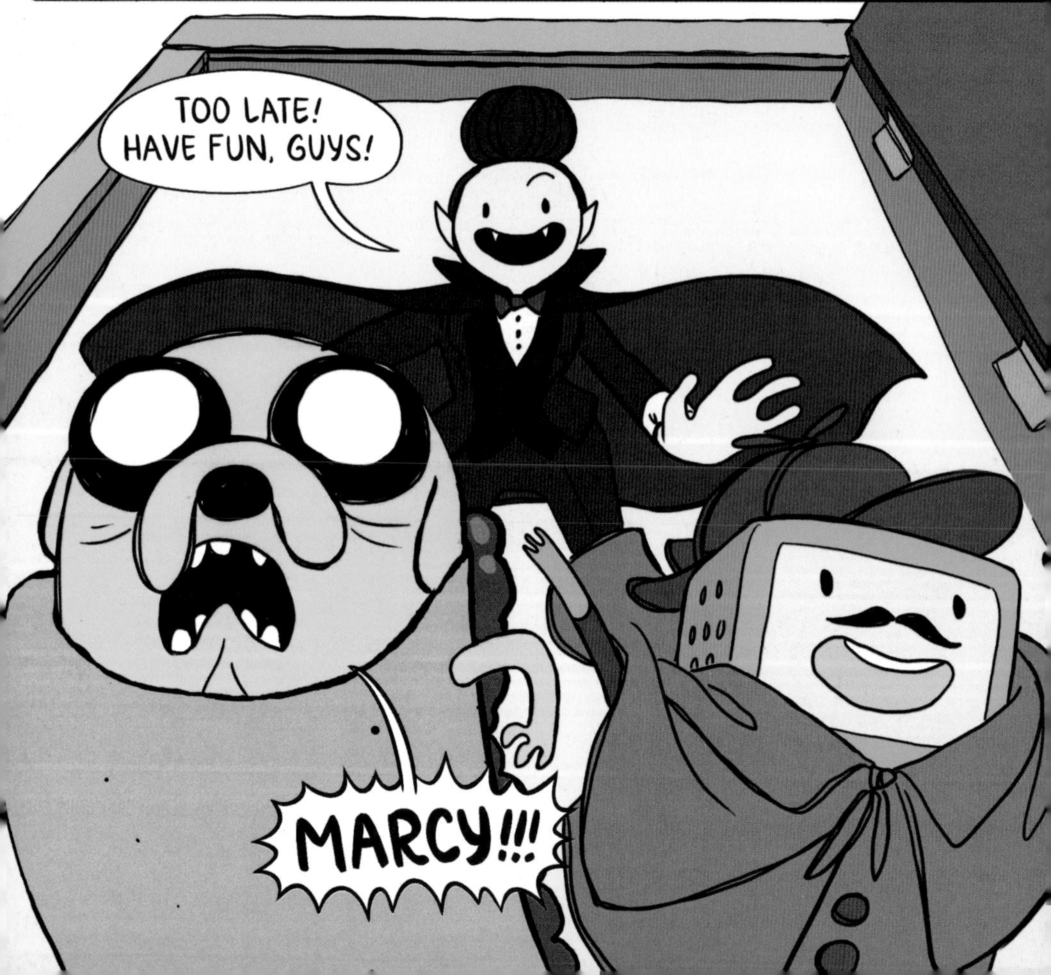
TOO LATE! HAVE FUN, GUYS!
MARCY!!!

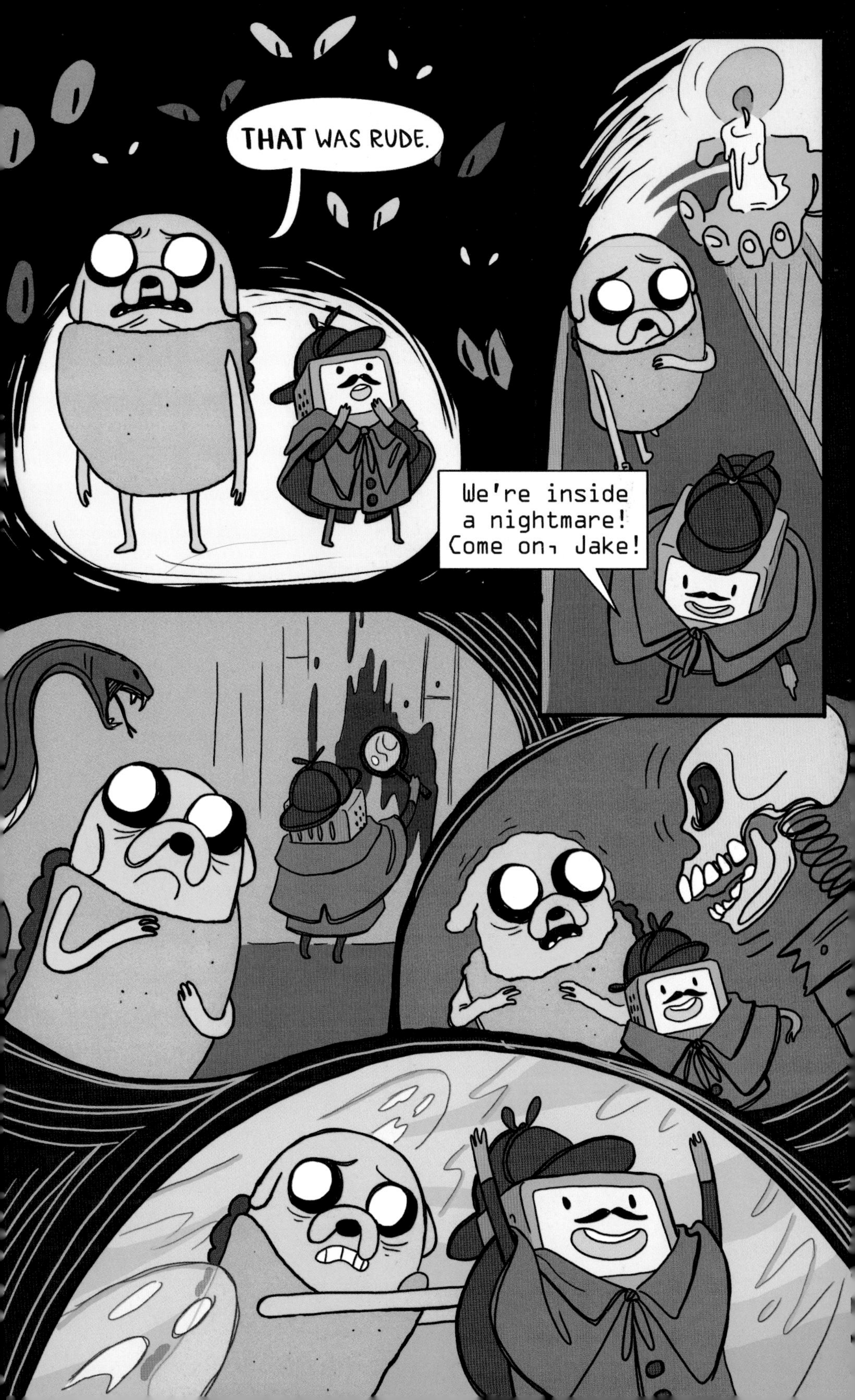
THAT WAS RUDE.
We're inside a nightmare! Come on, Jake!

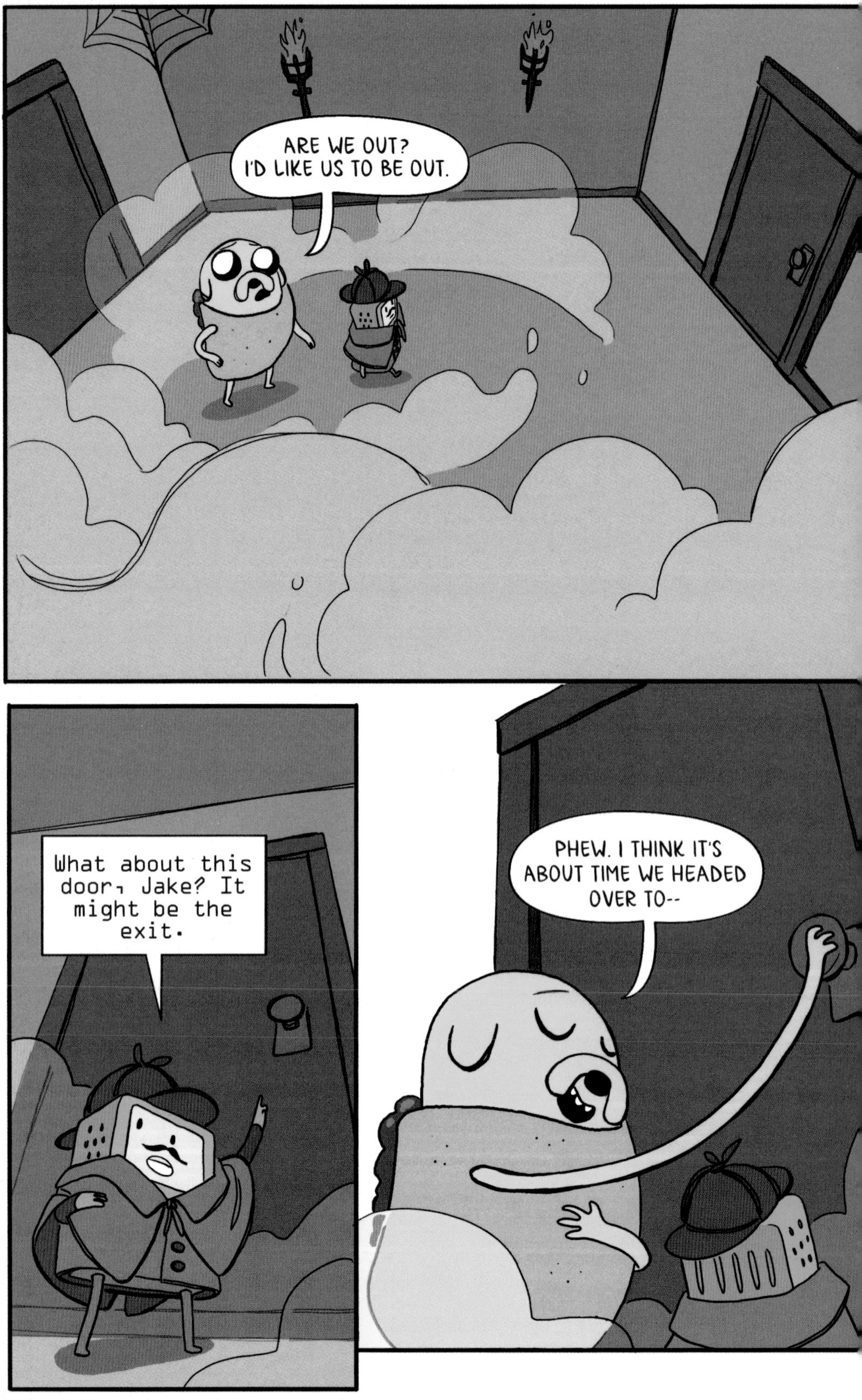
ARE WE OUT? I'D LIKE US TO BE OUT.
What about this door, Jake? It might be the exit.
PHEW. I THINK IT'S ABOUT TIME WE HEADED OVER TO--

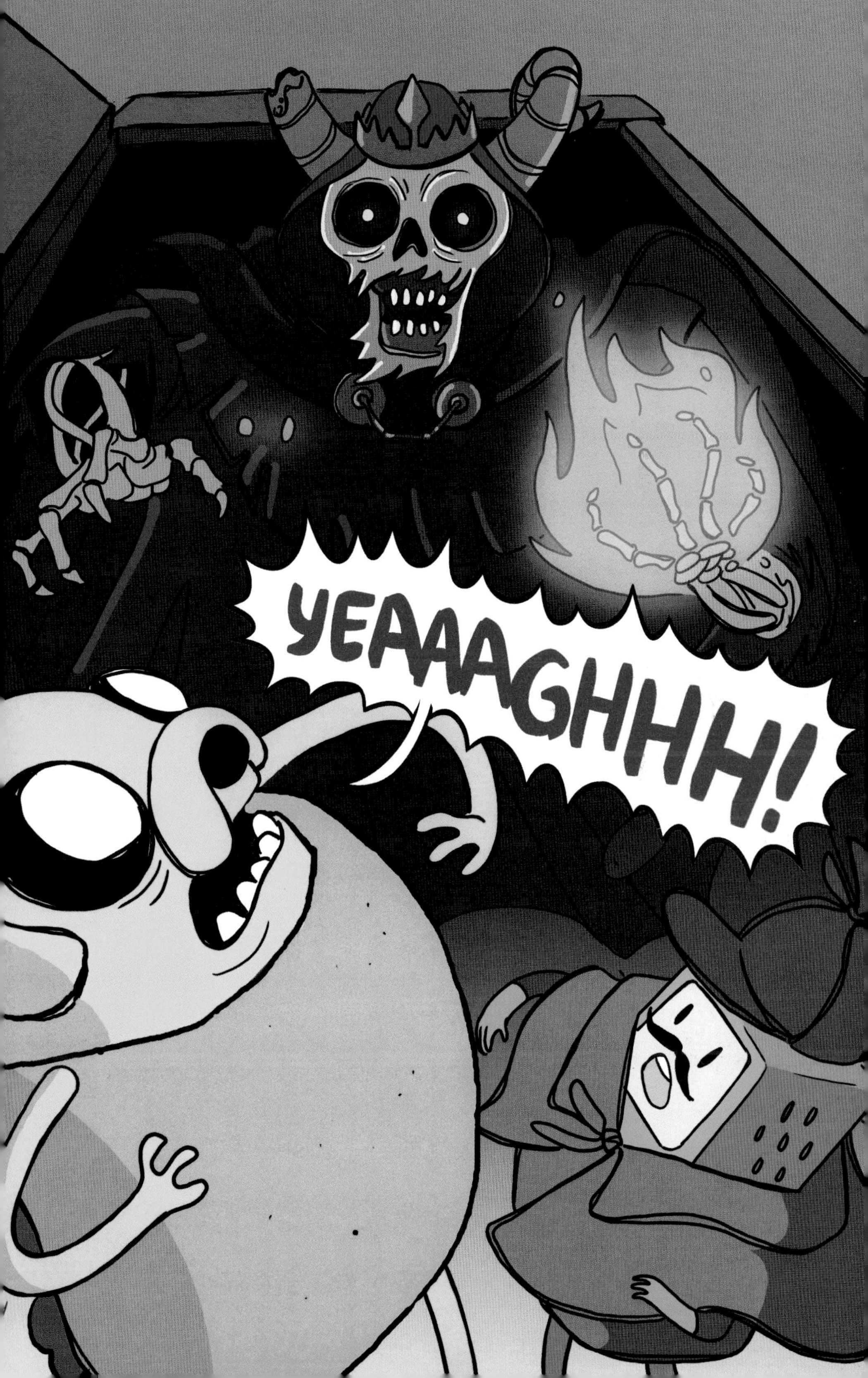
YEAAAAGHHHH!

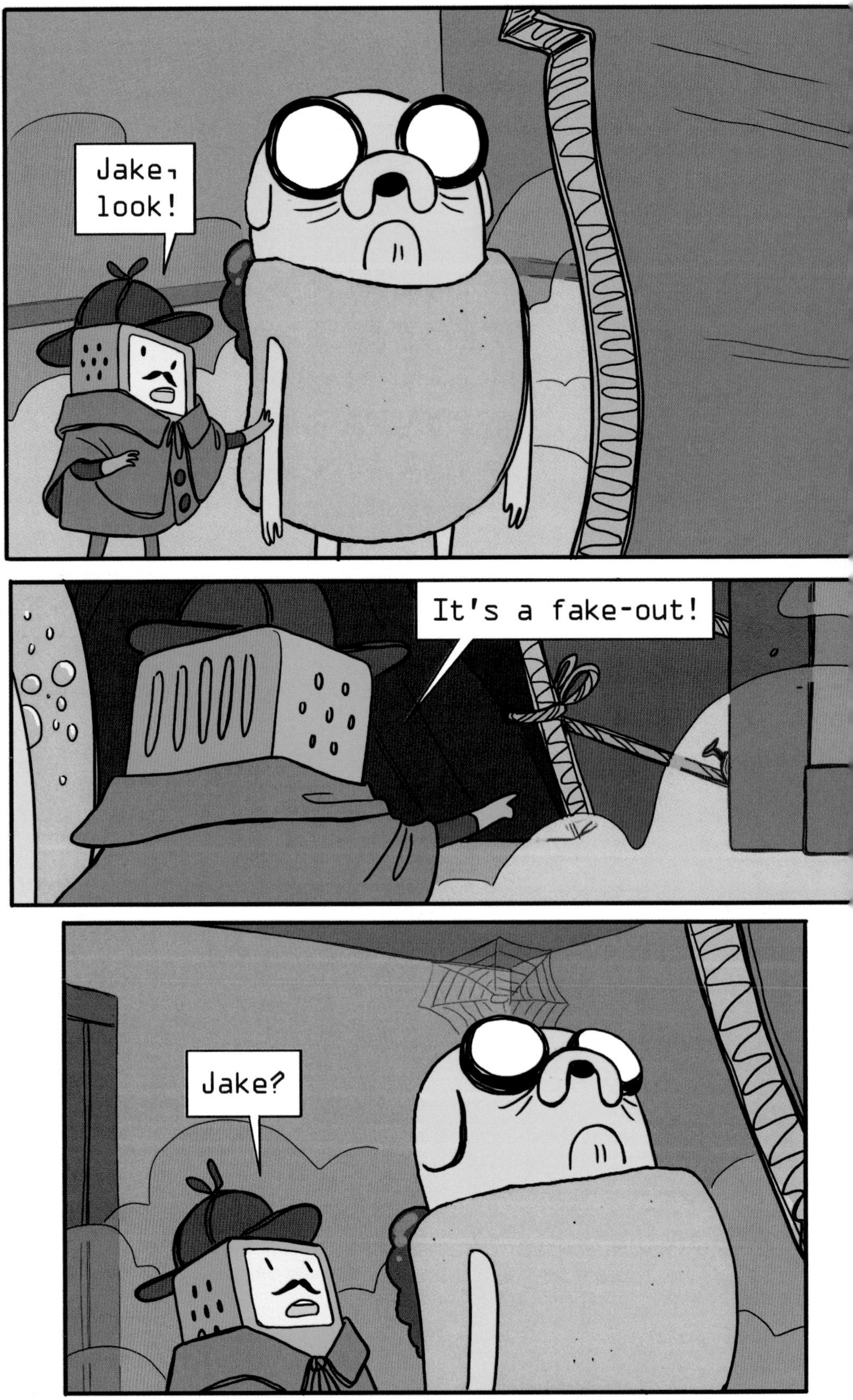
Jake, look!
It's a fake-out!
Jake?

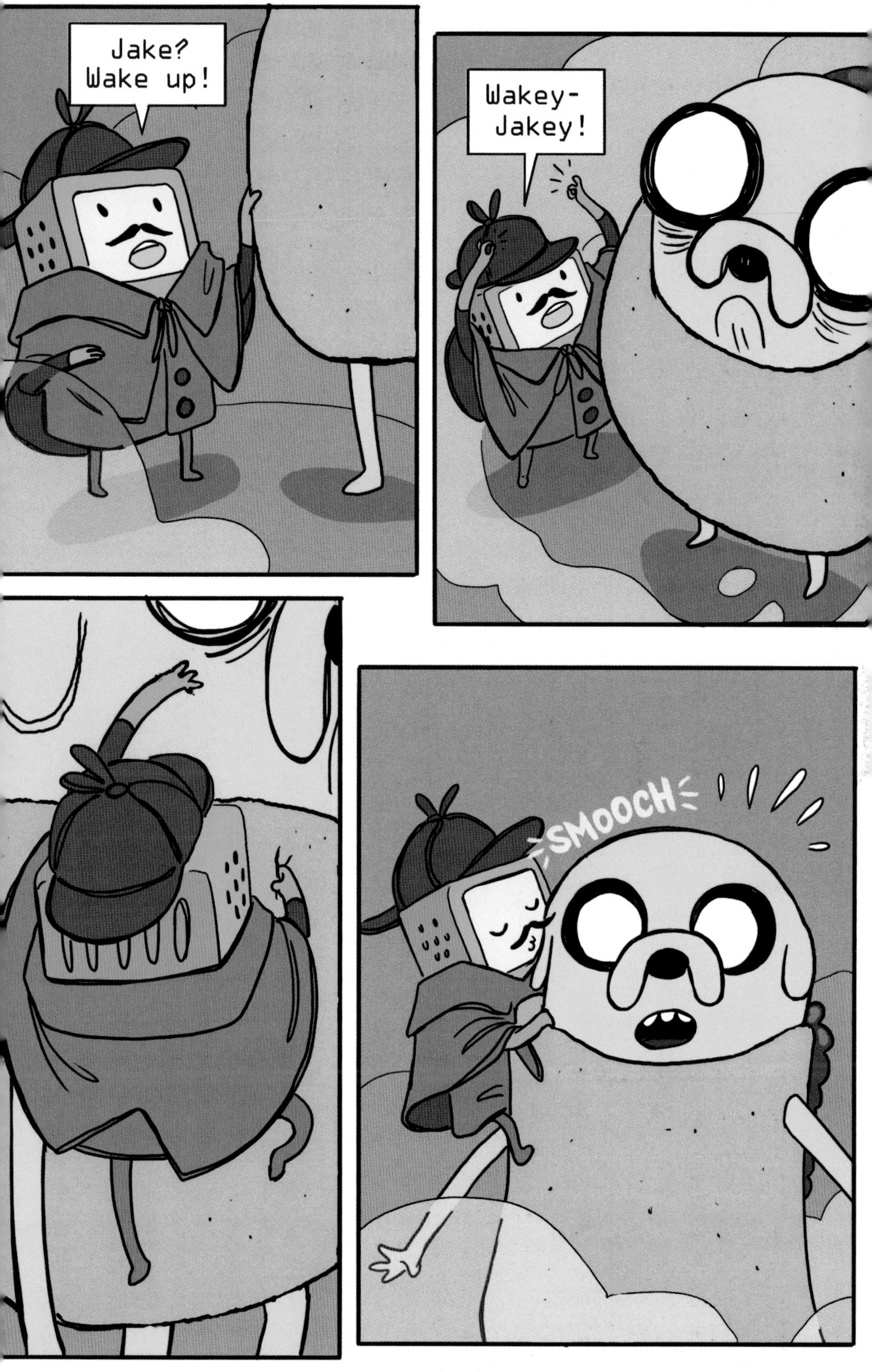
Jake?
Wake up!
Wakey-
Jakey!
SMOOCH

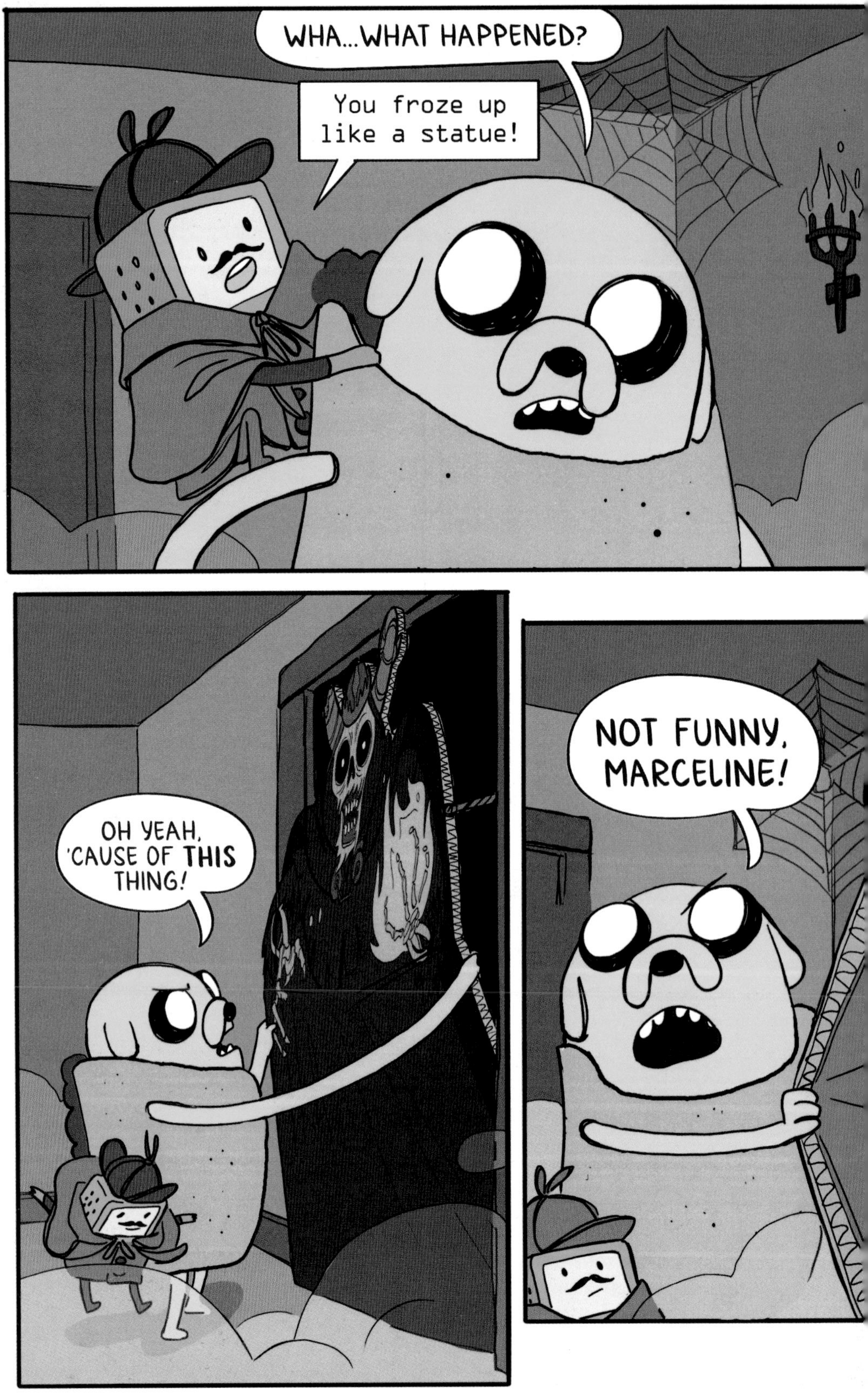
WHA...WHAT HAPPENED?
You froze up like a statue!
OH YEAH, 'CAUSE OF **THIS** THING!
NOT FUNNY, MARCELINE!

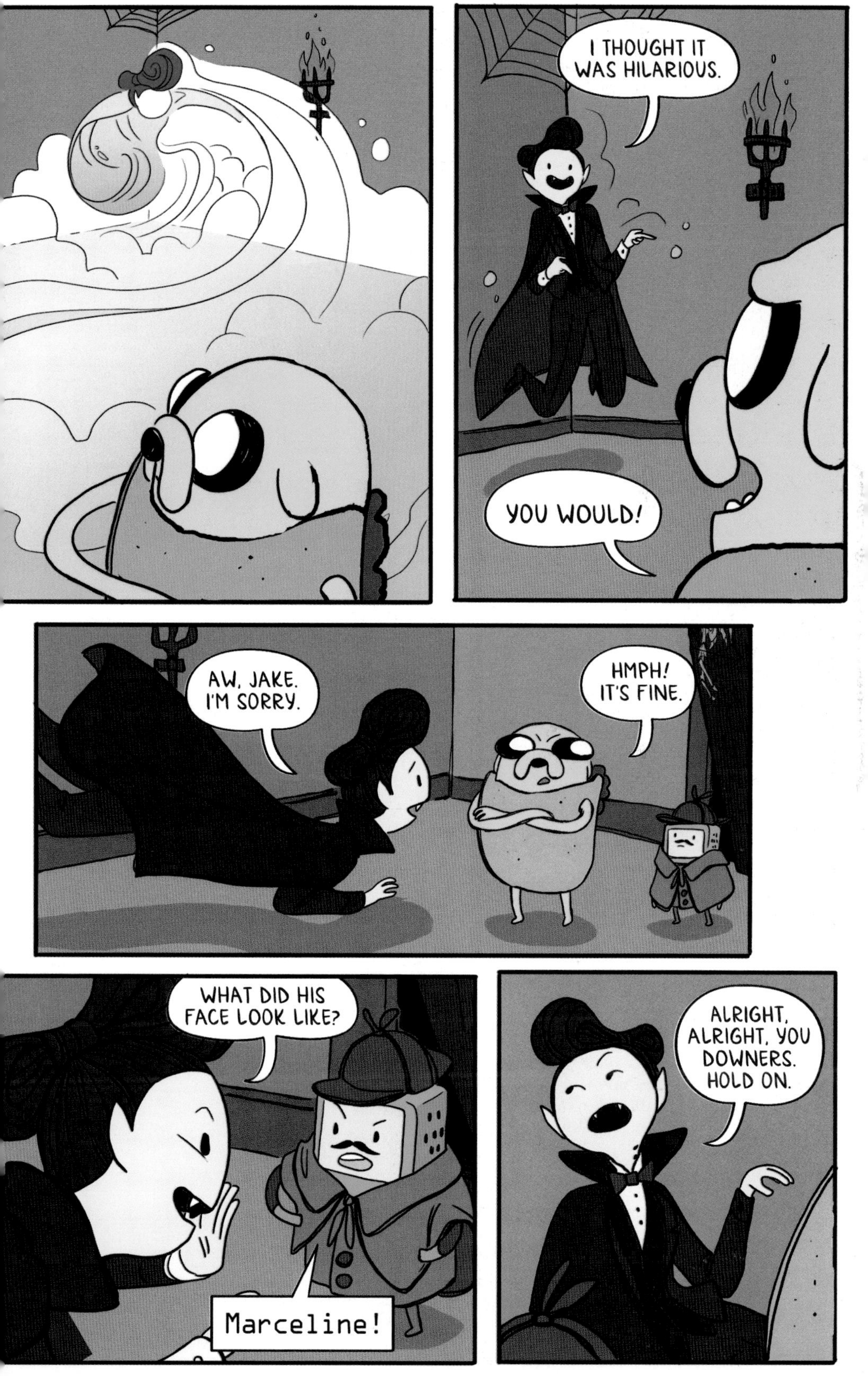
I THOUGHT IT WAS HILARIOUS.
YOU WOULD!
AW, JAKE. I'M SORRY.
HMPH! IT'S FINE.
WHAT DID HIS FACE LOOK LIKE?
Marceline!
ALRIGHT, ALRIGHT, YOU DOWNERS. HOLD ON.

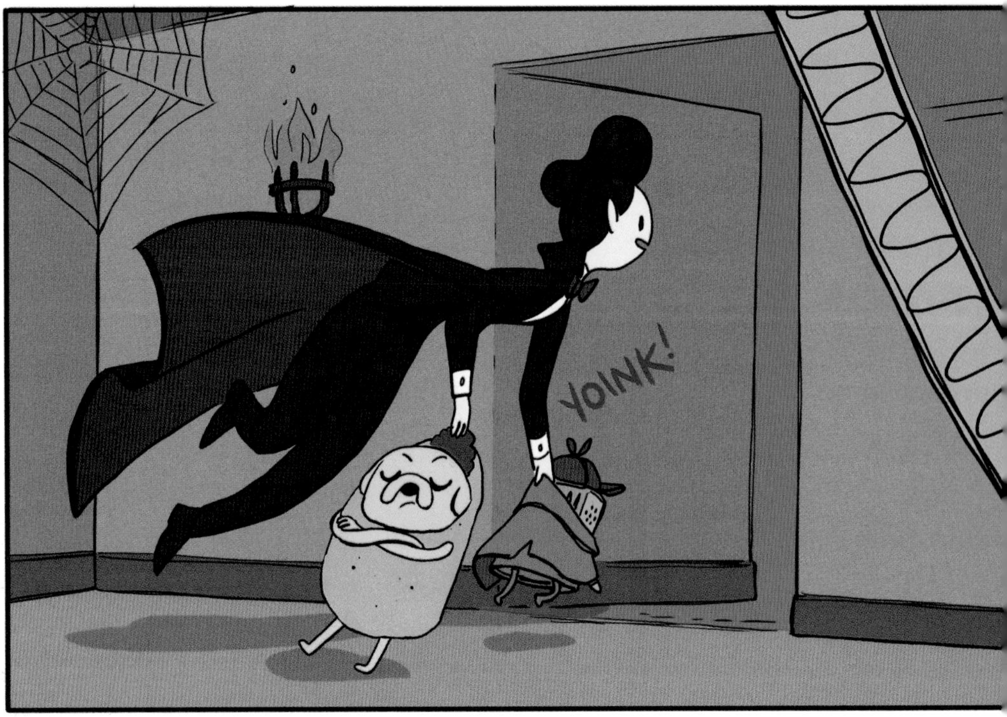
YOINK!

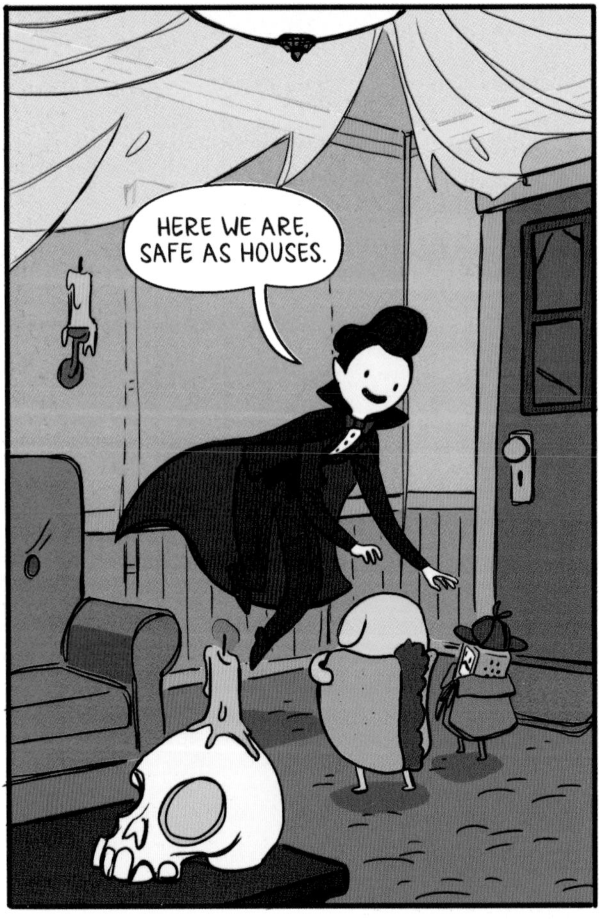
HERE WE ARE,
SAFE AS HOUSES.

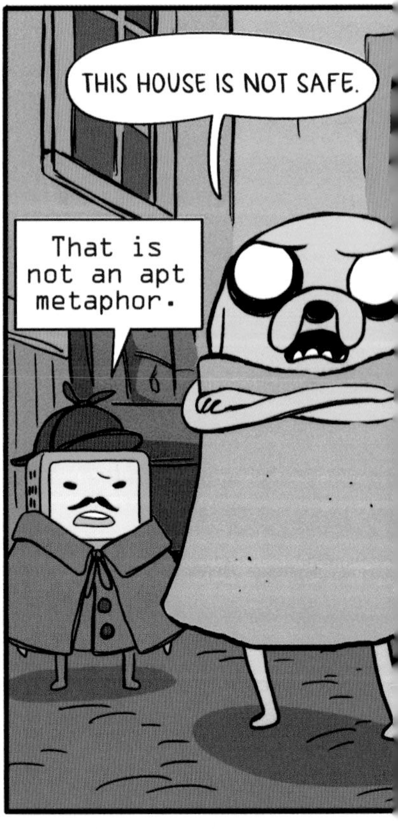
THIS HOUSE IS NOT SAFE.
That is not an apt metaphor.

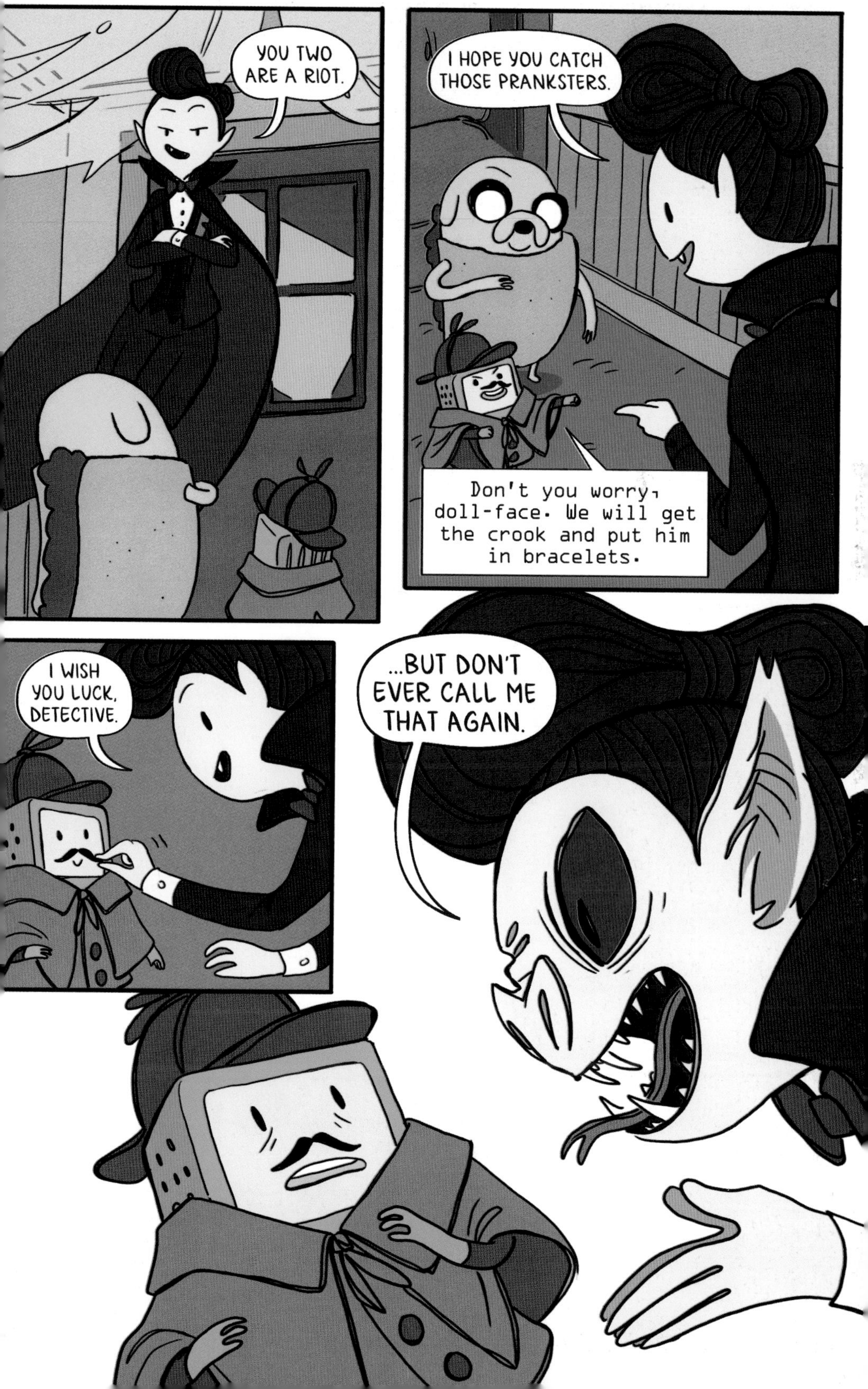
YOU TWO ARE A RIOT.
I HOPE YOU CATCH THOSE PRANKSTERS.
Don't you worry, doll-face. We will get the crook and put him in bracelets.
I WISH YOU LUCK, DETECTIVE.
...BUT DON'T EVER CALL ME THAT AGAIN.

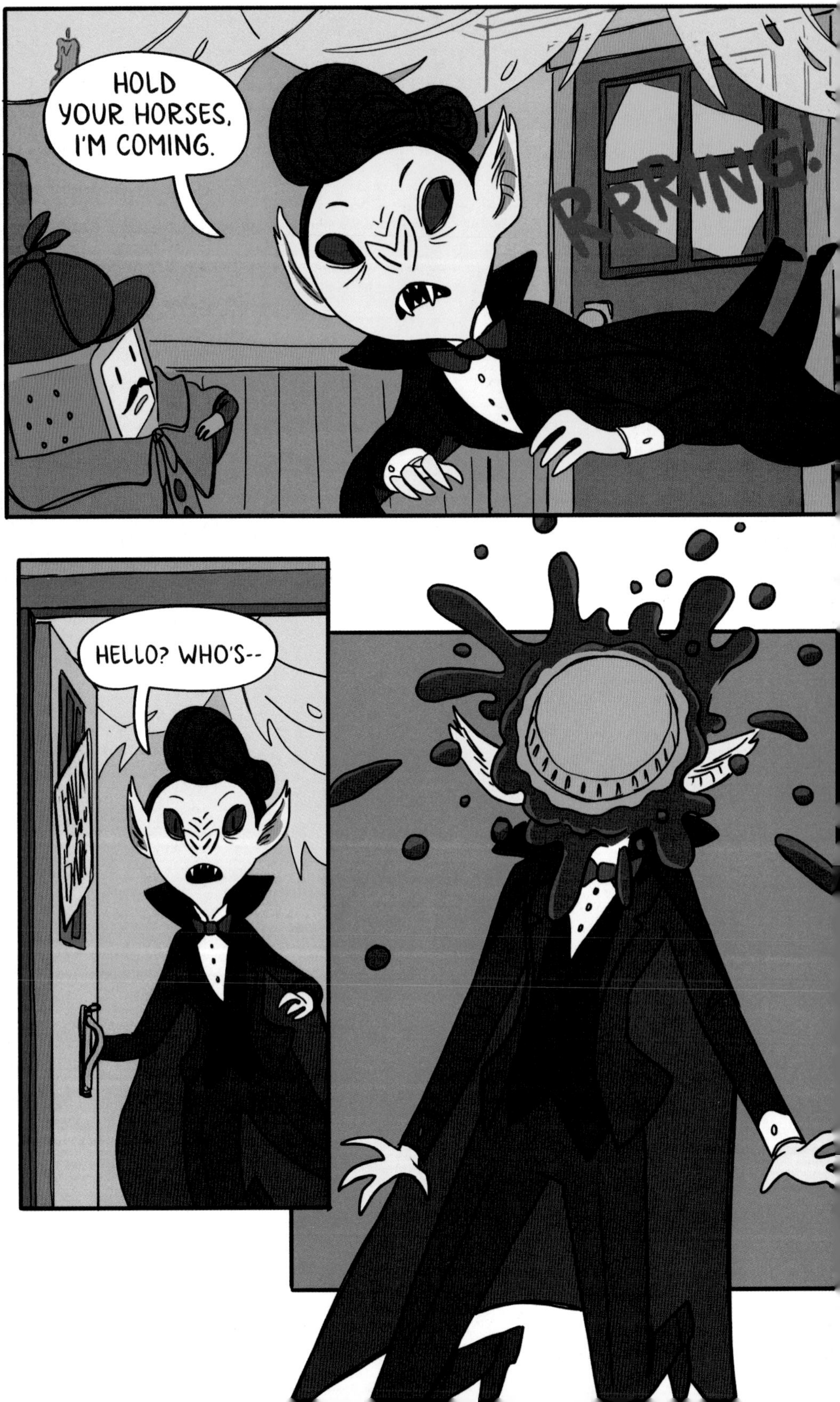
HOLD YOUR HORSES, I'M COMING.
RRRING!
HELLO? WHO'S--

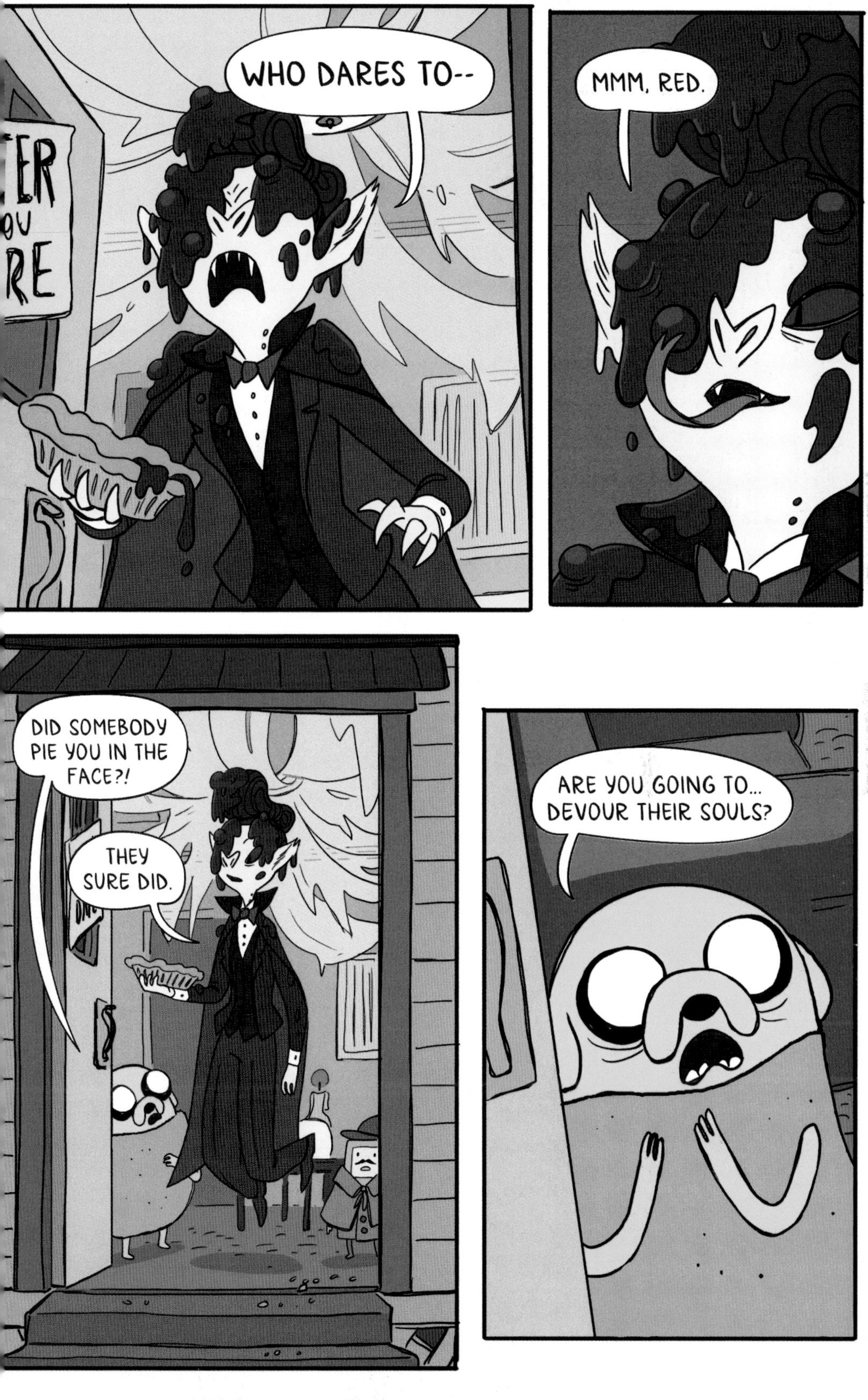
WHO DARES TO--
MMM, RED.
DID SOMEBODY PIE YOU IN THE FACE?!
THEY SURE DID.
ARE YOU GOING TO... DEVOUR THEIR SOULS?

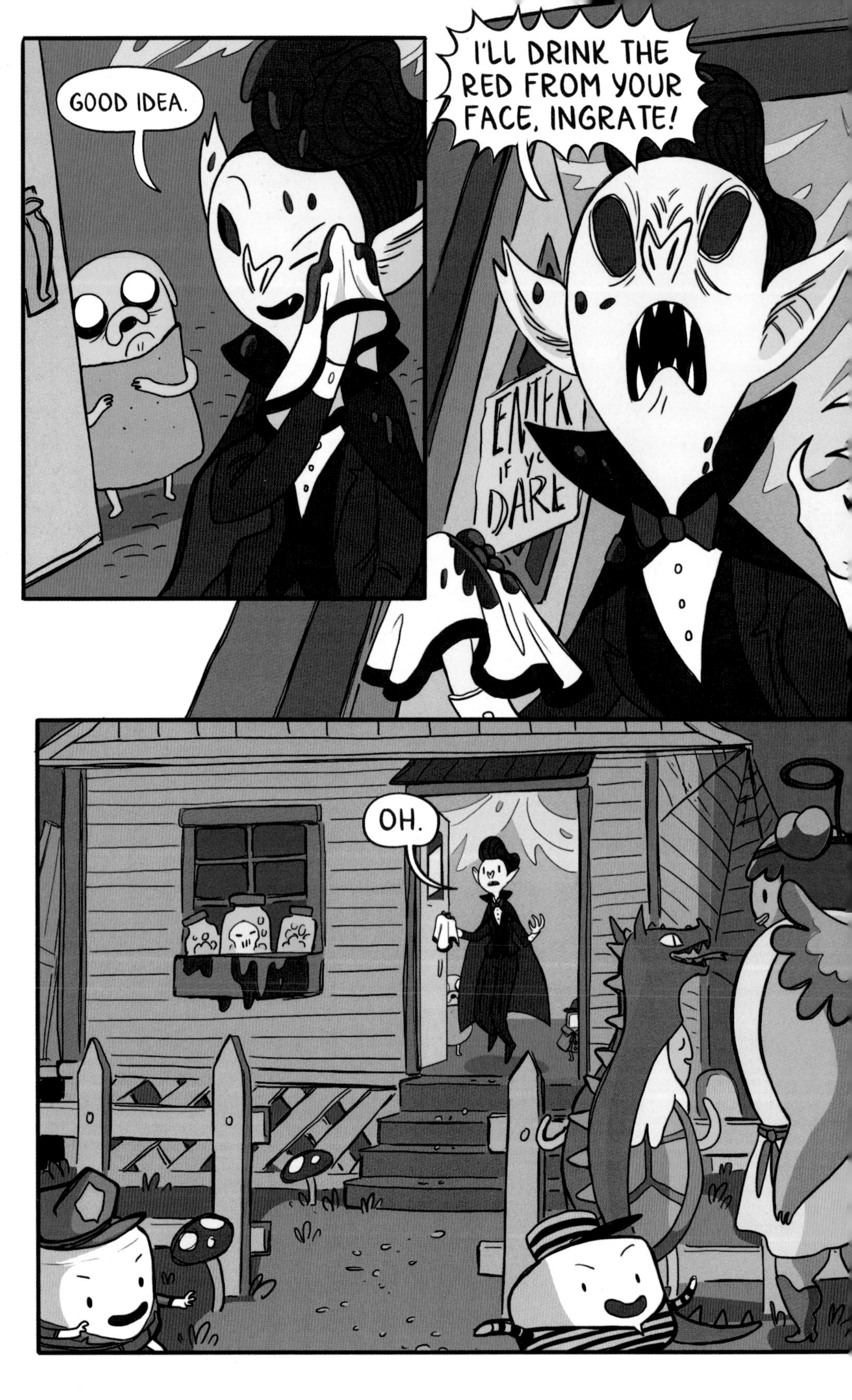

GOOD IDEA.
I'LL DRINK THE RED FROM YOUR FACE, INGRATE!
ENTER IF YO DARE
OH.

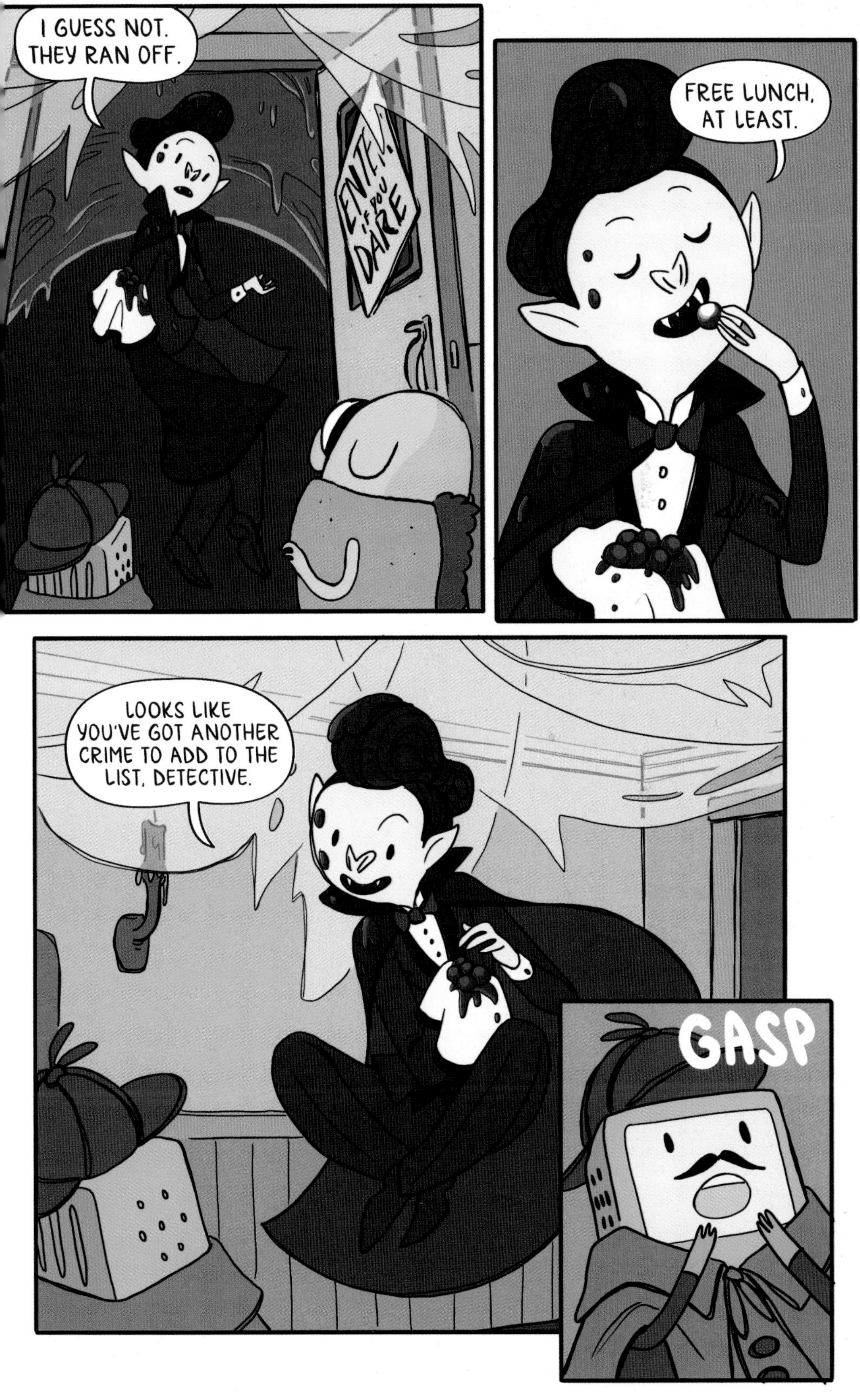
I GUESS NOT. THEY RAN OFF.
ENTER IF YOU DARE
FREE LUNCH, AT LEAST.
LOOKS LIKE YOU'VE GOT ANOTHER CRIME TO ADD TO THE LIST, DETECTIVE.
GASP

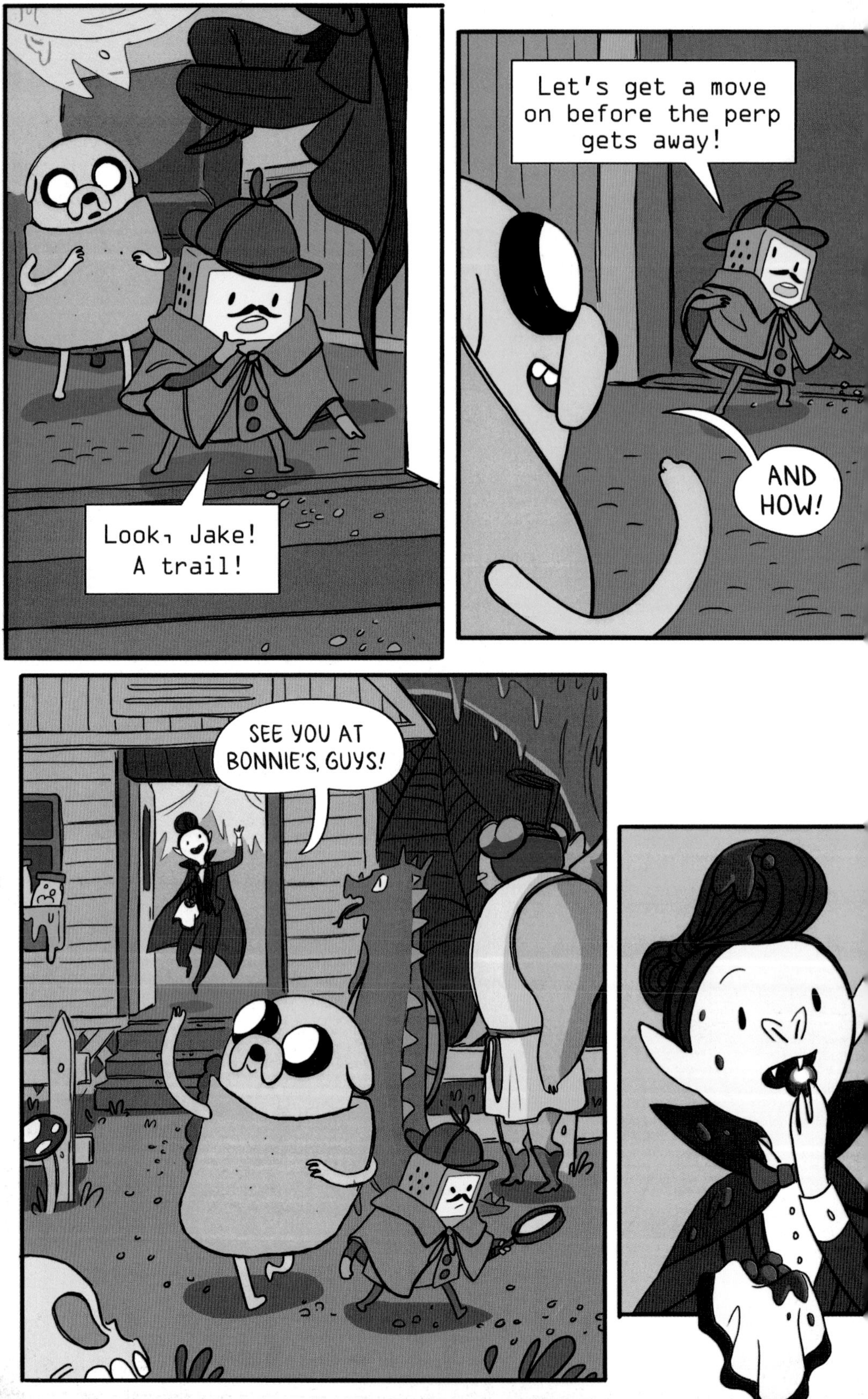
Look, Jake! A trail!
Let's get a move on before the perp gets away!
AND HOW!
SEE YOU AT BONNIE'S, GUYS!

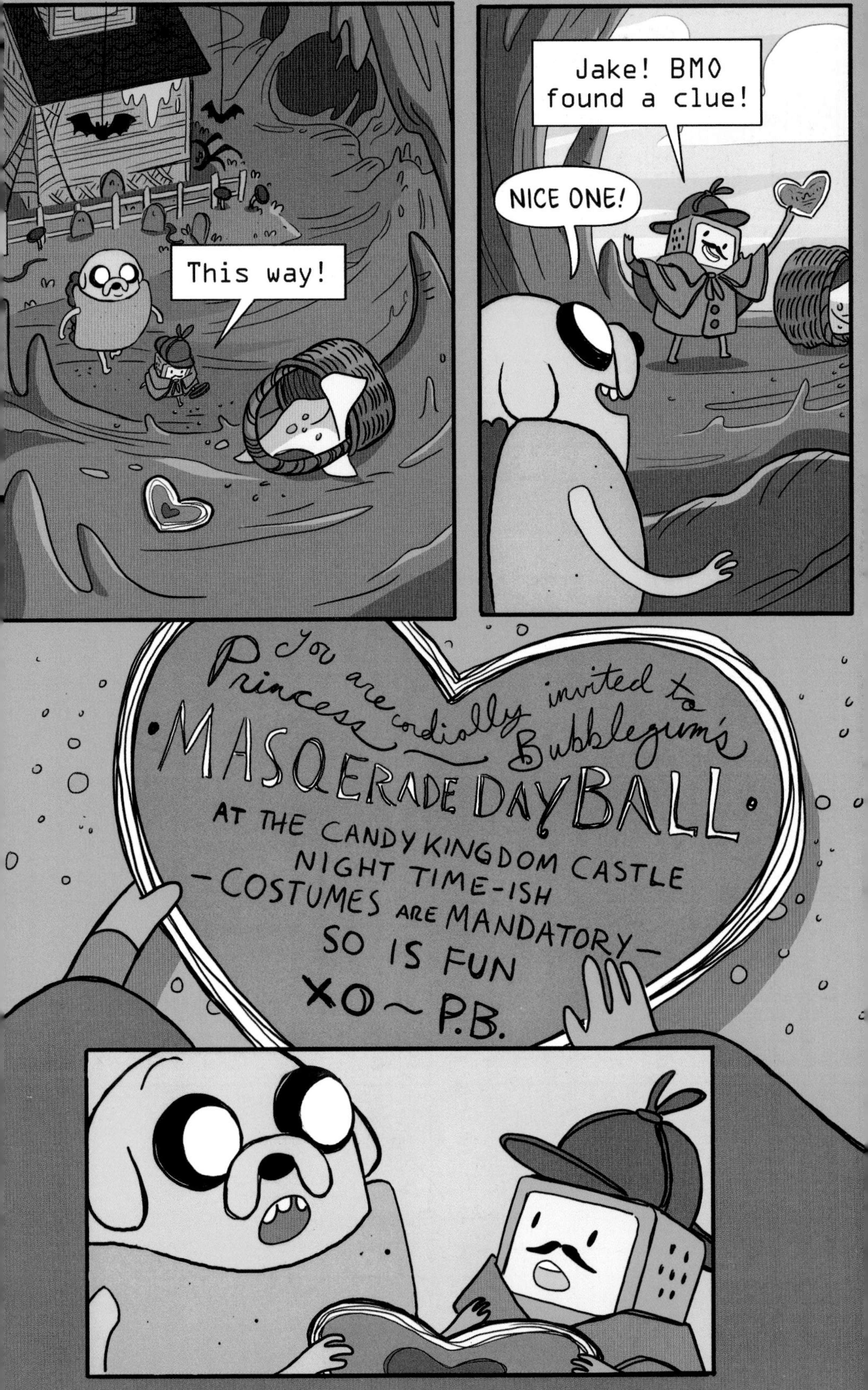
This way!
Jake! BMO found a clue!
NICE ONE!
You are cordially invited to
Princess Bubblegum's
MASQERADE DAY BALL
AT THE CANDY KINGDOM CASTLE
NIGHT TIME-ISH
-COSTUMES ARE MANDATORY-
SO IS FUN
XO ~ P.B.

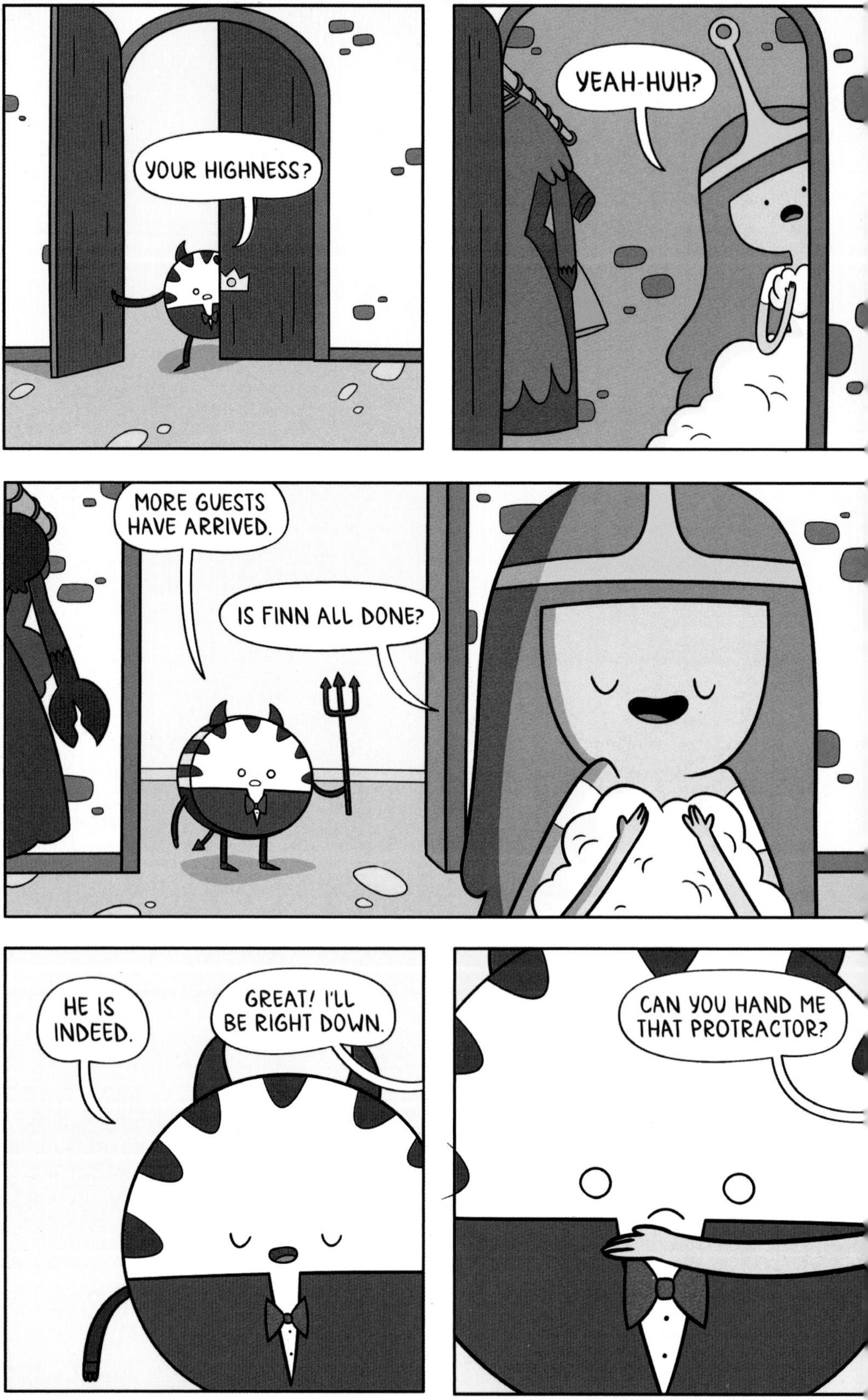
YOUR HIGHNESS?
YEAH-HUH?
MORE GUESTS HAVE ARRIVED.
IS FINN ALL DONE?
HE IS INDEED.
GREAT! I'LL BE RIGHT DOWN.
CAN YOU HAND ME THAT PROTRACTOR?

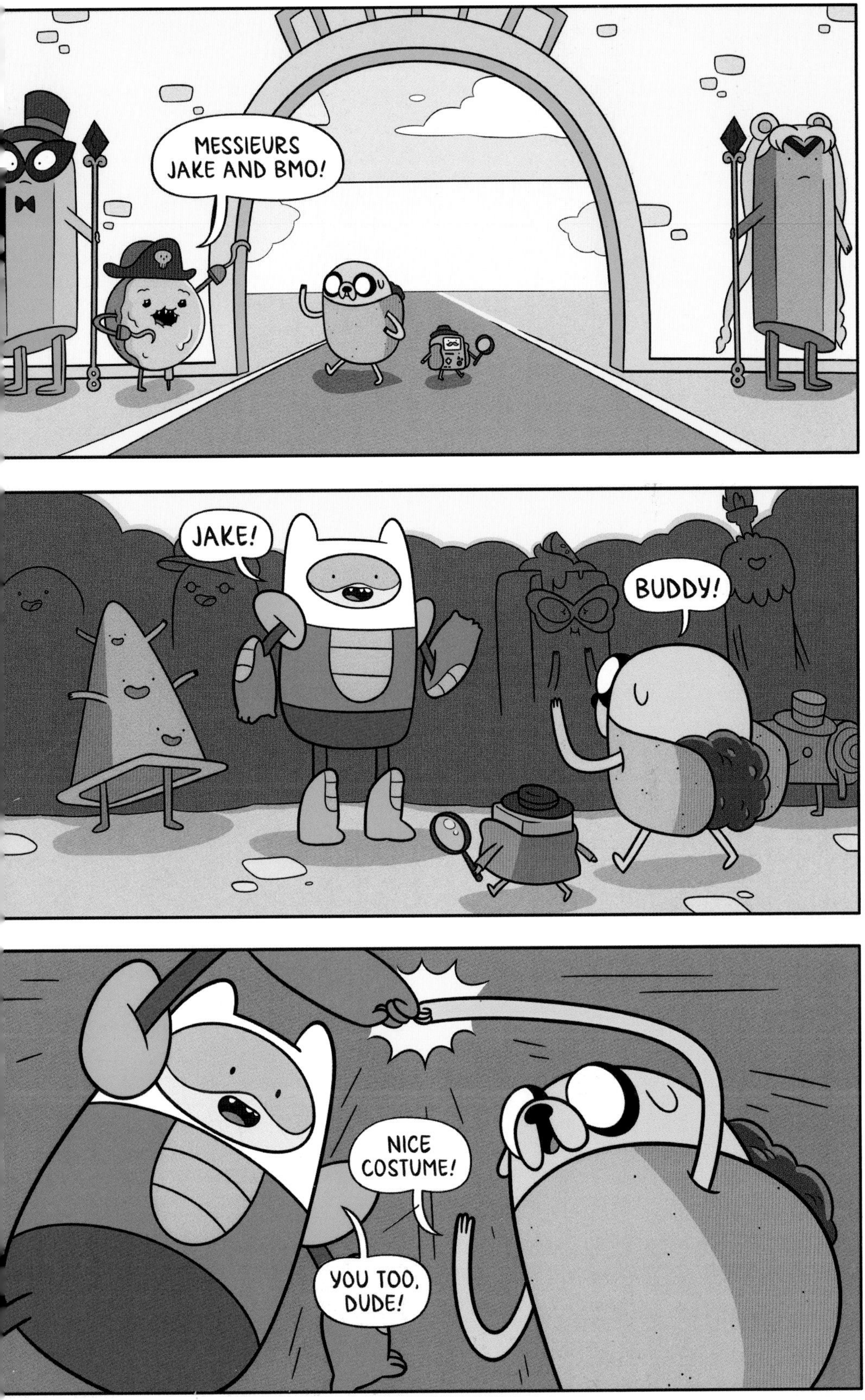

MESSIEURS JAKE AND BMO!
JAKE!
BUDDY!
NICE COSTUME!
YOU TOO, DUDE!

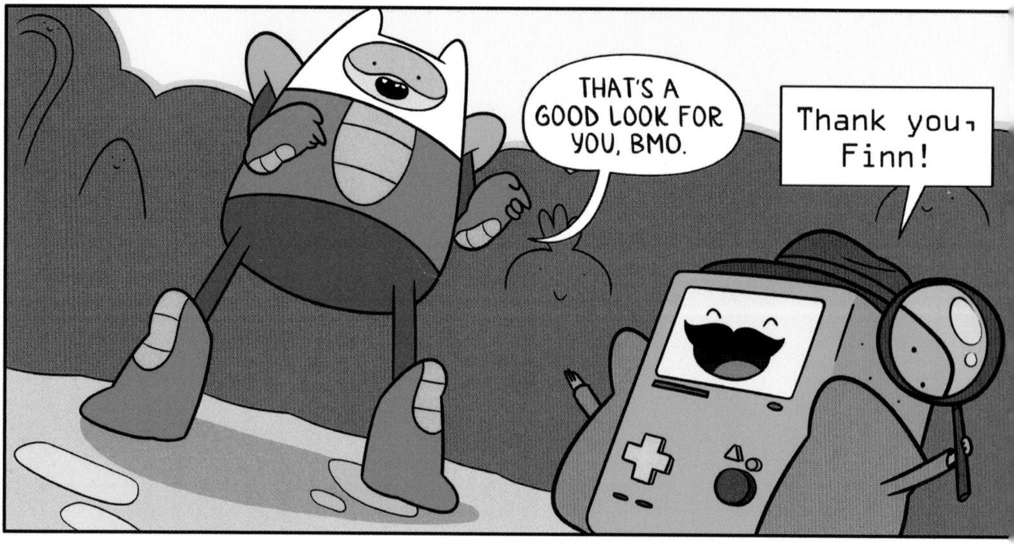
THAT'S A GOOD LOOK FOR YOU, BMO.
Thank you, Finn!

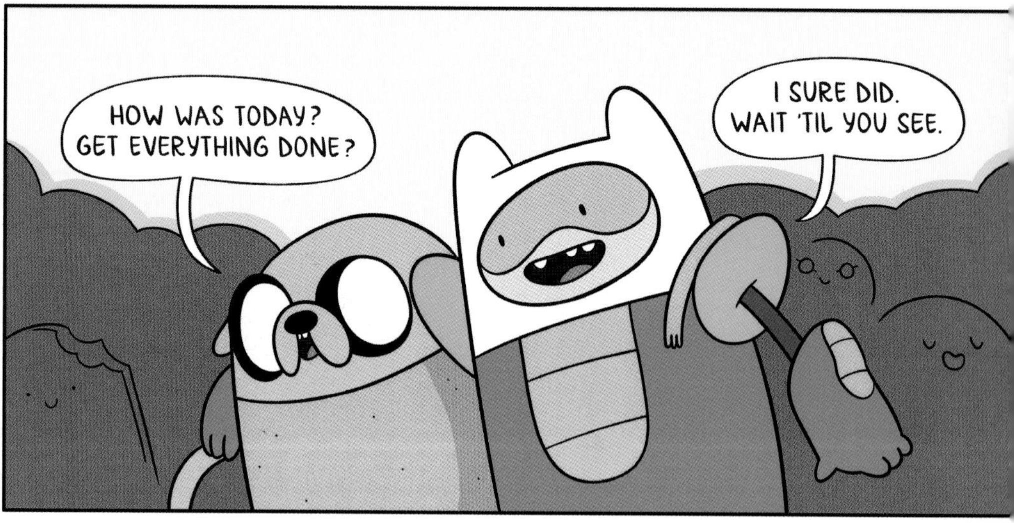
HOW WAS TODAY? GET EVERYTHING DONE?
I SURE DID. WAIT 'TIL YOU SEE.

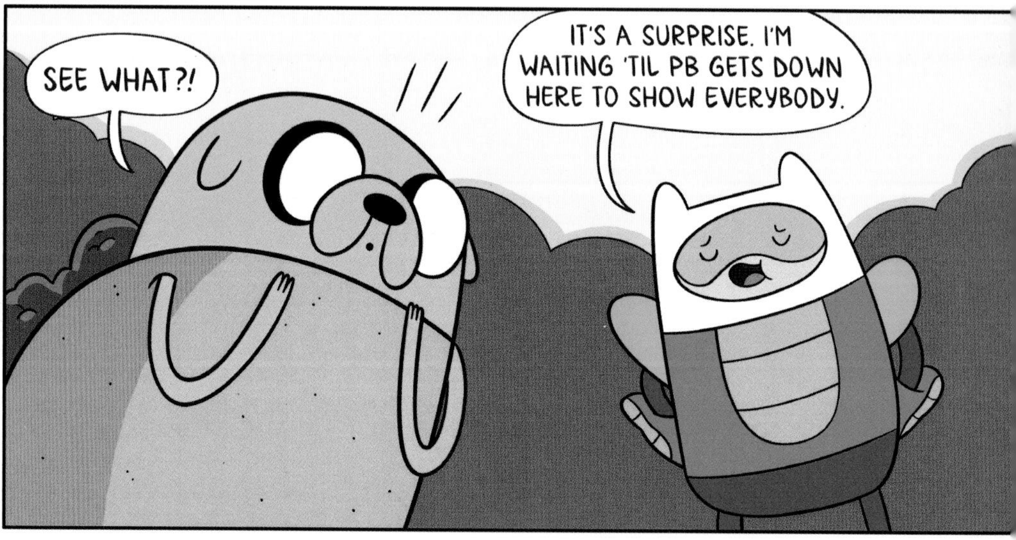
SEE WHAT?!
IT'S A SURPRISE. I'M WAITING 'TIL PB GETS DOWN HERE TO SHOW EVERYBODY.

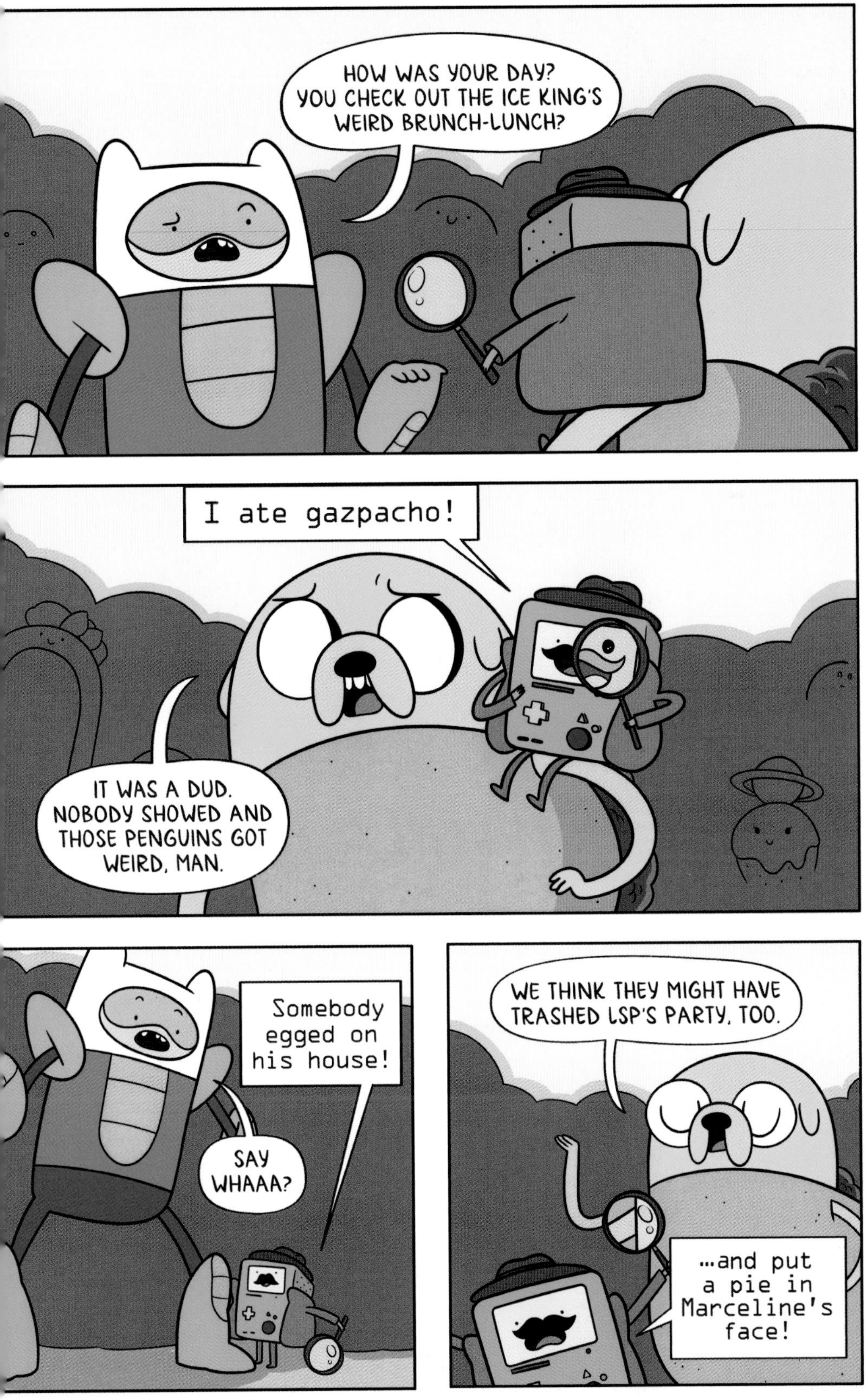
HOW WAS YOUR DAY? YOU CHECK OUT THE ICE KING'S WEIRD BRUNCH-LUNCH?
I ate gazpacho!
IT WAS A DUD. NOBODY SHOWED AND THOSE PENGUINS GOT WEIRD, MAN.
Somebody egged on his house!
SAY WHAAA?
WE THINK THEY MIGHT HAVE TRASHED LSP'S PARTY, TOO.
...and put a pie in Marceline's face!

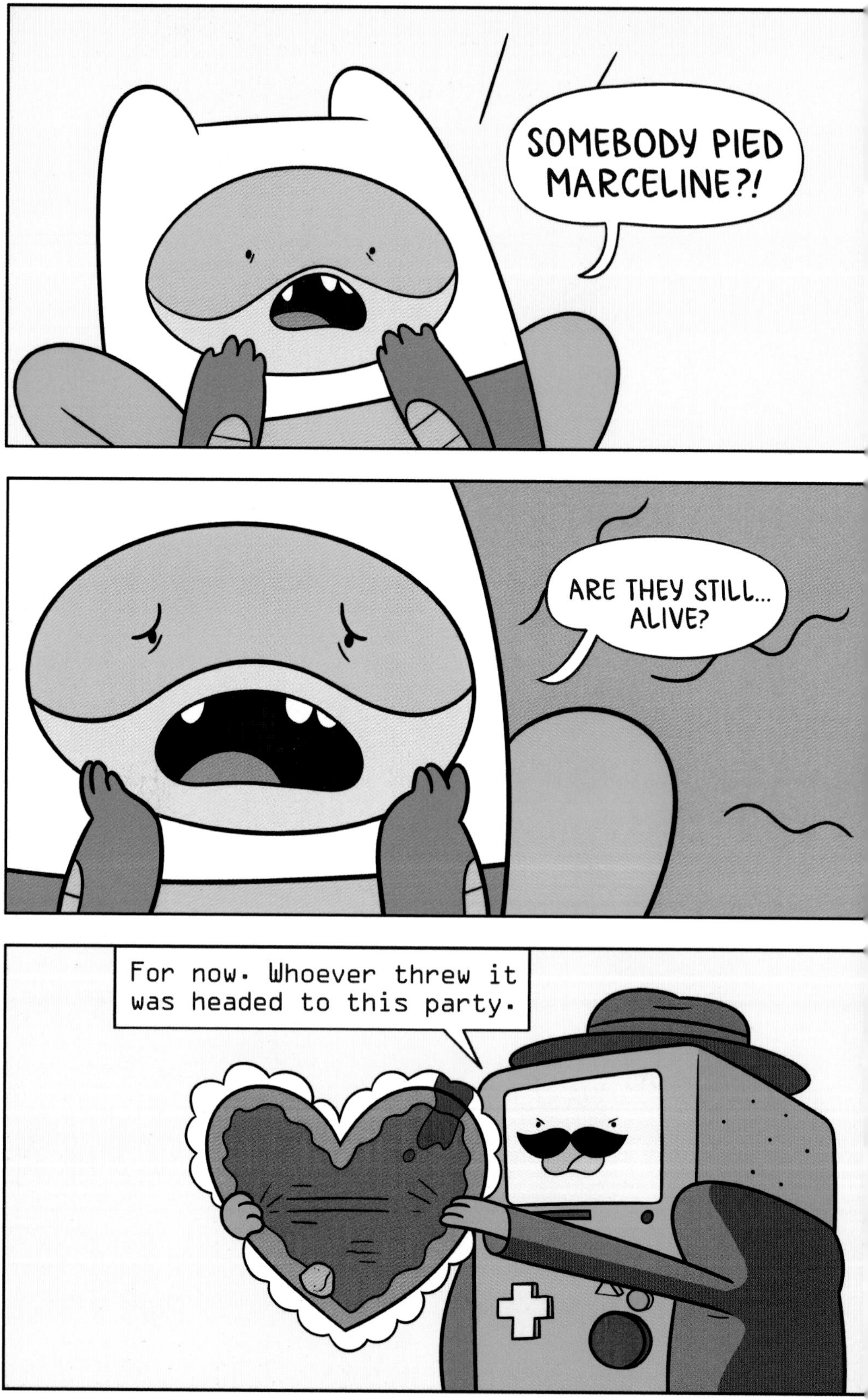
SOMEBODY PIED MARCELINE?!
ARE THEY STILL... ALIVE?
For now. Whoever threw it was headed to this party.

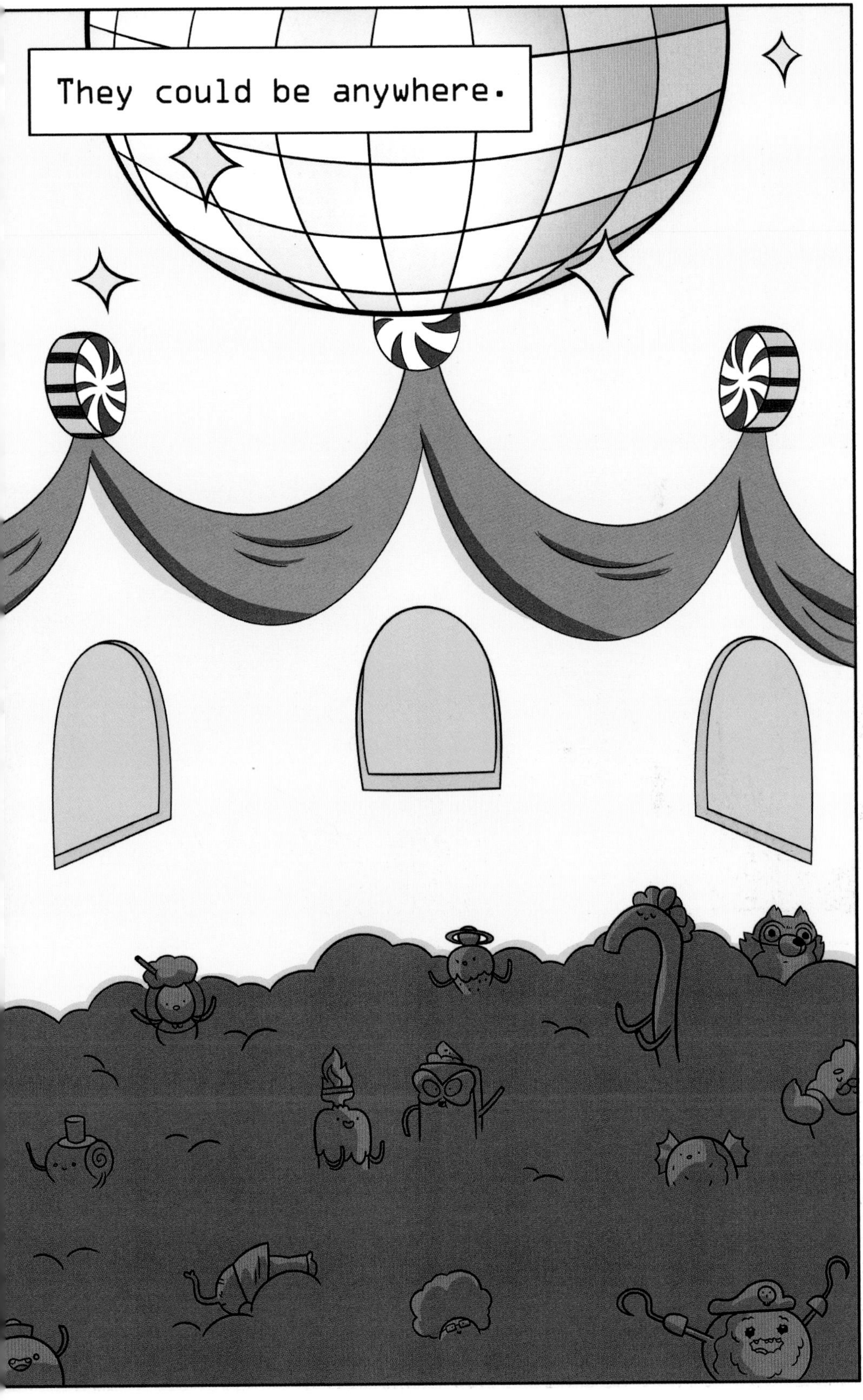
They could be anywhere.

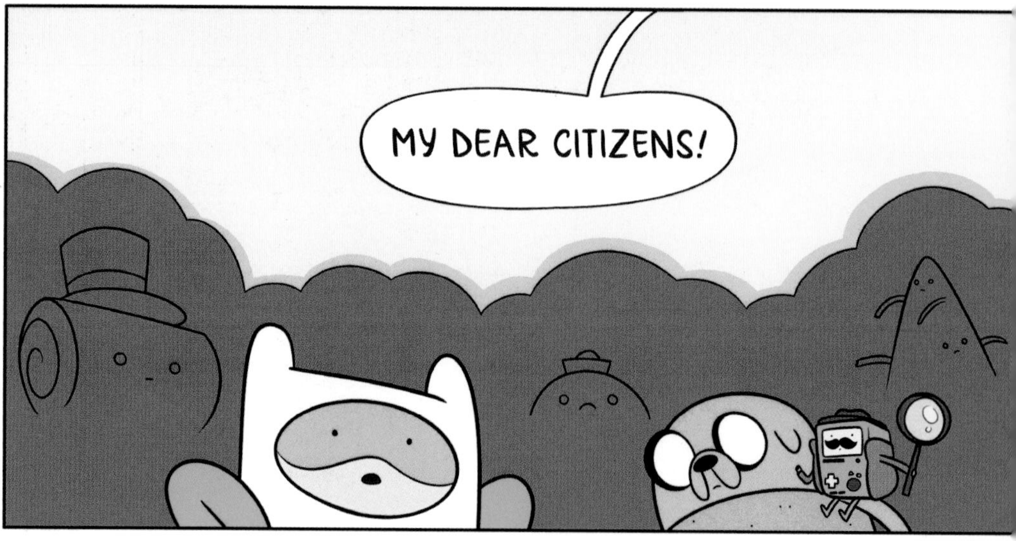
MY DEAR CITIZENS!

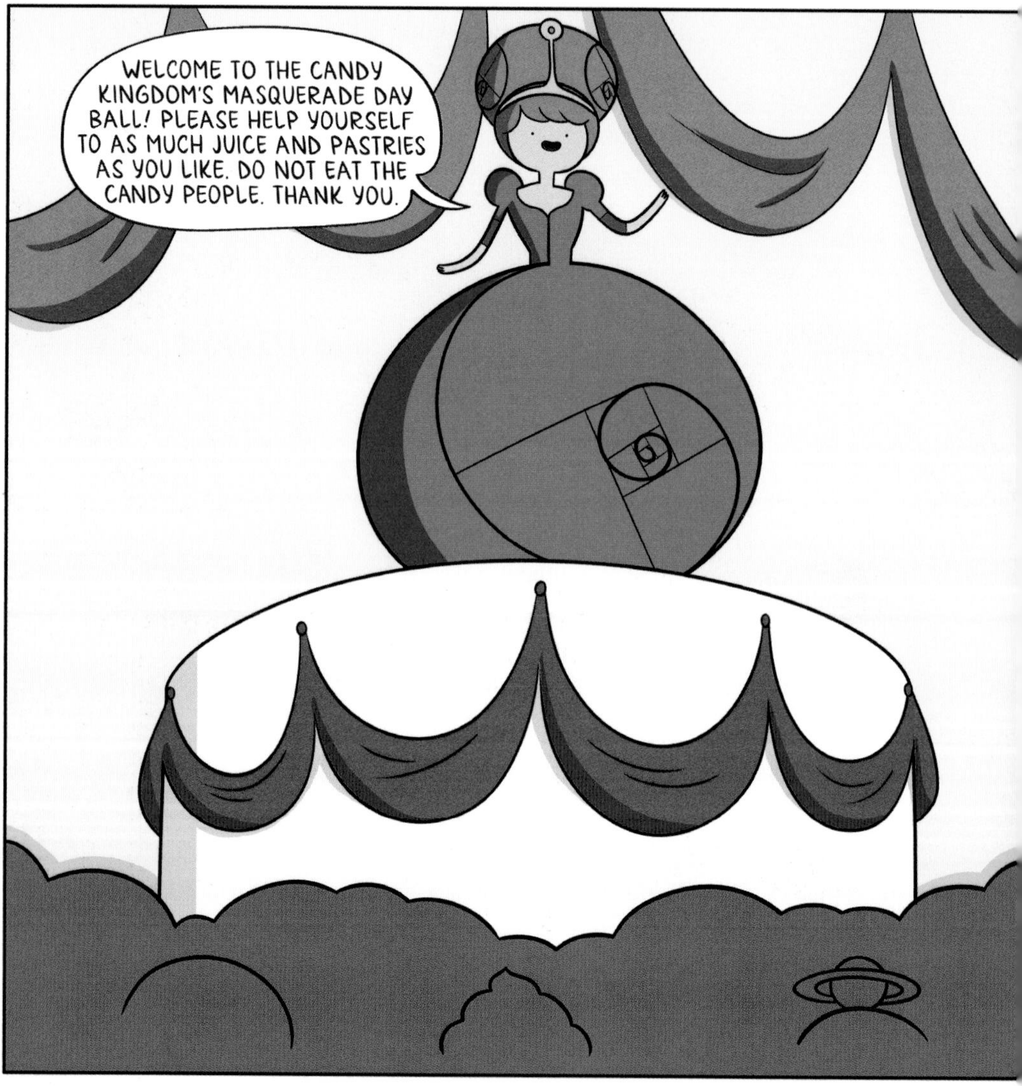
WELCOME TO THE CANDY KINGDOM'S MASQUERADE DAY BALL! PLEASE HELP YOURSELF TO AS MUCH JUICE AND PASTRIES AS YOU LIKE. DO NOT EAT THE CANDY PEOPLE. THANK YOU.

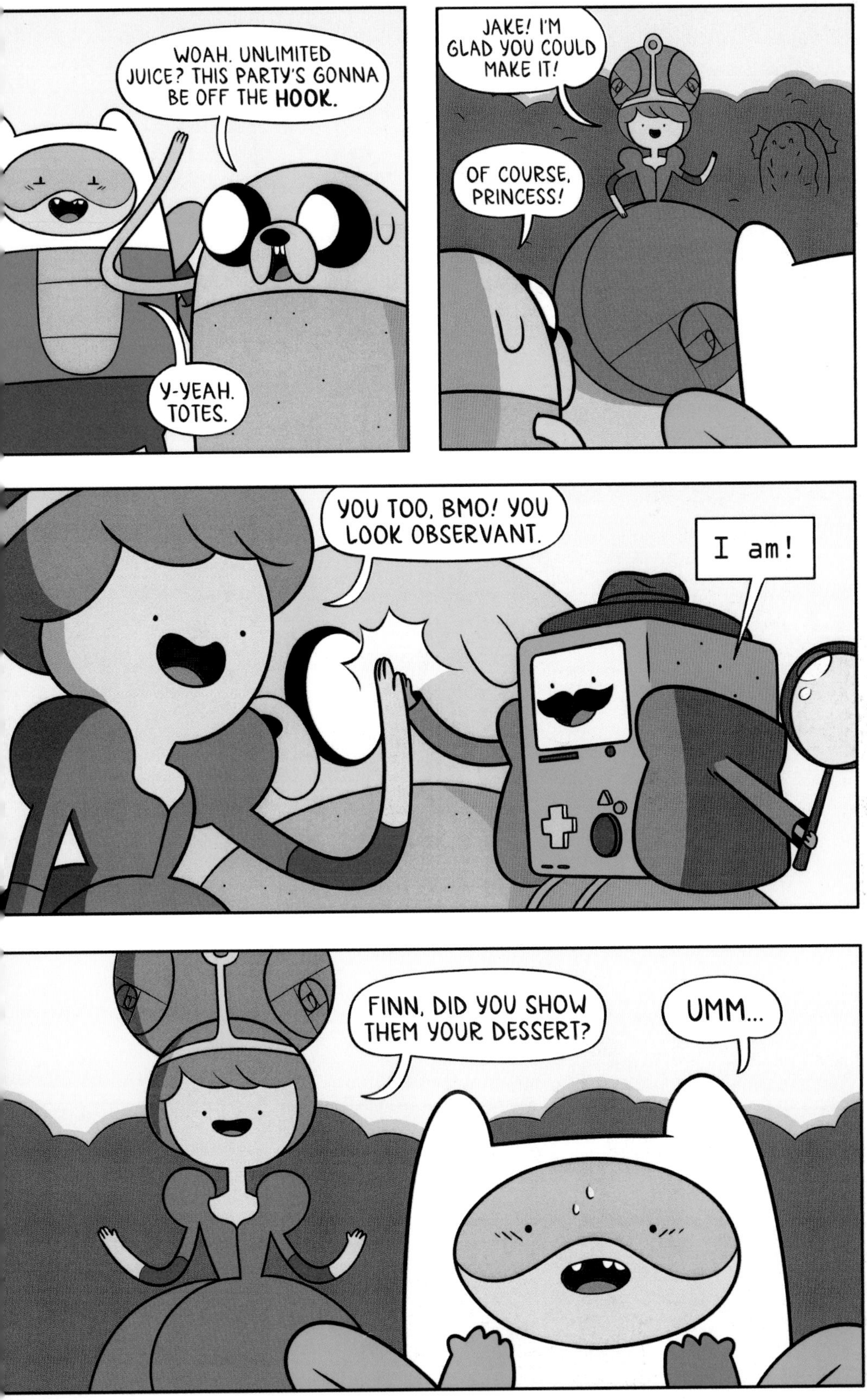
WOAH. UNLIMITED JUICE? THIS PARTY'S GONNA BE OFF THE **HOOK.**
Y-YEAH. TOTES.
JAKE! I'M GLAD YOU COULD MAKE IT!
OF COURSE, PRINCESS!
YOU TOO, BMO! YOU LOOK OBSERVANT.
I am!
FINN, DID YOU SHOW THEM YOUR DESSERT?
UMM...

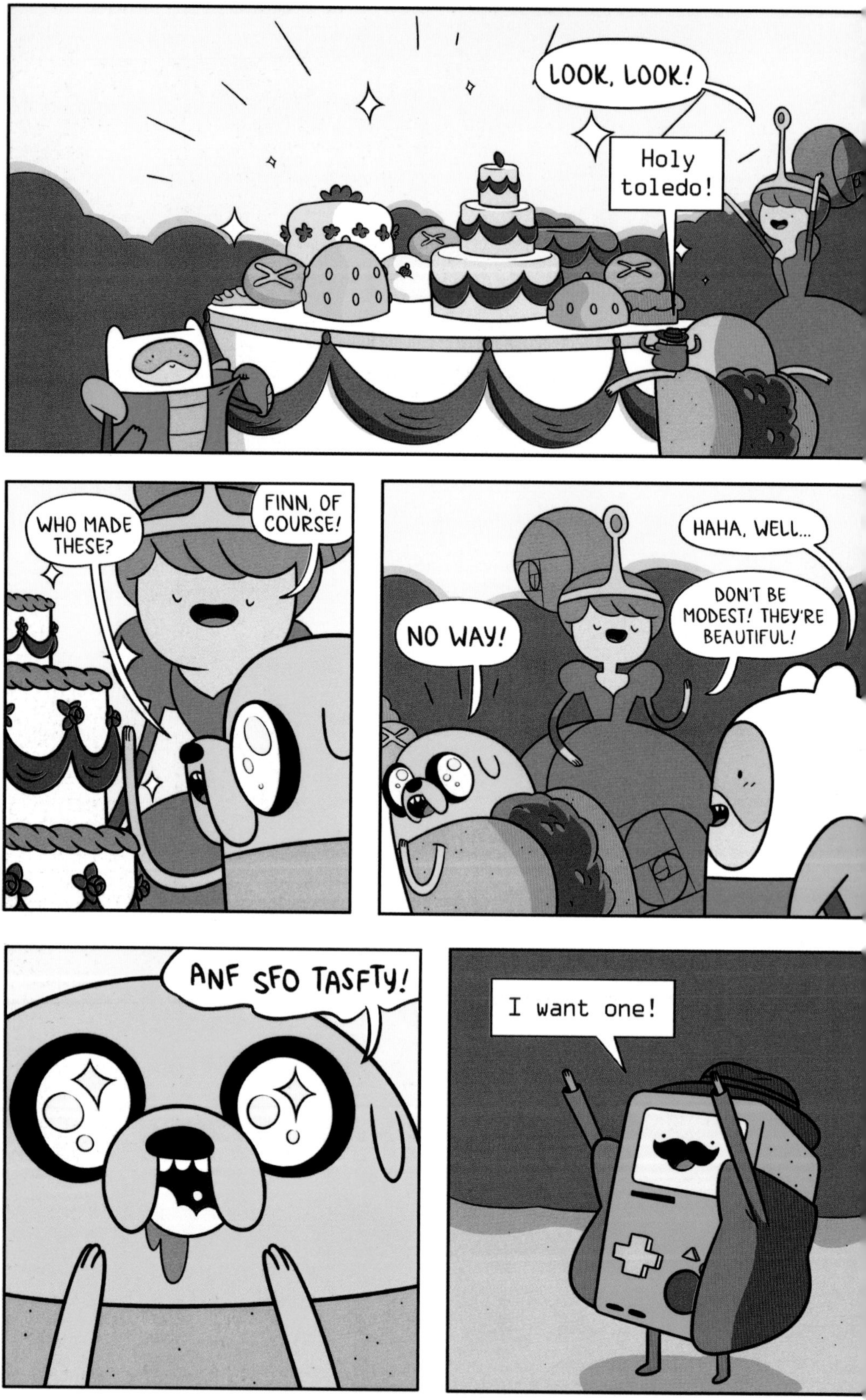
LOOK, LOOK!
Holy toledo!
WHO MADE THESE?
FINN, OF COURSE!
HAHA, WELL...
NO WAY!
DON'T BE MODEST! THEY'RE BEAUTIFUL!
ANF SFO TASFTY!
I want one!

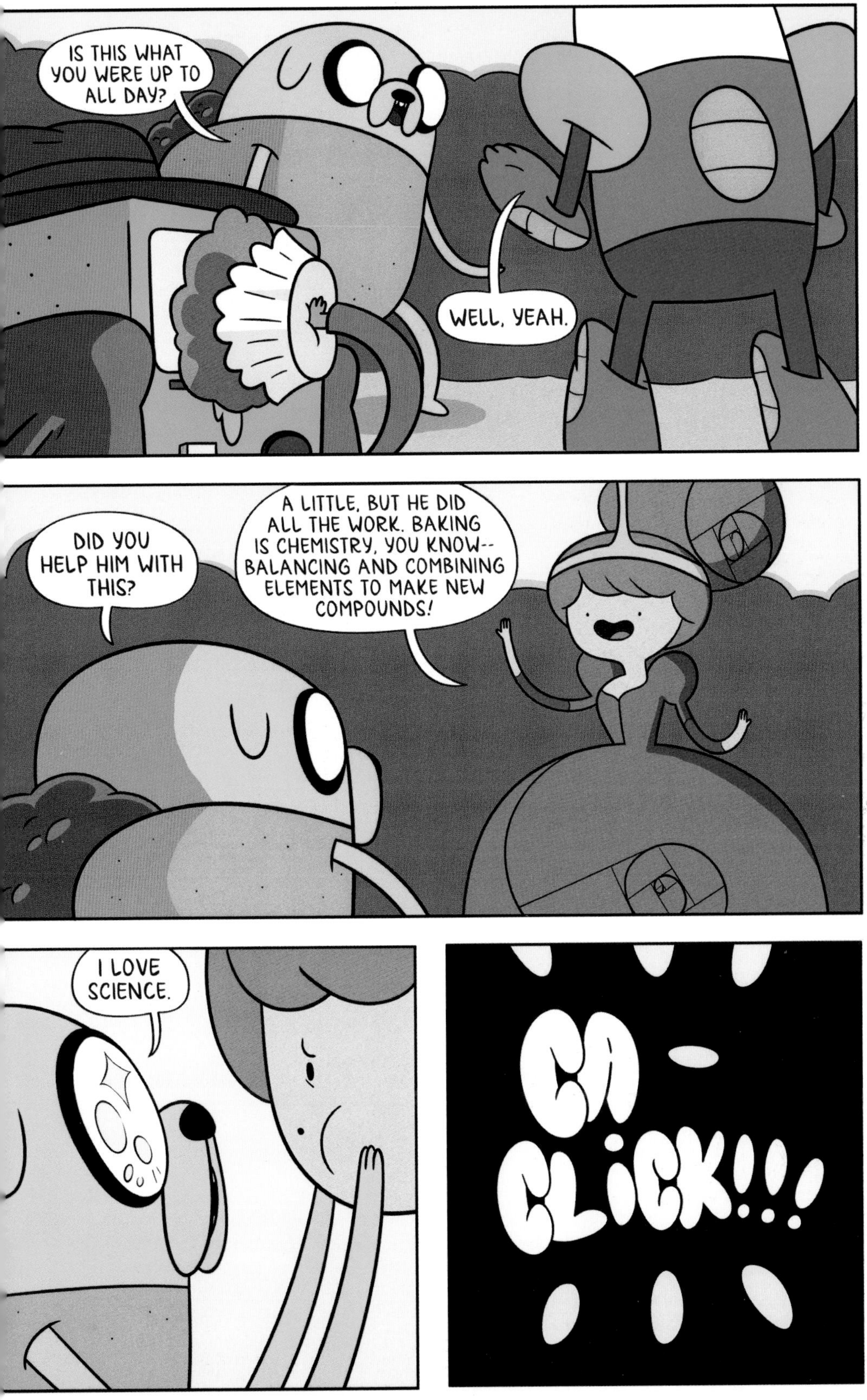
IS THIS WHAT YOU WERE UP TO ALL DAY?
WELL, YEAH.
DID YOU HELP HIM WITH THIS?
A LITTLE, BUT HE DID ALL THE WORK. BAKING IS CHEMISTRY, YOU KNOW-- BALANCING AND COMBINING ELEMENTS TO MAKE NEW COMPOUNDS!
I LOVE SCIENCE.
CA-CLICK!!!

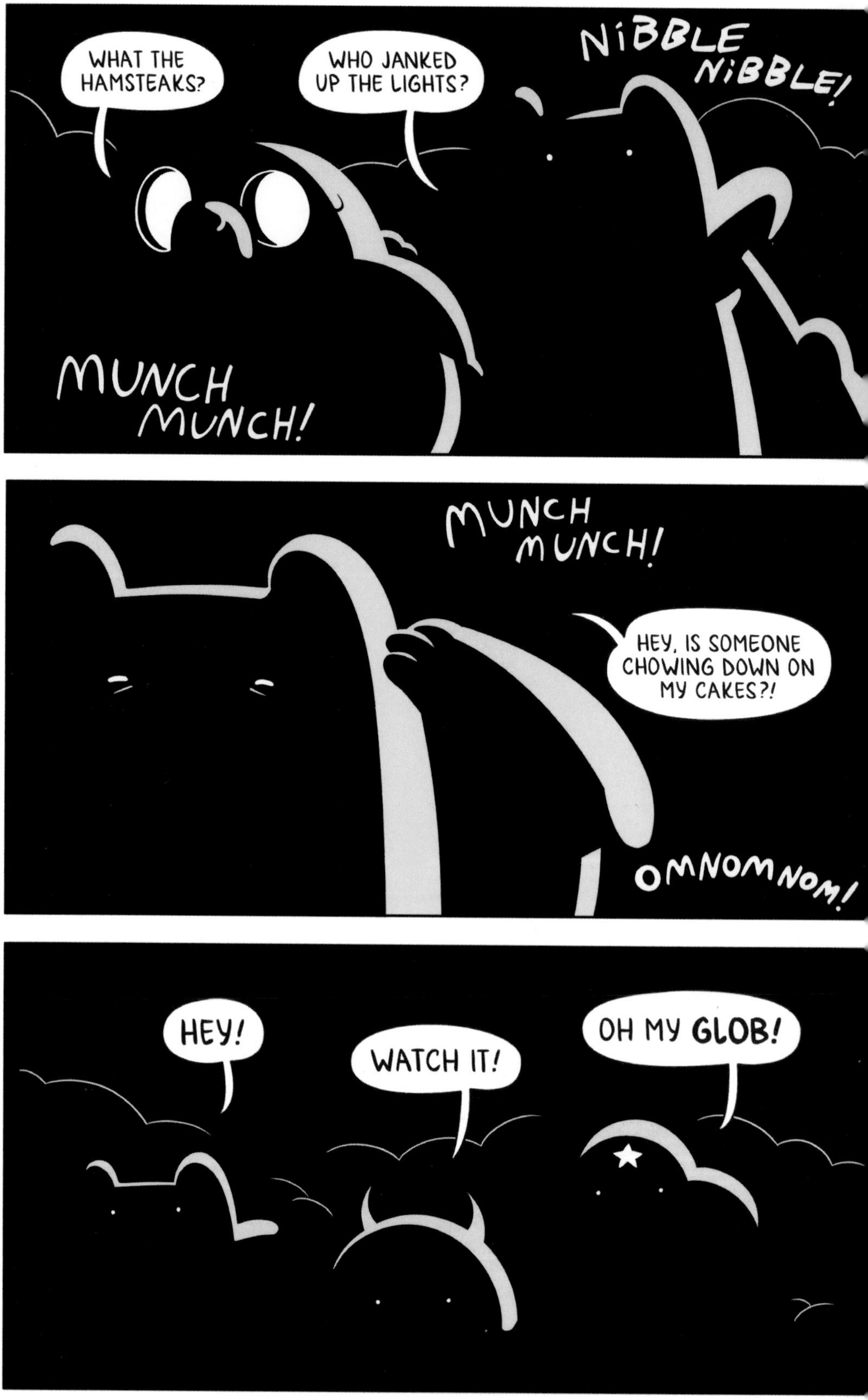
WHAT THE HAMSTEAKS?
WHO JANKED UP THE LIGHTS?
NIBBLE NIBBLE!
MUNCH MUNCH!
MUNCH MUNCH!
HEY, IS SOMEONE CHOWING DOWN ON MY CAKES?!
OMNOMNOM!
HEY!
WATCH IT!
OH MY **GLOB**!

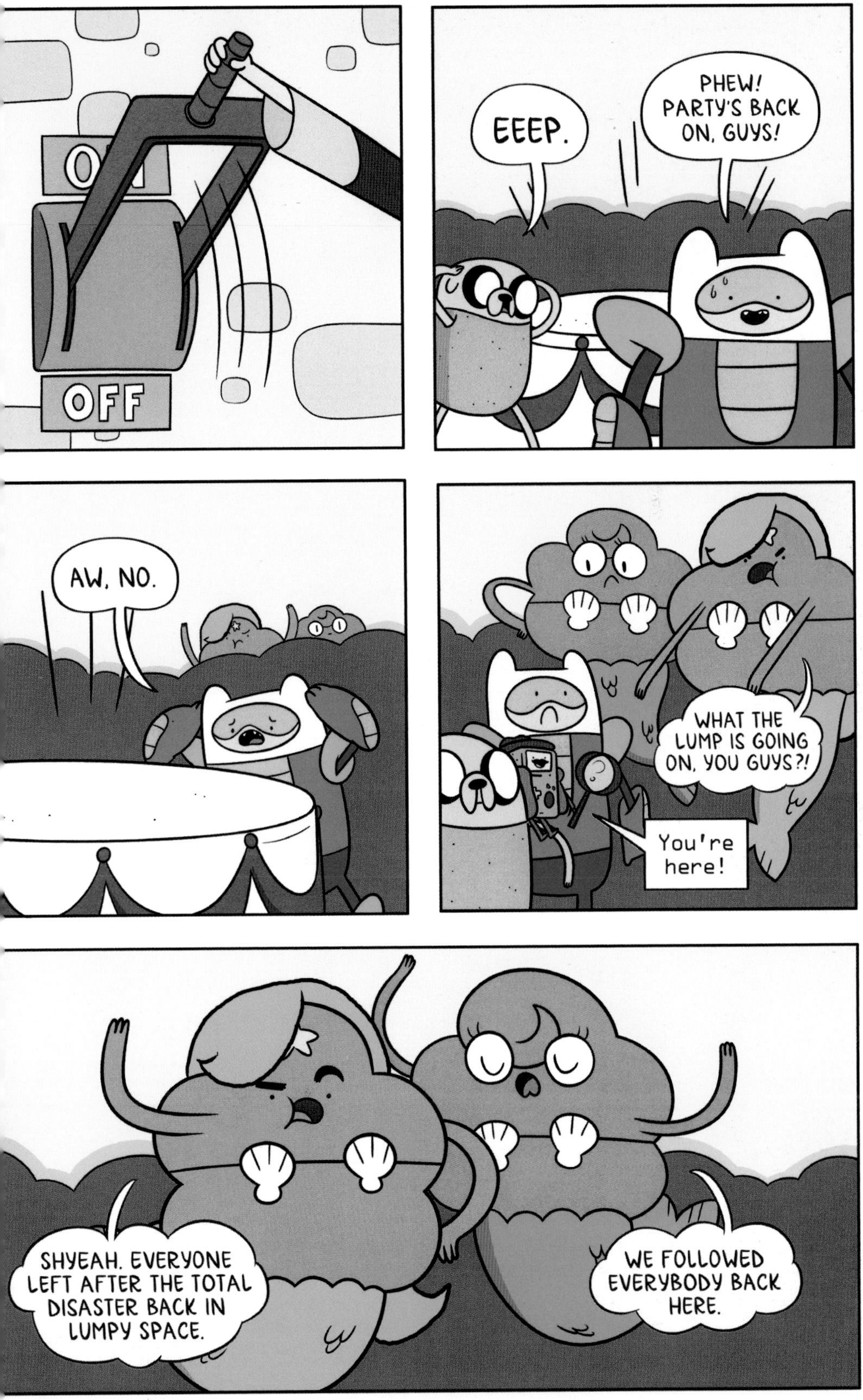
OFF
EEEP.
PHEW! PARTY'S BACK ON, GUYS!
AW, NO.
WHAT THE LUMP IS GOING ON, YOU GUYS?!
You're here!
SHYEAH. EVERYONE LEFT AFTER THE TOTAL DISASTER BACK IN LUMPY SPACE.
WE FOLLOWED EVERYBODY BACK HERE.

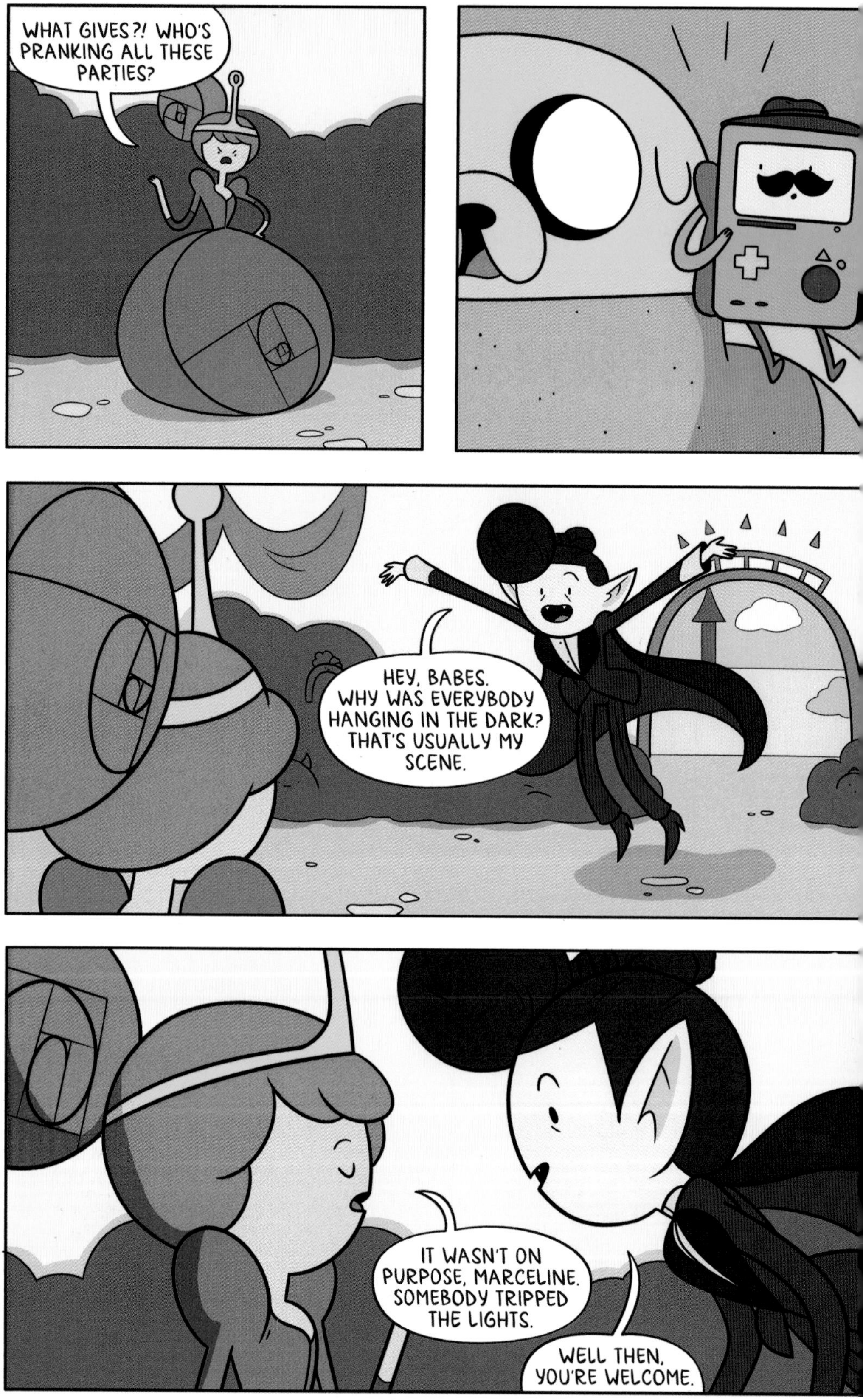
WHAT GIVES?! WHO'S PRANKING ALL THESE PARTIES?
HEY, BABES. WHY WAS EVERYBODY HANGING IN THE DARK? THAT'S USUALLY MY SCENE.
IT WASN'T ON PURPOSE, MARCELINE. SOMEBODY TRIPPED THE LIGHTS.
WELL THEN, YOU'RE WELCOME.

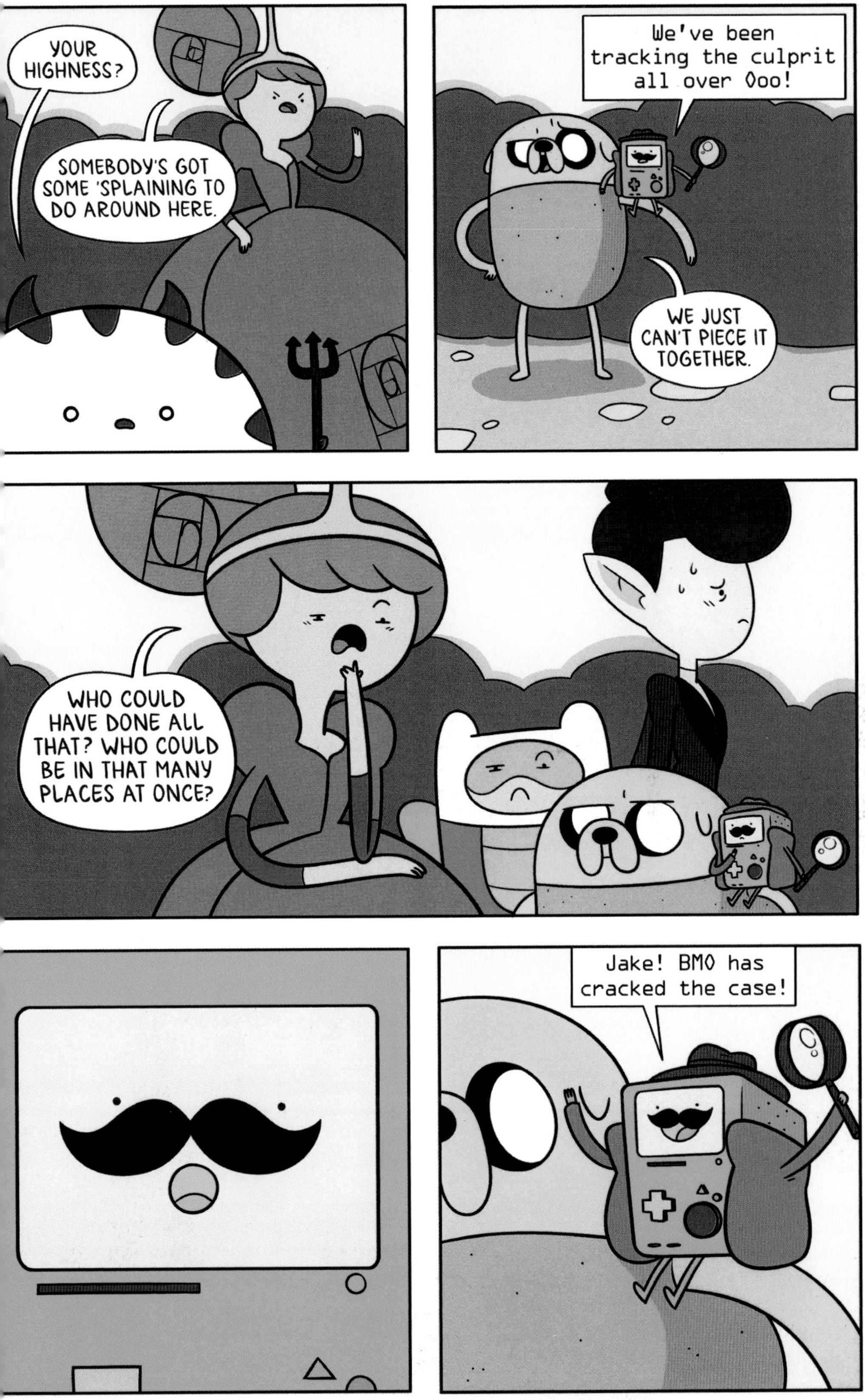

YOUR HIGHNESS?
SOMEBODY'S GOT SOME 'SPLAINING TO DO AROUND HERE.
We've been tracking the culprit all over Ooo!
WE JUST CAN'T PIECE IT TOGETHER.
WHO COULD HAVE DONE ALL THAT? WHO COULD BE IN THAT MANY PLACES AT ONCE?
Jake! BMO has cracked the case!

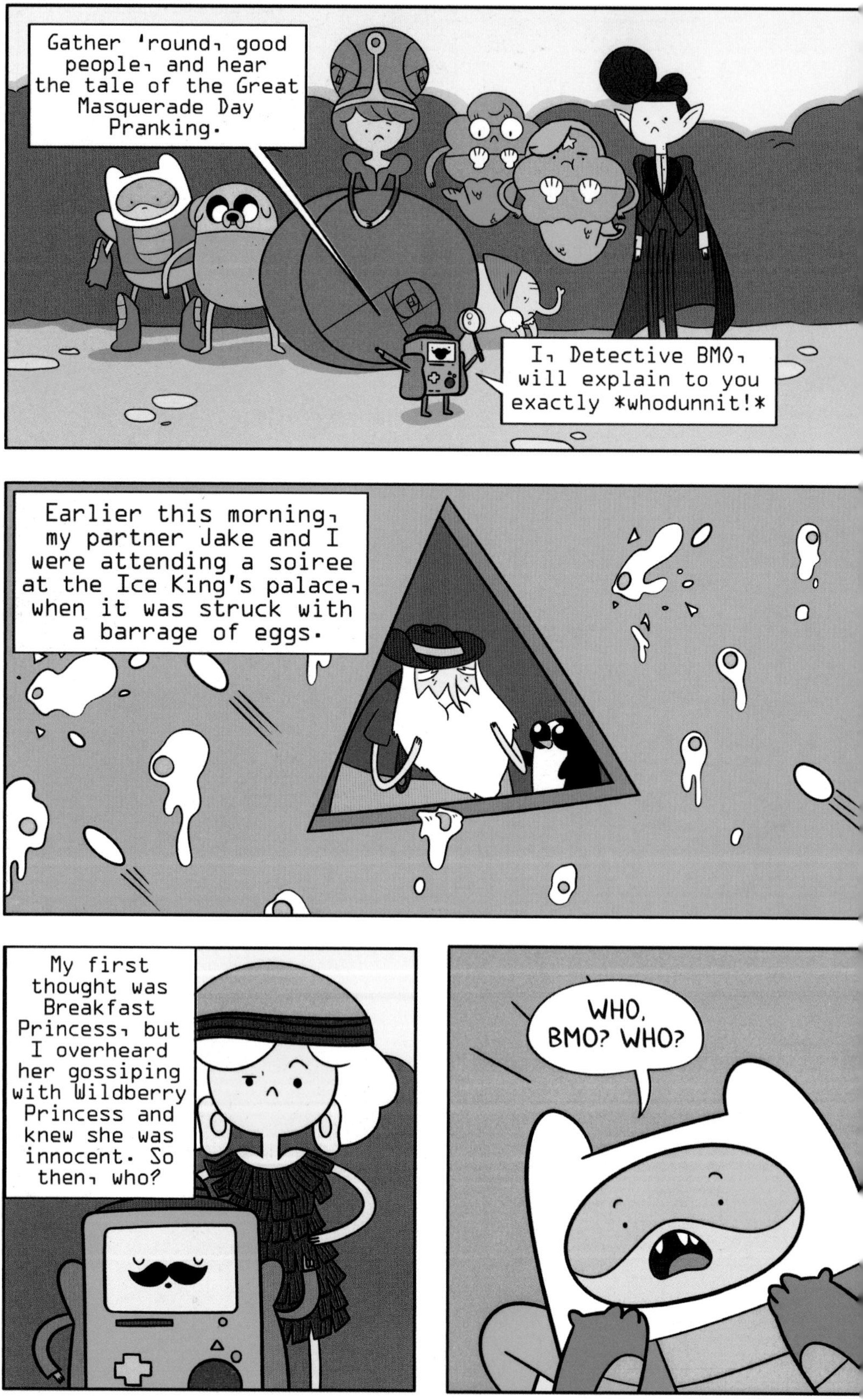

Gather 'round, good people, and hear the tale of the Great Masquerade Day Pranking.
I, Detective BMO, will explain to you exactly *whodunnit!*
Earlier this morning, my partner Jake and I were attending a soiree at the Ice King's palace, when it was struck with a barrage of eggs.
My first thought was Breakfast Princess, but I overheard her gossiping with Wildberry Princess and knew she was innocent. So then, who?
WHO, BMO? WHO?

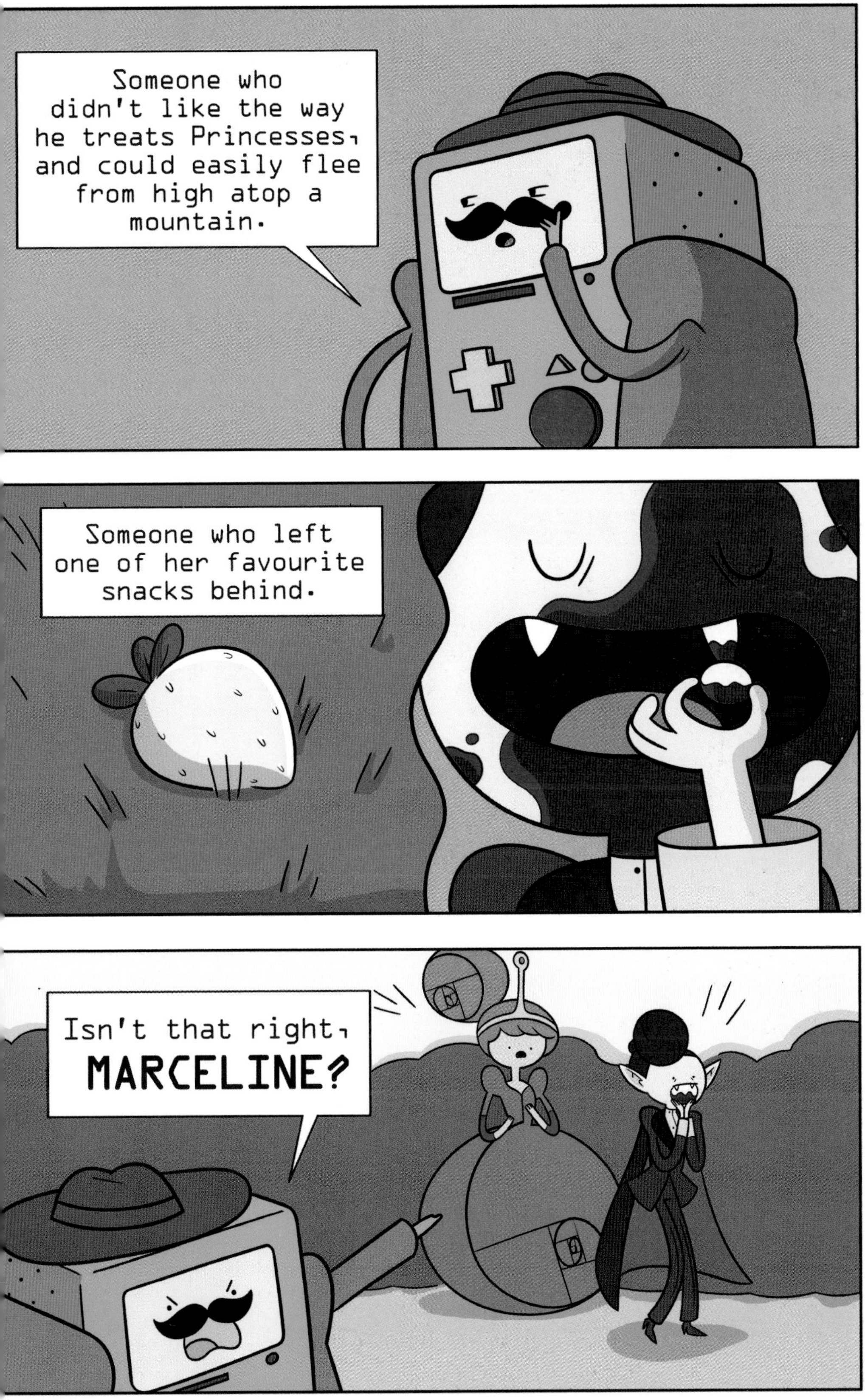
Someone who didn't like the way he treats Princesses, and could easily flee from high atop a mountain.
Someone who left one of her favourite snacks behind.
Isn't that right, MARCELINE?

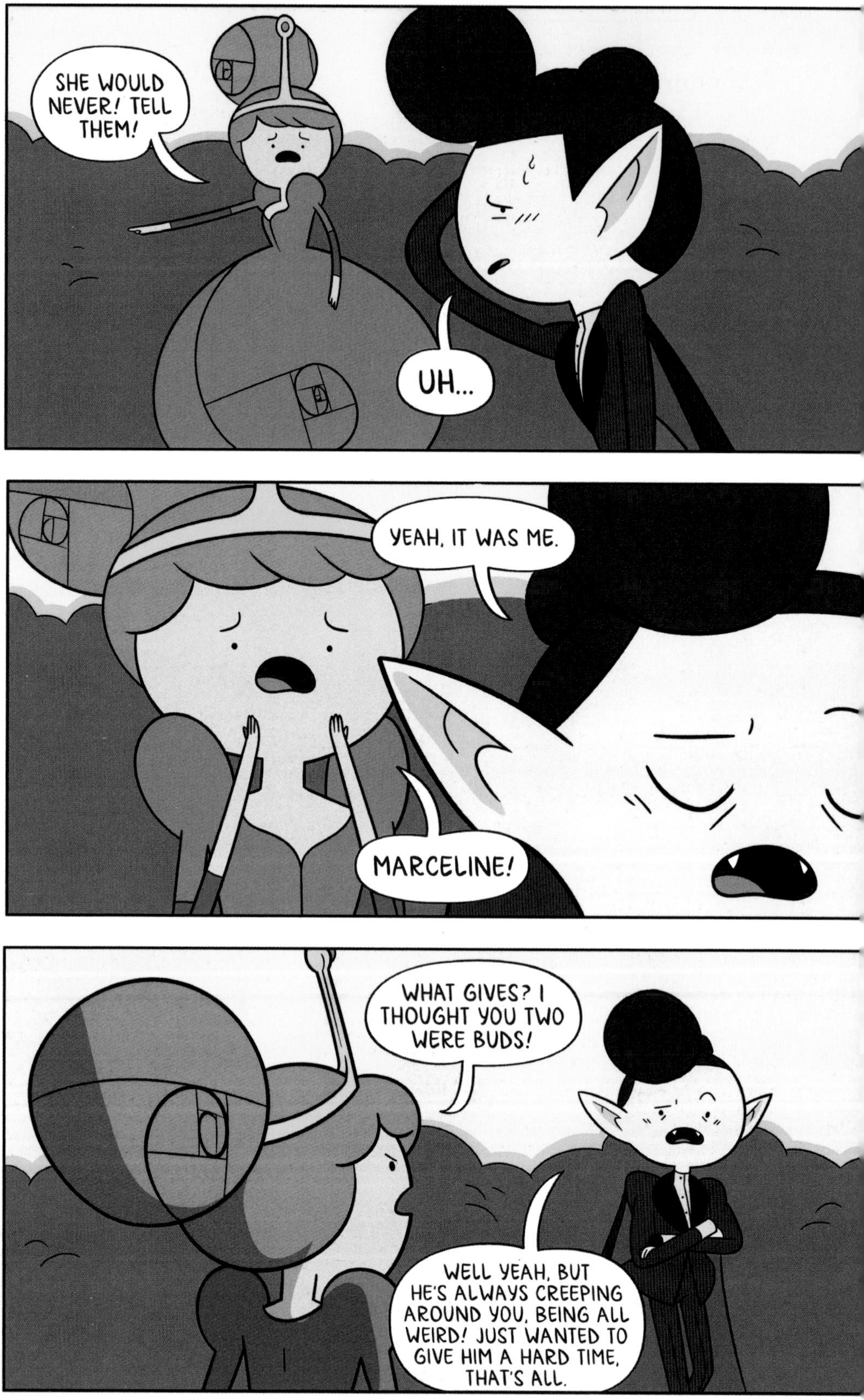
SHE WOULD NEVER! TELL THEM!
UH...
YEAH, IT WAS ME.
MARCELINE!
WHAT GIVES? I THOUGHT YOU TWO WERE BUDS!
WELL YEAH, BUT HE'S ALWAYS CREEPING AROUND YOU, BEING ALL WEIRD! JUST WANTED TO GIVE HIM A HARD TIME, THAT'S ALL.

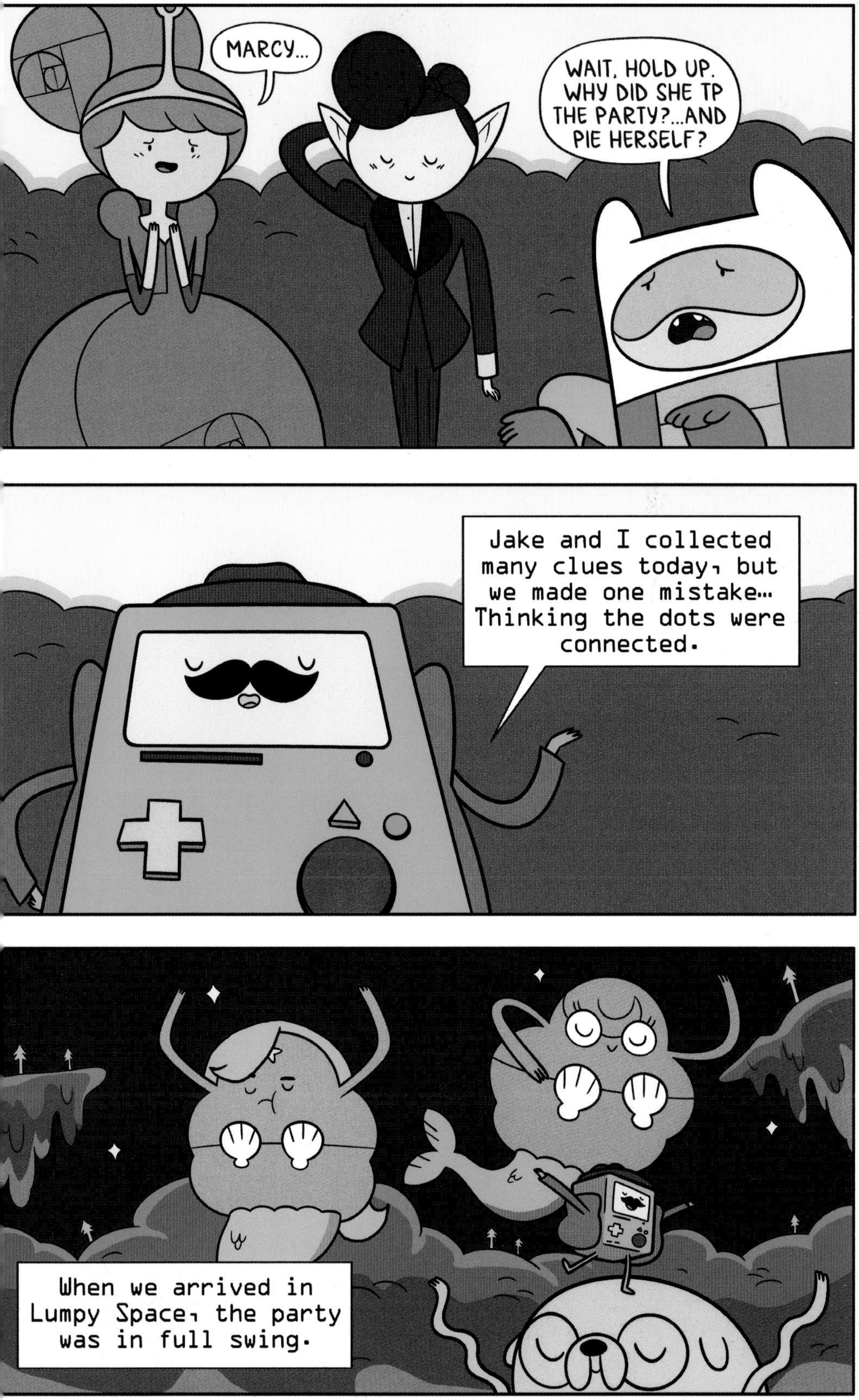
MARCY...
WAIT, HOLD UP. WHY DID SHE TP THE PARTY?...AND PIE HERSELF?
Jake and I collected many clues today, but we made one mistake... Thinking the dots were connected.
When we arrived in Lumpy Space, the party was in full swing.

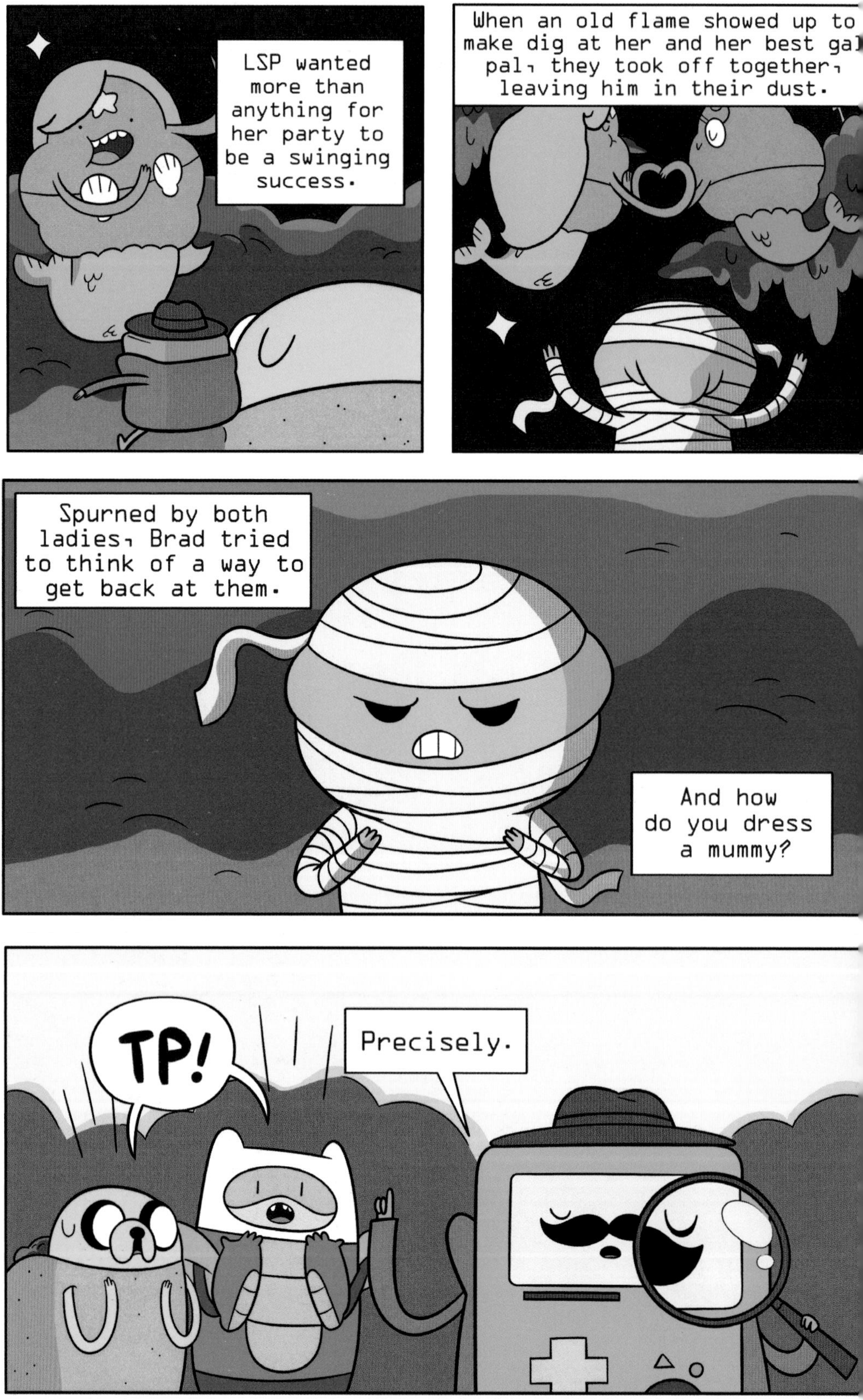
LSP wanted more than anything for her party to be a swinging success.
When an old flame showed up to make dig at her and her best gal pal, they took off together, leaving him in their dust.
Spurned by both ladies, Brad tried to think of a way to get back at them.
And how do you dress a mummy?
TP!
Precisely.

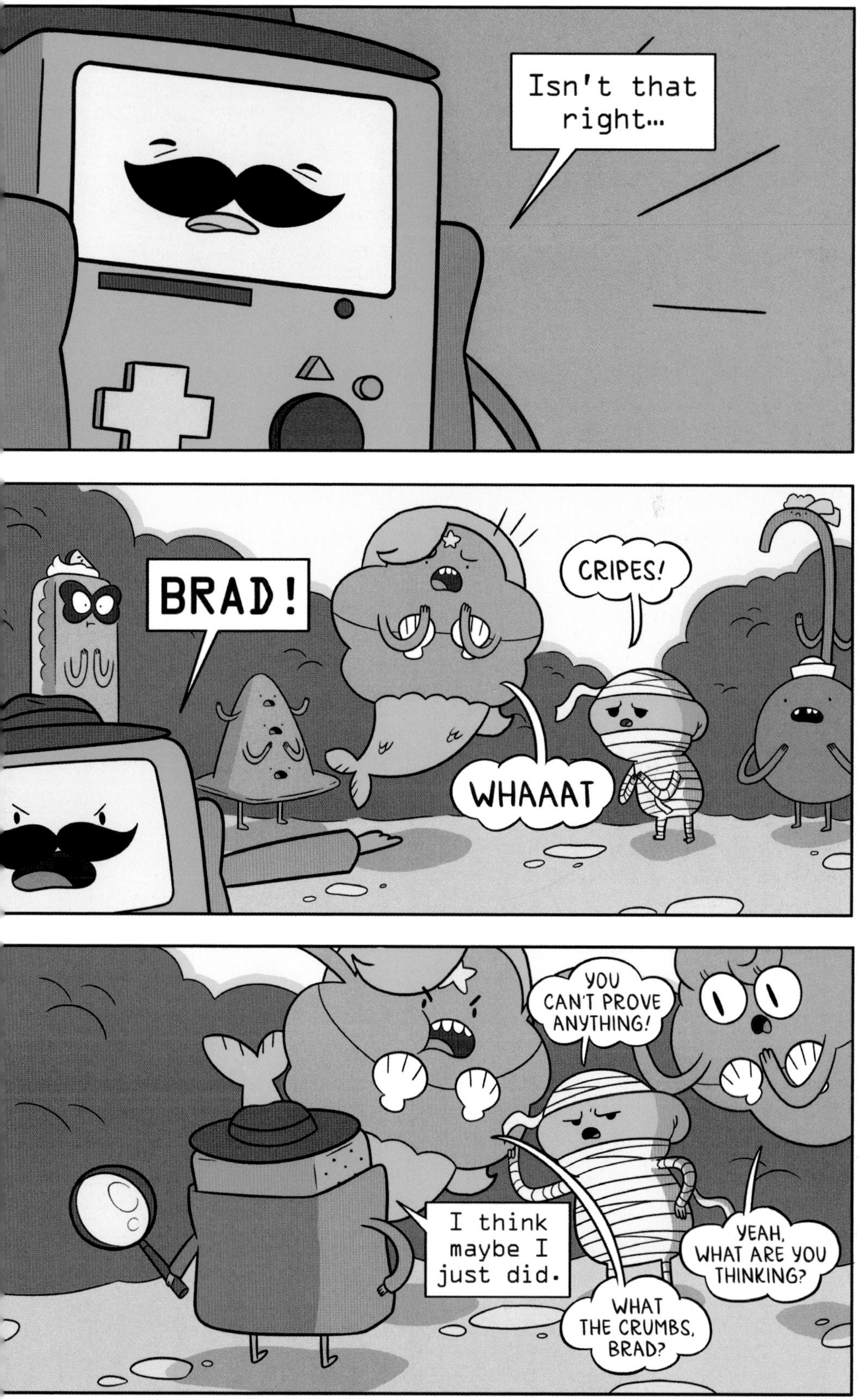
Isn't that right...
BRAD!
CRIPES!
WHAAAT
YOU CAN'T PROVE ANYTHING!
I think maybe I just did.
YEAH, WHAT ARE YOU THINKING?
WHAT THE CRUMBS, BRAD?

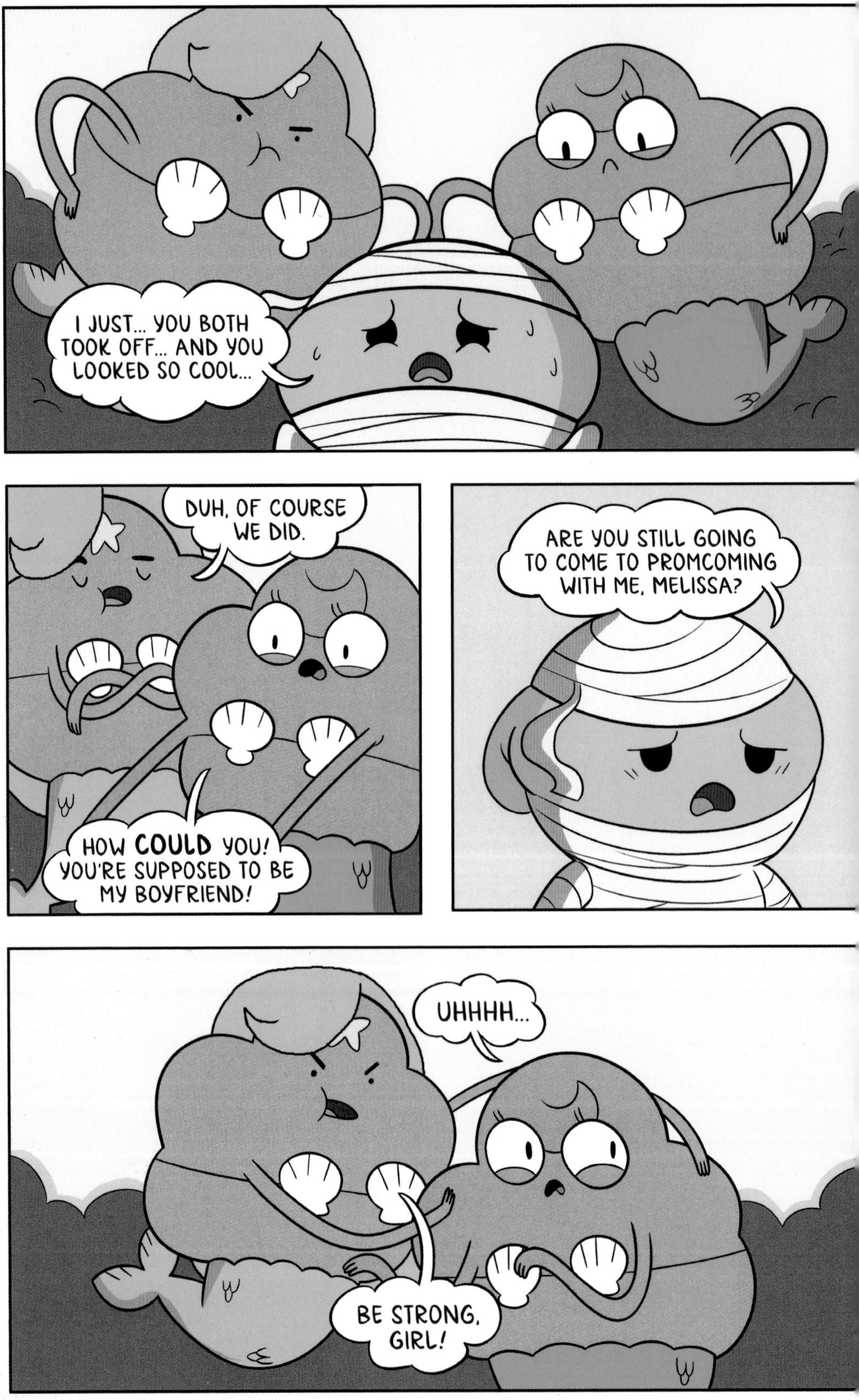
I JUST... YOU BOTH TOOK OFF... AND YOU LOOKED SO COOL...
DUH, OF COURSE WE DID.
HOW **COULD** YOU! YOU'RE SUPPOSED TO BE MY BOYFRIEND!
ARE YOU STILL GOING TO COME TO PROMCOMING WITH ME, MELISSA?
UHHHH...
BE STRONG, GIRL!

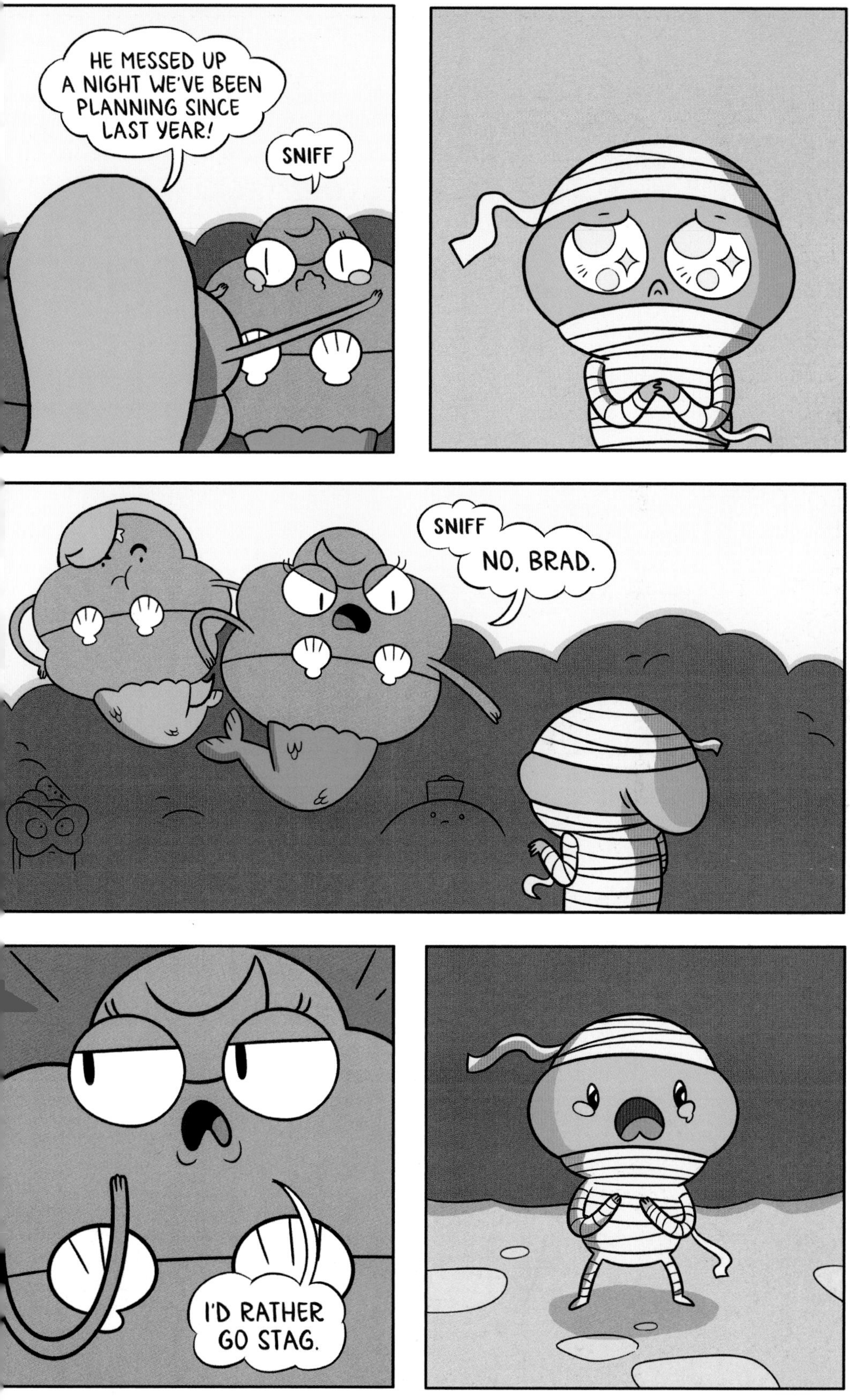
HE MESSED UP A NIGHT WE'VE BEEN PLANNING SINCE LAST YEAR!
SNIFF
SNIFF
NO, BRAD.
I'D RATHER GO STAG.

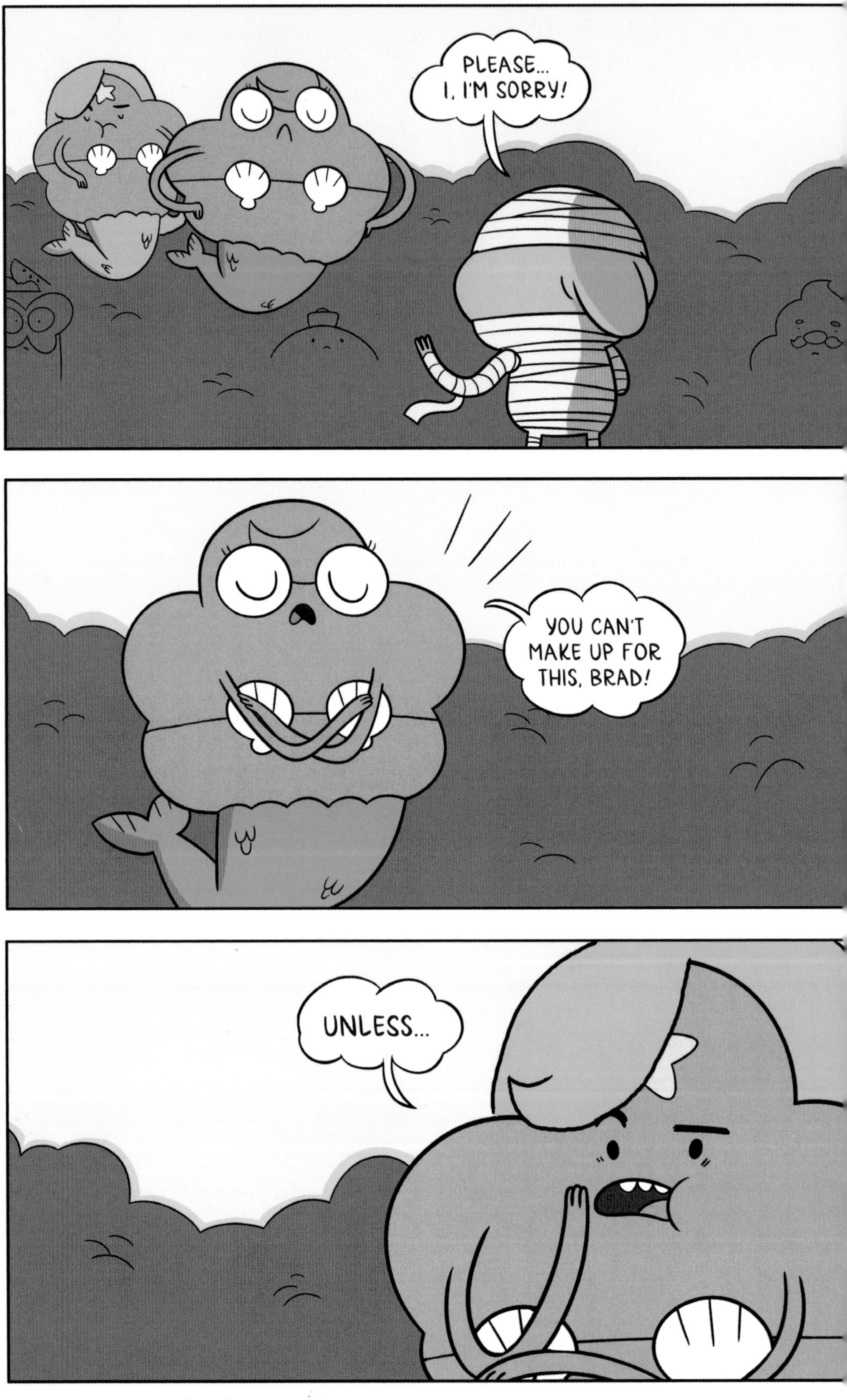
PLEASE...
I, I'M SORRY!
YOU CAN'T
MAKE UP FOR
THIS, BRAD!
UNLESS...

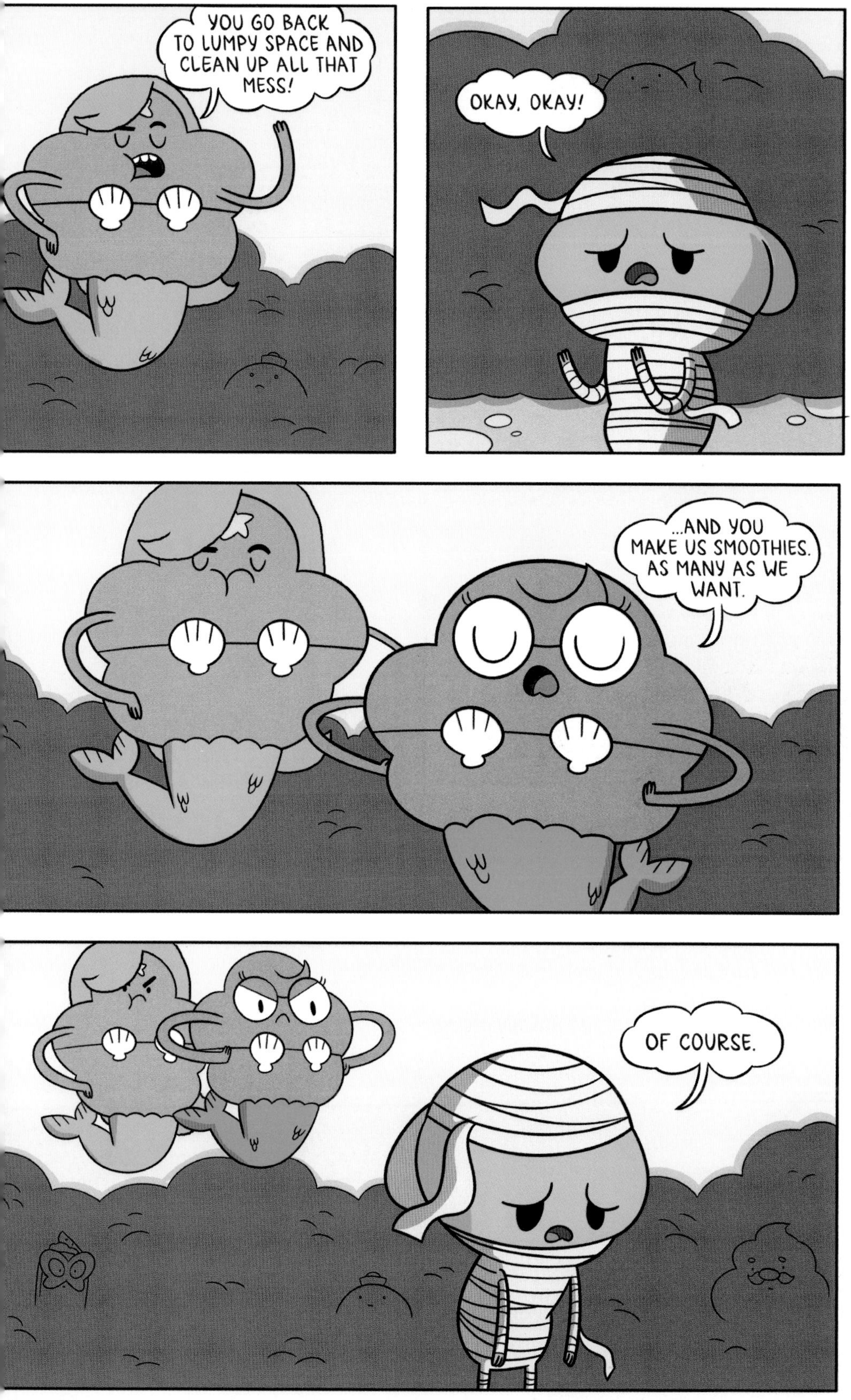
YOU GO BACK TO LUMPY SPACE AND CLEAN UP ALL THAT MESS!
OKAY, OKAY!
...AND YOU MAKE US SMOOTHIES. AS MANY AS WE WANT.
OF COURSE.

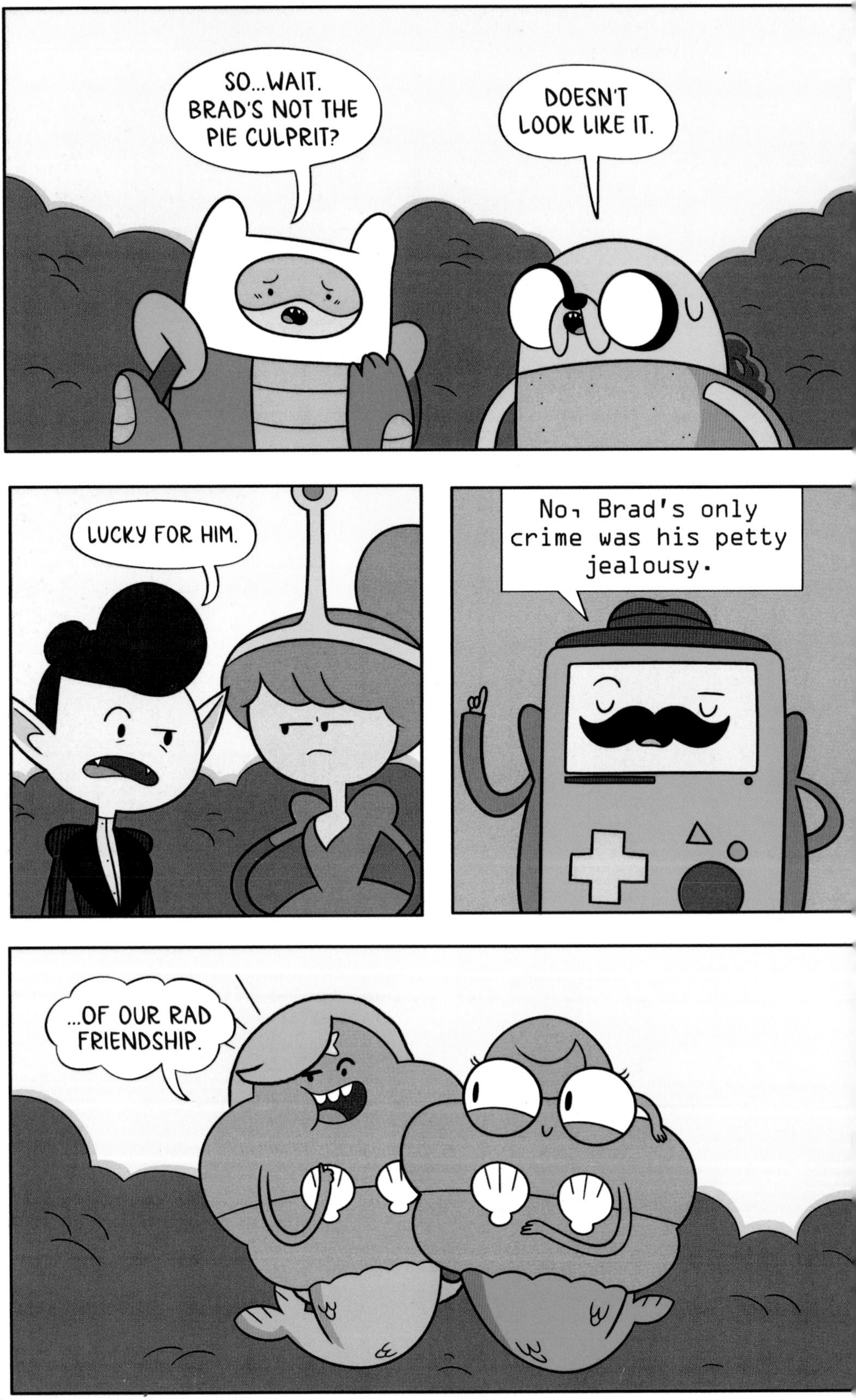

SO...WAIT. BRAD'S NOT THE PIE CULPRIT?
DOESN'T LOOK LIKE IT.
LUCKY FOR HIM.
No, Brad's only crime was his petty jealousy.
...OF OUR RAD FRIENDSHIP.

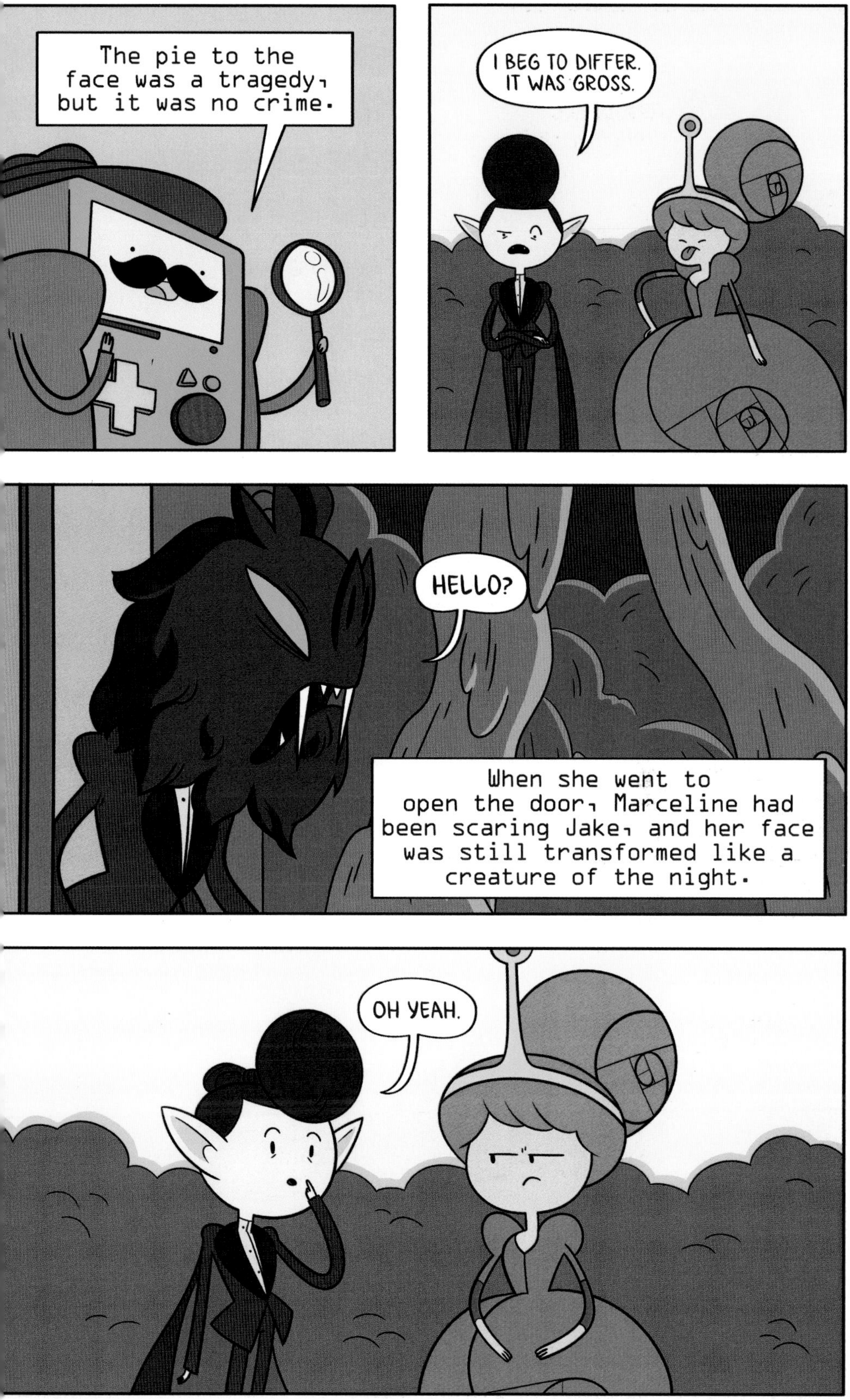

The pie to the face was a tragedy, but it was no crime.
I BEG TO DIFFER. IT WAS GROSS.
HELLO?
When she went to open the door, Marceline had been scaring Jake, and her face was still transformed like a creature of the night.
OH YEAH.

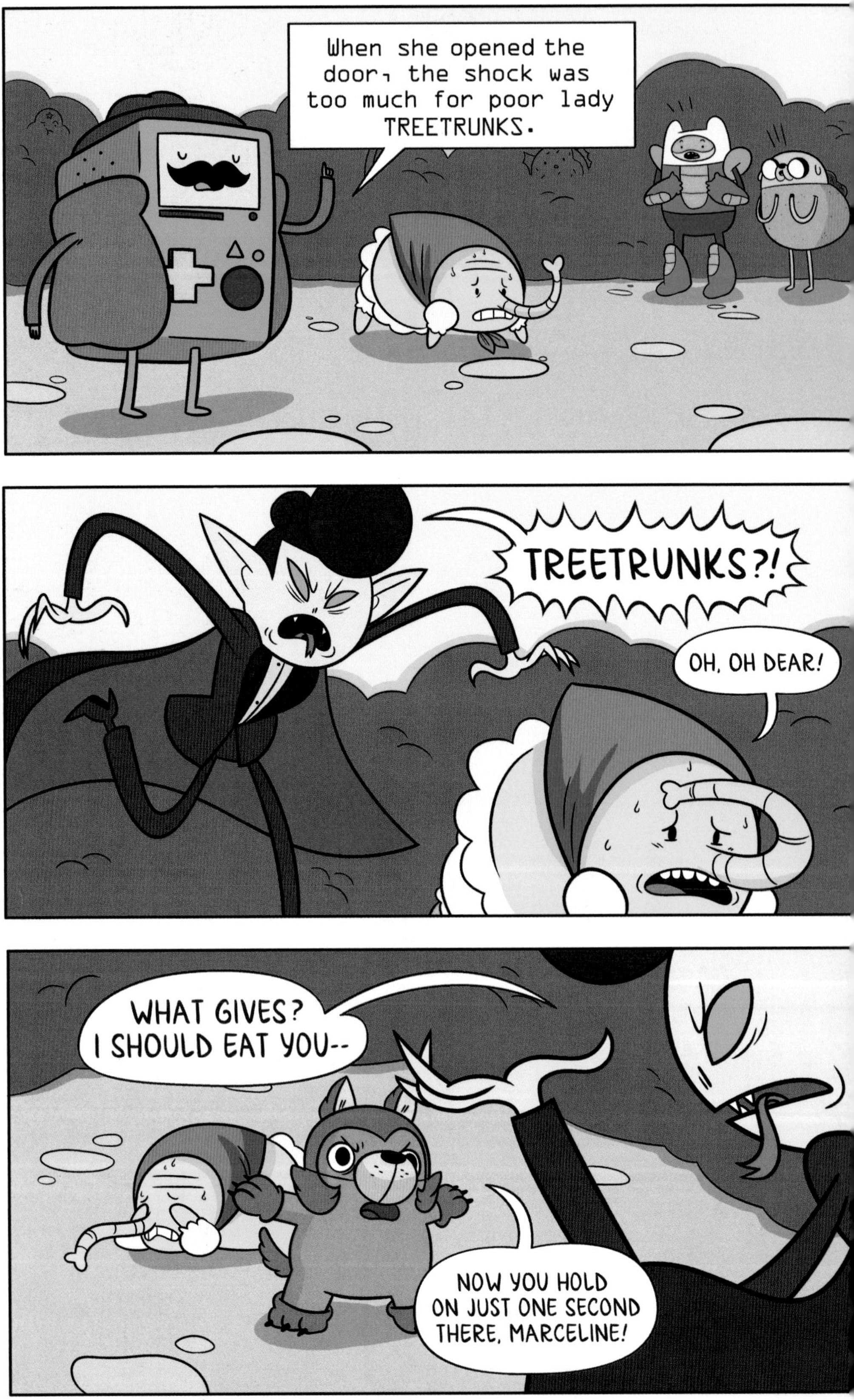
When she opened the door, the shock was too much for poor lady TREETRUNKS.
TREETRUNKS?!
OH, OH DEAR!
WHAT GIVES? I SHOULD EAT YOU--
NOW YOU HOLD ON JUST ONE SECOND THERE, MARCELINE!

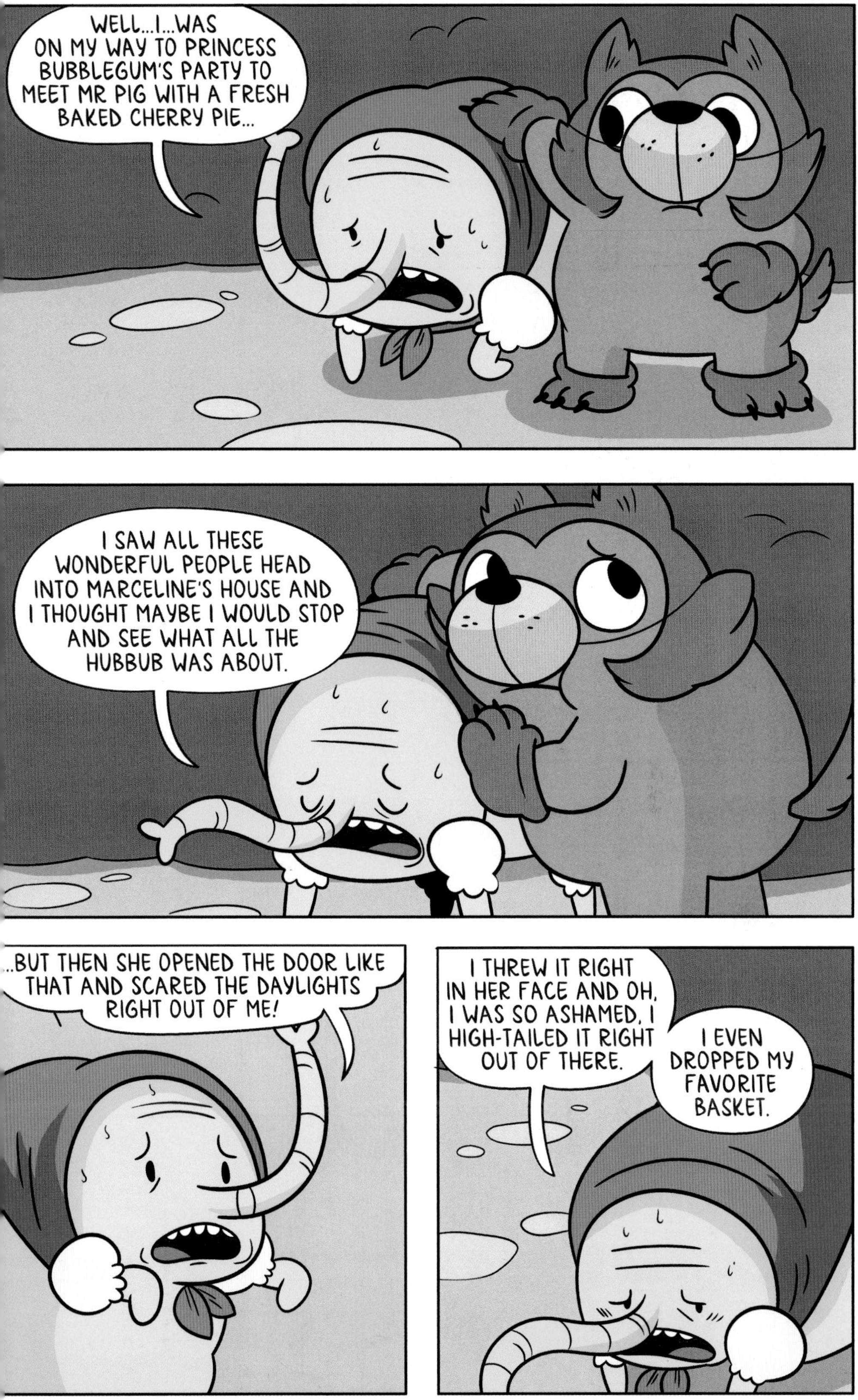
WELL...I...WAS ON MY WAY TO PRINCESS BUBBLEGUM'S PARTY TO MEET MR PIG WITH A FRESH BAKED CHERRY PIE...
I SAW ALL THESE WONDERFUL PEOPLE HEAD INTO MARCELINE'S HOUSE AND I THOUGHT MAYBE I WOULD STOP AND SEE WHAT ALL THE HUBBUB WAS ABOUT.
...BUT THEN SHE OPENED THE DOOR LIKE THAT AND SCARED THE DAYLIGHTS RIGHT OUT OF ME!
I THREW IT RIGHT IN HER FACE AND OH, I WAS SO ASHAMED, I HIGH-TAILED IT RIGHT OUT OF THERE.
I EVEN DROPPED MY FAVORITE BASKET.

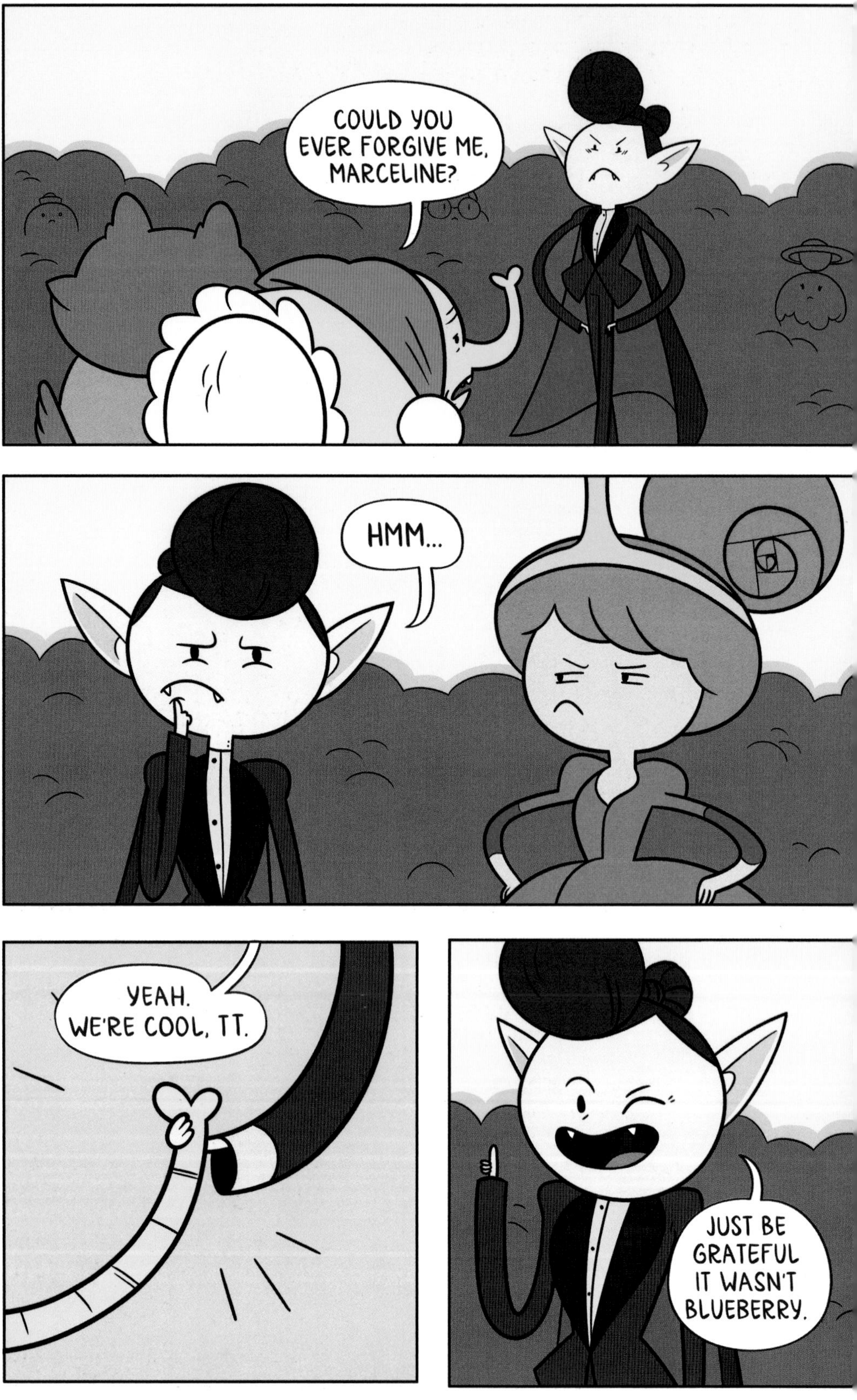
COULD YOU EVER FORGIVE ME, MARCELINE?
HMM...
YEAH. WE'RE COOL, TT.
JUST BE GRATEFUL IT WASN'T BLUEBERRY.

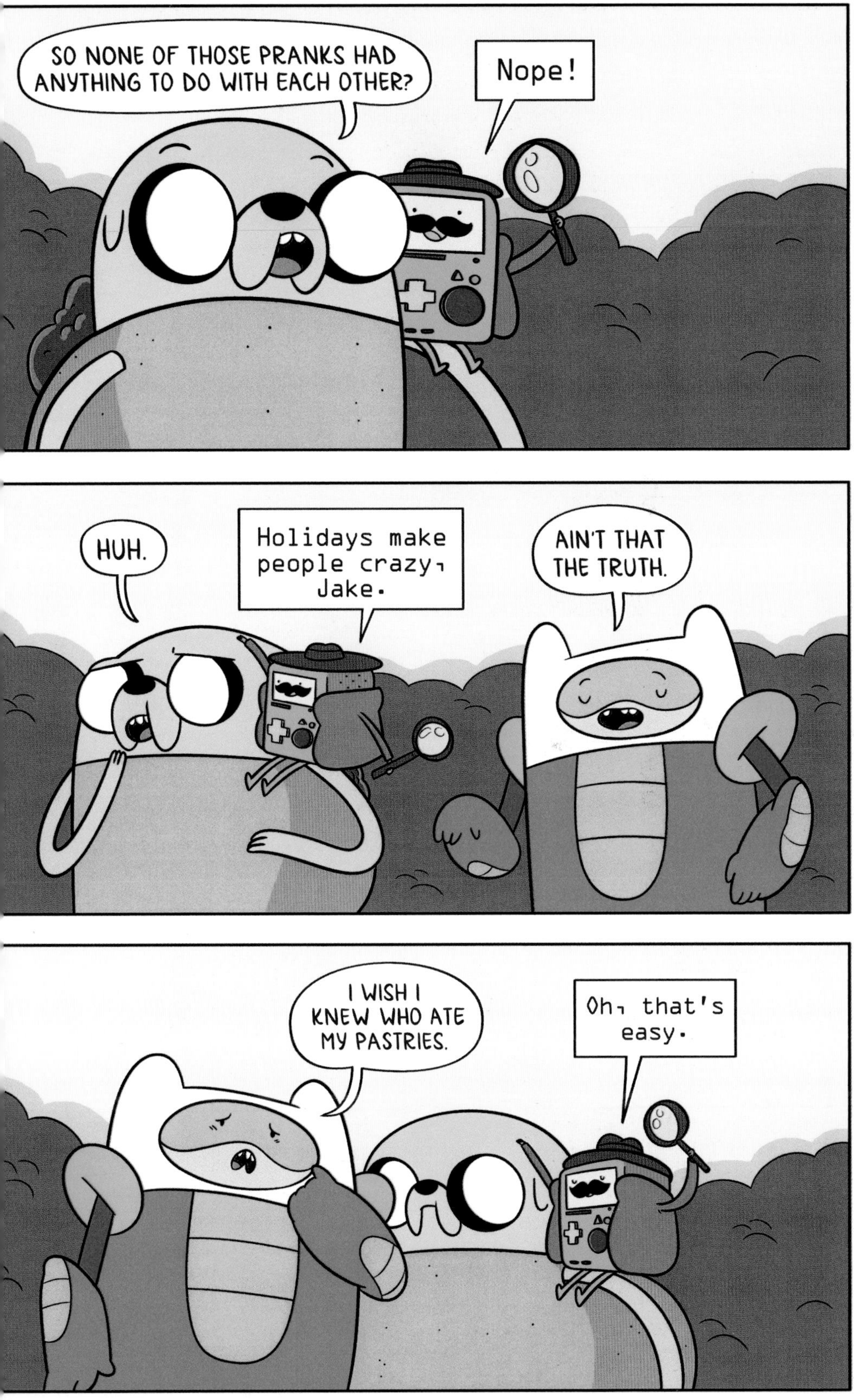
SO NONE OF THOSE PRANKS HAD ANYTHING TO DO WITH EACH OTHER?
Nope!
HUH.
Holidays make people crazy, Jake.
AIN'T THAT THE TRUTH.
I WISH I KNEW WHO ATE MY PASTRIES.
Oh, that's easy.

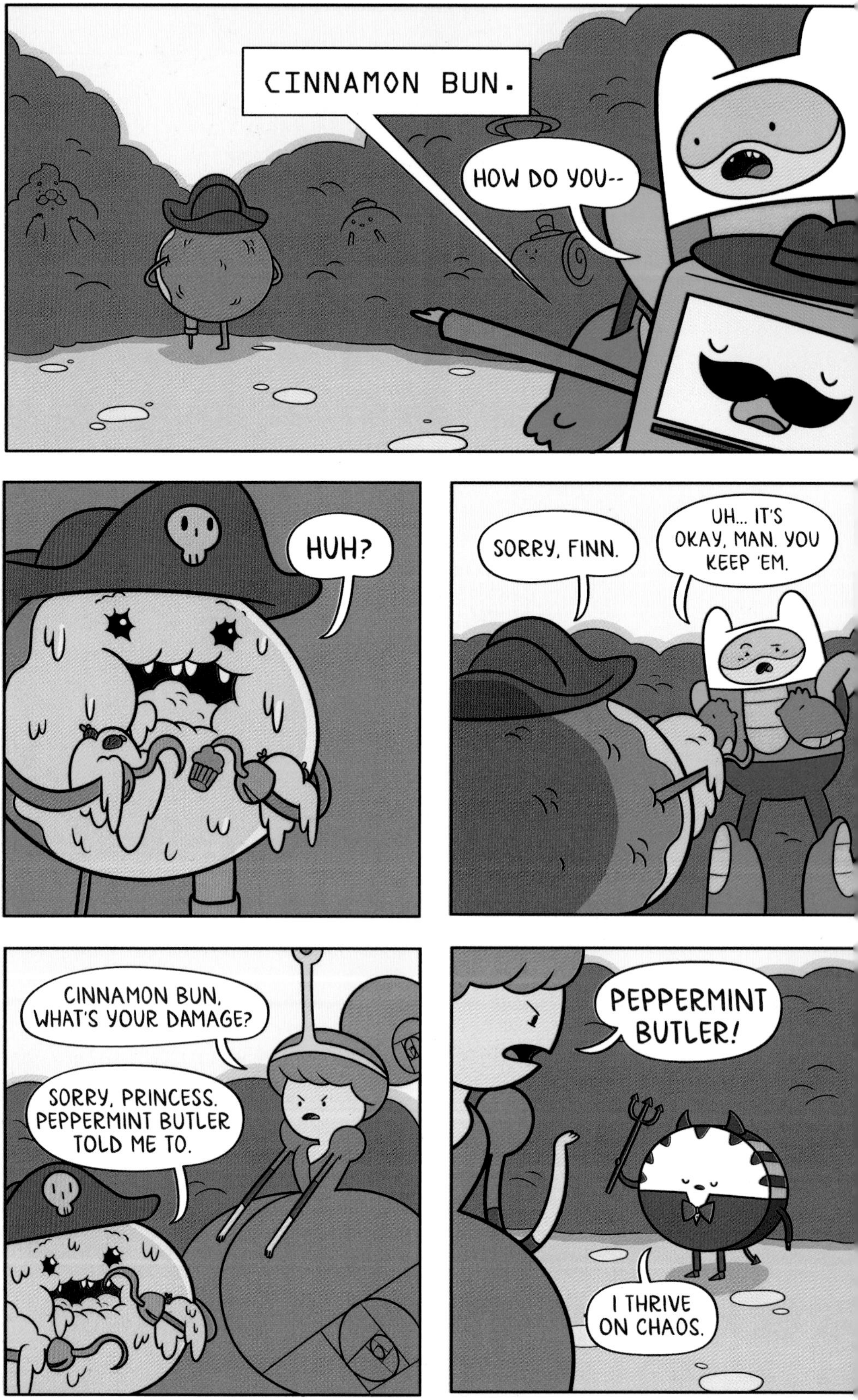
CINNAMON BUN.
HOW DO YOU--
HUH?
SORRY, FINN.
UH... IT'S OKAY, MAN. YOU KEEP 'EM.
CINNAMON BUN, WHAT'S YOUR DAMAGE?
SORRY, PRINCESS. PEPPERMINT BUTLER TOLD ME TO.
PEPPERMINT BUTLER!
I THRIVE ON CHAOS.

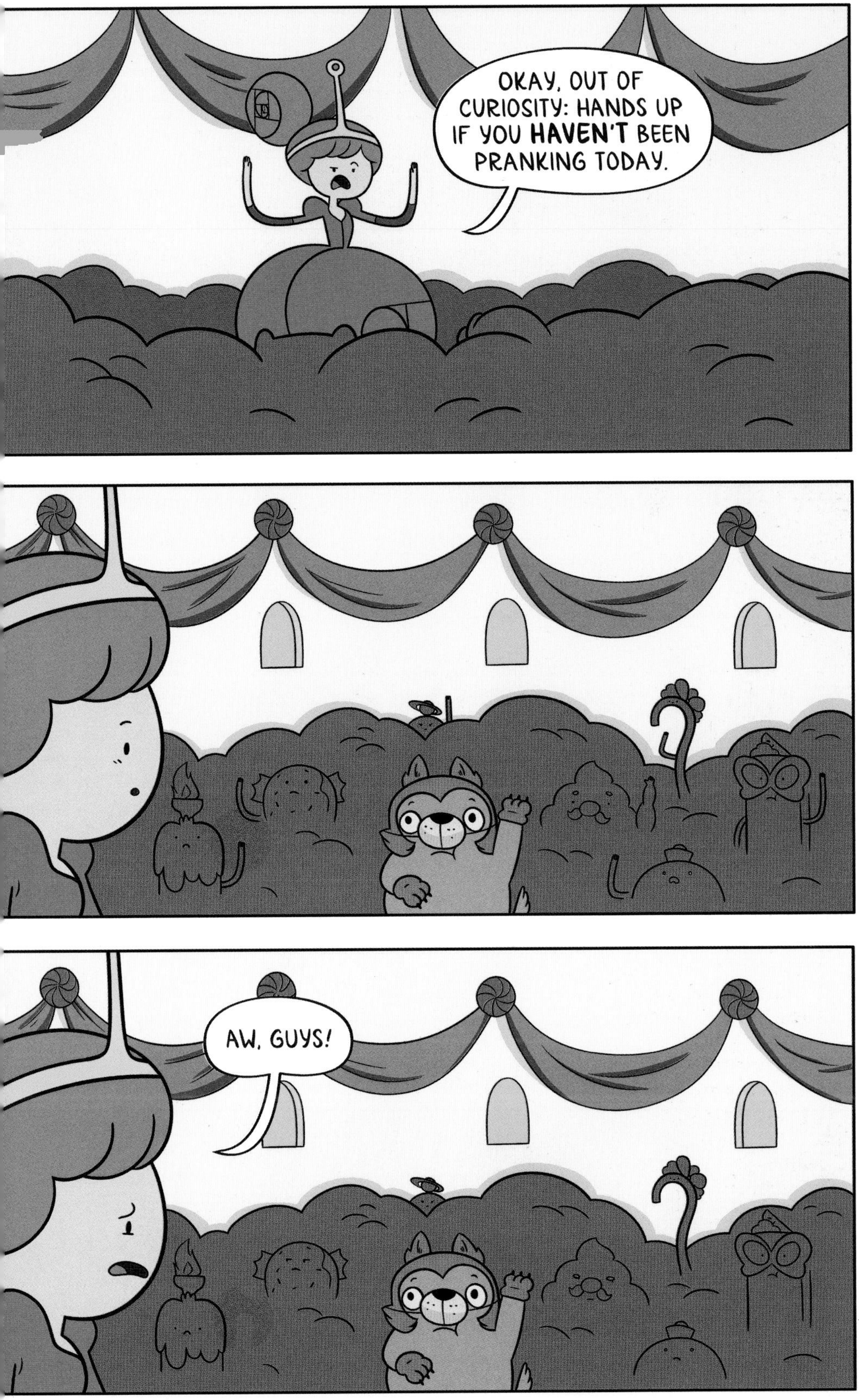
OKAY, OUT OF CURIOSITY: HANDS UP IF YOU **HAVEN'T** BEEN PRANKING TODAY.
AW, GUYS!

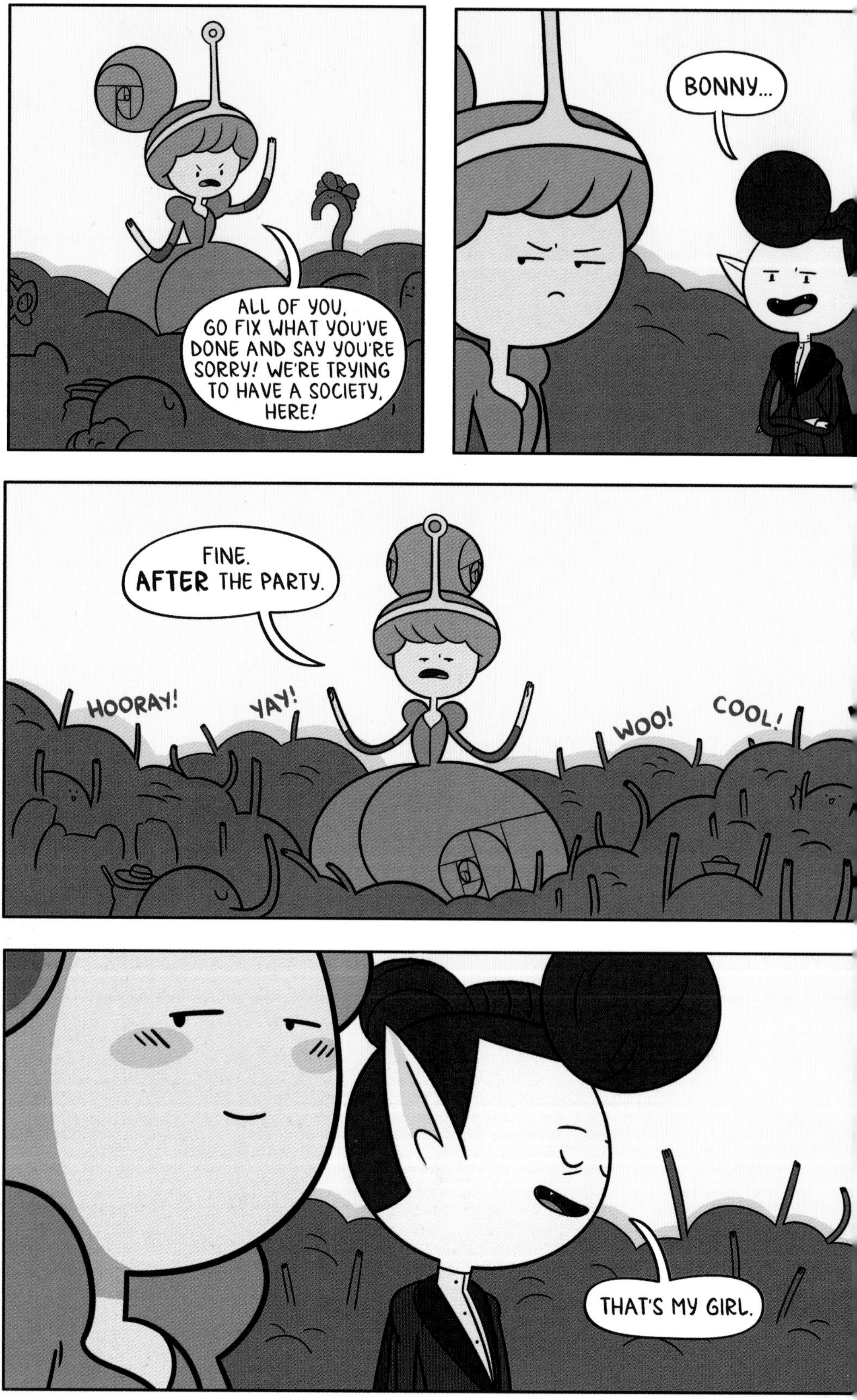
ALL OF YOU, GO FIX WHAT YOU'VE DONE AND SAY YOU'RE SORRY! WE'RE TRYING TO HAVE A SOCIETY, HERE!
BONNY...
FINE. **AFTER** THE PARTY.
HOORAY!
YAY!
WOO!
COOL!
THAT'S MY GIRL.

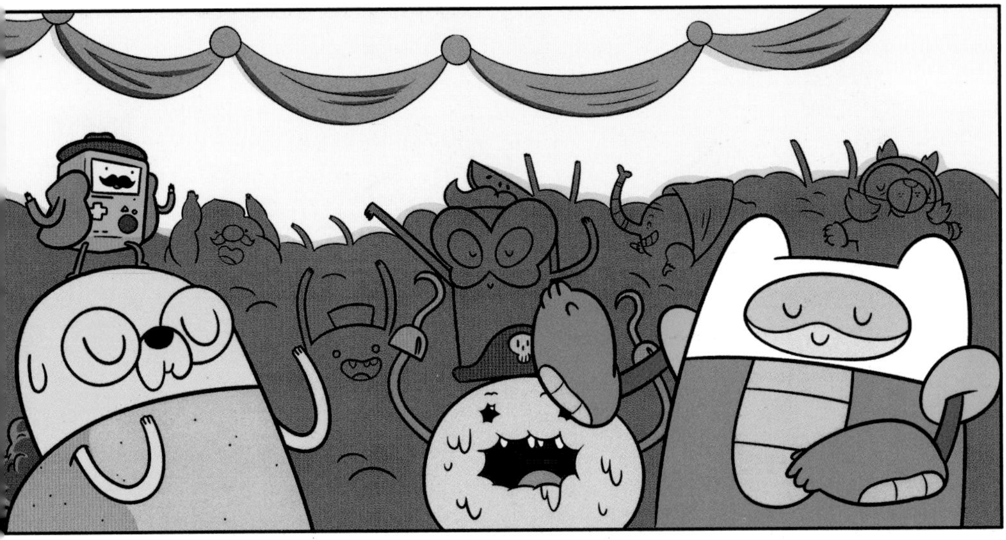

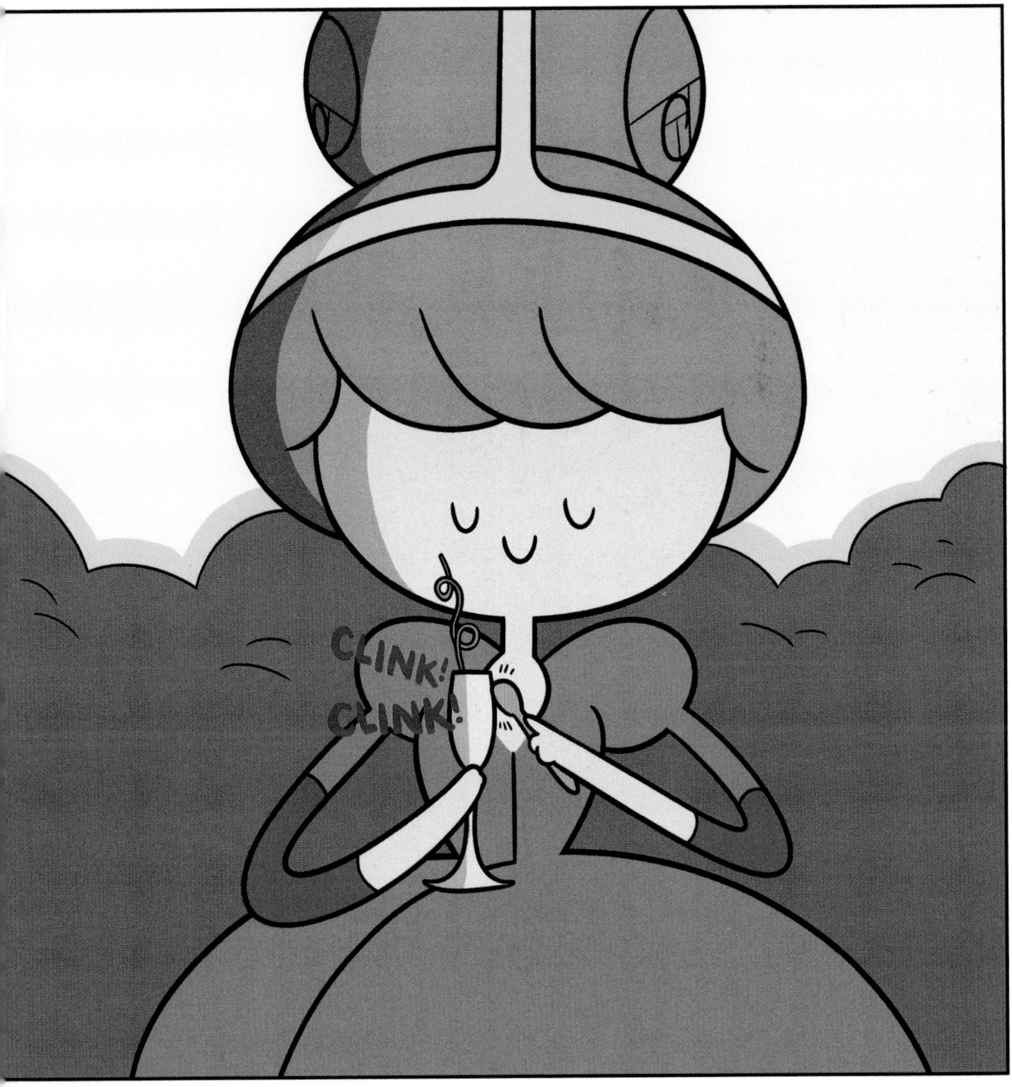
CLINK! CLINK!

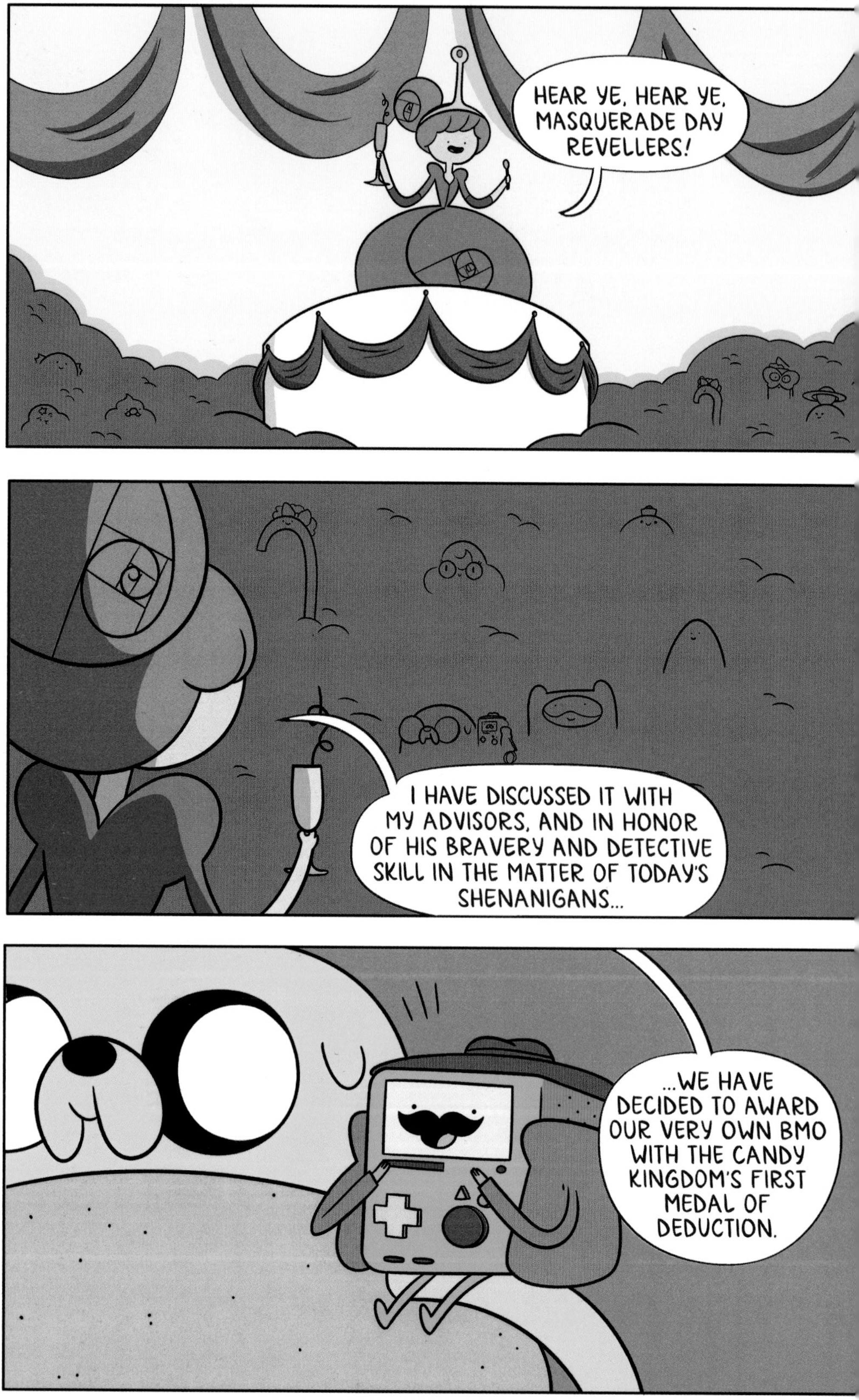
HEAR YE, HEAR YE, MASQUERADE DAY REVELLERS!
I HAVE DISCUSSED IT WITH MY ADVISORS, AND IN HONOR OF HIS BRAVERY AND DETECTIVE SKILL IN THE MATTER OF TODAY'S SHENANIGANS...
...WE HAVE DECIDED TO AWARD OUR VERY OWN BMO WITH THE CANDY KINGDOM'S FIRST MEDAL OF DEDUCTION.

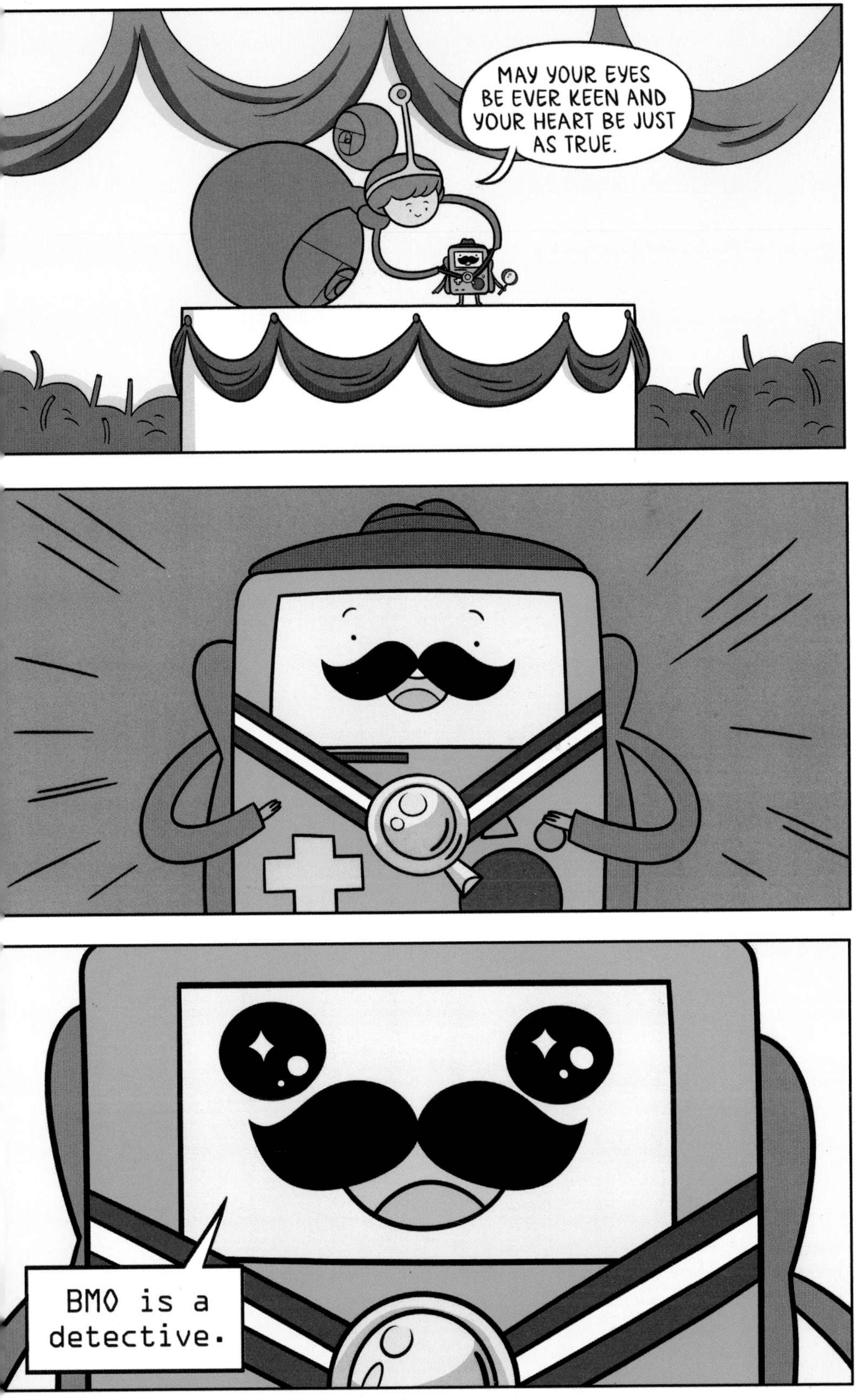
MAY YOUR EYES BE EVER KEEN AND YOUR HEART BE JUST AS TRUE.
BMO is a detective.

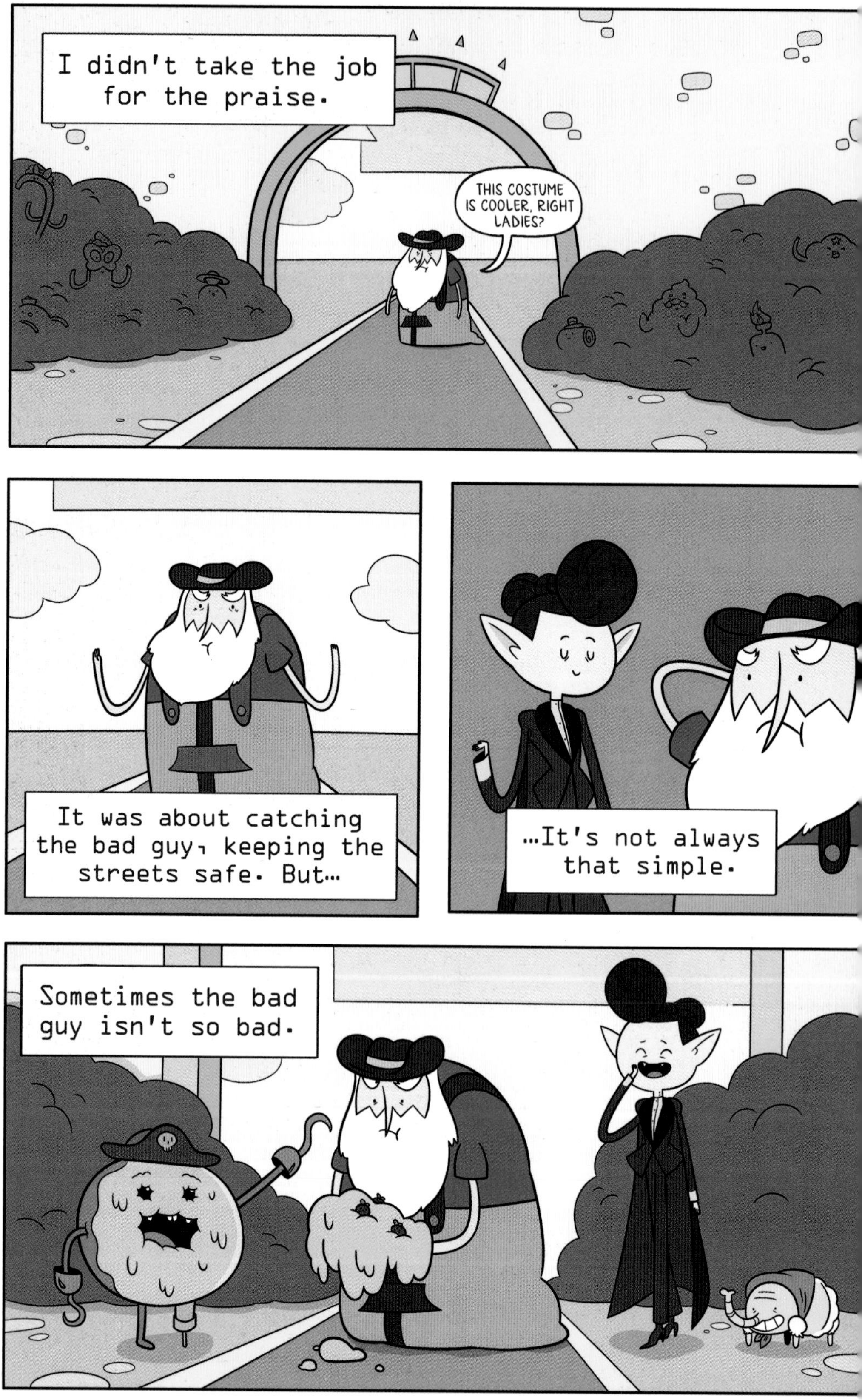
I didn't take the job for the praise.
THIS COSTUME IS COOLER, RIGHT LADIES?
It was about catching the bad guy, keeping the streets safe. But...
...It's not always that simple.
Sometimes the bad guy isn't so bad.

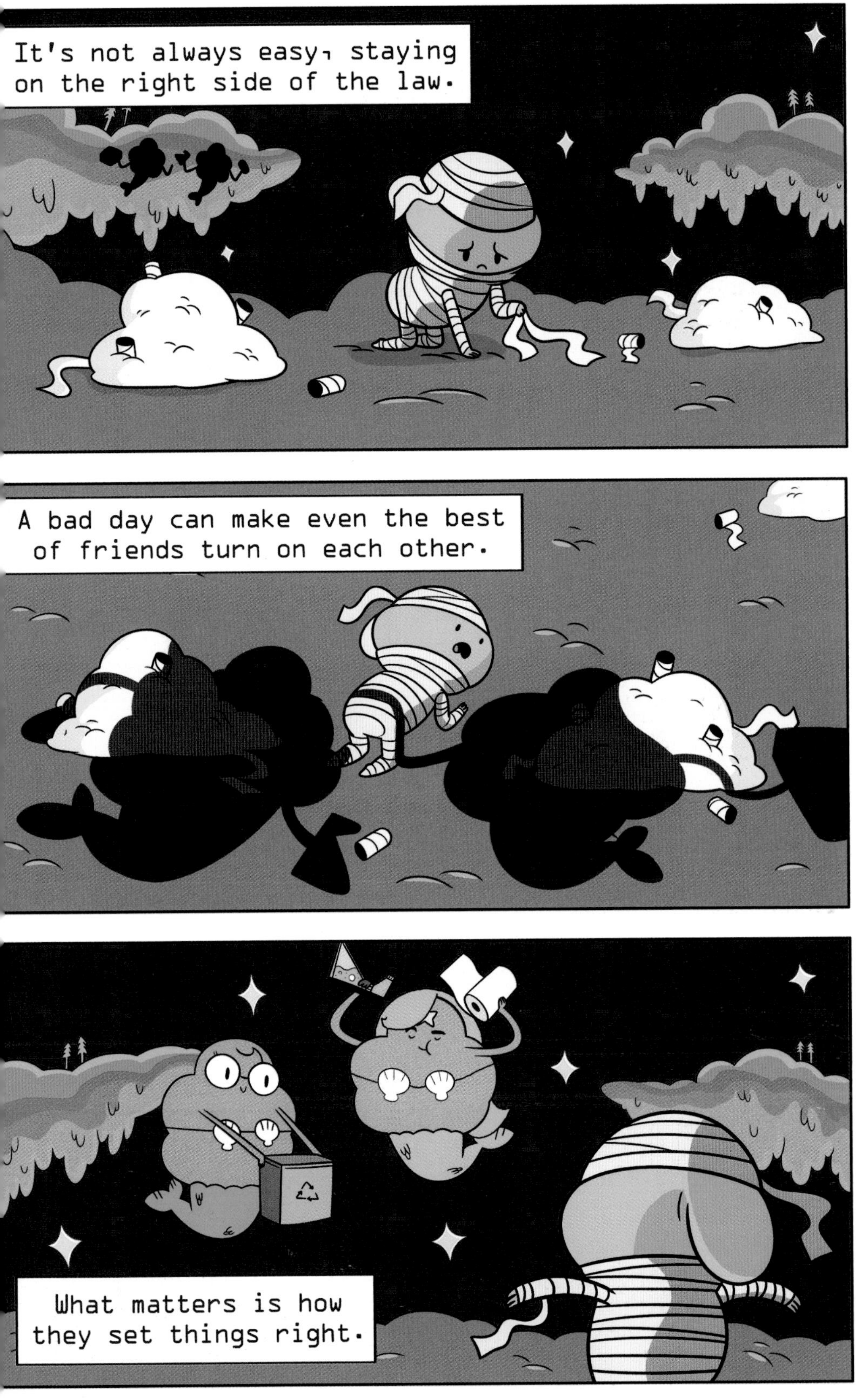
It's not always easy, staying on the right side of the law.
A bad day can make even the best of friends turn on each other.
What matters is how they set things right.

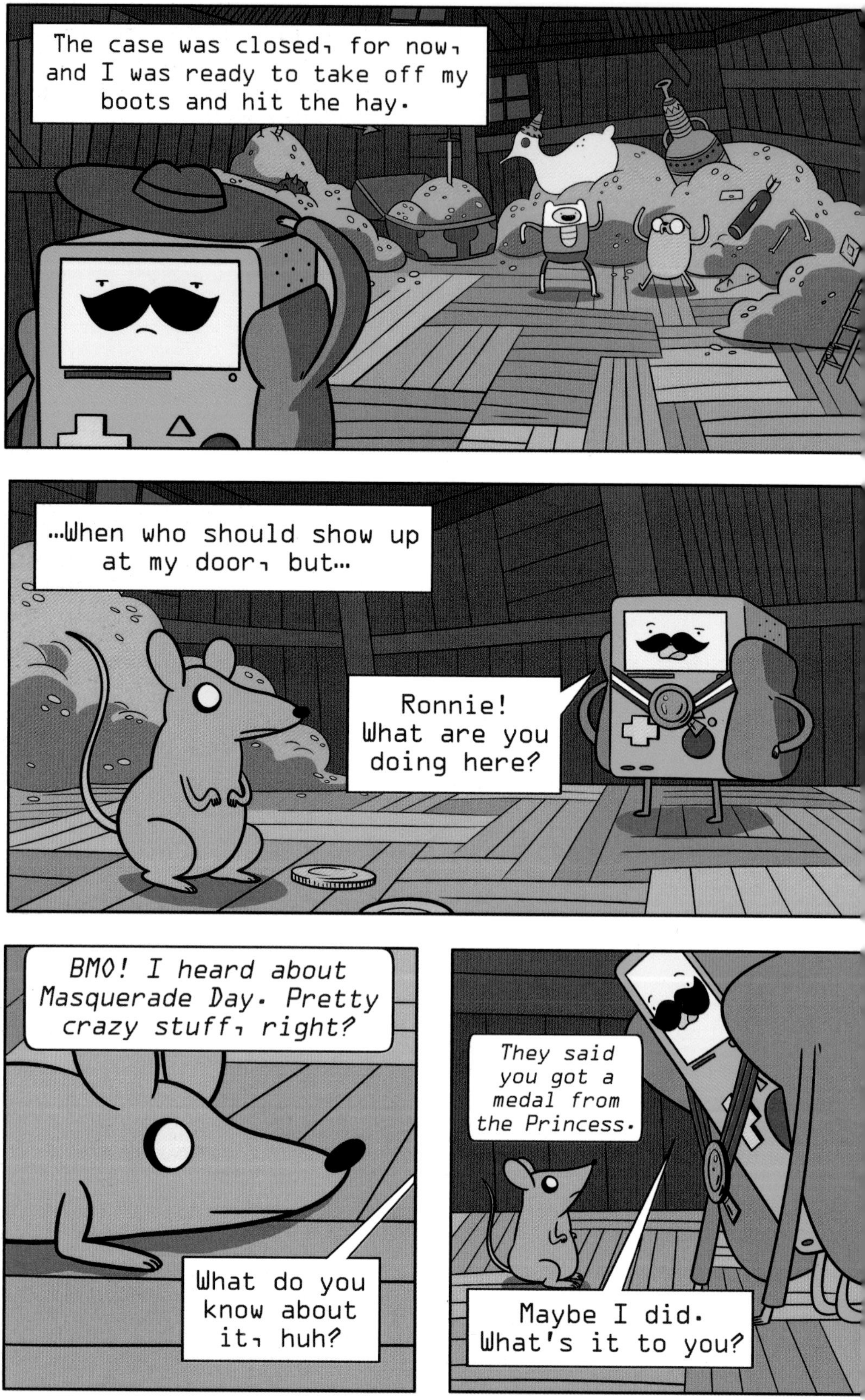
The case was closed, for now, and I was ready to take off my boots and hit the hay.
...When who should show up at my door, but...
Ronnie! What are you doing here?
BMO! I heard about Masquerade Day. Pretty crazy stuff, right?
What do you know about it, huh?
They said you got a medal from the Princess.
Maybe I did. What's it to you?

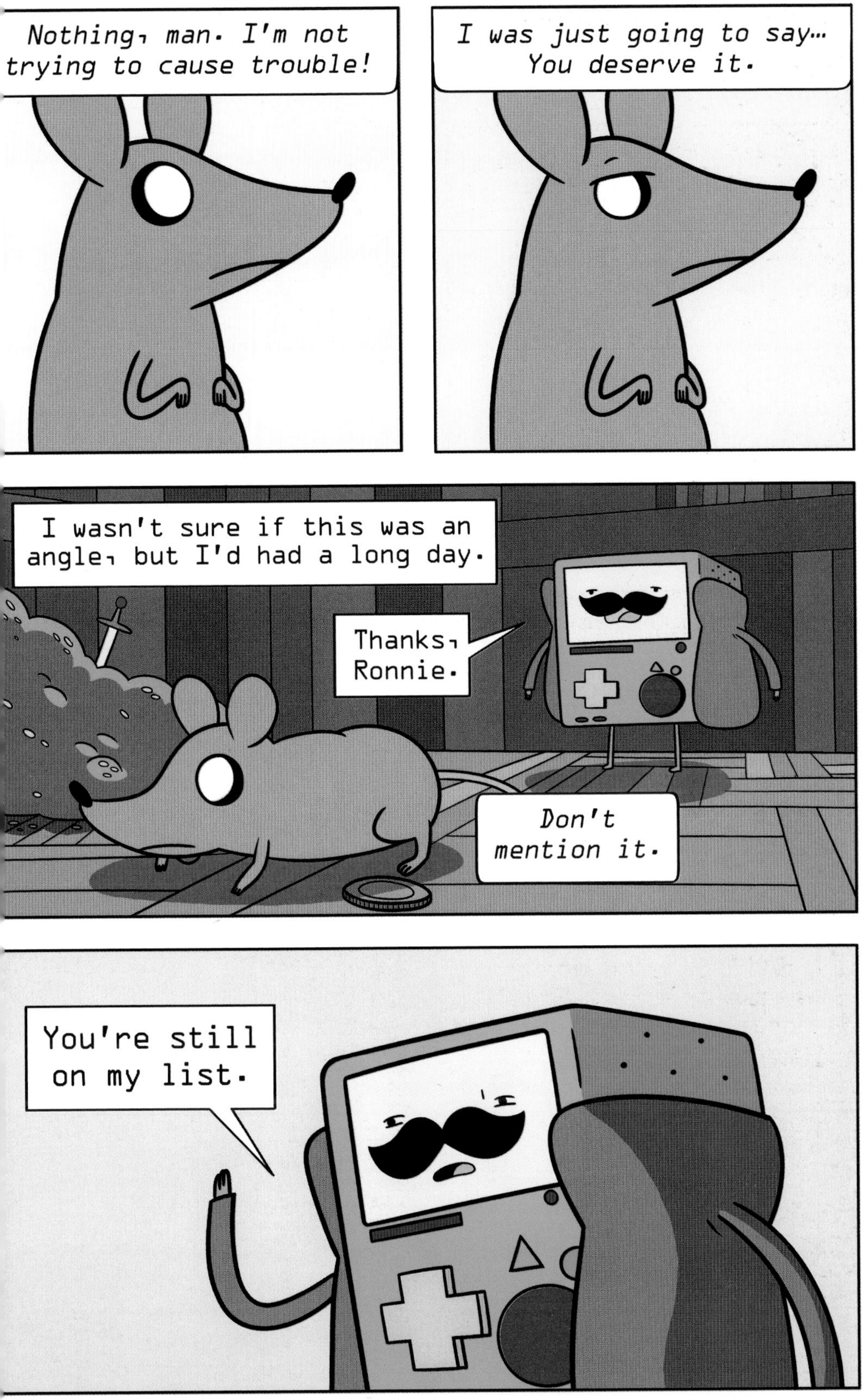
Nothing, man. I'm not trying to cause trouble!
I was just going to say... You deserve it.
I wasn't sure if this was an angle, but I'd had a long day.
Thanks, Ronnie.
Don't mention it.
You're still on my list.

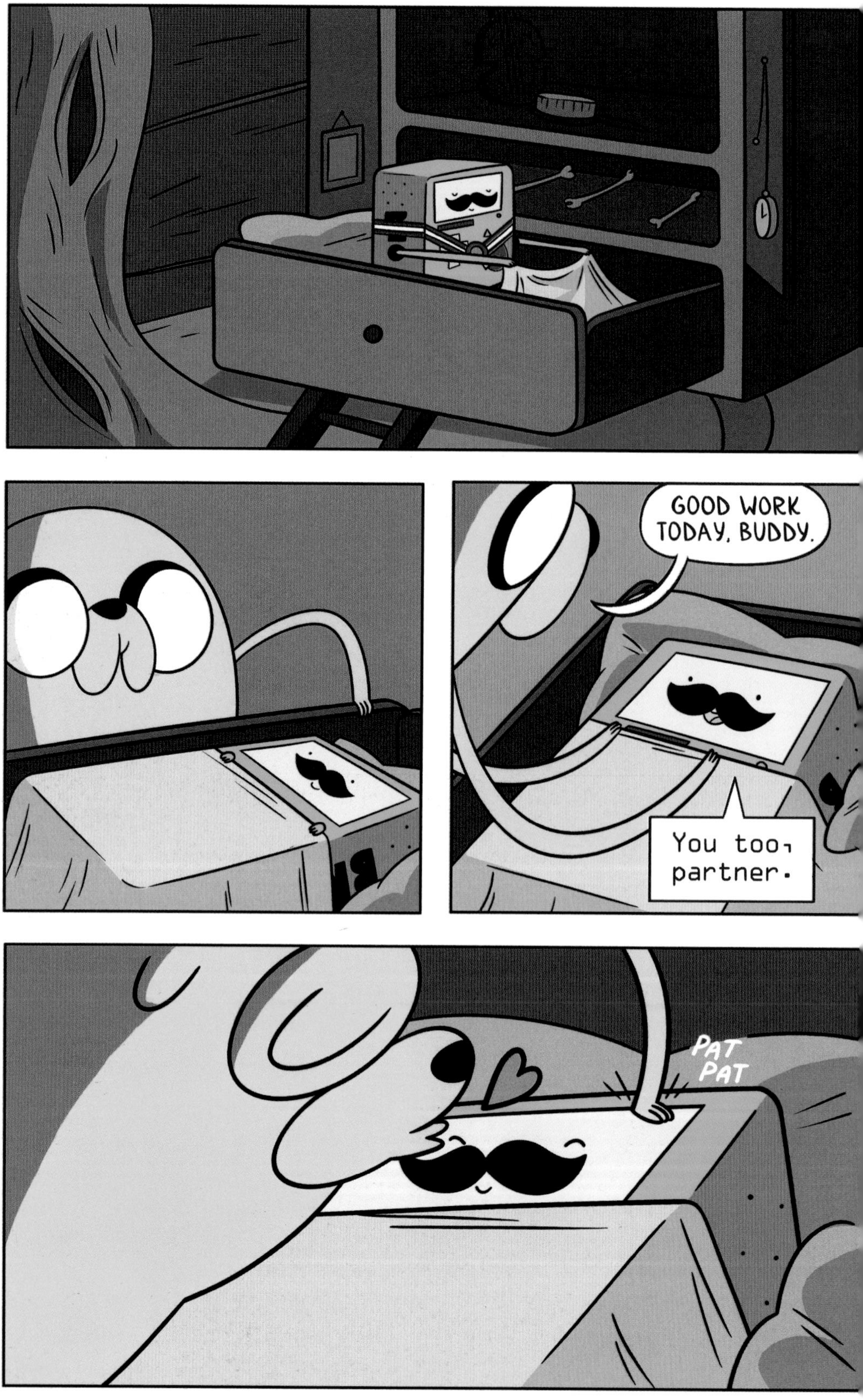
GOOD WORK TODAY, BUDDY.
You too, partner.
PAT PAT

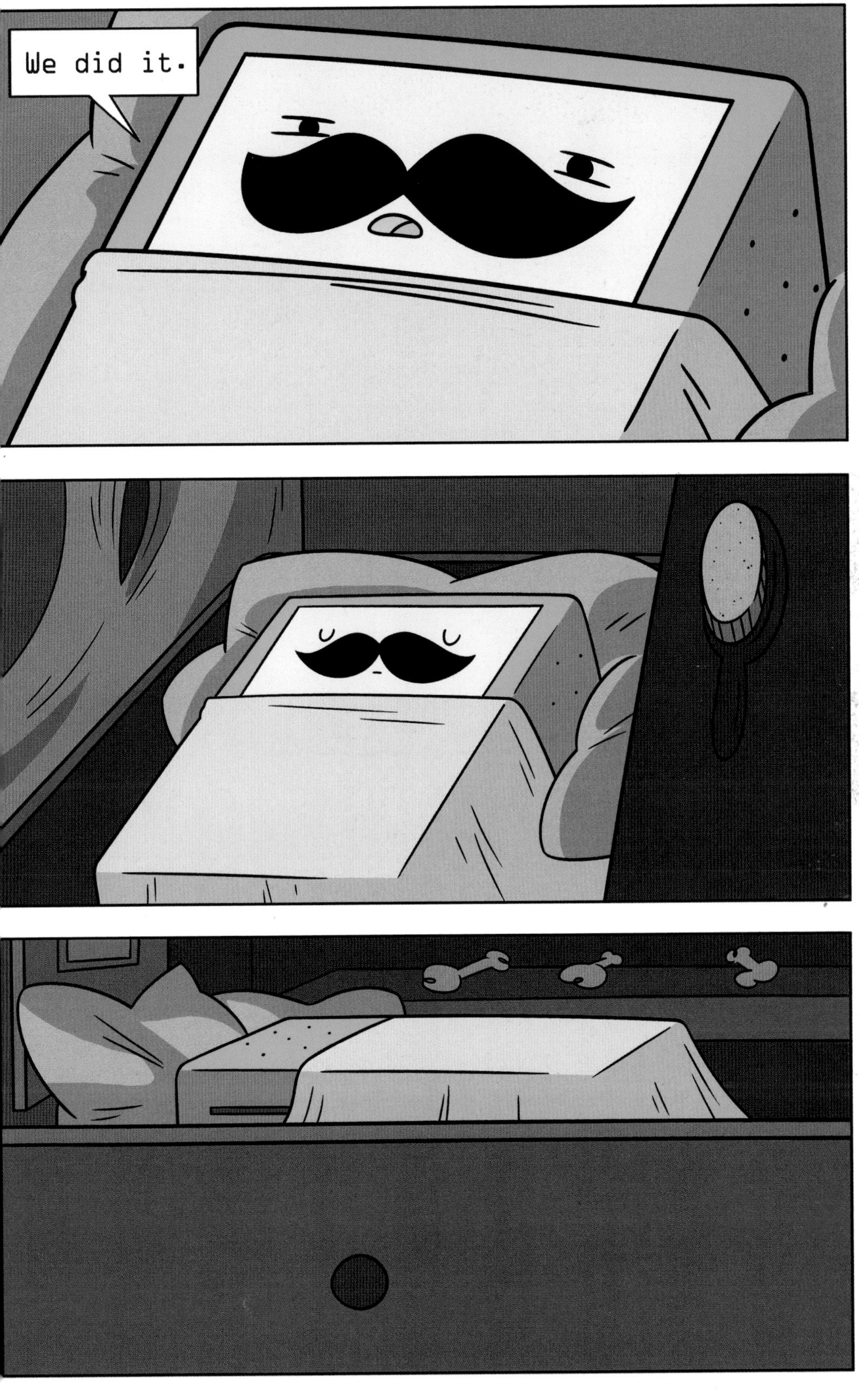
We did it.

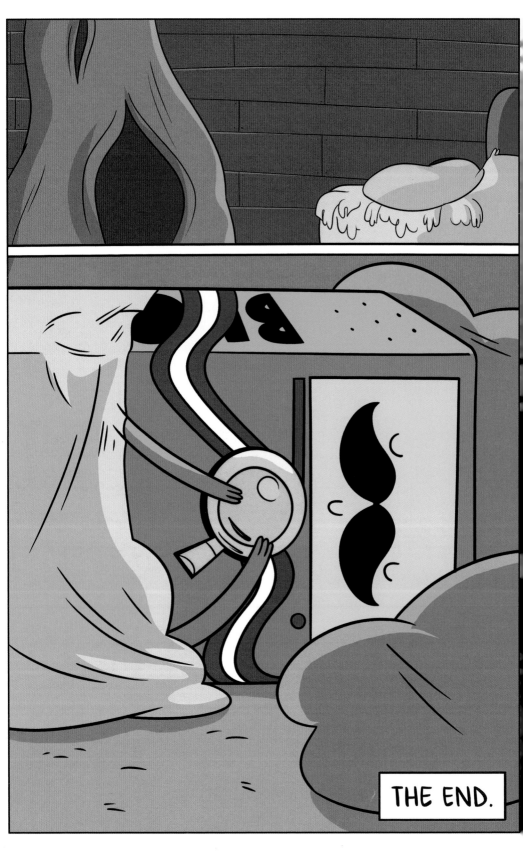

THE END.

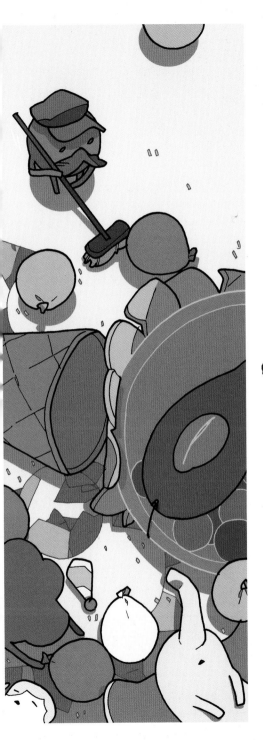

STARCHY
meredith mcclaren

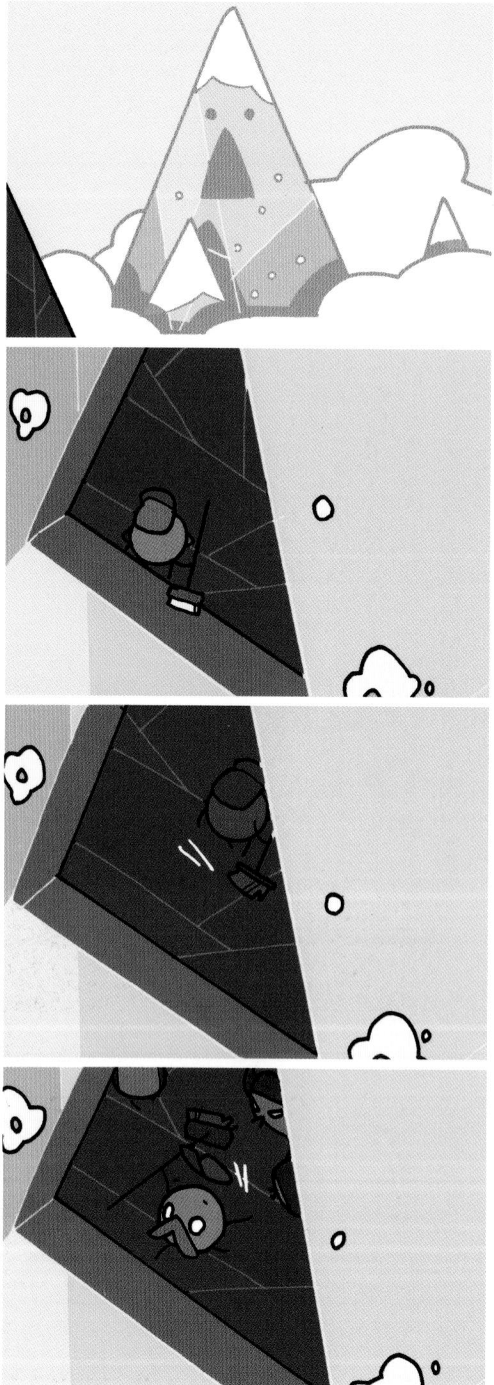

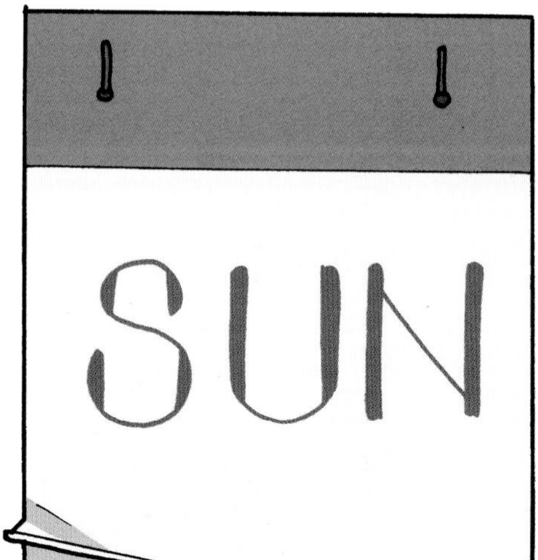
SUN

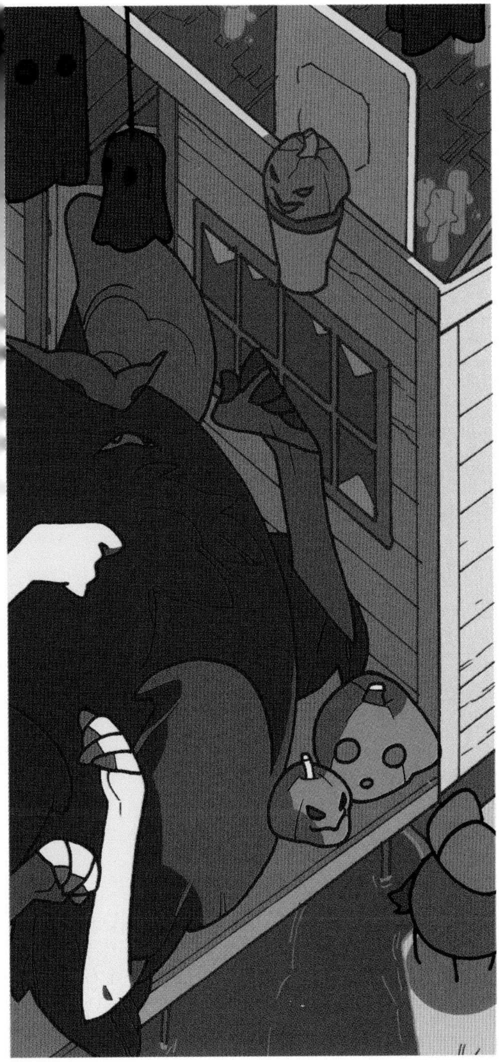

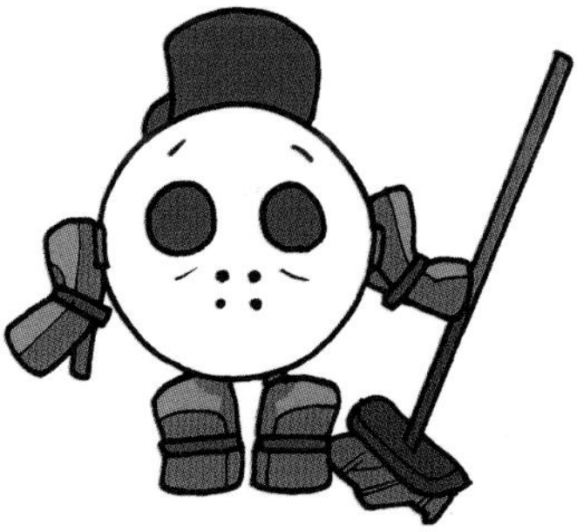

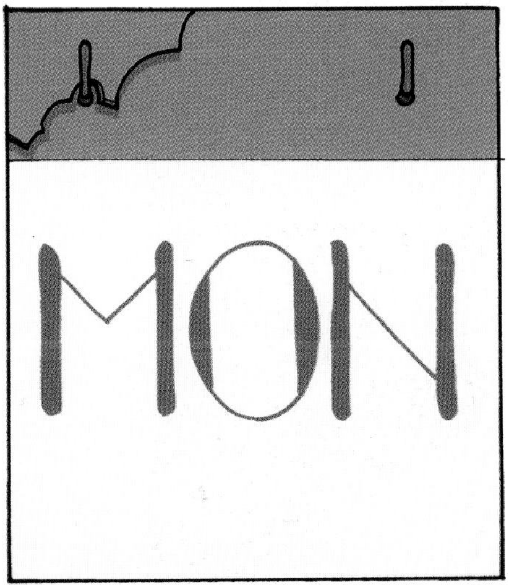
MON

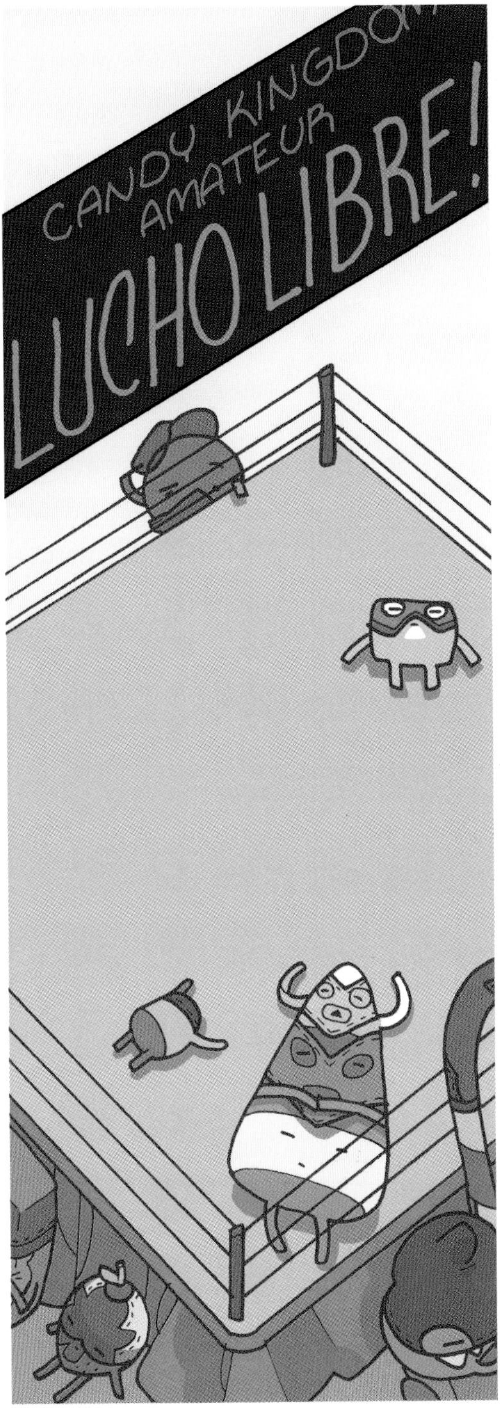
CANDY KINGDOM AMATEUR
LUCHO LIBRE!

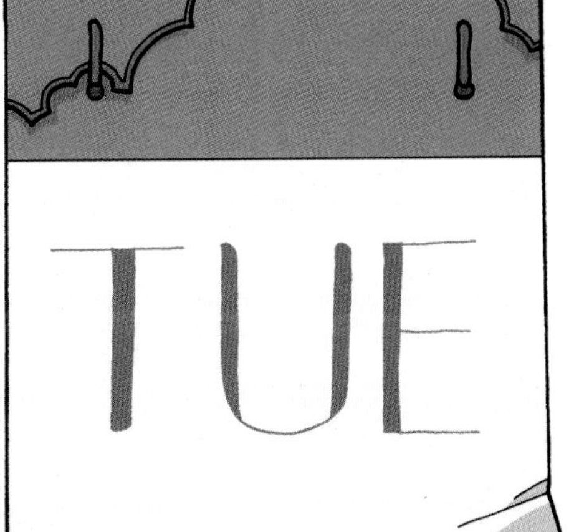
TUE

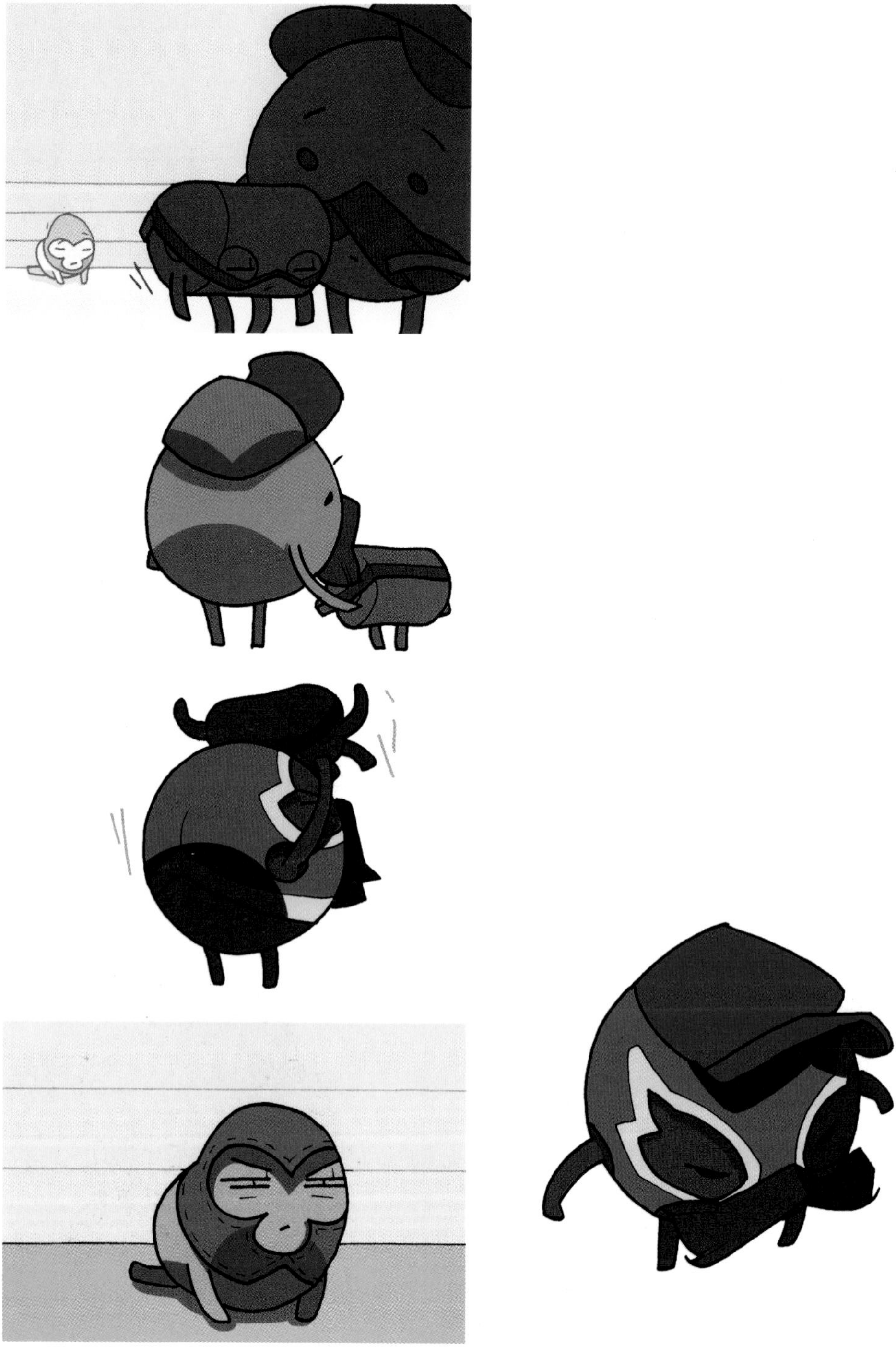

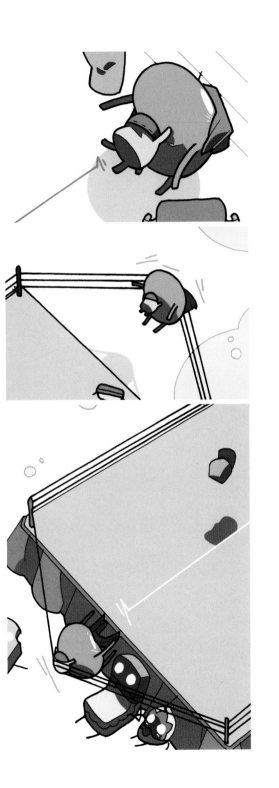

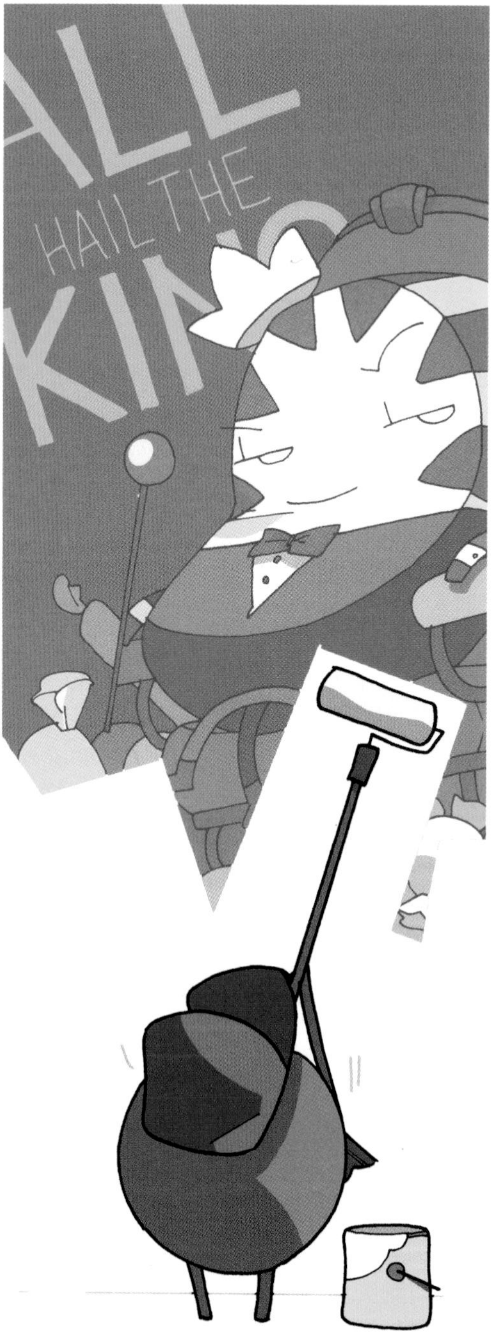
HAIL THE

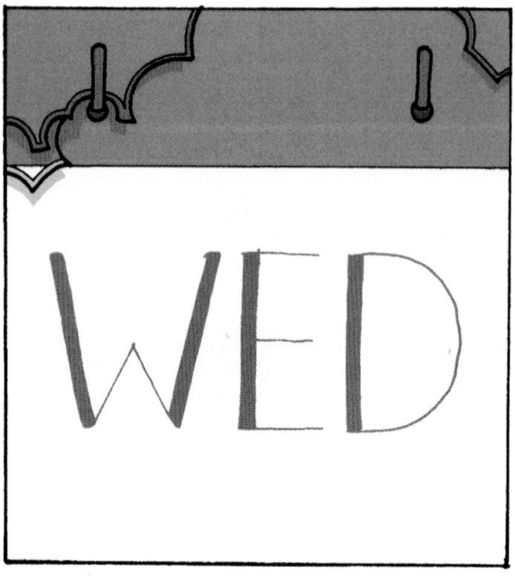
WED

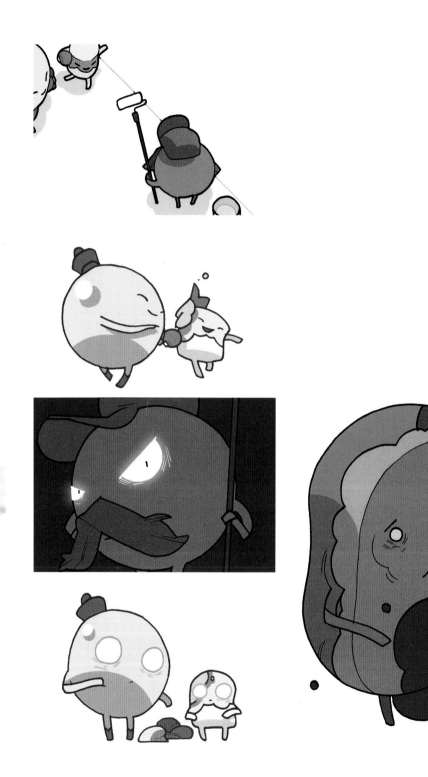

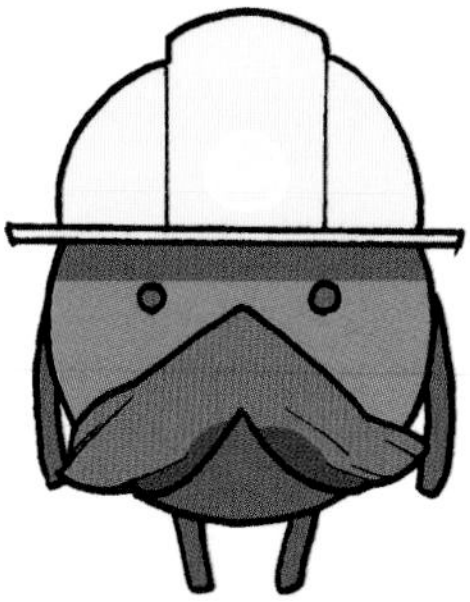

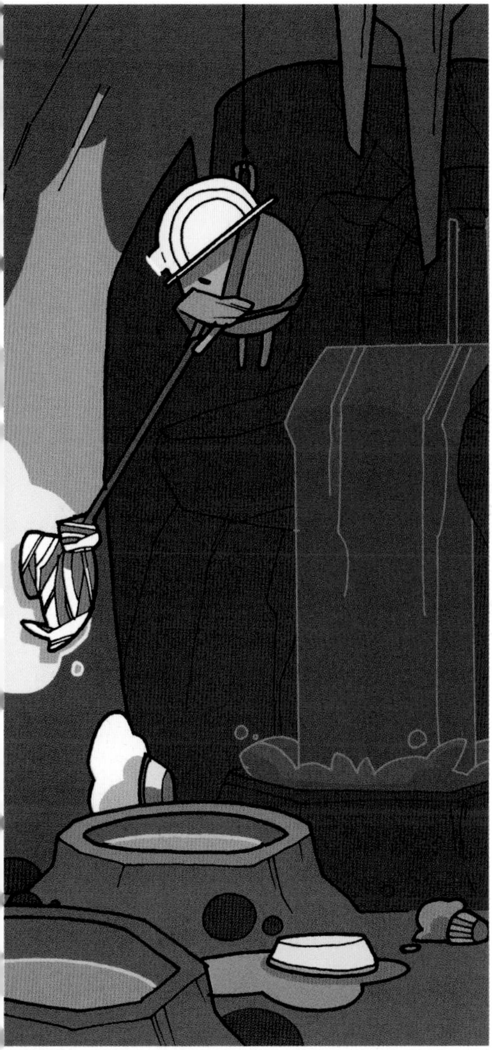

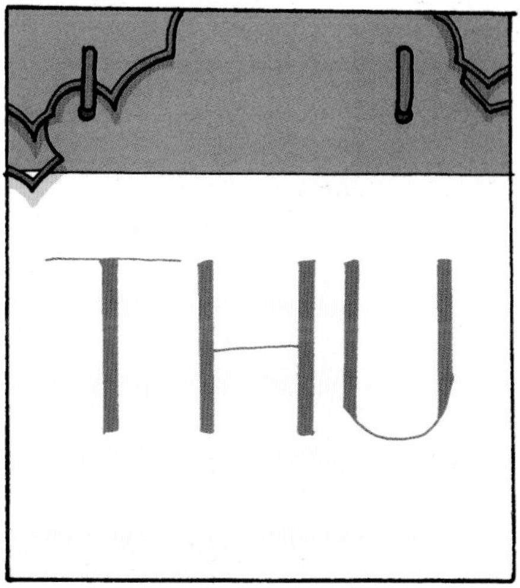
THU

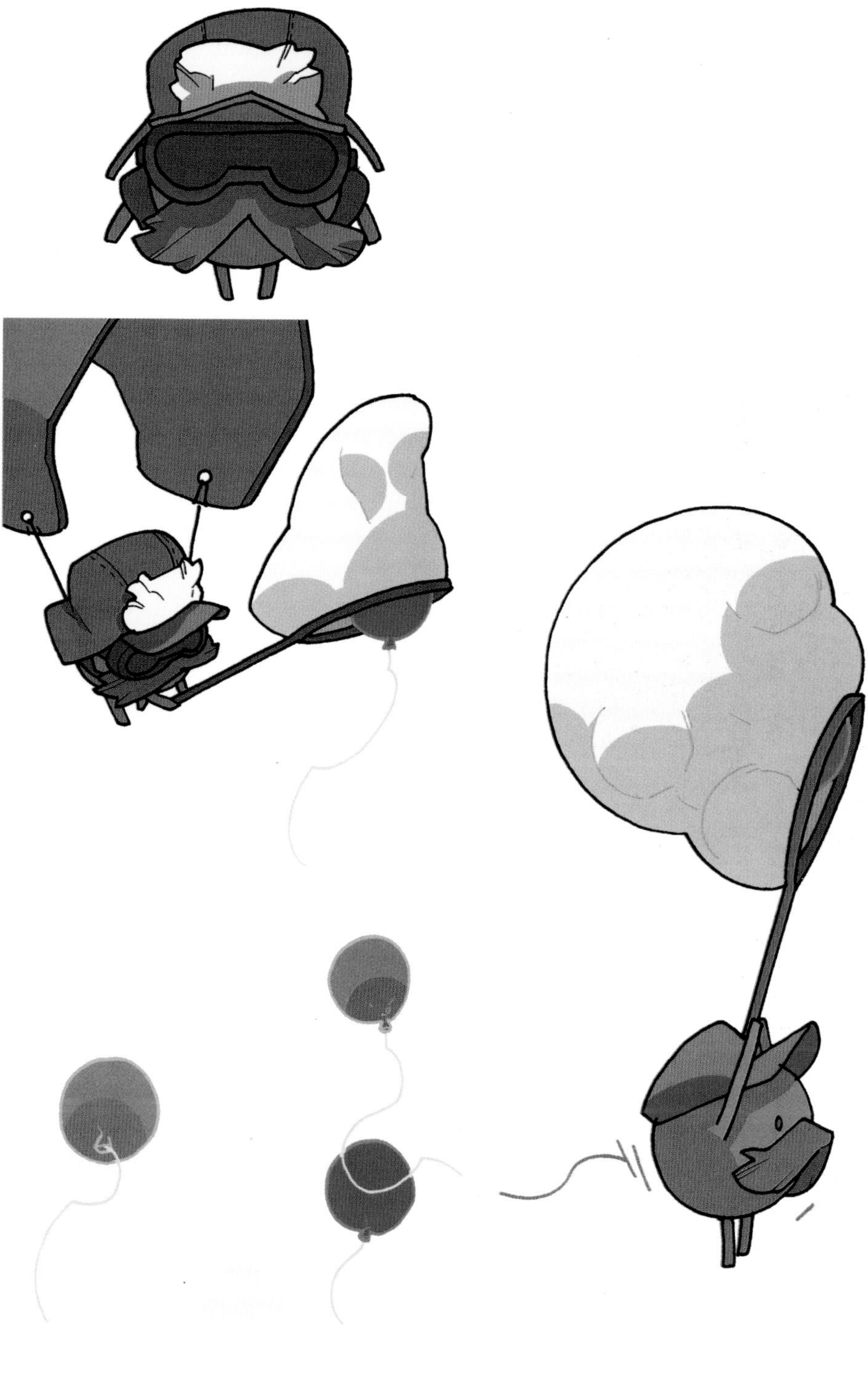

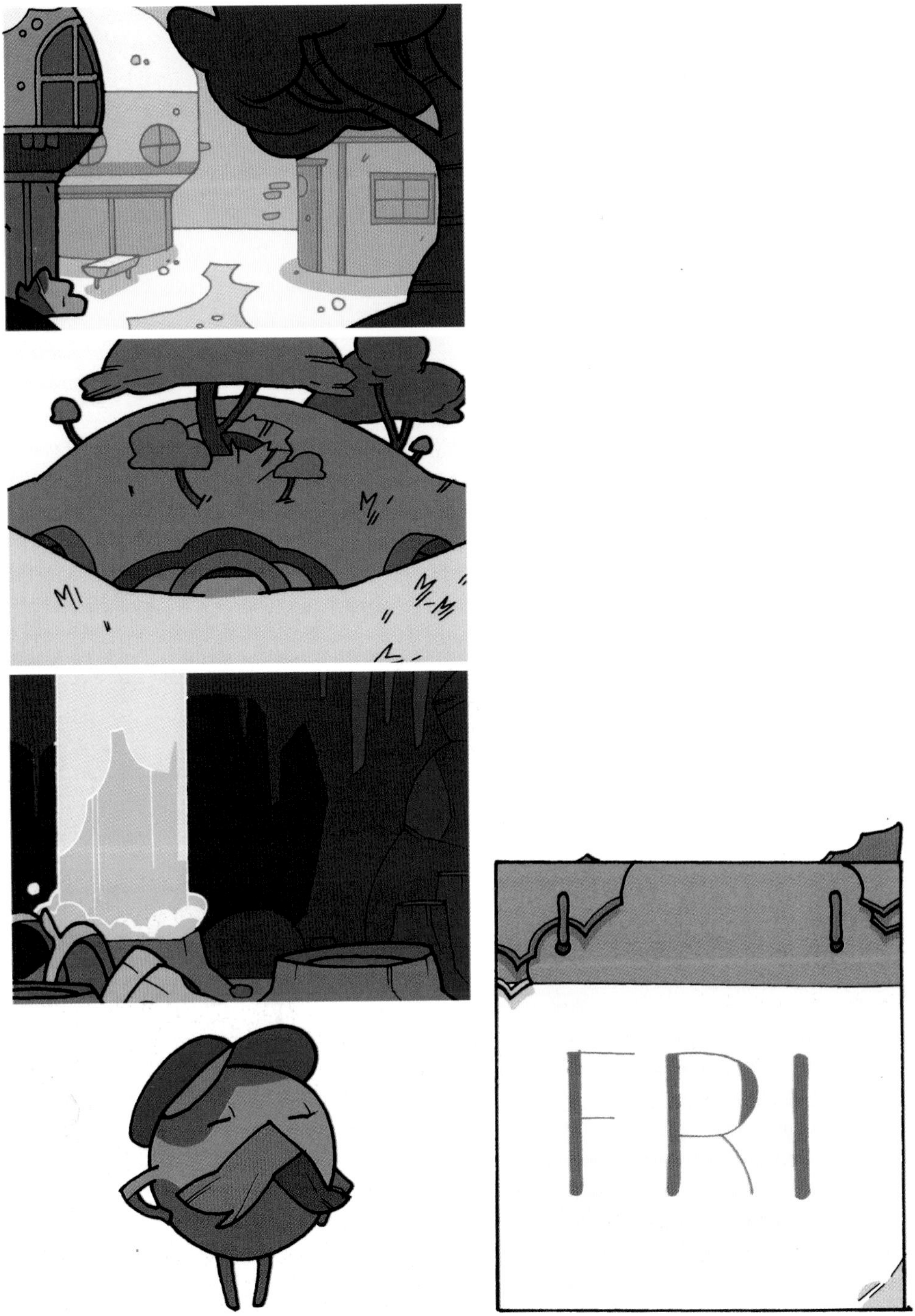
FRI

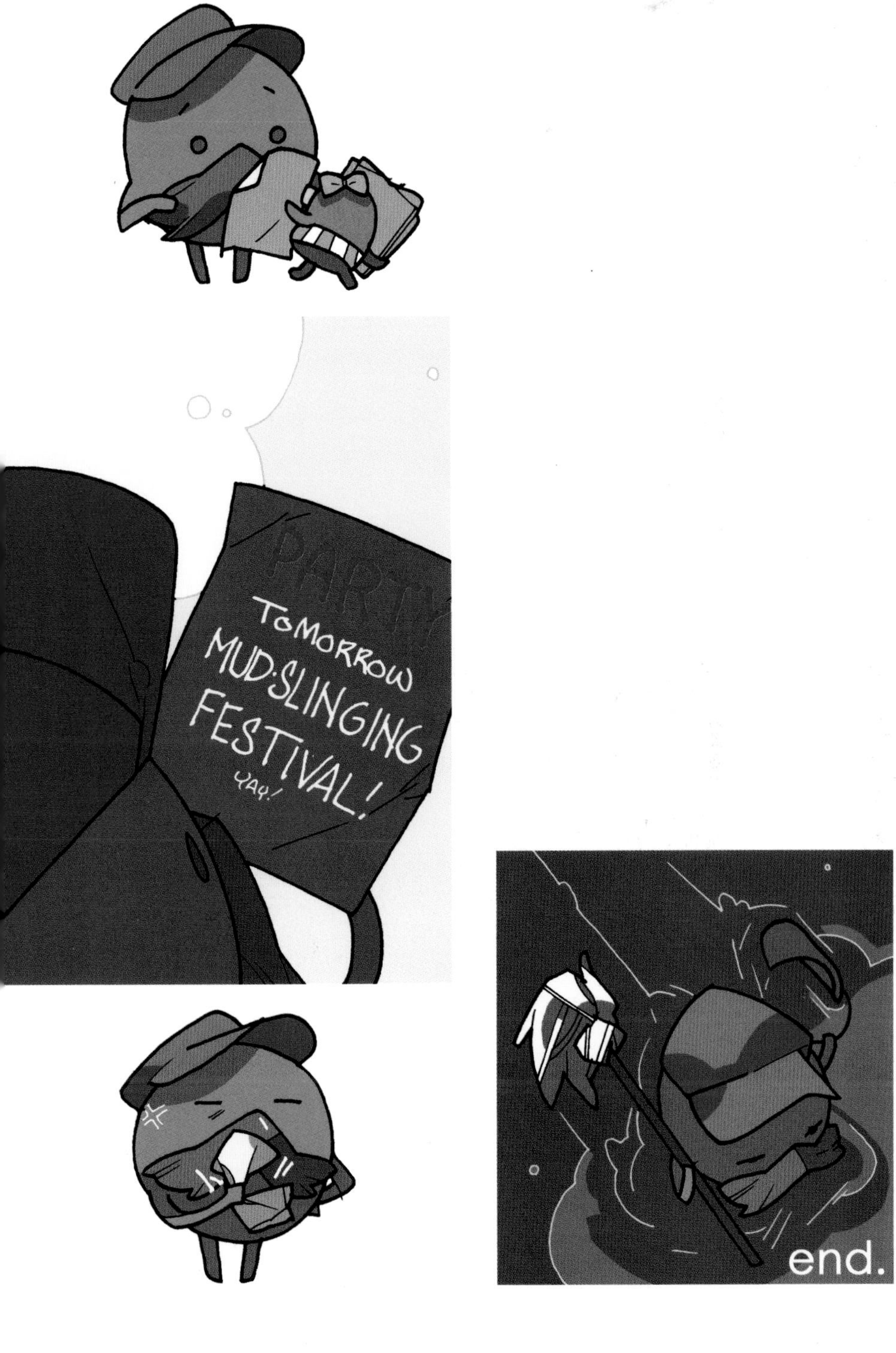
PARTY
TOMORROW
MUD-SLINGING
FESTIVAL!
YAY!
end.

THE FOUR CASTLES

SPRING 2016

Written by Josh Trujillo
Art by Zachary Sterling